LEONARDO DA VINCI

Treasures from the Biblioteca Reale, Turin

Tesori dalla Biblioteca Reale, Torino

LEONARDO DA VINCI

Treasures from the Biblioteca Reale, Turin   Tesori dalla Biblioteca Reale, Torino

Edited by / A cura di
PAOLA SALVI

With a Proem to the Codex Huygens by / Con un Proemio al *Codice Huygens* di
CARLO PEDRETTI

HAPAX
EDITORE

This volume has been published in conjunction with the exhibition
Leonardo da Vinci: Tresaures from the Biblioteca Reale, Turin
Questo volume è stato pubblicato in occasione della mostra
Leonardo da Vinci. Tesori dalla Biblioteca Reale, Torino

The Morgan Library & Museum, New York
October 25, 2013—February 2, 2014

Under the Auspices of the President of the Italian Republic
Sotto l'Alto Patronato del Presidente della Repubblica Italiana

2013 ANNO DELLA CULTURA ITALIANA
YEAR OF ITALIAN CULTURE

2013 — Year of Italian Culture in the United States
2013 – Anno della Cultura Italiana negli Stati Uniti

Leonardo da Vinci: Treasures from the Biblioteca Reale, Turin was organized by the Morgan Library & Museum and the Ministero Italiano degli Affari Esteri (Italian Ministry of Foreign Affairs), the Ministero Italiano dei Beni e delle Attività Culturali e del Turismo (Ministry of Italian Cultural Heritage and Activities and of Tourism), the Embassy of Italy in Washington, D.C., and the Biblioteca Reale, Turin, in collaboration with the Italian Cultural Institute of New York and la Fondazione NY.

It was made possible with generous support from the estate of Alex Gordon, the T. Kimball Brooker Foundation, Jean-Marie and Elizabeth Eveillard, Diane A. Nixon, and Mr. and Mrs. Seymour R. Askin, Jr., and from Giunti Editore, Finmeccanica S.p.A., Fondazione Bracco and Tenaris SA.

It is part of *2013 — Year of Italian Culture in the United States*, an initiative held under the Auspices of the President of the Italian Republic, organized by the Italian Ministry of Foreign Affairs and the Embassy of Italy in Washington, D.C. with the support of Corporate Ambassadors, Eni S.p.A., and Intesa Sanpaolo S.p.A.

Italian Ministry of Foreign Affairs
Ministry of Italian Cultural Heritage and Activities and of Tourism
General Direction of the Department for the General Administration of Libraries, Cultural Institutions and Author's Rights
Regional Direction for the Cultural and Landscape Heritage of Piedmont
Embassy of Italy in Washington, D.C.
Biblioteca Reale, Turin
Italian Cultural Institute of New York
la Fondazione NY

Leonardo da Vinci. Tesori dalla Biblioteca Reale, Torino è stata organizzata dalla Morgan Library & Museum e dal Ministero Italiano degli Affari Esteri, dal Ministero Italiano dei Beni e delle Attività Culturali e del Turismo, dall'Ambasciata Italiana a Washington, D.C. e dalla Biblioteca Reale di Torino, in collaborazione con l'Istituto Italiano di Cultura di New York e la Fondazione NY.

L'evento è stato reso possibile grazie al generoso sostegno di Alex Gordon, della Fondazione T. Kimball Brooker, di Jean-Marie ed Elizabeth Eveillard, di Diane A. Nixon, dei coniugi Seymour R. Askin Jr., di Giunti Editore, Finmeccanica S.p.A., Fondazione Bracco e Tenaris SA.

L'evento fa parte delle celebrazioni del *2013 – Anno della Cultura Italiana negli Stati Uniti*, organizzate dal Ministero Italiano dei Beni e delle Attività Culturali e del Turismo e dall'Ambasciata Italiana a Washington, D.C. sotto l'Alto Patronato del Presidente della Repubblica Italiana e con il supporto degli Ambasciatori aziendali Eni S.p.A. ed Intesa Sanpaolo S.p.A.

Ministero Italiano degli Affari Esteri
Ministero Italiano dei Beni e delle Attività Culturali e del Turismo
Direzione Generale per le biblioteche, gli istituti culturali e il diritto d'autore
Direzione Regionale per i Beni Culturali e Paesaggistici del Piemonte
Ambasciata Italiana a Washington, D.C.
Biblioteca Reale di Torino
Istituto Italiano di Cultura di New York
la Fondazione NY

Edited by | A cura di:
Paola Salvi

Texts | Testi:
Carlo Pedretti
Annalisa Perissa Torrini
Paola Salvi

Catalogue entries | Schede dei disegni:
Paola Salvi (PS)
Annalisa Perissa Torrini (Leonardeschi)

Translations | Traduzioni:
From Italian to English | Dall'italiano all'inglese:

Katherine M. Clifton (KMC):
Leonardo da Vinci: "Birds and Other Things" /
Leonardo da Vinci: "uccelli et altre cose"
Appendix / *Appendice*
Catalogue: Drawings by Leonardo / Catalogo: Disegni di Leonardo
Codex on the Flight of Birds / *Codice sul volo degli uccelli*
Codex Huygens - Folios chosen by PS / *Codice Huygens* - Fogli scelti da PS
Coordination of translators / Coordinamento dei traduttori

Margaret A. Kenneally:
Leonardo and His School: The Importance of Drawing /
Leonardo e la sua scuola. Il primato del disegno
Catalogue: Drawings by Leonardeschi / Catalogo: Disegni dei Leonardeschi

Joyce Holmes:
Treasures by Leonardo from the Biblioteca Reale, Turin /
Tesori leonardiani dalla Biblioteca Reale di Torino

From English to Italian | Dall'inglese all'italiano:

Sara Taglialagamba:
Proem to the Codex Huygens / Proemio al *Codice Huygens*

Editorial project coordination | Coordinamento progetto editoriale:
Riccardo Lorenzino
Designed by | Grafica: De Gregorio – Torino
Page layout | Impaginazione: In•Stile – Torino
Editing | Redazione: Federica Scomparin
Printed by | Stampa: Graf Art – Venaria (TO)

ISBN 978-88-88000-60-2

© 2014 Hapax Editore – Torino
Texts © 2013 the Authors
Tel. + 39 011 3119037 – Fax + 39 011 3083336
e-mail: info@hapax.it – www.hapax.it

CONTENTS
SOMMARIO

FOREWORDS
PREFAZIONI

Few artists in history can legitimately claim the title universal genius. Leonardo da Vinci, whose creative prowess and infinitely inventive spirit have been a source of fascination from his day to the present, is one of the rare exceptions. It is thus a particular honor for the Morgan Library & Museum to present a splendid group of drawings by this extraordinary Renaissance master, together with representative examples by some of the artists in his orbit, from the exceptionally rich holdings of the Biblioteca Reale in Turin. Like the Morgan, the Biblioteca Reale is a repository of rare and historically significant works on paper—manuscripts, books, and drawings—a kinship that makes a partnership between our two institutions especially fitting.

Drawings (and paintings) by Leonardo da Vinci are scarce in this country. From the time of his death and in the succeeding centuries works from his hand were relentlessly sought, most voraciously by royal and aristocratic collectors. The majority eventually came to reside in European collections, with the richest and most important concentration of his drawings now in the Royal Library at Windsor Castle. The Morgan Library & Museum, which has one of the largest—and, by American standards, oldest—collections of old master drawings in the United States, boasts only one autograph sheet by the artist. Several of the ideas Leonardo investigated, in both words and images, for his planned *Treatise on Painting*, are, however, echoed in an important late sixteenth-century manuscript in the Morgan's collection attributed to the Lombard artist Carlo Urbino. Known as the Codex Huygens, it is discussed in an essay in the present catalogue by Carlo Pedretti, and selected pages have been included in the exhibition. The Morgan's Codex Huygens provides a fascinating lens onto some of the scientific and theoretical ideas that engaged this profound mind, thus supplementing the rich presentation of Leonardo as a draftsman afforded by the drawings generously lent by the Biblioteca Reale.

Pochi artisti nel corso della storia possono legittimamente rivendicare il titolo di *genio universale*. Leonardo da Vinci, la cui coraggiosa creatività e l'infinito spirito d'inventiva continuano sin dalla sua epoca ad affascinare l'umanità, costituisce una di queste rare eccezioni. È pertanto un particolare onore per la Morgan Library & Museum presentare una splendida raccolta di disegni di questo straordinario maestro del Rinascimento, insieme con altri significativi esempi di alcuni artisti della sua cerchia, provenienti dall'eccezionale patrimonio artistico della Biblioteca Reale di Torino.

Come la Morgan, la Biblioteca Reale è una miniera di documenti cartacei rari e straordinariamente significativi – manoscritti, libri e disegni – un'affinità che rende particolarmente proficuo l'incontro fra le nostre due Istituzioni.

I disegni (e i dipinti) di Leonardo da Vinci sono rari nel nostro Paese. Dall'epoca della sua morte e nei secoli successivi, i suoi lavori sono stati ricercati con incessante bramosia, soprattutto da collezionisti appartenenti a famiglie reali e aristocratiche. La gran parte di queste opere giunse infine a concentrarsi nelle collezioni europee, delle quali quella della Royal Library di Windsor Castle è oggi la più ricca e importante. La Morgan Library & Museum, che possiede una delle più ampie – e, per gli standard americani, antiche – collezioni degli Stati Uniti di disegni di Maestri del passato, vanta soltanto un foglio autografo di Leonardo. Molte delle idee su cui il grande artista si soffermò per l'ormai perduto manoscritto del progettato *Trattato della Pittura*, hanno comunque avuto eco in un importante manoscritto appartenente alla collezione della Morgan, e risalente alla fine del XVI secolo, attribuito all'artista lombardo Carlo Urbino. Conosciuto come *Codice Huygens*, costituisce il tema del contributo di Carlo Pedretti al presente volume, ed alcune delle sue pagine sono esposte nella mostra newyorkese. Il *Codice Huygens* della Morgan permette un'affascinante messa a fuoco di alcune delle riflessioni scientifiche e teoriche che attirarono la fervida mente di Leonardo, arricchendo la preziosa presentazione della sua attività di disegnatore offerta dalle opere generosamente prestate dalla Biblioteca Reale.

The exhibition *Leonardo da Vinci: Treasures from the Biblioteca Reale, Turin* was organized by the Morgan Library & Museum and the Italian Ministry of Foreign Affairs, the Ministry of Italian Cultural Heritage and Activities and of Tourism, the Embassy of Italy in Washington, D.C., and the Biblioteca Reale in Turin in collaboration with the Italian Cultural Institute of New York and la Fondazione NY. It is part of the *Year of Italian Culture in the United States*. For proposing the exhibition and helping to bring it into existence we are enormously grateful to Riccardo Viale, Director of the Italian Cultural Institute, New York, and Renata Rosati, Head of Cultural Programs of la Fondazione NY. We are deeply appreciative of the support of Giovanni Saccani, Director of the Biblioteca Reale, Turin. For their contributions to the present catalogue, thanks are due to Paola Salvi, Annalisa Perissa Torrini, and Carlo Pedretti. Grateful acknowledgment is due to them, as well as to Edina Adam, John Alexander, Benjamin Bailes, Linden Chubin, Alex Confer, Susan Eddy, Simone Grant, Margaret Holben Ellis, Patricia Emerson, Anita Masi, Susan Miller, Patrick Milliman, Christine Nelson, Marilyn Palmeri, Paula Pineda, Alanna Schindewolf, Thomas Shannon, Kristina Stillman, Deborah Winard, Linda Wolk-Simon, and many others.

The exhibition was made possible with generous support from the estate of Alex Gordon, the T. Kimball Brooker Foundation, Jean-Marie and Elizabeth Eveillard, Diane A. Nixon, and Mr. and Mrs. Seymour R. Askin, Jr., and from Giunti, Finmeccanica, Fondazione Bracco and Tenaris. To all of them I wish to express our heartfelt thanks.

William M. Griswold
Director, The Morgan Library & Museum

La mostra *Leonardo da Vinci. Tesori dalla Biblioteca Reale, Torino* è stata organizzata dalla Morgan Library & Museum, dal Ministero Italiano degli Affari Esteri, dal Ministero Italiano dei Beni e delle Attività Culturali e del Turismo, dall'Ambasciata Italiana a Washington, D.C. e dalla Biblioteca Reale di Torino, in collaborazione con l'Istituto Italiano di Cultura di New York e la Fondazione NY, e fa parte degli eventi dell'*Anno della Cultura Italiana negli Stati Uniti*.

Per aver proposto la mostra e aver contribuito a darle vita esprimiamo la nostra gratitudine a Riccardo Viale, Presidente dell'Istituto Italiano di Cultura di New York e Renata Rosati, Responsabile dei Programmi culturali de la Fondazione NY. Esprimiamo un profondo apprezzamento per il supporto di Giovanni Saccani, Direttore della Biblioteca Reale di Torino. Per i loro contributi a questo catalogo ringraziamo Paola Salvi, Annalisa Perissa Torrini, e Carlo Pedretti. A loro va la nostra grata riconoscenza, così come a Edina Adam, John Alexander, Benjamin Bailes, Linden Chubin, Alex Confer, Susan Eddy, Simone Grant, Margaret Holben Ellis, Patricia Emerson, Anita Masi, Susan Miller, Patrick Milliman, Christine Nelson, Marilyn Palmeri, Paula Pineda, Alanna Schindewolf, Thomas Shannon, Kristina Stillman, Deborah Winard, Linda Wolk-Simon, e molti altri.

La mostra è stata resa possibile grazie al generoso sostegno economico di Alex Gordon, Jean-Marie ed Elizabeth Eveillard, Diane A. Nixon, i coniugi Seymour R. Askin, Jr., nonché di Giunti, Finmeccanica, Fondazione Bracco e Tenaris. A tutti loro desidero esprimere il nostro più sentito grazie.

William M. Griswold
Direttore della Morgan Library & Museum

Since September 2012, the Biblioteca Reale in Turin has greeted visitors with a fresh configuration, offering a combined museum and library to the public, readers, and scholars alike.

The new structure of the Biblioteca Reale is the result of the evolution of the Polo Reale Progetto, a single, vast museum in the former royal center of the city, which includes the Palazzo Reale, the Armeria Reale, the Biblioteca Reale itself, the Galleria Sabauda, the Museo Archeologico, and the Giardini Reali.

Since April 16, the Biblioteca Reale has also been linked to the Armeria Reale, on the floor above, thanks to the reopening to the public of the great staircase commissioned by King Carlo Alberto and closed to the public in 1961. The staircase was restored by the Italian Ministry of Cultural Heritage and Activities and of Tourism, with the support of the Consulta per la Valorizzazione dei Beni Artistici e Culturali di Torino, and is now presented to the public in its original state, with the collection of ancient stone plaques purchased by King Carlo Alberto once again *in situ*.

The library's reading room has been relocated in a specially designed area—with access limited only to readers in order to guarantee the utmost privacy and silence—in the second part of the monumental hall decorated by Pelagio Palagi (1775–1860), a painter, sculptor, and decorator of interiors from Bologna, who for many years worked at the Court of Savoy. The first part of the hall hosts a display of the permanent collections with a selection of items linked to the history of the Library, bindings and volumes of particular importance, all exhibited in cabinets specially refurbished for the occasion.

An important aspect of the Biblioteca Reale's new image is the multimedia system installed in the two entrance halls, thanks to the generous contribution of the Consulta per la Valorizzazione dei Beni Artistici e Culturali di Torino. Visitors can explore the digital collections of the library as well as the cultural heritage of Piedmont through the resources of the system.

Dal 28 settembre 2012 la Biblioteca Reale di Torino si presenta al pubblico con un nuovo assetto espositivo, garantendo così sia ai visitatori sia ai lettori e agli studiosi la doppia funzione di museo e di biblioteca.

La nuova veste della Biblioteca Reale trova la sua ragione nell'evoluzione del Progetto del Polo Reale di Torino, un unico grande museo nel centro aulico della città che comprende Palazzo Reale, Armeria Reale, la stessa Biblioteca Reale, la Galleria Sabauda, il Museo Archeologico e i Giardini Reali.

Dal 16 aprile 2013 la Biblioteca Reale è inoltre collegata alla sovrastante Armeria Reale grazie alla riapertura al pubblico dello Scalone commissionato dal re Carlo Alberto e chiuso al pubblico nel 1961. Lo Scalone, restaurato dal Ministero dei Beni e delle Attività Culturali e del Turismo con il sostegno dalla Consulta per la Valorizzazione dei Beni Artistici e Culturali di Torino, viene restituito alla fruizione pubblica nel suo aspetto originario, con la collezione di lapidi antiche acquistate dal re Carlo Alberto, ricollocate nell'originaria posizione.

La sala di consultazione della Biblioteca trova oggi spazio in un'area apposita ad accesso limitato solo per i lettori (a cui vengono garantiti così maggiore privacy e silenzio), collocata nella seconda parte del Salone monumentale decorato da Pelagio Palagi (1775-1860), pittore, scultore, decoratore d'interni, di origine bolognese, impiegato a lungo presso la corte sabauda. La prima parte del Salone, invece, ospita una esposizione delle collezioni permanenti, con una selezione di manufatti legati alla storia dell'Istituto, legature di pregio nonché volumi di particolare rilievo, all'interno di vetrine appositamente rinnovate per l'occasione.

Punto forte di questa nuova immagine della Biblioteca Reale è l'allestimento multimediale installato nelle due sale di ingresso: grazie al prezioso contributo della Consulta per la Valorizzazione dei beni artistici e culturali di Torino sono stati installati dispositivi multimediali, sia per poter navigare attraverso le collezioni digitali dell'Istituto, sia per promuovere e valorizzare, anche attraverso video emozionali, i beni culturali piemontesi.

Il nuovo allestimento cerca anche di far vivere ai visitatori il progetto di *Wunderkammer* che Carlo Alberto ha per-

The new installation of the museum also gives visitors the opportunity to experience the *Wunderkammer* that King Carlo Alberto intended to create, thanks to important acquisitions of manuscripts, drawings and other *objets d'art*, which are presented partly in the original and partly in digital form.

The *Self-Portrait* and the Codex on the Flight of Birds by Leonardo da Vinci, to mention just two of the precious works preserved in the Biblioteca Reale—the latter being exhibited in New York on this prestigious occasion—can be admired and studied by all in the digital version, which can easily be consulted on the touchscreen monitors of the Library.

The term "library-museum" has precise philological meanings in the concept of its founder, Carlo Alberto. He wanted a study library open to all and a showcase of the dynasty's grandeur for the benefit of foreign diplomats and guests at the Court of Savoy.

Today, this original vision of the Library is offered as a precious *unicum* to visitors to the Polo Reale, thus further contributing to the already rich array of cultural institutions in our city and the state-owned cultural heritage of Piedmont.

Mario Turetta
*Regional Director for the Cultural
and Landscape Heritage of Piedmont*

seguito con acquisizioni importanti sia di manoscritti sia di disegni sia di oggetti d'arte che vengono presentati in parte in originale, in parte in formato elettronico.

L'*Autoritratto* e il *Codice sul volo degli uccelli* di Leonardo da Vinci, per citare due esempi di preziose opere conservate alla Biblioteca Reale, la seconda delle quali esposta in questa prestigiosa occasione newyorkese, potranno così essere ammirati e studiati da tutti attraverso la versione digitale, liberamente consultabile nei monitor *touchscreen* della Biblioteca.

La "biblioteca-museo" ha precisi riferimenti filologici nella stessa volontà del suo fondatore, re Carlo Alberto, che voleva una biblioteca di studio aperta a tutti e sede espositiva della "grandeur sabauda" nei confronti dei diplomatici stranieri e degli ospiti della corte sabauda.

Oggi questa visione originaria della Biblioteca è offerta come un unicum prezioso al visitatore del Polo Reale, ampliando così una già ricca offerta culturale e museale della nostra città e del patrimonio culturale statale in Piemonte.

Mario Turetta
*Direttore Regionale per i Beni Culturali
e Paesaggistici del Piemonte*

Our public libraries play a central role locally and nationally, offering information services, training and education and preserving and safeguarding the nation's bibliographic heritage.

They are *places of written memories* and must combine the need to safeguard their collections with the more proactive work of providing access to and understanding of their content, in cooperation with national and international institutions operating in the cultural sector.

Conservation and management are the two principles set out in Article 9 of the Italian Constitution, which states: "The Republic promotes the development of culture and scientific and technical research. It safeguards the landscape and the historical and artistic heritage of the nation."

Although conservation and management differ in their object, purpose and prescriptive power, the link between projects for cultural promotion and the protection of the national heritage — the product of erstwhile cultural activities, the objects that were produced, the buildings and landscapes that bear witness to them — is evident.

Preservation requires the analysis of potential risks to the historical patrimony; plans for controlling and maintaining the collections, periodic inspection of the storage sites to check for any environmental, biological or chemical risks, followed by suitable proposals for conservation and restoration; inspection and maintenance of the utility systems; precautions to be taken when transferring and moving material and assessment of their correct application; preparation of emergency plans and equipment; management of loan procedures in the case of participation in cultural events; identification of potential risks for architectural structures.

To enact policies for the management of cultural heritage means adopting sustainable and responsible strategies; the current generation must ensure that it is preserved for the enjoyment of generations to come.

Heritage, culture, research and *development* are an indivisible whole: our artistic, architectural, landscape, figurative, musical, literary, humanistic, and linguistic heritage and the creativity of the Italian people comprise our identity and role of our nation in the world.

Le *Biblioteche Pubbliche Statali* rivestono un ruolo centrale in ambito locale e nazionale attraverso l'erogazione di servizi informativi, formativi e culturali e conservando e tutelando il patrimonio bibliografico della Nazione.

Quali *luoghi della memoria scritta*, esse coniugano le esigenze di tutela con i più dinamici momenti di valorizzazione e promozione della visibilità e conoscenza del proprio posseduto, anche grazie alla cooperazione con istituzioni nazionali ed internazionali che operano nel settore culturale.

Conservazione e valorizzazione costituiscono i due principi fondamentali di cui si compone l'art. 9 della Costituzione: "La Repubblica promuove lo sviluppo della cultura e la ricerca scientifica e tecnica. Tutela il paesaggio e il patrimonio storico e artistico della Nazione".

Sebbene si tratti di principi diversi per oggetto, finalità e forza precettiva, è manifesta l'interconnessione tra il piano della promozione culturale e quello della protezione del patrimonio identitario, quale prodotto delle attività culturali pregresse, nella loro materializzazione concreta, nelle *cose mobili* ed *immobili* che ne sostanziano il valore.

La conservazione prevede l'analisi dei rischi potenziali cui è soggetto il patrimonio; un piano di controllo e manutenzione delle collezioni; periodica verifica dei depositi per accertare eventuali situazioni di rischio ambientale, biologico e chimico, con opportune proposte di intervento conservativo e di restauro; accertamento dell'adeguatezza e del funzionamento degli impianti; adozione di misure cautelative nella definizione delle modalità di circolazione e movimentazione del materiale e verifica della loro corretta applicazione; predisposizione del piano e degli strumenti per l'emergenza; gestione delle procedure di prestito in caso di partecipazione a manifestazioni culturali; individuazione dei rischi potenziali della struttura architettonica.

Attuare politiche di valorizzazione del patrimonio culturale significa, d'altra parte, adottare strategie sostenibili e responsabili nei confronti del bene culturale, avendo la generazione presente il dovere di assicurarne piena fruibilità da parte dei posteri.

Patrimonio, cultura, ricerca e *sviluppo* sono elementi di un tutto inscindibile: il nostro patrimonio artistico, architettonico, paesaggistico, figurativo, musicale, letterario, umanistico, la nostra

Loans of works are, of course, important for the development of our cultural heritage: they encourage the effective exchange of our national past, keeping alive the memory of our most prestigious history and displaying exhibits that are often rare or unique, and at the same time, promoting the legacy of our country at the international level, confirming Italy's role as a cultural leader worldwide; a role that is capable of generating a more widespread and significant interest in the magnificent cultural heritage of the nation, producing positive and long-lasting social and economic benefits.

The union between Tourism and Culture is a formidable driving force for our cultural diplomacy. Presenting these treasures to Europeans and non-Europeans, and making our contribution to *ad hoc* exhibitions and events, is a positive response to the generalized demand for international culture, guaranteeing more extensive and direct enjoyment of our heritage, broadening participation in cultural activities and laying the foundations for a permanent flow of visitors to Italy.

The event in which the Biblioteca Reale in Turin plays a leading role, with the loan of the Codex on the Flight of Birds and other precious drawings by Leonardo da Vinci, his pupils and followers to the exhibition at the Morgan Library & Museum, can be seen in this context.

This presentation of our precious bibliographical legacy, as part of the *Year of Italian Culture in the United States* is therefore a fundamental opportunity for consolidating the bonds that unite Italy and the United States and for creating new connections, for encouraging the meeting of diverse cultures, integration and dialogue among peoples, strengthening reciprocal understanding and raising awareness of the value of cultural heritage as the wealth of humanity as a whole.

Rossana Rummo
*Ministry of Italian Cultural Heritage
and Activities and of Tourism
Director General, Department for the
Administration of Libraries,
Cultural Institutions and Author's Rights*

lingua, la creatività degli italiani sono, infatti, il correlativo della nostra identità e del ruolo italiano nel panorama mondiale.

I prestiti di opere rientrano a pieno titolo nell'attività di valorizzazione del patrimonio: essi favoriscono la concreta circolazione dei nostri retaggi storici ed identitari, mantengono viva la memoria del nostro passato più prestigioso e costante l'attenzione nei confronti di un materiale ostensivo spesso unico e raro. Inoltre, rappresentano il più efficace veicolo per confermare il potenziale storico del nostro Paese in una dimensione internazionale e per suggellare il ruolo di capofila culturale nel mondo rivestito dall'Italia, tale da generare un più diffuso e significativo interesse intorno al ricchissimo patrimonio della Nazione e produrre positive e durature ricadute sociali ed economiche.

Il connubio Turismo e Cultura è un formidabile volano per la nostra diplomazia culturale. Presentare i prodotti della cultura alla popolazione europea ed extra-europea, anche portando propri contributi in percorsi espositivi promossi *ad hoc*, significa rispondere positivamente alla richiesta generalizzata dell'offerta culturale internazionale e qualificarne l'entità, vuol dire garantire il diritto alla più ampia e diretta fruizione del patrimonio, estendere la base partecipativa alle attività culturali, nonché gettare le basi per flussi permanenti di visitatori in Italia.

In tale contesto si inserisce, a pieno titolo, l'iniziativa che vede protagonista la Biblioteca Reale di Torino con il prestito alla mostra allestita presso la Morgan Library & Museum del *Codice sul volo degli uccelli* e di altri preziosissimi disegni di Leonardo da Vinci e di allievi e seguaci.

La valorizzazione del nostro prezioso patrimonio bibliografico nell'ambito dell'*Anno della Cultura Italiana negli Stati Uniti* costituisce, pertanto, un'occasione fondamentale per consolidare i legami che uniscono l'Italia all'America e per crearne nuovi, per favorire l'incontro delle diversità culturali, l'integrazione e il dialogo tra i popoli, per rafforzare reciproca conoscenza e sensibilizzare sul valore del bene culturale come ricchezza per l'umanità intera.

Rossana Rummo
*Ministero dei Beni e delle Attività Culturali e del Turismo
Direttore Generale per le biblioteche,
gli istituti culturali e il diritto d'autore*

On May 24, 2012, following the great celebratory exhibition at the Reggia di Venaria Reale (Turin) on the occasion of the 150th anniversary of the Unification of Italy, a study day was held at the Biblioteca Reale in Turin to discuss future research on the library's prestigious collection of works by Leonardo and to offer an overview of major international exhibitions and appreciation of the precious collection of drawings by Leonardo. This underlined the Biblioteca Reale's great commitment to the preservation of Leonardo's heritage, even though the first major exhibition devoted to Leonardo in the last century, organized in Milan (at the height of the Fascist regime and probably with the intention of glorifying the greatness of the Italian genius), included works from Italy and abroad but none from the Biblioteca Reale in Turin.

In the year since the meeting of May 2012, works by Leonardo from the Biblioteca Reale have been and are still on display in important national and international exhibitions, beginning with the Paris exhibition *La "Sainte Anne" l'ultime chef-d'œuvre de Léonard de Vinci* (*"Saint Anne": Leonardo da Vinci's Ultimate Masterpiece*), which included an exquisite drawing by a follower of Leonardo (15716 D.C.).

In December 2012, the Codex on the Flight of Birds arrived at the Pushkin Museum of Fine Arts in Moscow, where it remained until February 11, 2013, for the exhibition *Italian Drawings from the Collections of the Pushkin Museum of Fine Arts*.

The Codex was on display until recently at the National Air and Space Museum of the Smithsonian Institution in Washington, D.C., an event organized by the Italian Ministry of Foreign Affairs, the Ministry of Italian Cultural Heritage and Activities and of Tourism, the Embassy of Italy in Washington, D.C., and the Biblioteca Reale in Turin, as part of the *Year of Italian Culture in the United States*.

The exhibition *Leonardo da Vinci. L'uomo universale* (*Leonardo da Vinci: Universal Man*) at the Gallerie dell'Accademia di Venezia (Venice 2013) features four drawings from Turin, including the *Proportional Study of the Face and the Eye*, which was chosen as the title image of the exhibition.

Il 24 maggio del 2012 si teneva presso la Biblioteca Reale di Torino una "Giornata di studi" che intendeva fare il punto sull'avanzamento delle ricerche sulla prestigiosa collezione leonardiana della BRT, dopo la grande mostra celebrativa dei 150 anni dell'Unità d'Italia tenuta presso la Reggia di Venaria Reale (Torino), e offrire una panoramica sulle grandi mostre e sulla valorizzazione internazionale del prezioso nucleo di disegni di Leonardo. Emergeva così la grande attenzione posta nella valorizzazione del patrimonio leonardiano della BRT, anche se nella prima grande occasione del secolo scorso (nel 1939, in pieno clima fascista e con il probabile intento di glorificare la grandezza del genio italiano) venne allestita una mostra a Milano dedicata a Leonardo da Vinci con disegni e autografi che giunsero dall'Italia e dall'estero, mentre nulla pervenne dalla Biblioteca Reale di Torino.

Dall'occasione di confronto del maggio 2012 è trascorso poco più di un anno, durante il quale i disegni di Leonardo della BRT sono stati e sono presenti in mostre nazionali e internazionali di grande rilievo, a partire dall'esposizione parigina *La "Sainte Anne" l'ultime chef-d'œuvre de Léonard de Vinci* (*La "Sant'Anna". L'ultimo capolavoro di Leonardo da Vinci*), dove era esposto lo squisito disegnino di seguace (15716 D.C.).

Nel dicembre dello stesso anno il *Codice sul volo degli uccelli* è approdato al Museo Puskin di Mosca dove vi è rimasto fino all'11 febbraio 2013, per l'esposizione *Mostra sui disegni italiani dalle collezioni del Museo Puskin*.

Si è appena conclusa l'esposizione del Codice al National Air and Space Museum dello Smithsonian di Washington, D.C., organizzata dal Ministero Italiano degli Affari Esteri, dal Ministero dei Beni e delle Attività Culturali e del Turismo, dall'Ambasciata d'Italia a Washington, D.C. e dalla Biblioteca Reale di Torino, nel quadro dell'*Anno della Cultura Italiana negli Stati Uniti*.

La mostra *Leonardo da Vinci. L'uomo universale*, presso le Gallerie dell'Accademia di Venezia (Venice 2013), ha esposto quattro disegni della collezione, tra cui lo *Studio proporzionale del volto e dell'occhio*, che è stato scelto come immagine guida della mostra.

Now, on the occasion of the *Year of Italian Culture in the United States*, the Morgan Library & Museum in New York is hosting the exhibition *Leonardo da Vinci: Treasures from the Biblioteca Reale, Turin* (October 25, 2013–February 2, 2014). The exhibition, organized in collaboration with the Italian Cultural Institute of New York, will display almost the entire corpus of drawings by Leonardo and the Leonardeschi from the Biblioteca Reale in Turin. The focus of the exhibition is the Codex on the Flight of Birds; the drawings by Leonardo will play a supporting role and are thematically and graphically linked to it. Another highlight of the exhibition is the *Head of a Young Woman*, presumed to be a study for the angel in the *Virgin of the Rocks*. The gentle face of a young woman, drawn in metalpoint with highlights in white, is Turin's most renowned drawing next to the *Self-Portrait* and has rightly been described as 'the most beautiful drawing in the world'.

Giovanni Saccani
Director, Biblioteca Reale, Turin

Ora, sempre in occasione dell'*Anno della Cultura Italiana negli Stati Uniti*, la Morgan Library di New York ospita la grande esposizione leonardiana dal titolo *Leonardo da Vinci. Tesori dalla Biblioteca Reale*, Torino, dal 25 ottobre 2013 al 2 febbraio 2014. La mostra, che ha visto anche l'impegno dell'Istituto Italiano di Cultura a New York, espone quasi tutto Il corpus dei disegni di Leonardo da Vinci e dei Leonardeschi posseduti dalla Biblioteca Reale di Torino. L'esposizione ha come nucleo centrale il *Codice sul volo degli uccelli*; i disegni di Leonardo fanno da cornice al *Codice* e sono a esso collegati tematicamente e graficamente. Splendido cammeo dell'esposizione è la *Testa di fanciulla* (presunto studio per l'angelo della *Vergine delle rocce*), accompagnato dai disegni dei Leonardeschi. Il dolcissimo volto di fanciulla, eseguito a punta metallica con lumeggiature di biacca, è il disegno più celebre della raccolta torinese dopo *l'Autoritratto* e non a torto è definito il disegno più bello del mondo.

Giovanni Saccani
Direttore della Biblioteca Reale di Torino

Within the range of cultural exchanges promoted by la Fondazione NY, this exhibition of drawings by Leonardo and the Leonardeschi assumes particular importance due to the relevance of the works on display, and the contempory nature of its message.

Leonardo's genius, from his sublime art to the visionary design of flying machines, anticipates our times in which the synthesis of art and function is common, and the two are often pursued together.

Painter, architect, scientist, inventor, and designer of terrifying war machines, Leonardo spanned the whole field of creativity with a consistent intensity and sense of purpose. Once again he shows us that diversity has meaning only within the framework of a discipline. I believe this is a lesson that is still valid today.

It is the aim of la Fondazione to provide a platform for the investigation of the relationship between utility and beauty in any field and at the highest possible level.

We are particularly grateful to the Biblioteca Reale in Turin for lending these precious documents and to the Morgan Library & Museum for hosting this exhibition. I cannot think of a more appropriate or better place to exhibit drawings by Leonardo than the Morgan Library, whose architecture elegantly relates to both the Renaissance and our time.

Massimo Vignelli
President, la Fondazione NY

All'interno degli scambi culturali promossi dalla Fondazione, questa mostra dei disegni di Leonardo e dei Leonardeschi, assume una particolare importanza dovuta alla rilevanza delle opere esposte, ed alla contemporaneità del suo messaggio.

Il genio di Leonardo, dalla sua sublime arte ai visionari disegni delle macchine volanti, anticipa i nostri tempi dove la sintesi tra arte e funzione è sovente perseguita.

Pittore, architetto, scienziato, inventore, designer di spaventose macchine da guerra, Leonardo opera in tutto il campo della creatività con coerente intensità e determinazione. Ancora una volta ci mostra come la diversità abbia un significato solo se all'interno metodologico di una disciplina. Io credo che sia una lezione ancora valida, sia oggi che domani.

È uno dei fini della Fondazione quello di provvedere una piattaforma per approfondire il rapporto tra utilità e bellezza, in ogni campo, al massimo livello.

Siamo particolarmente grati, alla Biblioteca Reale di Torino per averci prestato questi preziosi documenti e alla Morgan Library & Museum per aver ospitato questa mostra.

Non posso immaginare un posto migliore e più appropriato per esporre i disegni di Leonardo, dove l'architettura dell'edificio si relaziona elegantemente sia con il Rinascimento che con il nostro tempo.

Massimo Vignelli
Presidente de la Fondazione NY

What sets Leonardo da Vinci apart from other artists is the way he was able to infuse life and soul into his portraits. One look at the *Mona Lisa* or the *Lady with an Ermine* will make the viewer realize that his paintings are more than attractive pictures rendered with extreme attention to detail, and with a realistic and precise representation of the human face. In his pictures there is something more—a conceptual leap that only Leonardo was able to bring to the world of Renaissance art. As we can see in the *Last Supper*, Leonardo was a keen psychologist in addition to being an accomplished scientist, artist, and engineer. He studied the world around him in 360 degrees. Every aspect of nature was of interest to him. No text or philosophy alone, whether by Aristotle or by any scholar of his time, could satisfy his quest for knowledge. He used empirical and experimental means and methods to explore problems and find unique and original solutions. This explains his insatiable curiosity about every aspect of nature and his numerous studies of the human body, of the development of the fetus in the womb, of the flight of insects and birds, of the shapes of rocks and clouds, of the harmony of sounds, of the life of plants, of the laws of waves and clouds. Many aspects of the material world were investigated by Leonardo "the experimental scientist" and later by Leonardo "the artist and inventor" in order to achieve practical goals in both painting and military and civil engineering. Perhaps more than any other artist, Leonardo consistently achieved his artistic goals through a comprehensive approach to problem solving and a unique capacity for universal epistemological understanding.

It is through this scientific curiosity, addressing every possible field, that Leonardo arrived at the profound psychological insights that animate his portraits and enhance their realism. It was known that Leonardo spent much time observing the work in progress on his paintings. It seems that he was concerned with simulating the psychological, and behavioral realities of the subjects of his paintings, while also anticipating each painting's impact on the minds its audience. This is evident in the *Last Supper*, for example in the figure of Judas: he is physically

Quello che caratterizza Leonardo da Vinci rispetto a tutti gli altri artisti è di essere stato capace d'infondere la vita e l'anima nei suoi ritratti. Guardando la *Gioconda* o la *Dama con l'Ermellino* ci si accorge che non si tratta solo di bei quadri, con una cura perfetta dei dettagli, con una rappresentazione realistica e plastica del volto umano. Vi è qualcosa di più, un salto concettuale che solo Leonardo fu in grado di introdurre nell'arte Rinascimentale. Egli, come illustra bene l'*Ultima Cena*, era un acuto psicologo oltreché un grande scienziato, artista e ingegnere. Nel suo studio della realtà era capace di farsi domande a 360 gradi. Ogni aspetto della natura lo interessava. Nessun testo, che fosse di Aristotele o degli eruditi del suo tempo, lo soddisfaceva. Non applicava alcun principio cumulativo o di autorità della conoscenza, ma voleva dare su ogni problema una sua risposta e una soluzione originale, possibilmente di tipo empirico e sperimentale. Da qui la sua curiosità insaziabile su ogni aspetto della natura, che lo ha portato a studiare il corpo umano, la crescita del feto, il volo degli insetti e degli uccelli, le forme delle rocce e delle nubi, l'armonia dei suoni, la vita vegetale, le leggi delle onde e delle nubi. I molti aspetti della realtà venivano scandagliati da scienziato sperimentale e poi da tecnologo ed erano utilizzati per raggiungere obiettivi pratici nella pittura come nella tecnologia militare e civile. Come, e forse più di ogni altro genio universale, raggiungeva i suoi obiettivi utilizzando un potente modello inclusivo di *problem solving* e, si potrebbe dire, anche una capacità unica di *universal epistemological understanding*.

Proprio da questa sua curiosità scientifica a tutto campo nasceva la sua capacità di *insight* psicologico che gli permetteva di dare vita ai suoi ritratti. Era noto che Leonardo passasse molto tempo ad osservare il lavoro in corso dei suoi dipinti. Sembra che la sua preoccupazione fosse di simulare la reale dinamica psicologica e comportamentale dei soggetti dei suoi quadri, e cercare di anticipare l'impatto che il dipinto poteva avere nella testa degli osservatori. Ciò è evidente nell'*Ultima Cena*. Si pensi soltanto alla figura di Giuda, partecipante alla cena ma completamente isolato psicologicamente

present, yet emotionally and morally isolated from the rest of the apostles. Leonardo instinctively applied rules of empathy and theories of mind which are now studied in the neurocognitive and neuroaesthetic sciences.

However, the appearance of life and true human emotion in Leonardo's subjects can also be attributed to his mastery of an artistic device with psychophysical and perceptual elements: *sfumato*. In *sfumato* the confluence of an evanescent outline and blended colors create a form that always leaves something to the viewer's imagination. Leonardo understood that in order to make an image come alive, the viewer must be intrigued by a certain element of mystery in the subject. Well-defined contours and precise shapes tend to crystallize the image and render it too rigid and static.

The exhibition *Leonardo da Vinci: Treasures from the Biblioteca Reale, Turin* at the Morgan Library & Museum, featuring a collection of drawings from the Biblioteca Reale in Turin and organized in collaboration with the Italian Cultural Institute and la Fondazione NY, gives an idea of Leonardo's multifaceted genius.

The Codex on the Flight of Birds combines the exactness and open-mindedness of the scientist with the impeccable graphic and pictorial techniques of the artist. The *Head of a Young Woman*, which served as a study for the angel in the *Virgin of the Rocks*, allows us to grasp his ability to provoke an empathic response in the viewer to the subjects of his paintings. Like the other drawings by Leonardo featured in the exhibition, these highlight the nuances and unique qualities of Leonardo, who was able to apply to his art all he discovered and invented in his scientific and investigative research.

Leonardo da Vinci: Treasures from the Biblioteca Reale, Turin is part of the *Year of Italian Culture in the United States*, celebrating the extraordinary, unsurpassed excellence of Italian Renaissance art.

Riccardo Viale
Director, Italian Cultural Institute of New York

e moralmente dal gruppo. Leonardo, in definitiva, applicava inconsapevolmente le leggi dell'empatia e della teoria della mente, che oggi sono studiate dalle scienze neurocognitive e dalla neuroestetica.

Vi è però anche un accorgimento su basi psicofisiche e percettologiche che spiega l'apparenza di vita dei suoi ritratti. Si tratta della famosa invenzione dello "sfumato": il contorno evanescente ed i colori pastosi fanno confluire una forma nell'altra lasciando sempre un margine alla nostra immaginazione. Leonardo capì che per rendere vivente un'immagine bisogna lasciare allo spettatore qualcosa da indovinare. Contorni troppo definiti e forme troppo precise cristallizzano l'immagine e la rendono statuaria.

La mostra *Leonardo da Vinci. Tesori della Biblioteca Reale, Torino*, organizzata dalla Morgan Library sulla base di parte della collezione della Biblioteca Reale di Torino, con la collaborazione dell'Istituto Italiano di Cultura e de la Fondazione NY, ci da un'idea della genialità multiforme di Leonardo.

Il *Codice sul volo degli uccelli* fonde rigore e spregiudicatezza scientifica a impeccabile tecnica grafica e pittorica. La *Testa di fanciulla*, ritenuto lo studio per il volto dell'angelo della *Vergine delle rocce*, pur attraverso la semplicità cromatica e formale di un disegno, fa cogliere quella capacità, prima citata, di attivazione empatica della psicologia e della vita delle sue figure. Entrambi, come gli altri disegni di Leonardo presenti nella mostra, riaffermano le assolute peculiarità di Leonardo, capace di mettere al servizio della bellezza tutti gli strumenti che il suo genio scientifico indagatore era capace di scoprire e di inventare.

Leonardo da Vinci. Tesori della Biblioteca Reale, Torino fa parte dei grandi eventi dell'*Anno della Cultura Italiana negli Stati Uniti*, come espressione della straordinaria, insuperabile grandezza dell'arte del Rinascimento italiano.

Riccardo Viale
Direttore dell'Istituto Italiano di Cultura di New York

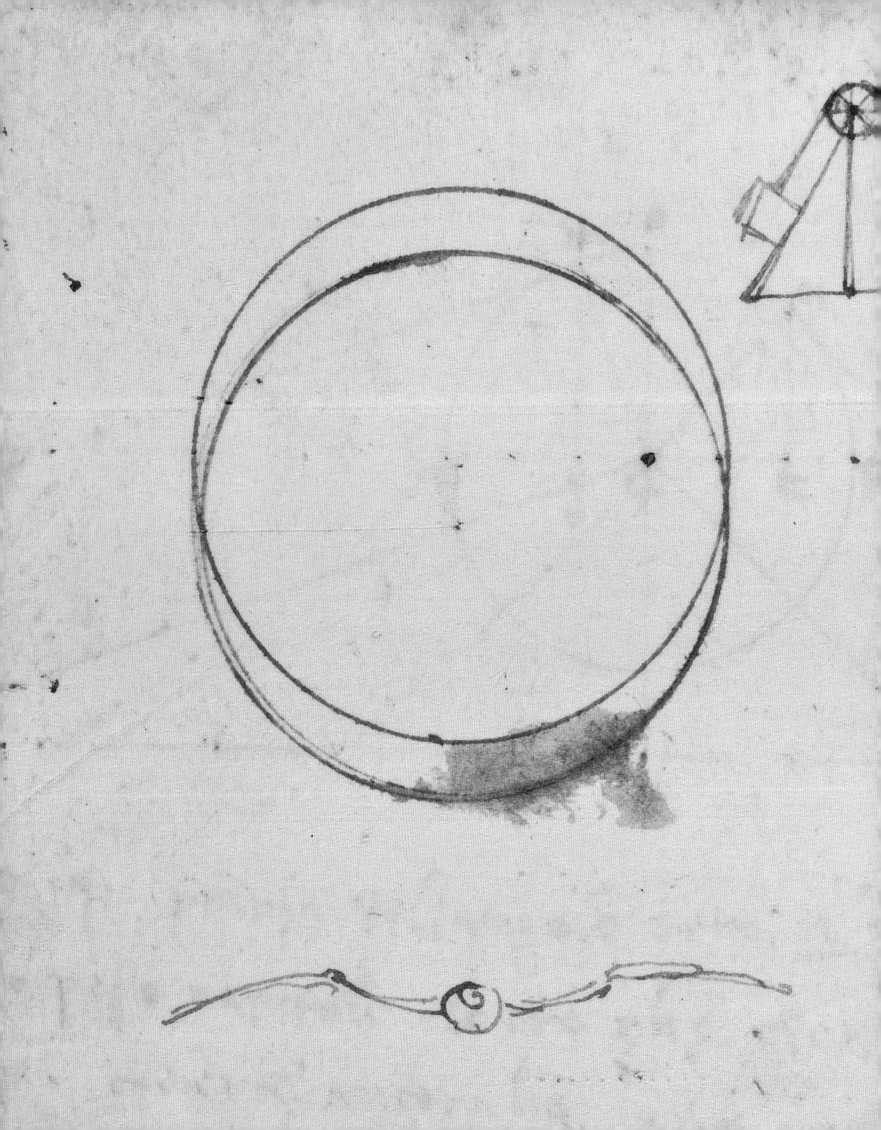

LEONARDO DA VINCI

TREASURES FROM THE BIBLIOTECA REALE, TURIN

TESORI DALLA BIBLIOTECA REALE, TORINO

DRAWINGS BY LEONARDO
DISEGNI DI LEONARDO

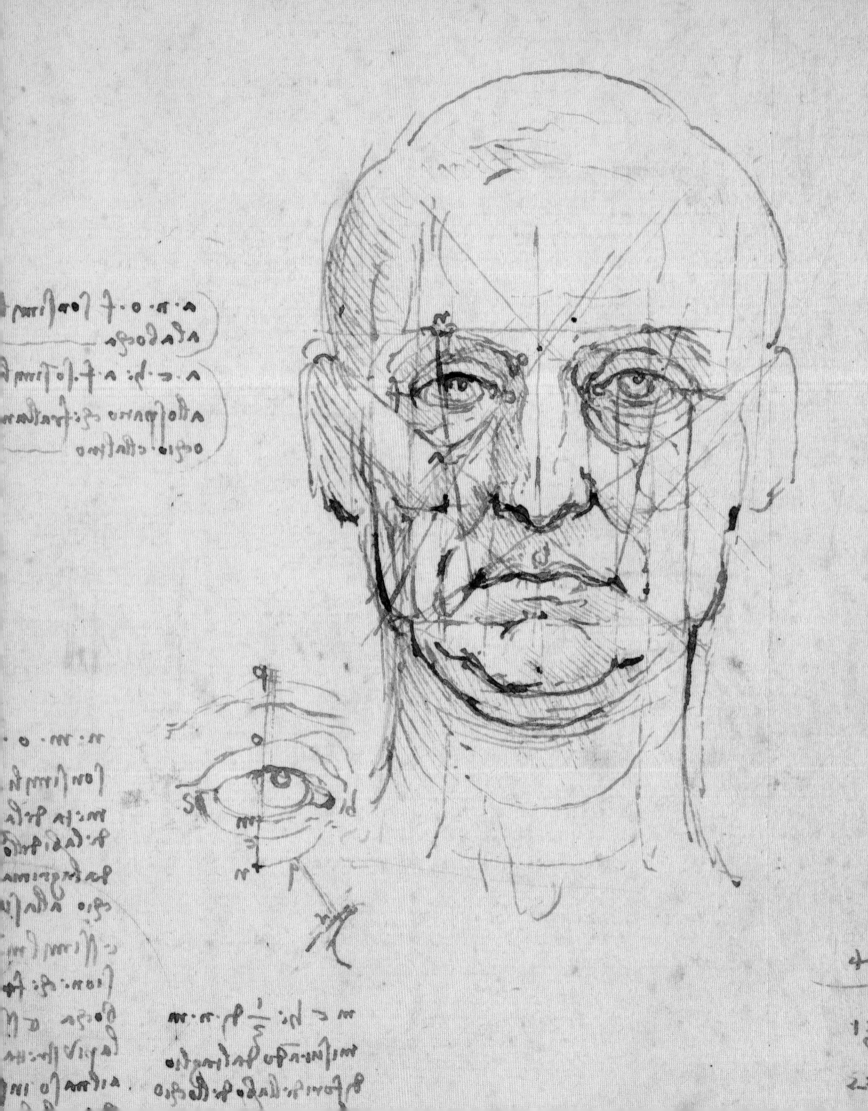

Treasures by Leonardo from the Biblioteca Reale, Turin

Tesori leonardiani dalla Biblioteca Reale di Torino

Paola Salvi

The group of autograph works by Leonardo at the Biblioteca Reale in Turin consists of the Codex on the Flight of Birds and thirteen drawings,[1] with subjects ranging from studies of the human face, proportions, figure and anatomy to studies of horses, nature, and weapons of war derived from antiquity. In addition, the collection comprises a considerable number of sheets by Leonardo's pupils and followers, the so-called Leonardeschi. A great many of these treasures are on display in this exhibition, the highlights of which can be identified in two exceptional works: the Codex on the Flight of Birds (cat. 9) and the *Head of a Young Woman* (cat. 1), presumed to be a preparatory study for the angel in Leonardo's *Virgin of the Rocks*.

The complexity and variety of material in the Codex on the Flight of Birds (see also my essay "Leonardo da Vinci: 'Birds and Other Things'" in this volume, pp. 55–93) are typical of Leonardo. He habitually and intentionally combined different topics on one sheet, uniting various aspects of reality. His pages are also crowded with notes and sketches related not by topic but by his need to immediately capture a thought or observation, with the intention of later developing it or putting it into order. Thus the codex has provided the outline for developing an exhibition sequence which, through the collection itself, helps visitors to comprehend the polyhedral nature of Leonardo and the variety of his studies.

The Codex on the Flight of Birds explores the movement of an animate body, the related issues of weight and balance, and the range of motion of each part, beginning with the limits imposed by the osteoarticular system and the power of the muscular apparatus. Leonardo's method of studying the anatomy and functionality of the locomotor apparatus of birds is not unlike the way he approaches the study of the human body: he uses a comparative principle that is also seen in Manuscript G, taken up again in the *Treatise on Painting*, in which he observes that "all terrestrial animals have a certain resemblance in their parts, that is, their muscles, sinews, and bones, and

La collezione di autografi di Leonardo da Vinci della Biblioteca Reale di Torino consta del *Codice sul volo degli uccelli* e di un nucleo di 13 disegni,[1] che spaziano dallo studio del volto alla ritrattistica, dagli studi anatomici e di figura a quelli proporzionali, da quelli di soggetto naturalistico a quelli del cavallo, fino alla progettazione di congegni bellici di derivazione antica. A questo prezioso nucleo si aggiunge un cospicuo numero di fogli di cosiddetti Leonardeschi, allievi e seguaci. Gran parte di questi tesori della Collezione torinese sono esposti in questa mostra, che trova il proprio filo conduttore in due opere eccezionali: il *Codice sul volo degli uccelli* (cat. 9) e il presunto studio per l'angelo della *Vergine delle rocce* (cat. 1).

La complessità e la varietà di materie del *Codice sul volo degli uccelli* (si veda anche il mio saggio "Leonardo da Vinci: 'uccelli et altre cose'" in questo volume, pp. 55-93) sono tipiche di Leonardo. Da un lato, ciò è determinato da una intenzionale modalità di pensiero, che tende a riunire vari aspetti della realtà, dall'altro, si deve alla consuetudine ad affollare le proprie carte con argomenti vari, associati dalla necessità di fissare immediatamente un pensiero o un'osservazione, destinandone ad una fase successiva lo sviluppo o la riordinazione. Il *Codice* mi ha offerto così la traccia per costruire, mediante la Collezione stessa, un percorso espositivo che aiutasse a comprendere anche la poliedricità di Leonardo e la varietà dei suoi studi.

L'orizzonte generale che emerge dal *Codice sul volo degli uccelli* comprende il movimento di un corpo animato, con tutti i problemi che riguardano il peso, l'equilibrio, le possibili escursioni dei vari segmenti dello stesso, a partire dai limiti posti dal sistema osteo-articolare e dalla potenza dell'apparecchio muscolare. Il metodo di studio dell'anatomia e della funzionalità dell'apparato locomotore degli uccelli non è dissimile da quello adottato per il corpo umano, secondo un principio comparativo che emerge anche nel *Ms. G*, ripreso nel *Libro di pittura*, laddove Leonardo precisa che "tutti li animali terrestri han similitudine di membra, cioè muscoli, nervi e ossa, e nulla si variano se non in lunghezza o in grossezza, come sarà dimostro nell'anatomia".[2] La frequente comparazione istituita tra alcune parti del corpo dell'uccello e dell'uomo (come nel foglio 16 r del

these do not vary except in length or in breadth, as will be shown in the [book on] anatomy."[2] The frequent comparison of certain parts of the body of the bird with those of the man (see, for example, fol. 16 recto)[3] or, in other studies, those of the horse links the codex to the *Musculature of the Legs* (cat. 6a) and, in turn, to the of sense of power expressed by the figure standing stalwartly on his legs in *Hercules with the Nemean Lion* (cat. 8) and to the splendid *Nudes for the "Battle of Anghiari"* (cat. 7), regarded as preparatory studies for Leonardo's now lost mural in the Palazzo Vecchio in Florence. The study of the muscular strength of the body, starting from the power in the legs, anchored to the trunk by the pelvic girdle and moved by a powerful complex of elements in which the gluteal muscles stand out, can be linked to the Codex on the Flight of Birds, where the system of propulsion suggested for working the flying machine is based on the alternating thrust of the operator's lower limbs. On the anatomical sheet Windsor RL 19005 verso, K/P 141 verso, Leonardo wrote: "The principal, the greatest and most powerful muscles which are in man are the buttocks. These are of marvellous power as is demonstrated on the occasion of force exerted by a man in lifting weights."[4] This strength, transformed into a driving force, is what activates the great artificial bird, shown in his studies on various sheets, including fol. 88 recto of Manuscript B (fig. 6), which contains mathematical calculations.[5] Leonardo envisioned other instruments that would be powered by the motion of human legs, such as a boat with vertical blades (based on medieval models) on fol. 945 recto (ex 344 r-b) of the Codex Atlanticus.

The adductor strength of the thighs and calves is what allows the rider to grip the flanks of the horse. It is thus no coincidence that the Turin sheet for the *Battle of Anghiari* (cat. 7) contains sketches of horse and rider at a trot and at full gallop. The position of the figure in the top right foreground is taken up again, like a visual quotation, in the artist's superb anatomical sheet Windsor RL 12625 recto, K/P 95 recto, whose drawings and notes set up direct comparisons between the human limb and the legs of the horse, with an occasional reference to birds: "Draw the knee of a man bent like that of the horse." "To match the bone structure of a horse with that of a man you will make the man on tip-toe in drawing his legs." "Make a man on tip-toe in order that you may better liken man to other animals." "Connection of fleshy muscles with bones without any tendon or

Codice),[3] ma pure, in altri studi, con parti del cavallo, ha reso naturale che al fascicolo sul volo fossero associati gli *Studi di muscolatura degli arti inferiori* (cat. 6a), cui si ricollegano, per la potenza espressa dalla figura saldamente poggiante sulle gambe, l'*Ercole con il leone nemeo* (cat. 8) e lo splendido foglio di *Nudi per la* Battaglia di Anghiari (cat. 7), considerato preparatorio per il perduto affresco di Palazzo Vecchio a Firenze. L'attenzione alla prestanza del corpo a partire dalla potenza muscolare degli arti di sostegno, ancorati al tronco tramite il cingolo pelvico e mossi da un forte complesso di elementi tra cui spicca la muscolatura glutea, è riconducibile al *Codice sul volo* anche per il sistema di propulsione ipotizzato per azionare la macchina volante, basato proprio sulla spinta alternata degli arti inferiori. Nel foglio anatomico RL 19005 v, K/P 141 v, Leonardo ha scritto. "Li principali e li magglori e il più potenti muscoli che sieno nell'uomo sono le sue natiche. Queste so<n> di maravigliosa potenzia, come si dimostra nel loco della forza fatta dall'uomo nel suo alzar de' pesi".[4] A questa forza, trasformata in forza motrice, è affidato il compito di azionare il grande uccello artificiale, come dimostrano gli studi contenuti in svariati fogli, tra cui i calcoli del foglio 88 r del *Ms. B* (fig. 6).[5] La propulsione umana generata dalla potenza degli arti inferiori è prevista anche per il funzionamento di altri strumenti, tra cui un'imbarcazione a pale verticali (costruita sulla base di modelli medievali), come risulta dal foglio 945 r (ex 344 r-b) del *Codice Atlantico*.

La forza adduttoria delle cosce e delle gambe consente anche la presa a morsa sul tronco del cavallo nell'esercizio dell'equitazione. Non è quindi un caso che il foglio torinese per la *Battaglia di Anghiari* (cat. 7) presenti gli schizzi di cavallo e cavaliere al trotto e al galoppo sfrenato, mentre la posizione della figura in primo piano a destra è ripresa, come una citazione, nel meraviglioso foglio anatomico di Windsor RL 12625 r, K/P 95 r. Esso contiene disegni e note dedicati alla diretta comparazione tra l'arto umano e quello equino, con richiamo anche agli uccelli: "Figura il ginocchio dell'omo piegato come quel del cavallo"; "Per equiparare l'ossatura del cavallo a quella dell'omo farai l'omo in punta di piedi nella figurazione delle gambe"; "Fa' l'omo in punta di piedi acciò che tu assimigli meglio l'omo alli altri animali"; "Congiunzione de' muscoli carnoso colle ossa, senza alcun nervo o cartilagine. E 'l simile farai di più animali e uccelli".[6]

Dei tre disegni di zampe di cavallo che la Biblioteca possiede, sono qui esposti il doppio foglio giuntato con *Studi della muscolatura delle zampe anteriori di un cavalllo* (cat. 4), datato al 1480 circa, e il più tardo (c. 1508) foglio con *Studi delle zampe posteriori di un cavallo* (cat. 5), nel quale si ravvisa l'intervento di Francesco Melzi.

gristle [cartilage]. And you will make the same in many animals and birds."[6]

The Biblioteca Reale, Turin, owns three studies of horses' legs, two of which are included in the Morgan exhibition: the double folio with *Studies of the Musculature of a Horse's Forelegs* (cat. 4), dated ca. 1480, and the ca. 1508 *Studies of the Hindquarters of a Horse* (cat. 5), in which the hand of Francesco Melzi can be recognized.

The themes of anatomy, movement and maintaining balance, whether still or in motion, also link these autograph sheets with the Codex on the Flight of Birds through the drawing of a leg, upside-down on fol. 17 verso (cat. 9, pl. XXXVI), which in turn is related to Windsor RL 12637 recto, K/P 9 recto (fig. 13).

The Morgan Library & Museum shared my wish to see the Turin drawings flanked by the Codex Huygens, which was partly copied from Leonardo's lost manuscript on human movements (according to Erwin Panofsky "circular, continuous and uniform movement").[7] The codex also contains folios on human and equine proportions, anatomy, perspective, and theory of light and shade. Amongst the proportion-

I temi del corpo umano, del movimento e dell'equilibrio in posizione statica e dinamica, riuniscono i fogli citati e il *Codice sul volo* anche per il disegno di gamba presente, capovolto, alla carta 17 v (cat. 9, tav. XXXVI), riconducibile al foglio anatomico RL 12637 r, K/P 9 r (fig. 13).

La Morgan Library & Museum non poteva non condividere il mio desiderio di vedere affiancata ai disegni torinesi una selezione dal *Codice Huygens*, lì conservato, che contiene la testimonianza a noi rimasta dei perduti disegni di Leonardo sul moto del corpo umano, indicato da Panofsky come "del moto circolare continuo e uniforme".[7] Il *Codice Huygens* contiene anche fogli dedicati alle proporzioni umane e del cavallo, all'anatomia, alla prospettiva e alla teoria delle ombre. Tra gli studi proporzionali, si possono citare, a titolo esemplificativo: il foglio 53 r (fig. 43), che riproduce, invertito, lo studio proporzionale a Windsor RL 12607 r, K/P 21 r; il foglio 54 r (fig. 42), che riproduce lo studio proporzionale del volto del foglio 236 r delle Gallerie dell'Accademia di Venezia; il foglio 65 r, che riproduce lo studio proporzionale della gamba e del piede dei fogli RL 19136-19139 v, K/P 31 v e i rapporti mano/piede come nel foglio di Windsor RL 19133 r, K/P 29 r; il foglio 77 r (fig. 44), che corrisponde al foglio RL 12294 r, con lo studio proporzionale

FIG. 2

LEONARDO DA VINCI
*Studies of Scythed Chariots /
Studi di carri d'assalto muniti
di falci,* ca. 1485
Pen and brown ink on paper /
Penna e inchiostro su carta
210 x 292 mm
Turin, Biblioteca Reale
(15583 D.C.)

al studies we may mention as examples fol. 53 recto (fig. 43), which repeats the proportional study from Windsor RL 12607 recto, K/P 21 recto; fol. 54 recto (fig. 42), which reproduces the face on a sheet at the Gallerie dell'Accademia in Venice (236 recto); fol. 65 recto, which shows the proportional study of the leg and the foot on Windsor RL 19136–19139 verso, K/P 31 verso and the relations between the hand and the foot on RL 19133 recto, K/P 29 recto; fol. 77 recto (fig. 44) corresponding to RL 12294 recto, with the proportional study of the foreleg of the horse, etc. The history of the Codex Huygens, the current state of research on it and potential consequent interpretations are summarized by Carlo Pedretti in his essay significantly entitled "Proem to the Codex Huygens" (see pp. 151–67 in this volume).

It is well known that, for Leonardo, drawing was not only an artistic practice but also an act of scientific knowledge. This is abundantly clear in the scrupulous descriptive accuracy of the *Two Studies of Insects* (cat. 3). The beetle and the dragonfly are drawn in minute detail, like a scientific illustration, yet they are also vibrantly alive, a quality that relates them to Leonardo's study of flight.[8] Another drawing in Turin depicts moths circling a flame, a symbol of knowledge according to an ancient allegory introduced in different versions over time (cat. 6b).

The *Three Views of a Bearded Man* (cat. 2), in which the subject is shown in frontal, three-quarter, and profile views (the three typical views of representation), has also been linked with the Codex on the Flight of Birds, not in direct relation to Leonardo's studies, but through the observations of critics. Indeed, Luigi Firpo (1991)[9] identified a resemblance between the three-quarter view in this drawing and a face in red chalk faintly visible on a folio of the codex (cat. 9, pl. XXII).

The sheet of three bearded heads—a skillful intermingling of precise detailing, rough outlining, and sketching so light that it amounts to mere suggestion—leads us directly to the second iconic work of this exhibition, the *Head of a Young Woman* (cat. 1), considered to be a preparatory sketch for the first version of Leonardo's *Virgin of the Rocks* (Musée du Louvre, Paris).

This drawing, emblem of the Turin collection, was allegedly called by Bernard Berenson the "most beautiful drawing in the world."[10] It is beyond doubt one of the most significant and charming works in the artistic panorama of the Renaissance. All of

della zampa anteriore del cavallo, ecc. La storia del *Codice Huygens*, lo stato degli studi e le prospettive che potrebbero aprirsi sono qui illustrati da Carlo Pedretti nel suo saggio dal significativo titolo "Proemio al *Codice Huygens*" (si veda in questo volume pp. 151-67).

Come noto, il disegno è per Leonardo pratica artistica che diviene pure atto di conoscenza scientifica. Questo assunto trova un esempio significativo, sul fronte propriamente naturalistico, nell'acribia descrittiva dei *Due studi di insetti* (cat. 3). Il coleottero e la libellula sono dettagliatamente raffigurati in ogni loro parte, come in un'illustrazione scientifica, tuttavia vivi e vibranti e pertanto da ricondurre anch'essi agli studi sul volo.[8] Non manca, nella Collezione torinese, un riferimento al valore simbolico del roteare delle farfalle intorno al fuoco, secondo un'allegoria della conoscenza presentata nel tempo in diverse versioni (cat. 6b).

Anche le *Tre vedute di testa virile con barba* (cat. 2), disegno nel quale il soggetto è raffigurato di fronte, di tre quarti e di profilo (le tre vedute tipiche della raffigurazione artistica), hanno un collegamento con il *Codice sul volo degli uccelli*, seppure non sul piano diretto e leonardiano, ma sul fronte delle interpretazioni critiche. Luigi Firpo (1991)[9] ha

FIG. 3

LEONARDO DA VINCI
Profile of a Man Crowned with Laurel / Testa virile di profilo incoronata di alloro,
ca. 1506–10
Red chalk and brown ink on paper / Sanguigna e inchiostro su carta
168 x 125 mm
Turin, Biblioteca Reale
(15575 D.C.)

Leonardo's greatest stylistic qualities can be found in the representation of the face, the impact of the gaze, the graphic synthesis, and expressive intensity of the line. The subject, drawn from life, is depicted in three-quarter view and is seen slightly from behind. The symmetry of the page is maintained by the merest hint of the line of the left shoulder. She is looking over her shoulder, like someone responding to a voice. Her hair, loosely gathered, and her simple hat, perhaps more a cap, suggest a domestic, common setting, as I have recently pointed out.[11] The position of her body, the turn of her head and neck, the line of the trapezius muscle that so accurately indicates the profile of her shoulder, the shape of her nose, the angle of her glance, and the slight bulging of her eyes, in my opinion confirm that the drawing is a preparatory study

infatti voluto ravvisare una somiglianza tra la veduta di tre quarti di questo disegno e quella sovrascritta della carta 10 v del *Codice* (cat. 9, tav. XXII).

La triplice testa barbuta, che deriva, sul piano grafico, dal sapiente dosaggio di parti descritte nel dettaglio e di zone sommariamente delineate, o addirittura solo suggerite dall'abbozzo, ci conduce direttamente alla seconda opera simbolo e 'timone' di questa mostra: la *Testa di fanciulla* (cat. 1), ritenuto uno studio per la prima versione della *Vergine delle rocce* (conservata al Louvre di Parigi).

Il disegno, emblema della Biblioteca Reale e ormai ovunque accompagnato dalla definizione, attribuita a Bernard Berenson, di "più bel disegno del mondo",[10] è senza dubbio una delle opere più significative e affascinanti nel panorama artistico rinascimentale, e contiene *in nuce* le 'qualità' stilistiche di Leonardo per quanto riguarda la rap-

FIG. 4

LEONARDO DA VINCI
Proportion Studies of the Head and the Eye /
Studi di proporzioni del volto e dell'occhio, ca. 1489–90
Pen and brown ink on paper /
Penna e inchiostro su carta
144 x 116 and 197 x 160 mm
Turin, Biblioteca Reale
(15576–15574 D.C. recto)

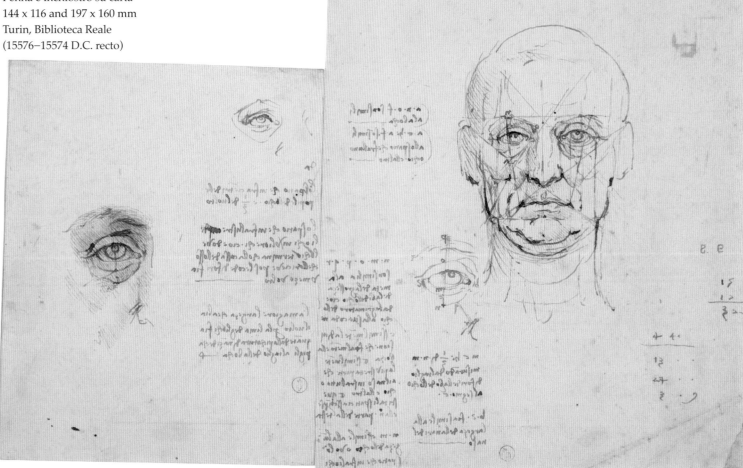

for the first version of the *Virgin of the Rocks*. Therefore, it is to be regarded as a life drawing that was reworked and idealized, becoming the angel on the right of the painting in the Louvre. The drawing retains graceful elements which derive from Leonardo's training in the workshop of Verrocchio and presages the search for animation that would feature in the artist's successive studies of the face and its possible expressions (culminating in Leonardo's theory of *moti mentali,* motions of the mind). For these reasons, this drawing provides a perfect link to the drawings by the Leonardeschi on display, a section that includes the *Study of the Angel in Verrocchio's "Baptism of Christ"* (cat. 10), and brings together numerous studies of heads, as discussed in Annalisa Perissa Torrini's essay in this volume (pp. 183–96).

For these treasures, the journey to New York is justified by the prestige of the Morgan Library and the related works in its collection.[12] I must also mention the autograph drawings by Leonardo which remain in Italy. Concurrently with this exhibition, the *Proportion Studies of the Head and the Eye* (15576 D.C. and 15574

presentazione del volto, l'importanza dello sguardo, la sintesi grafica e l'intensità espressiva del segno. Il soggetto è un ritratto dal vero di fanciulla, eseguito in veduta di tre quarti da una posizione del corpo latero-posteriore, con la simmetria della pagina segnata dalla spalla sinistra, appena accennata. Il capo, infatti, si volge indietro, come avviene a chi si volti ad un richiamo. La capigliatura sommariamente raccolta e il semplice copricapo, forse una cuffia, come ho recentemente evidenziato, fanno supporre un contesto domestico e popolare.[11] La posizione della figura, l'impostazione del capo sul collo, la linea del muscolo trapezio che definisce correttamente il profilo della spalla, la forma del naso, la posizione dello sguardo e la caratteristica un poco sporgente degli occhi, continuano a tenere, a parere di chi scrive, questo splendido disegno collegato alla prima versione della *Vergine delle rocce*. Si tratterebbe, quindi, di uno studio dal vero che ha trovato rielaborazione e idealizzazione nell'angelo a destra del dipinto del Louvre. Il disegno conserva elementi di grazia derivanti dall'esperienza formativa di Leonardo alla bottega del Verrocchio, e presagisce la ricerca dell'animazione che sarà propria dei successivi studi sui volti e sulle loro possibili

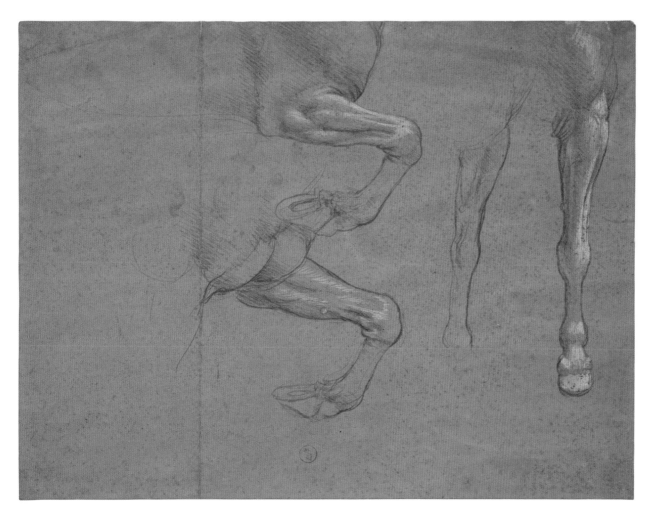

FIG. 5

LEONARDO DA VINCI
Studies of the Forelegs of a Horse / Studi delle zampe anteriori di un cavallo
Metalpoint heightened with white on blue prepared paper /
Punta metallica e lumeggiature di biacca su carta preparata azzurra
154 x 205 mm
Turin, Biblioteca Reale
(15580 D.C.)

D.C. recto; fig. 4) were temporarily in Venice for the exhibition *Leonardo da Vinci. L'uomo universale* (*Leonardo da Vinci: Universal Man*) at the Gallerie dell'Accademia, displayed in the company of Leonardo's *Vitruvian Man* and exceptional drawings with studies of the face in profile (Gallerie dell'Accademia 228 and 236, and Windsor, RL 12601 recto, K/P 19 recto), not to mention other elegant proportional studies also from the Royal Collection at Windsor, hung together in a section dedicated to the human proportion that I had the honor of curating.[13] The same exhibition in Venice also included other sheets from Turin: *Studies of Scythed Chariots* (15583 D.C.; fig. 2); *Studies of the Forelegs of a Horse* (15580 D.C.; fig. 5); and *Profile of a Man Crowned with Laurel* (15575 D.C.; fig. 3). Presiding over the "Sala Leonardo" of the Biblioteca Reale in Turin, home to all these treasures, remains Leonardo himself, in his *Self-Portrait* (15571 D.C.; fig. 1).

Between 2011 and 2012, on the occasion of the 150th anniversary of the Unification of Italy, all the autograph drawings by Leonardo from the Turin collection were on display in the Venaria Reale (just a few miles from Turin) in a spectacular exhibition (*Leonardo. Il Genio, il Mito* [*Leonardo: The Genius, the Myth*]) designed by Dante Ferretti. The section of the exhibition dedicated to these drawings (*Il genio e il suo volto* [*The Genius and His Face*]) was given an unusual slant, on the basis of the themes represented in the collection. Individual drawings, or groups on similar topics, from the Biblioteca Reale were shown alongside prestigious works by Leonardo on loan from national and international collections, to allow an examination of the specific subjects of the sheets or groups of sheets entirely from the original works.[14] The celebrated Turin collection thus demonstrated that a profound understanding of the graphic work and main research areas of the artist could be acquired through the collection itself. Indeed, the exhibition was also an opportunity for new observations and important comparisons, including, for the first time, a direct comparison of the *Self-Portrait* with the profile study of Leonardo at Windsor (RL 12726 recto) and the copy at the Ambrosiana (F 263 inf., 1 bis).[15] Thus in-depth, ongoing studies could be launched. It must be hoped that the meeting of the treasures of Turin's Biblioteca Reale and those of New York's Morgan Library & Museum gives rise to equally fertile developments in the field of Leonardo scholarship.[16]

espressioni (compiendosi con la teoria dei "moti mentali"). Per queste ragioni, esso costituisce in mostra un 'link' d'eccezione con i disegni di Leonardeschi, sezione che si apre con lo *Studio di angelo nel "Battesimo di Cristo" del Verrocchio* (cat. 10) e riunisce numerosi studi di teste, per i quali si rinvia al saggio di Annalisa Perissa Torrini (pp. 183-96).

Nel contesto di uno spostamento transoceanico di tale entità, giustificato dal prestigio dell'Istituzione ospitante e dalle opere leonardesche che essa conserva,[12] corre l'obbligo di menzionare i disegni autografi di Leonardo rimasti in Italia: nello stesso periodo di questa mostra gli *Studi di proporzioni del volto e dell'occhio* (15576 e 15574 D.C. r riuniti; fig. 4) hanno raggiunto Venezia per la mostra *Leonardo da Vinci. L'uomo universale*, alle Gallerie dell'Accademia, trovandosi in 'compagnia' dell'*Uomo vitruviano* e degli eccezionali studi proporzionali del volto in profilo (Gallerie dell'Accademia, 228 e 236, e Windsor, RL 12601 r, K/P 19 r), nonché di altri raffinati studi proporzionali provenienti dalla Collezione Reale a Windsor, raccolti in una sezione dedicata alle proporzioni del corpo umano che ho avuto l'onore di curare.[13] Anche gli *Studi di carri d'assalto muniti di falci* (carri falcati) (15583 D.C.; fig. 2), gli *Studi di zampe anteriori di un cavallo* (15580 D.C.; fig. 5), la *Testa virile di profilo incoronata di alloro* (15575 D.C.; fig. 3), hanno partecipato alla mostra veneziana. A presiedere la 'casa', la Sala Leonardo della Biblioteca Reale di Torino dove tutti questi tesori sono conservati, è rimasto Leonardo stesso, cioè il suo *Autoritratto* (15571 D.C.; fig. 1).

Tra il 2011 e il 2012, nell'occasione della celebrazione del 150esimo anniversario dell'Unità d'Italia, tutti gli autografi di Leonardo furono esposti alla Reggia di Venaria Reale (a pochi chilometri da Torino), nel contesto di una spettacolare mostra (*Leonardo. Il Genio, il Mito*) con l'allestimento di Dante Ferretti. Alla sezione che li raccoglieva (intitolata *Il Genio e il suo volto*) si intese dare un taglio particolare, guidato dai soggetti presenti nella Collezione. A singoli disegni o gruppi di analogo tema della Biblioteca si riunirono così prestigiosi prestiti nazionali e internazionali, a completare e approfondire, esclusivamente attraverso originali, l'argomento specifico di quel foglio o gruppo di fogli.[14] La prestigiosa Collezione torinese dimostrava così di poter far conoscere ad ampio raggio l'attività grafica e le principali tematiche di ricerca dell'artista. La mostra divenne inoltre occasione di nuovi studi e di confronti importanti, tra cui, per la prima volta, quello, diretto, tra l'*Autoritratto*, il volto di Leonardo in profilo conservato a Windsor (RL 12726 r) e la copia dell'Ambrosiana (F 263 inf., 1 bis),[15] consentendo riflessioni che continuano ad oggi. Ci si augura che anche l'incontro tra i tesori della Biblioteca Reale di Torino e alcuni della Morgan Library & Museum di New York sia origine di altrettanto fertile sviluppo degli studi.[16]

¹ The autograph drawings by Leonardo in the Biblioteca Reale, Turin, are: *Self-Portrait* (15571 D.C.); *Head of a Young Woman (Study for the Angel in the "Virgin of the Rocks")* (15572 D.C. recto and verso, featuring a sketch of ornamental motif inside an oval); *Studies of Scythed Chariots* (15583 D.C.); *Three Views of a Bearded Man* (15573 D.C.); *Proportion Studies of the Head and the Eye* (15574–76 D.C. recto and verso, including studies for machine parts); *Profile of a Man Crowned with Laurel* (15575 D.C.); *Nudes for the "Battle of Anghiari" and Other Figure Studies* (15577 D.C. recto and verso, including a charcoal sketch of a figure, probably not autograph); *Hercules with the Nemean Lion* (15630 D.C.); *Musculature of the Legs* (15578 D.C. recto and verso, including a poetic composition and a figure sitting near a fire with flying moths); *Studies of the Musculature of a Horse's Forelegs* (15579 D.C.); *Studies of the Forelegs of a Horse* (15580 D.C.); *Studies of the Hindquarters of a Horse*, with intervention by Francesco Melzi (15582 D.C.); *Two Studies of Insects* (15581 D.C.). Regarding the *Head of an Old Man* (15585 D.C.), attributed to Cesare da Sesto, it must be noted that Carlo Pedretti (Pedretti 2011, pp. 41–51) has recently raised the possibility that it might be by Leonardo (see also S. Taglialagamba in Venaria Reale [Turin], 2011–12, pp. 123–24, cat. 1.28).

² Manuscript G, fol. 5 verso, see Marinoni 1986–90, Manuscript G, 1989, pp. 9–10 (English translation KMC), and Pedretti 1995, vol. I, p. 183.

³ Cf. herein p. 127.

⁴ Keele and Pedretti 1979–80, vol. II, p. 518.

⁵ See also my essay dedicated to the Codex on the Flight of Birds in this volume, pp. 55–93.

⁶ Keele and Pedretti 1979–80, vol. I, p. 298.

⁷ Panofsky 1962, pp. 97–98.

⁸ See cat. 3, p. 38, for further drawings and annotations by Leonardo on insects and their flight, to which must be added the annotation of Manuscript G, 5 verso, taken up again in the *Treatise on Painting*, chapter 79: "Then there are the aquatic animals which are of many varieties, for which I shall not persuade the painter to make up a rule, since the varieties are almost infinite, and the same applies to the insect species," see Marinoni 1986–90, Manuscript G, 1989, p. 10 (English translation KMC), and Pedretti 1995, vol. I, p. 184.

⁹ Firpo 1991, pp. XXII–XXIII.

¹⁰ See cat. 1, p. 32.

¹¹ Salvi in Venaria Reale (Turin) 2011–12, pp. 60–63, cat. 1.1a.

¹² For catalogue entries on drawings by Leonardo and the Leonardeschi at the Morgan Library & Museum, see Pedretti 1993.

¹³ Salvi 2013b, pp. 40–57. See also Venice 2013, "Studi di proporzioni del corpo umano," pp. 86–97, cat. I_01 (Gallerie dell'Accademia, Venice, 228); cat. I_02 (Biblioteca Reale, Turin, 15574–76 D.C. recto); I_03 (Gallerie dell'Accademia, Venice, 236 recto and verso); I_04 (Royal Library, Windsor, RL 12601 recto, K/P 19 recto); I_05 (Royal Library, Windsor, RL 12606 recto, K/P 20 recto); I_06 (Royal Library, Windsor, RL 12607 recto, K/P 21 recto); I_07 (Royal Library, Windsor, RL 12304 recto, K/P 28 recto); I_08 (Royal Library, Windsor, RL 19132 recto, K/P 27 recto). My own recent studies have shown the derivation of the so-called *Vitruvian Man* not only from Vitruvius but also from the *Tabulae dimensionum hominis* of *De statua* of Leon Battista Alberti. See also Salvi 2012a. The drawings displayed in the Venice exhibition further emphasize this derivation. For the importance Leonardo attached to the eye and the sense of sight, see Salvi 2012b.

¹⁴ See Salvi 2011, pp. 27–40, where the author recalls, through quotations from Leonardo manuscripts, the themes underlying the grouping of the drawings in the exhibition.

¹⁵ See Salvi in Venaria Reale (Turin) 2011–12, pp. 36–37 and pp. 106–13, cats. 1.19, 1.20, 1.21.

¹⁶ I would like to thank Carlo Pedretti and Annalisa Perissa Torrini; Giovanna Giacobello Bernard, Clara Vitulo and the staff of the Biblioteca Reale; new friends and colleagues at the Morgan Library & Museum; and amongst many others, Ernani Orcorte, photographer, Monica Taddei of the Biblioteca Leonardiana in Vinci and Giuseppe Garavaglia of the Ente Raccolta Vinciana in Milan.

¹ I disegni autografi di Leonardo della Biblioteca Reale di Torino sono i seguenti: *Autoritratto* (15571 D.C.); *Testa di fanciulla* (presunto studio per l'angelo della *Vergine delle rocce*) (15572 D.C. recto e verso, al verso è uno schizzo di motivo ornamentale entro ovale); *Studi di carri d'assalto muniti di falci* (carri falcati) (15583 D.C.); *Tre vedute di testa virile con barba* (15573 D.C.); *Studi di proporzioni del volto e dell'occhio* (15574-76 D.C. recto e verso, al verso sono studi di parti di una macchina); *Testa virile di profilo incoronata di alloro* (15575 D.C.); *Nudi per la "Battaglia di Anghiari" e altri studi di figura* (15577 D.C. recto e verso, al verso schizzo a carboncino della figura centrale, di dubbia autografia); *Ercole con il leone nemeo* (15630 D.C.); *Studi di muscolatura degli arti inferiori* (15578 D.C. recto e verso, al verso sono un componimento poetico e una figura presso il fuoco con farfalle volanti); *Studi di muscolatura delle zampe anteriori di un cavallo* (15579 D.C.); *Studi delle zampe anteriori di un cavallo* (15580 D.C.); *Studi delle zampe posteriori di un cavallo*, con intervento di Francesco Melzi (15582 D.C.); *Due studi di insetti* (15581 D.C.). Corre l'obbligo di segnalare che per la *Testa senile* (15585 D.C.), attribuita a Cesare da Sesto, recentemente Carlo Pedretti (Pedretti 2011, pp. 41-51) ha avanzato l'ipotesi di una autografia di Leonardo (si veda anche la scheda, di S. Taglialagamba, 1.28, pp. 123-24, in Venaria Reale [Turin] 2011-12).

² *Ms. G*, f. 5 v, Marinoni 1986-90, *Il manoscritto G*, 1989, pp. 9-10; Pedretti 1995, vol. I, p. 183.

³ Cfr. qui p. 127, *infra*.

⁴ Keele and Pedretti 1980-84, vol. III, p. 518.

⁵ Si veda in questo stesso volume il mio saggio dedicato al *Codice sul volo degli uccelli*, *infra*, pp. 55-93.

⁶ Keele and Pedretti 1980-84, vol. II, p. 298.

⁷ Panofsky 1962, pp. 97-98.

⁸ Si veda cat. 3, p. 38, *infra*, per gli ulteriori disegni e annotazioni di Leonardo sugli insetti e il loro volo, cui sarà da aggiungere l'annotazione del *Ms. G*, f. 5 v, ripresa nel *Libro di pittura*, cap. 79: "Ecci poi li animali d'acqua che sono di molte varietà, [del]li quali non persuaderò il pittore che vi facia regola, perché son quasi d'infinite varietà, e così li animali insetti", Marinoni 1986-90, *Il manoscritto G*, 1989, p. 10; Pedretti 1995, vol. I, p. 184.

⁹ Firpo 1991, pp. XXII-XXIII.

¹⁰ Si veda la scheda 1, dedicata al disegno, in questo stesso volume, p. 32, *infra*.

¹¹ Salvi in Venaria Reale (Turin) 2011-12, pp. 60-63, cat. 1.1a.

¹² Per la catalogazione dei disegni di Leonardo e dei Leonardeschi della Morgan Library & Museum, si veda Pedretti 1993.

¹³ Cfr. Salvi 2013b, pp. 40-57. Si veda anche in Venice 2013 la Sezione "Studi di proporzioni del corpo umano", pp. 86-97, cat. I_01 (Gallerie dell'Accademia, Venezia, 228); I_02 (Biblioteca Reale, Torino, 15574-76 D.C. r); cat. I_03 (Gallerie dell'Accademia, Venezia, 236 recto e verso); I_04 (Royal Library, Windsor, RL 12601 r, K/P 19 r); I_05 (Royal Library, Windsor, RL 12606 r, K/P 20 r); I_06 (Royal Library, Windsor, RL 12607 r, K/P 21 r); I_07 (Royal Library, Windsor, RL 12304 r, K/P 28 r); I_08 (Royal Library, Windsor, RL 19132 r, K/P 27 r). Studi recenti di chi scrive hanno dimostrato la derivazione del cosiddetto *Uomo vitruviano*, oltre che da Vitruvio, dalle *Tabulae dimensionum hominis* del *De statua* di Leon Battista Alberti. Si veda Salvi 2012a. I disegni esposti nella mostra veneziana evidenziano ulteriormente questa derivazione. Per l'importanza assegnata da Leonardo all'occhio e al senso della vista si veda Salvi 2012b.

¹⁴ Si veda Salvi 2011, pp. 27-40, dove sono richiamati, attraverso citazioni dai manoscritti di Leonardo, i temi riferibili ai raggruppamenti di disegni in mostra.

¹⁵ Cfr. Salvi 2011, pp. 36-37. Si vedano anche le schede, di P. Salvi, relative ai tre disegni in Venaria Reale (Turin) 2011-12, cat. 1.19, 1.20, 1.21, pp. 106-13.

¹⁶ Mi fa piacere ringraziare qui Carlo Pedretti e Annalisa Perissa Torrini; Giovanna Giacobello Bernard, Clara Vitulo e il personale della Biblioteca Reale; i nuovi amici e colleghi della Morgan Library & Museum; fra molti altri, Ernani Orcorte, fotografo, Monica Taddei della Biblioteca Leonardiana di Vinci e Giuseppe Garavaglia dell'Ente Raccolta Vinciana di Milano.

1

LEONARDO DA VINCI (1452–1519)

recto

Head of a Young Woman (Study for the Angel in the "Virgin of the Rocks")
Testa di fanciulla (studio per l'Angelo della "Vergine delle rocce")
ca. 1483–85

Metalpoint heightened with white on buff prepared paper
Punta metallica e lumeggiature di biacca su carta preparata ocra chiaro
181 x 159 mm (7 ⅛ x 6 ¼ inches)

verso

Sketch of an Ornamental Motif within an Oval
Schizzo di motivo ornamentale entro ovale

Pen and brown ink on metalpoint
Penna e inchiostro bruno su traccia di punta metallica

Turin, Biblioteca Reale
(15572 D.C. recto and verso)

Literature / Bibliografia: Richter (1833) 1939, vol. I, p. 377, no. XLII; Berenson 1903, vol. I, p. 154, vol. II, p. 61, no. 1084; Clark 1939, p. 46; Giglioli 1944, p. 102, pl. LXXII; Bertini in Turin 1950, pp. 14–15, cat. 19; Brunetti in Florence 1952, p. 27, cat. 32; Bertini 1958, p. 35, no. 218; Wallace 1966, pp. 144–45; Pedretti in Turin 1975, pp. 8–9, cat. 2; Griseri 1978, no. 9; Pedretti 1990, pp. 84–86, no. 2; Pedretti in Turin 1990, pp. 42–43, cat. 11; Pedretti in Giacobello Bernard 1990, pp. 106–7; Kemp in Washington, D.C. 1991–92, pp. 272–73, cat. 171; Turin 1998–99, pp. 74–77, cat. II.3; Marani in Milan 2001, pp. 120–21, cat. 25; Pedretti in Turin 2003–4, pp. 55–57, cat. 14; Pedretti in Turin 2006, pp. 38–39, cat. I.3; O'Grody in Birmingham and San Francisco 2008–9, pp. 14–17, cat. 1; Marani 2011a, pp. 16–17; Marani 2011b, pp. 20–21; Syson in London 2011–12, p. 117; Salvi in Venaria Reale (Turin) 2011–12, pp. 60–63, cat. 1.1a–1.1b; Taglialagamba in Pedretti 2012, pp. 31–32, no. 1.

Described by Bernard Berenson as "one of the finest achievements of all draughtsmanship" (Berenson 1903), this famous drawing by Leonardo has also been spoken of as "the masterpiece owned by the *Biblioteca Reale* in Turin, a wonder amongst wonders" (Giglioli 1944); Kenneth Clark (Clark 1939) called it "one of the most beautiful, I dare say, in the world." This is probably the origin of the phrase attributed to Berenson in 1952, in an unspecified context, when he supposedly called it "the most beautiful drawing in the world" (see Pedretti, Turin 1975, p. 9). The girl is seen from behind, looking over her shoulder, a pose typical of Leonardo. The angel on the left (painted by Leonardo) in Andrea del Verrocchio's *Baptism of Christ* is seen in the same pose, as is the angel on the right in the first version of the *Virgin of the Rocks,* in the Louvre. In all three cases the figure is seen from behind or in three-quarter profile, the body still and the head turned on the supple neck in a smooth movement that combines the mobility of neck (spinal column) and head (pivoting of the atlas vertebra on the epistropheus). In Verrocchio's *Baptism,* the angel, kneeling slightly to the rear of the central figure of Christ, is seen from behind, a position that permits the head to be turned in profile toward the main scene. The angel in the first version of the *Virgin of the Rocks,* on the other hand, has a pose that allows for the head to be turned in a three-quarter profile. The angel's gaze is directed beyond the painting, and draws the observer's attention to the central figure, the Virgin, toward whom the angel is pointing. The angel's pose is similar to that of the young woman in the present sheet, which was drawn from life. Here the trunk is in a fixed posture, and the movements of neck, head, face, and, finally, gaze follow one another in a sequence that re-

Già indicato da Bernard Berenson come "one of the finest achievements of all draughtsmanship" (Berenson 1903), questo celebre disegno di Leonardo è stato considerato "capolavoro posseduto dalla *Biblioteca Reale* di Torino, meraviglia tra le meraviglie" (Giglioli 1944). Kenneth Clark (Clark 1939) lo ha definito "one of the most beautiful, I dare say, in the world". Da qui, forse, la frase attribuita a Berenson nell'anno 1952, in un contesto non precisato, che avrebbe designato il foglio come "il più bel disegno del mondo" (si veda Pedretti in Turin 1975, p. 9). La figura presenta la caratteristica impostazione leonardiana del 'ritratto di spalla', che si trova sia nell'angelo a sinistra del *Battesimo* di Andrea del Verrocchio (di mano di Leonardo), sia in quello a destra nella prima versione della *Vergine delle rocce*, conservata al Louvre di Parigi. In tutti e tre questi casi la figura è collocata in veduta posteriore o di tre quarti posteriore, con il busto fisso e la testa ruotata verso la spalla con un movimento morbido che deriva dalla mobilità combinata del collo (rachide cervicale) e della testa (rotazione dell'atlante sul perno dell'epistrofeo). Nel *Battesimo* del Verrocchio, dove l'angelo è posto totalmente di schiena e leggermente arretrato rispetto alla figura centrale del Cristo, la testa si volge verso la scena principale mostrando il profilo. Nell'angelo della prima versione della *Vergine delle rocce*, invece, la posizione del busto consente il voltare della testa di tre quarti, con lo sguardo diretto all'esterno del quadro, a richiamare l'attenzione dell'osservatore sulla figura centrale della Vergine, mostrata con l'indice destro. Questa posizione è la stessa del disegno torinese, un ritratto dal vero, impostato sulla base della postura fissa del tronco sul quale si susseguono i movimenti del collo, della testa, del volto e infine dello sguardo, in una sequenza che ricorda i numerosi disegni e schizzi che Leonardo ha realizzato tra la fine degli anni Settanta e gli inizi degli anni Ottanta, tra cui lo studio al British Museum di Londra, raffigurante la Vergine

33

calls numerous Leonardo drawings and sketches made between the late 1470s and early 1480s, including the study at the British Museum of the Virgin and Child with a cat (1856,0621.1 verso). A sheet at Windsor (RL 12513) includes eighteen studies of the possible positions of the female head and neck with respect to the trunk, seen from various angles. Clark (Clark 1968–69, vol. I, p. 90) assigned it to Leonardo's Florentine period: "They are, of course, perfectly authentic, and evidence of Leonardo Florentine training, and above all of his debt to his master." A superb study of hands at Windsor (RL 12558) that is technically and stylistically very close to the Turin drawing has been dated between 1478 and 1480 (Clark 1968–69, vol. I, pp. 104–5). These drawings appear to be closely related. For this reason, when the date of one is changed, the dating of the others is generally reviewed.

Möller (1916) and Ochenkowsky (1919) suggested a link with the portrait of Cecilia Gallerani, as she appears in the so-called *Lady with an Ermine* in Cracow. Marani (Marani 2011a and Marani 2011b) has dated the drawing to around 1490, considering it stylistically similar to the series of skulls from 1489, an opinion I have questioned (see Salvi in Venaria Reale [Turin] 2011–12, p. 62). In the exhibition catalogue for *Leonardo da Vinci: Painter at the Court of Milan* (London 2011–12), the present sheet was discussed with the above-mentioned Windsor sheets (RL 12513 and RL 12558) and the *Portrait of a Woman in Profile* (RL 12505), and all were assigned to Leonardo's Milanese period, around 1490 (Syson in London 2011–12, pp. 114–17, cats. 11, 12, 13): "It is now possible to construct a coherent group of metalpoint drawings, all from 1490 or a little before, which includes not just these two works [RL 12558, RL 12505] and the horse studies, but also studies of an infant [RL 12569 recto] and two superb drawings of women's heads in Paris [Louvre 2376] and Turin [the present drawing]." For Windsor RL 12513, an association with the *Lady with an Ermine* has been suggested, given the similarity between the sketch on the far left of the sheet and the position of the head and neck of the famous painting (Syson in London 2011–12, pp. 118–19, cat. 13).

In order to evaluate this new theory, we should turn to Clark's considerations on Windsor RL 12505 (Clark 1968–69, vol. I, p. 88): "Between 1482, the period of the last silver-point drawings for the *Adoration*, and 1495, when he seems to have abandoned this medium altogether, we have little datable evidence of Leonardo's silver-point style. It is therefore difficult to say where in this period we must place this beautiful and famous profile. In favor of an early date we may say that the paper is very similar to that of the hands, '588 [*sic*, '558], and the studies of heads, '513. The simple head-dress is characteristically Florentine and can be paralleled in numerous Florentine portraits. In the Mainardi portrait formerly in the Kaiser-Friedrich Museum, Berlin, No. 83, head-dress and type of sitter are surprisingly similar. I have found no instance of this coiffure in Milan, where the head-dresses were bejewelled and formal. Against this, the technique seems to be closer to the late than early drawings of horses."

con il Bambino e un gatto (1856,0621.1 v). Un foglio conservato a Windsor, RL 12513, contiene diciotto studi raffiguranti le possibilità di movimento della testa e del collo femminili sul tronco, in varie vedute. Clark (Clark 1968-69, vol. I, p. 90) lo ha assegnato al periodo fiorentino: "They are, of course, perfectly authentic, and evidence of Leonardo Florentine training, and above all of his debt to his master". Il superbo foglio RL 12558, raffigurante studi di mani, è tecnicamente e stilisticamente molto vicino al disegno torinese ed è stato datato al 1478-80 (Clark 1968-69, vol. I, pp. 104-5). Questi disegni paiono tutti in stretta relazione tra loro. Per questa ragione, con lo spostamento cronologico di uno si tende a rivedere anche la datazione degli altri.

Per il disegno di Torino, Möller (1916) e Ochenkowsky (1919) avevano ipotizzato un collegamento con il ritratto di Cecilia Gallerani, come compare nel celebre dipinto *La Dama con l'ermellino*, conservato a Cracovia. Pietro Marani (Marani 2011a e Marani 2011b), ha riferito il disegno al 1490 circa, ritenendolo stilisticamente vicino alla serie dei crani del 1489 (opinione da chi scrive non condivisa, si veda Salvi in Venaria Reale [Turin] 2011-12, p. 62). Nel catalogo della recente mostra londinese (London 2011-12) dedicata a *Leonardo da Vinci: Painter at the Court of Milan*, i tre disegni citati (Torino, Windsor RL 12513 e RL 12558) e il *Ritratto di donna in profilo*, RL 12505, sono stati riuniti e assegnati tutti al periodo milanese, intorno al 1490 (Syson in London 2011-12, pp. 114-17, catt. 11, 12, 13): "It is now possible to construct a coherent group of metalpoint drawings, all from 1490 or a little before, which includes not just these two works [RL 12558, RL 12505] and the horse studies, but also studies of an infant [RL 12569 r] and two superb drawings of women's heads in Paris [Louvre 2376] and Turin [il disegno di cui si sta scrivendo]". Per il foglio RL 12513 è proposta una relazione con la *Dama con l'ermellino* per la similitudine tra lo schizzo all'estremo sinistro del foglio e la posizione di testa e collo nel celebre dipinto (Syson in London 2011-12, pp. 118-19, cat. 13).

Per valutare questa nuova ipotesi mi sembra siano da riprendere le riflessioni di Clark per il foglio RL 12505 (Clark 1968-69, vol. I, p. 88), che scrive: "Between 1482, the period of the last silver-point drawings for the *Adoration*, and 1495, when he seems to have abandoned this medium altogether, we have little datable evidence of Leonardo's silver-point style. It is therefore difficult to say where in this period we must place this beautiful and famous profile. In favour of an early date we may say that the paper is very similar to that of the hands, '588 [*sic*! '558], and the studies of heads, '513. The simple head-dress is characteristically Florentine and can be paralleled in numerous Florentine portraits. In the Mainardi portrait formerly in the Kaiser-Friedrich Museum, Berlin, No. 83, head-dress and type of sitter are surprisingly similar. I have found no instance of this coiffure in Milan, where the head-dresses were bejewelled and formal. Against this, the technique seems to be closer to the late than early drawings of horses".

L'uso della punta metallica su carta preparata, medium piuttosto rigido, riduce le variazioni stilistiche nell'ambito della produzione di uno stesso artista, cosicché risultano importanti altri aspetti del disegno. Nel caso delle opere citate, sono a mio avviso da proporre le seguenti osservazioni. Lo studio di mani (RL 12558) risente in maniera significativa dello stile del Verrocchio, e, in particolare, come da vari autori messo in evidenza, di quello del marmo conservato a Firenze (Museo del Bargello) conosciuto come

The use of metalpoint on prepared paper, a rather stiff medium, limits the stylistic variations within an artist's work, making other aspects of the drawing important. In the case of the works mentioned, I would like to make the following observations: Leonardo's study of hands (RL 12558) shows the strong influence of Verrocchio's style, in particular, as various authors have observed, the marble bust *Lady with a Bunch of Flowers,* at the Museo del Bargello. Rather than being a recollection of his master's work that emerged at the end of the 1480s (Syson in London 2011–12, p. 117), I believe that the similarity between the bust and the sheet of hands indicates that the drawing was done during the Florentine period, as proposed by Clark.

The eighteen head studies (RL 12513) should also be considered as dating from this Florentine period, since they coincide with the problems of representation that Leonardo posed for himself at that time. The similarity of the position of the head and neck between the sketch on the left of the sheet and the *Lady with an Ermine* (stressed by Syson in London 2011–12, p. 118) does not necessarily demand that the sheet be redated; since the sheet is a repertory of life studies, this head could have been used at a later date.

The Turin drawing is stylistically close to the sheets mentioned here, while the turning of the head and the facial features clearly link it to the first version of the *Virgin of the Rocks,* allowing us to date it around 1483–85. The drawing is typical of Leonardo's concise style: with just a few strokes, he captures the position of the subject, defining a few details with chiaroscuro, achieving an extreme lightness in the image that the eye of the observer reads as a whole, including the parts that are merely hinted at. It is, as Robert Wallace said, a "deceptively simple" drawing (Wallace 1966), and has great elegance and psychological penetration. The focal point is the gaze, directed at the viewer, yet not fixed: the slightly lowered eyelids just veil it. As the gaze of the angel in the *Virgin of the Rocks* in the Louvre serves to direct us toward the central scene, the gaze in the present sheet also directs us, but in this case to something unspecified. The present sheet was first identified by Richter (Richter 1883) as a life study for the painting, and the classification was confirmed by various authors, including Pedretti (Pedretti in Turin 1975, Pedretti 1990, Pedretti in Turin 2006) and this author (Salvi in Venaria Reale [Turin], 2011–12), so that this association has remained the most plausible. This drawing represents a milestone in portraiture for its vibrancy and psychological insight.

On the verso is an ornamental sketch, believed to be by Leonardo, depicting tangled ribbons, which recalls a recurrent motif in Leonardo's work (interlaced branches on the ceiling of the Sala delle Asse in Milan or the knots in the emblem of the Accademia Vinciana). Drawn within an oval that lies horizontal to the drawing on the recto, it has been considered a study for a decorative element for a book cover (Pedretti in Turin 1975, p. 8), but it could also be a project for a goldsmith to fashion into a jewel or medallion.

PS

Dama col mazzolino. Piuttosto che una reminescenza emersa alla fine degli anni '80 del Quattrocento (Syson in London 2011-12, p. 117), credo che questo aspetto indichi come appropriata una datazione al periodo fiorentino, secondo quanto proposto da Clark. Allo stesso tempo fiorentino è da mantenere la serie dei diciotto studi (RL 12513), poiché coincide con problemi di rappresentazione che Leonardo si poneva in quegli anni. La similitudine dell'impostazione di testa e collo tra lo schizzo a sinistra del foglio e la *Dama con l'ermellino* (messo in evidenza da Syson in London 2011-12, p. 118) non necessariamente comporta lo spostamento cronologico del disegno, che, contenendo un repertorio di posizioni studiate sul vero, può essere stato utilizzato anche a distanza di tempo.

Il foglio torinese rivela una vicinanza stilistica con i disegni citati, mentre la rotazione della testa e i tratti fisionomici lo collegano, con chiara evidenza, alla prima versione della *Vergine delle rocce,* consentendo una indicazione cronologica intorno al 1483-85. Lo stile sintetico è emblematico di Leonardo, che con pochi segni riesce a cogliere l'impostazione della figura, che definisce in alcuni particolari con il chiaroscuro, ottenendo una estrema leggerezza dell'immagine che l'occhio dell'osservatore riesce a leggere in modo unitario, anche in quelle parti solo abbozzate. È un disegno, quindi, "ingannevolmente semplice", come lo ha definito Robert Wallace (Wallace 1966), e di grande raffinatezza e penetrazione psicologica. Il punto focale è lo sguardo, diretto all'osservatore in maniera non fissa: un lievissimo abbassamento delle palpebre lo vela appena, evocando un rimando ad altro, come nell'angelo della *Vergine delle rocce* parigina, che indica infatti la scena centrale. Dal riconoscimento del Richter (Richter 1883) come studio dal vero per quest'opera, confermato fino ad oggi da vari autori e da Pedretti (Pedretti in Turin 1975, Pedretti 1990, Pedretti in Turin 2006), infine da chi scrive (Salvi in Venaria Reale [Turin] 2011-12), questo collegamento rimane il più attendibile. Nell'ambito della ritrattistica, questo delicato foglio costituisce una pietra miliare nel percorso di animazione e di resa psicologica del soggetto ritratto.

Al verso si trova uno schizzo ornamentale, ritenuto autografo, costituito da un intreccio di nastri che richiama un motivo ricorrente in Leonardo (rami della volta della Sala delle Asse a Milano e i nodi nell'emblema dell'Accademia Vinciana). È disegnato entro un ovale che ha l'asse maggiore trasversale al disegno del recto, ed è stato considerato uno studio per un elemento decorativo destinato a un piatto di legatura (Pedretti in Turin 1975, p. 8), ma anche un possibile progetto da utilizzare in oreficeria, per un gioiello o un clipeo.

PS

2

LEONARDO DA VINCI (1452–1519)

Three Views of a Bearded Man
Tre vedute di testa virile con barba
ca. 1502

Red chalk on paper
Sanguigna su carta
111 x 284 mm (4 ⅜ x 11 ³⁄₁₆ inches)
Turin, Biblioteca Reale
(15573 D.C.)

Literature / Bibliografia: Berenson 1903, vol. II, p. 61, no. 1085; Valentiner 1930, p. 60; Giglioli 1944, p. 145, pl. CLXVI; Valentiner 1950, p. 151; Bertini in Turin 1950, p. 16, cat. 26; Brunetti in Florence 1952, p. 37, cat. 53; Bertini 1958, p. 36, no. 225; Pedretti in Turin 1975, pp. 10–11, cat. 3; Pedretti 1990, pp. 86–88, no. 3; Pedretti in Turin 1990, pp. 46–47, cat. 13; Turin 1998–99, pp. 78–79, cat. II.4; Marani in Milan 2001, pp. 148–49, cat. 39; Pedretti in Turin 2006, pp. 42–43, cat. I.5; O'Grody in Birmingham and San Francisco 2008–9, pp. 24–27, cat. 3; Salvi in Venaria Reale (Turin) 2011–12, pp. 100–1, cat. 1.16.

These three studies of the same face, featuring a wind-blown but cared-for beard, reveal an unusual physiognomy, above all in the shape of the head, with its protruding chin. The sheet is undoubtedly a life study, in which Leonardo first drew the front view and then the three-quarter profile and full profile views. He focuses mostly on the lower part of the face, especially on the finely detailed beard, while merely sketching in the upper part of the head, which is bare in the en-face drawing. In the three-quarter profile and the full profile, the subject wears some sort of head covering, perhaps a biretta. The proposed dates for the sheet vary, from the period of the *Last Supper* to that of the later deluge drawings. Valentiner (1930 and 1950) proposed the date of 1502 and suggested that the sitter is Cesare Borgia (the military leader, known as *Il Valentino* and son of Pope Alexander VI), who employed Leonardo around that time. This identification is not unanimously accepted, mostly because of the considerable difference between the man depicted in this drawing and the extant portraits of the renowned leader (Pedretti 1990, in particular with reference to the copy at the Galleria degli Uffizi). Stylistically, however, the date seems plausible, perhaps extending a little before and after. The triple nature of the study suggests that it may have been intended for a painting, as these are the three principal viewpoints, or for sculpture, as they could represent the starting point for a portrayal in the round. With regard to the sitter, he could also be an individual encountered by chance, as suggested by Pedretti (Pedretti 1990) in accordance with Vasari's comments on Leonardo's visual curiosity (Vasari [1568] 1996, vol. I, pp. 630–31): "He was so delighted when he saw certain bizarre heads of men, with the beard or hair growing naturally, that he would follow one that pleased him a whole day, and so treasured him up in idea, that afterwards, on arriving home, he drew him as if he had had him in his presence. Of this sort there are many heads to be seen, both of women and of men."

PS

Questi tre studi di uno stesso volto, caratterizzato da una barba mossa e composta, rivelano una fisionomia particolare, soprattutto per la forma della testa, dal mento spinto in avanti. Si tratta senza dubbio di uno studio dal vero, nel quale Leonardo ha disegnato dapprima la veduta frontale e poi le altre di tre quarti e di profilo, definendole soprattutto nella zona bassa del volto, con una bella descrizione della barba, abbozzando invece la parte alta della testa, che è libera nella proiezione frontale, mentre nel disegno di tre quarti e in profilo il soggetto indossa una fascia o berretta. L'assegnazione cronologica oscilla in un ampio raggio temporale, dal periodo del *Cenacolo* al più tardo dei disegni del *Diluvio*. La data del 1502 è stata proposta da Valentiner contestualmente alla individuazione del soggetto in Cesare Borgia (il condottiero figlio di Papa Alessandro VI e denominato "il Valentino"), presso cui Leonardo si trovava in quel periodo. Tale identificazione (Valentiner 1930 e 1950) non ha trovato unanimità, soprattutto per una notevole differenza con l'iconografia nota del celebre condottiero (Pedretti 1990, in particolare, con riferimento alla copia della Galleria degli Uffizi). Stilisticamente, tuttavia, resta attendibile la data di esecuzione, magari ampliando un poco il torno temporale a monte e a valle, mentre la natura triplice dello studio potrebbe avere una destinazione per la pittura, trattandosi delle tre vedute classiche della riproduzione bidimensionale, ma anche per la scultura, poiché le stesse costituiscono i riferimenti di partenza per lo svolgimento a tutto tondo. Riguardo al soggetto, potrebbe trattarsi pure di uno schizzo effettuato su di un individuo incontrato per caso, come evidenzia Pedretti (Pedretti 1990), secondo quanto riferisce Vasari sulla curiosità visiva di Leonardo: "Piacevagli tanto quanto egli vedeva certe teste bizzarre, o con barbe o con capegli degli uomini naturali, che arebbe seguitato uno che gli fussi piaciuto, un giorno intero; e se lo metteva talmente nella idea, che poi arrivato a casa lo disegnava come se l'avesse avuto presente. Di questa sorte se ne vede molte teste e di femmine e di maschi" (Vasari [1568] 1878-85, vol. IV, p. 26).

PS

3

LEONARDO DA VINCI (1452–1519)

Two Studies of Insects
Due studi di insetti
ca. 1480 and ca. 1503–5

Pen and brown ink on red prepared paper, cut out and mounted on a secondary sheet
Penna e inchiostro su carta colorata in rosso, ritagliata in due frammenti montati su altro foglio
129 x 118 mm (5 ¹/₁₆ x 4 ⁵/₈ inches)

Turin, Biblioteca Reale
(15581 D.C.)

Literature/Bibliografia: Berenson 1903, vol. II, p. 61, no. 1093; Giglioli 1944, p. 139, pl. CLI; Bertini in Turin 1950, p. 15, cat. 22; Brunetti in Florence 1952, p. 23, cat. 26; Boden-heimer 1956, pp. 147–53; Bertini 1958, p. 35, no. 221; Pedretti in Turin 1975, pp. 29–30, cat. 13; Griseri 1978, no. 7; Pedretti 1990, pp. 98–99, no. 13; Tongiorgi Tomasi in Florence 1992, p. 193, cat. 9.15; Turin 1998–99, pp. 100–1, cat. II.13; Genoa 2001, p. 84, cat. I.132; Pedretti in Turin 2003–4, pp. 62–63, cat. 17; Pedretti in Turin 2006, pp. 62–63, cat. I.14; O'Grody in Birmingham and San Francisco 2008–9, pp. 54–55, cat. 11; Salvi in Venaria Reale (Turin) 2011–12, pp. 78–79, cat. 1.7.

These two exquisite drawings, cut out and mounted on a secondary sheet, portray two insects: a fairly common beetle and a dragonfly. According to some scholars, the latter is a *formicaleone* or typical Italian long-horned insect, "which can be recognized by the much thicker body than a dragonfly and the relatively long antennae" (Tongiorgi Tomasi in Pedretti 1990, p. 99). In the almost horizontal lines of the first drawing Pedretti identified "the emphatic strokes of the drawings from the period of the *Adoration of the Magi* (ca. 1481)." In the second drawing, he noted a "scratchy, spiky character similar to the drawings of brambles and plants in Windsor (not by Leonardo), RL 12426 and 12428, and similar sketches from the Codex Atlanticus, which indicate a period of Leonardo's activity around the time of the *Battle of Anghiari* and *Leda*" (Pedretti in Turin 2006). Each insect is drawn with great care for naturalistic detail and faithful representation of the parts, even the most insubstantial, such as the veining of the wings. The precision of the two drawings seems to emulate a taxidermic study. Nevertheless, they are to be associated with Leonardo's studies on flight, in particular with the project mentioned on fol. 3 recto of his Manuscript K, to devote one book, the third, of his planned treatise on flight to the "similarities of flight of birds, bats, fishes, animals insects" (English translation KMC). There are drawings of insects in the Codex Atlanticus, fol. 1051 verso (ex 377 v-b), that refer to the problem of weight: "when one rises, the other is lowered. The *pannicola* flies using four wings and when those at the front rise, those behind are lowered. But each pair must be sufficient to support its weight"; Ashburnham 2037, fol. 10 verso; Manuscript B, fol. 100 verso; Codex Arundel, fol. 36 recto. In Manuscript G, fol. 64 verso, Leonardo explains the flight of "the fourth species of butterfly, the devourer of winged ants," describing the insect in action, "with its four wings giving short and rapid flaps when it wants to prey on the tiny winged ants, moving at times the right forewing and the left hindwing, at other times the left forewing and the right hindwing, because the rudder formed by the tail does not increase or decrease the speed of its movement" (English translation KMC).

Questi due squisiti disegnini su carta ritagliata rappresentano due insetti, un cerambice, cioè un coleottero abbastanza comune, e una libellula. Secondo alcune opinioni quest'ultima sarebbe un formica-leone, "riconoscibile per il corpo assai più tozzo di quello di una Libellula e per le antenne relativamente lunghe" (Tongiorgi Tomasi in Pedretti 1990, p. 99). Per l'attribuzione dei disegni a Leonardo, Pedretti ha identificato nel segno quasi orizzontale del primo "il toc-co enfatico che caratterizza i disegni del tempo dell'*Adorazione dei magi* (circa 1481)", mentre nel segno dell'altro, ha rilevato il carattere "graffiante, spinoso, come nei disegni di rovi e piante a Windsor (non di Leonardo), RL 12426 e 12428, e schizzi a essi riferibili nel *Codice Atlantico*, che indicano un periodo dell'attività di Leonardo al tempo della *Battaglia di Anghiari* e della *Leda*" (Pedretti in Turin 2006). Rea-lizzati con la massima attenzione naturalistica, vi spicca la fedele rap-presentazione delle parti, anche le più fini, come le venature delle ali. Per tale precisione i due disegni sembrano emulare una preparazione tassidermica. Sono tuttavia da collegare agli studi sul volo, anche per la previsione, nel progetto del trattato enunciato nel foglio 3 r del *Ms. K*, di un libro (il terzo) dedicato al "volare in comune come d'uccelli, pipistrelli, pesci, animali insetti". Troviamo disegni di insetti nel *Codice Atlantico*, foglio 1051 v (ex 377 v-b), con attenzione al problema del peso: "quando l'una s'alz[a], l'altra abbassi. La pannicola vola con 4 alie e quando quelle dinanzi s'alzano, e quelle dirieto s'abbassano. Ma bisogna che ogni paio sia per sé sofficiente a sostenere tutto il peso"; nel foglio 10 v del manoscritto Ashburnham 2037; nel foglio 100 v del *Ms. B*, nel *Codice Arundel* (foglio 36 r). Nel foglio 64 v del *Ms. G* Leo-nardo descrive il modo di "volare della quarta spezie di parpaglioni, divoratori delle formiche alate", descrivendo l'insetto in azione con "le 4 sue alie nelli corti e revertiginosi corsi, quando vol predare le piccole formiche alate, movendo alcuna volta la destra dinanti e la sinistra dirieto, e <a>lcuna volta la sinistra dinanti e la destra dirieto, perché il timone fatto della coda non vale alla maggiore o minore velocità del suo moto".

PS

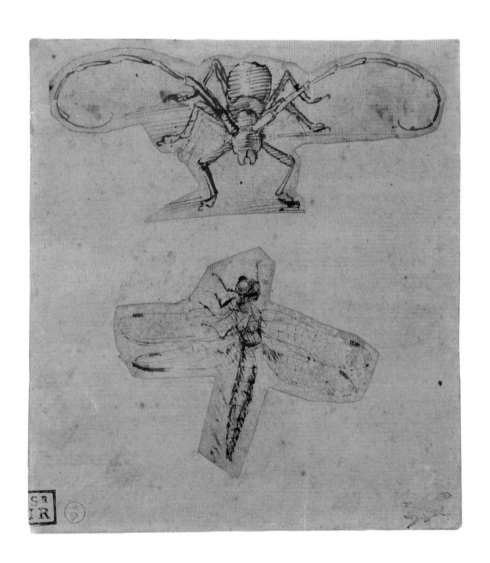

4

LEONARDO DA VINCI (1452–1519)

Studies of the Musculature of a Horse's Forelegs
Studi della muscolatura delle zampe anteriori di un cavallo
ca. 1480

Metalpoint on pale olive prepared paper
Punta metallica su carta preparata color verde chiaro
217 x 287 mm (8 9/16 x 11 5/16 inches)
Turin, Biblioteca Reale
(15579 D.C.)

Literature/Bibliografia: Berenson 1903, vol. II, p. 61, no. 1091; Bertini in Turin 1950, p. 15, cat. 23; Brunetti in Florence 1952, p. 30, cat. 39; Bertini 1958, p. 36, no. 222; Pedretti in Turin 1975, p. 26, cat. 10; Griseri 1978, no. 6; Pedretti 1990, pp. 96–97, no. 10; Turin 1998–99, pp. 94–95, cat. II.10; Pedretti in Turin 2006, pp. 56–57, cat. I.11; O'Grody in Birmingham and San Francisco 2008–9, pp. 42–45, cat. 8; Salvi in Venaria Reale (Turin) 2011–12, pp. 90–91, cat. 1.11.

Leonardo devoted much the same kind of attention to the study of horses as he did to the study of the human body. For the horse, too, he carried out a proportional evaluation that recalled ancient studies and undertook a morphological and anatomical investigation, analyzing the possibilities of movement and exploring various physical types. He studied horses throughout his lifetime, and produced drawings of them in preparation for his paintings and sculptures (the equestrian monuments to Francesco Sforza and Gian Giacomo Trivulzio).

This drawing, the earliest by Leonardo in the collection of the Biblioteca Reale, can be dated to his early Florentine period, between the *Adoration of the Shepherds* (ca. 1478), known only through some preparatory studies, and the *Adoration of the Magi*, dated 1481, at the Galleria degli Uffizi. This sheet can be directly linked to Windsor RL 12295 recto and RL 12296 recto, which Clark (Clark 1968–69, vol. I, p. 15) proposed were from this same period. A date of ca. 1480 for this drawing was therefore established by Pedretti (in Turin 1975 and Pedretti 1990).

The Turin sheet contains various views of a horse's forelegs, in a "natural" position and with one leg raised. The latter is the pose of the horse in traditional statuary, and the one Leonardo used in studies for the second equestrian monument to Sforza. As Pedretti (in Turin 1975) has pointed out, this classic pose can also be found in earlier drawings of horses at Windsor (RL 12312 recto and RL 12325 recto). Leonardo treats the horse above all as a subject to be understood anatomically and portrayed naturally, not as the crystallized figure that had been established in art. The sheet is occupied chiefly by sketches that analyze the musculature of the pectoral zone in side and front views, with some parts more defined by shading and others merely sketched in, similar to anatomical studies of the human body.

PS

Leonardo ha destinato agli studi del cavallo un'attenzione e un metodo speculari a quelli dedicati al corpo umano. Anche per questo soggetto è posta in essere una valutazione proporzionale, viene richiamato l'antico, è condotto uno studio morfologico e anatomico, vengono analizzate le possibilità di movimento, sono considerate le diverse tipologie di corporatura. Pure gli studi sul cavallo, infine, occupano praticamente tutto il corso della sua vita, sia per la progettazione scultorea (per i monumenti equestri a Francesco Sforza e a Gian Giacomo Trivulzio) sia per la raffigurazione pittorica.

Questo disegno, il più antico nella Collezione della Biblioteca Reale, è riferibile al primo periodo fiorentino, ad un lasso temporale tra l'*Adorazione dei pastori*, del 1478 circa, nota solo attraverso alcuni studi preparatori, e l'*Adorazione dei magi* della Galleria degli Uffizi, datata al 1481. Si tratta di disegni direttamente collegabili ai fogli a Windsor RL 12295 r e 12296 r, per i quali Clark (Clark 1968-69, vol. I, p.15) ha opportunamente proposto tale riferimento cronologico. Pedretti (in Turin 1975 e in Pedretti 1990) ha pertanto individuato una datazione intorno al 1480.

Il doppio foglio torinese contiene varie vedute delle zampe anteriori equine, sia in atteggiamento 'naturale', sia con richiamo alla consueta posizione sollevata e piegata della statuaria tradizionale, che sarà utilizzata negli studi per il secondo monumento equestre allo Sforza. Si tratta di una posizione classica che, come rileva Pedretti (in Turin 1975), si trova già nei disegni più antichi di cavalli (fogli a Windsor RL 12312 r e 12325 r). Negli studi del foglio torinese prevale tuttavia, al di là della postura prescelta, uno studio morfologico, dove il cavallo è un soggetto naturale da conoscere e raffigurare, e non una figura cristallizzata dalla consuetudine rappresentativa sedimentata nell'arte. La doppia pagina è così occupata da un susseguirsi di schizzi, dove è analizzata soprattutto la miologia della zona pettorale in veduta laterale e anteriore, con parti più definite dal chiaroscuro ed altre in abbozzo lineare, proprio come in un processo di conoscenza anatomica.

PS

41

5

LEONARDO DA VINCI (1452–1519) and FRANCESCO MELZI (1491/93–ca. 1570)

Studies of the Hindquarters of a Horse
Studi delle zampe posteriori di un cavallo
ca. 1508

Red chalk and traces of black chalk on paper
Sanguigna e tracce di pietra nera su carta
201 x 133 mm (7 15/16 x 5 1/4 inches)
Turin, Biblioteca Reale
(15582 D.C.)

Literature/Bibliografia: Bertini in Turin 1950, p. 15, cat. 25; Brunetti in Florence 1952, p. 30, cat. 40; Bertini 1958, p. 36, no. 224; Pedretti in Turin 1975, p. 28, cat. 12; Pedretti 1990, p. 98, no. 12; Turin 1998–99, pp. 98–99, cat. II.12; Pedretti in Turin 2006, pp. 60–61, cat. I.13; Perissa Torrini in Florence 2006–7b, pp. 103–4, cat. VII.1.h; O'Grody in Birmingham and San Francisco 2008–9, pp. 50–51, cat. 10; Salvi in Venaria Reale (Turin) 2011–12, pp. 94–95, cat. 1.13.

It is clear that this sheet was conceived and drawn by Leonardo, but the intervention of Francesco Melzi is unmistakable in the heavy overlaying (particularly in the study at top left) and the careful emulation of Leonardo's strokes. Pedretti (in Turin 2006) writes that the sheet is "entirely overdrawn by Melzi." The hindquarters of the horse are studied in several views and poses, including a mirrored representation of a hind leg (at top right), drawn with the same criteria as the mirror view of a human leg in cat. 6a. The sequence of drawings on the sheet seems to follow Leonardo's typical right-to-left pattern, beginning with the two legs in mirror view. Next is the drawing to the left, which has a hint of a flicked tail, followed at center by another leg with fine and masterly shading. The lower half of the sheet is taken up by two detailed drawings of hindquarters. The shading in the one at bottom right highlights the way the powerful muscles that attach the leg to the body appear on the body's surface, while the other drawing features the underlying musculature in a similar way to Windsor RL 12631 recto, K/P 89 recto "interposed between anatomy and the living" (Keele and Pedretti 1979–80, vol. I, p. 286).

According to Pedretti (in Turin 2006) the mirror view of the legs can be traced to drawings dated around 1493, such as Windsor RL 12301. He observes that the three views of the horse's hindquarters refer to other studies from the same period but are characterized by the style of the monument to Gian Giacomo Trivulzio (ca. 1508). The author considers these drawings to be related to Windsor RL 12333 recto, in which the study for the Sforza monument is completed by Melzi according to the style of the Trivulzio monument, and RL 12355 recto.

In addition, these sketches showing the power of the horse in motion are reminiscent of the studies for the *Battle of Anghiari*.

PS

Il foglio rivela pienamente la concezione e il disegno di Leonardo, ma risulta, nell'esecuzione, dall'intervento anche di Francesco Melzi, di cui si riconoscono la pesante ripassatura (soprattutto nel disegno in alto a sinistra) e la compìta emulazione del segno del Maestro. Pedretti (in Turin 2006) scrive: "interamente ripassato dal Melzi". Gli arti posteriori del cavallo sono studiati in diverse vedute e posizioni, compresa una rappresentazione speculare della zampa posteriore di un animale stante (in alto a destra), eseguita con il medesimo criterio adottato per le gambe umane raffigurate nel foglio della Biblioteca Reale 15578 (cat. 6a). La sequenza di disegni sembra seguire il procedere da destra a sinistra tipico di Leonardo: l'avvio sta nelle due zampe in veduta speculare; segue il disegno a sinistra con l'abbozzo di coda svolazzante; viene disegnata una ulteriore zampa al centro del foglio, chiaroscurata da un tratteggio fine e sapiente; infine, in basso, prima a destra e poi a sinistra, vengono disegnati in maniera dettagliata gli arti nel loro complesso. La possente muscolatura di attacco al tronco è evidenziata con due intensità chiaroscurali, che nel disegno a destra ricorda quella utilizzata per gli studi di morfologia esterna, e nel disegno a sinistra quella per la miologia sottocutanea, indicata come "interposta infra l'anatomia e 'l vivo" nel foglio RL 12631 r, K/P 89 r (Keele and Pedretti 1980-84, vol. II, p. 286).

Secondo Pedretti (in Turin 2006), le due zampe speculari sarebbero riconducibili a disegni databili al 1493, in rapporto con il foglio a Windsor RL 12301 r, mentre le tre vedute della parte posteriore intera dell'animale sarebbero in relazione con altri studi di Leonardo dello stesso periodo, ma caratterizzati da Melzi secondo lo stile del monumento al Trivulzio (c. 1508). L'autore mette in relazione tali disegni con i fogli di Windsor RL 12333 r (nel quale uno studio per il monumento Sforza è rifinito da Melzi secondo lo stile del monumento al Trivulzio) e RL 12355 r.

La potenza del corpo animale in azione, di cui si percepisce lo slancio, induce a considerare anche un riferimento agli studi per la *Battaglia di Anghiari*.

PS

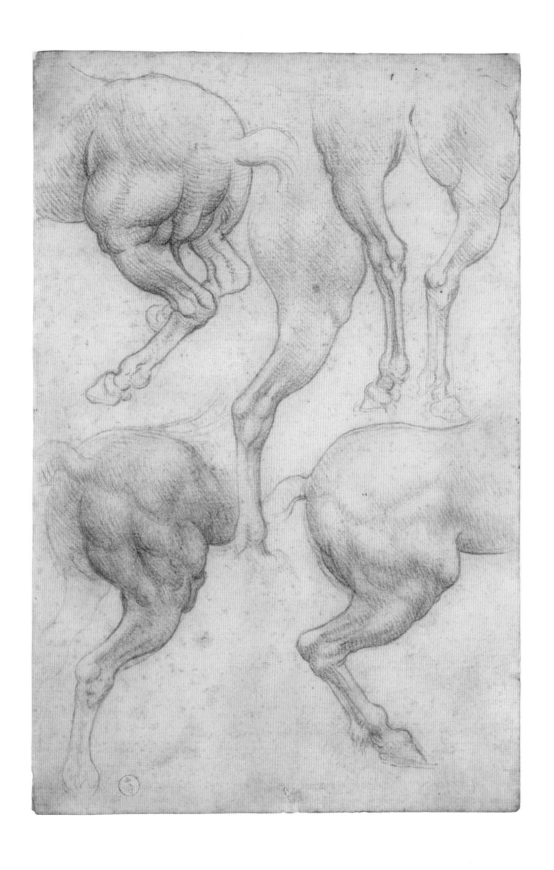

6a

LEONARDO DA VINCI (1452–1519)

Musculature of the Legs
Studi di muscolatura degli arti inferiori
ca. 1485–87

Pen and brown ink on paper
Penna e inchiostro bruno su carta
140 x 157 mm (5 ¹/₂ x 6 ³/₁₆ inches)
Turin, Biblioteca Reale
(15578 D.C. recto)

Literature/Bibliografia: Berenson 1903, vol. II, p. 61, no. 1090; Bertini in Turin 1950, p. 16, cat. 27; Brunetti in Florence 1952, p. 42, cat. 63; Bertini 1958, p. 36, no. 226; Clark 1968–69, vol. I, p. 132, vol. III, p. 56; Pedretti in Turin 1975, pp. 24–25, cat. 9; Pedretti 1990, pp. 94–96, no. 9; Turin 1998–99, pp. 90–91, cat. II.9 recto; Pedretti in Turin 2006, pp. 52–53, cat. I.10 recto; O'Grody in Birmingham and San Francisco 2008–9, pp. 32–35, cat. 5; Salvi in Venaria Reale (Turin) 2011–12, pp. 80–81, cat. 1.8a.

Throughout his life, Leonardo devoted a great deal of study to the lower limbs of man. In effect, this part of the body supports weight and allows physical stances attitudes and postures of man, thanks to both its osteoarticular structure and its powerful muscular system. The studies that Leonardo dedicated to this part of the body are therefore wide-ranging: anatomical (osteological and myological), of external morphology and comparative anatomy. They also include a category particular to Leonardo, which he calls "between anatomy and the living" (see Windsor RL 12631 recto), referring to his way of portraying the very muscular bodies of heroes and warriors. In this small sheet, proceeding from right to left, the first sketch is a pair of mirror views of the entire leg in profile, followed by an enlarged profile of the same figure, from the buttock to the foot, and then an anteromedial (from the front and toward the middle) view of both legs in a stance. The swift strokes depict the external appearance and at the same time demonstrate a precise understanding of what lies beneath the skin. The work was initially assigned to the years of the *Battle of Anghiari* (Berenson 1903), but Pedretti suggests a date of 1485–87 for stylistic reasons and because the sheet relates to topics on other sheets, including Windsor RL 12632 recto–RL 12634 recto, K/P 8 recto and RL 12637 recto, K/P 9 recto (ca. 1490–91; see fig. 13), which show a similar view, from the angle of the pelvis, with the groin and the development of the buttocks, to the feet. The sketch to the left, in which the right limb is pulled back and cut off by the margin of the sheet, is reminiscent of the Windsor drawing of the peripheral nerves (RL 12613 verso, K/P 1 recto), also dated 1485–87.

PS

Lo studio degli arti inferiori dell'uomo è affrontato da Leonardo con molta frequenza e particolare attenzione durante l'arco di tutta la sua attività. Si tratta infatti del distretto corporeo che regge il peso e consente gli atteggiamenti e le posture dell'uomo, sia attraverso la propria struttura osteo-articolare, sia attraverso il potente sistema muscolare. Gli studi che Leonardo dedica a questa parte del corpo sono quindi a tutto raggio: anatomici (osteologici e miologici), di morfologia esterna, di anatomia comparata, e di una natura del tutto particolare, intermedia tra lo stadio miologico e quello cutaneo, che egli definisce "infra l'anatomia e 'l vivo" (nel foglio anatomico a Windsor RL 12631 r), pensata per raffigurare in maniera corretta i corpi molto muscolosi di eroi e guerrieri. Nel piccolo disegno della Biblioteca Reale di Torino si ha uno svolgimento per vedute: procedendo da destra a sinistra, troviamo lo schizzo di tutto l'arto in proiezione laterale e speculare (destra e sinistra), il profilo ingrandito della stessa rappresentazione, dalla natica al piede, e, sulla sinistra una veduta antero-mediale dei due arti atteggiati. La conduzione grafica è veloce e rivela lo studio della morfologia esterna, che si avvale tuttavia di una precisa conoscenza sottocutanea. Inizialmente assegnato agli anni della *Battaglia di Anghiari* (Berenson 1903), è stato anticipato da Pedretti al 1485-87 per ragioni stilistiche e di affinità tematica con altri fogli, tra cui quelli a Windsor RL 12632 r-12634 r, K/P 8 r, e lo studio di posato realizzato su carta preparata in azzurro RL 12637 r, K/P 9 r (c. 1490-91; fig. 13), dei quali propone un analogo taglio, dalla delineazione del bacino, con la parte inguinale e lo sviluppo delle natiche, al piede. Nella figura di sinistra, l'arto destro portato indietro e tagliato dal margine del foglio è riconducibile al disegno dedicato ai nervi periferici RL 12613 v, K/P 1 r, datato anch'esso al 1485-87.

PS

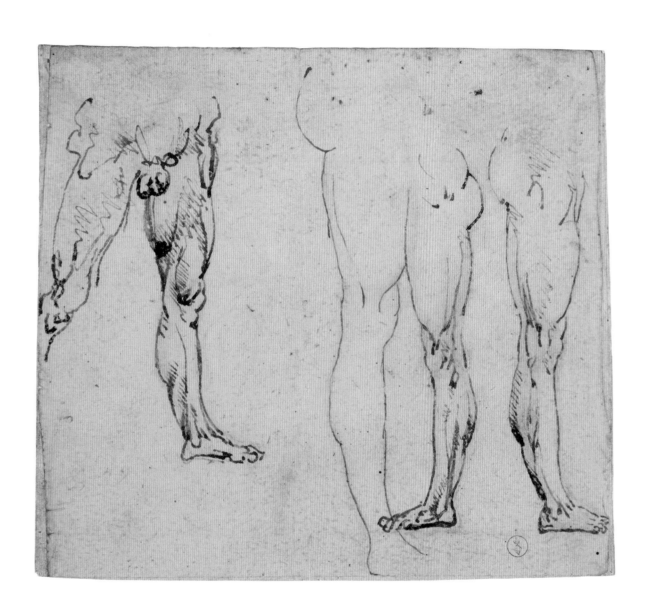

6b

LEONARDO DA VINCI (1452–1519)

Figure near a Fire and Moths
Figura presso il fuoco e farfalle volanti
ca. 1483–85

Pen and brown ink on paper
Penna e inchiostro bruno su carta
157 x 140 mm (6 ³⁄₁₆ x 5 ½ inches)
Turin, Biblioteca Reale
(15578 D.C. verso)

Literature/Bibliografia: Fumagalli 1939, p. 329; Bertini in Turin 1950, p. 16, cat. 27; Bertini 1958, p. 36, no. 226; Pedretti in Turin 1975, pp. 24–25, cat. 9; Pedretti 1990, pp. 94–96, no. 9; Turin 1998–99, pp. 92–93, cat. II.9 verso; Pedretti in Turin 2006, pp. 54–55, cat. I.10 verso; O'Grody in Birmingham and San Francisco 2008–9, pp. 32–35, cat. 5; Salvi in Venaria Reale (Turin) 2011–12, pp. 82–83, cat. 1.8b.

On the verso of the sheet showing the *Musculature of the Legs* (cat. 6a), oriented sideways with respect to the recto, are an allegorical sketch and a short poem on the same theme. The drawing portrays a figure sitting by a fire, busy stoking it, while numerous moths, sketched in as little circles, fly around the flames.

The poem reads (see Richter [1883] 1970, vol. II, p. 295, no. 1182):

blind ignorance misleads us thus
and delights with the results of lascivious joys
because it does not know the true light
because it does not know what is the true light
[ignorance]
vain splendour takes from us the power of being
behold for its vain splendour we go into the fire
thus blind ignorance does mislead us
that is blind ignorance so misleads us
that
o wretched mortals open your eyes

The theme of the "true light" appears in the Codex Atlanticus on fol. 187 recto (ex 67 r-a) and 692 recto (ex 257 r-b), both of which contain a fable about a moth and a flame. On fol. 187 recto, the "wandering moth" that burned its wings on a candle flame exclaimed, "O false light, how many of my kind you must have, in past times, shamefully deceived!" In the fable on fol. 692 recto the moral content is more explicit and can be directly linked to the poem on the Turin sheet. "As the wandering moth fluttered in the murky air, he saw a light, he flew toward it immediately and circling around it, he wondered greatly at such splendid beauty, and not being content only to see it, he hovered before it ready to do what he usually did with perfumed flowers; straightening his flight, boldly he passed into the light, and it burned the tips of his wings and his legs and other ornament"(Marinoni 1973–80, vol. III, p. 42; vol. VIII, p. 239. See for these two folios, Milan 2013, pp. 28–29, 34; English translation KMC). The Turin sheet is considered to date from an earlier period than the examples from the Codex Atlanticus, which dates from ca. 1490 (Pedretti in Turin 1975), and is consequently one of the artist's first observations on the topic. During the sixteenth century, the allegory was transformed positively, as a desire for knowledge, whose acquisition might come at the cost of death.

Il verso del foglio contenente gli *Studi di muscolatura degli arti inferiori* (cat. 6a) presenta, orientati trasversalmente rispetto al disegno del recto, uno schizzo allegorico e un componimento poetico di contenuto strettamente collegato. Nel disegno si distinguono una figura seduta presso un fuoco, intenta ad alimentarlo, e numerose farfalle, schizzate come piccoli cerchi, che roteano intorno alle fiamme.

Il commento poetico recita:

la ciecha ignjorāza chosi ci chōduce
e choleffetto dellasscivj sollazzj
per nō chonosciere la uera luce
per nō chonossciere qual sia la uera luce
(ignjorāza)
el uano splendor ci toglie lesser
b ⌠ *vedj che per lo splendor nel fu<o>cho andjamo*
 ⎸ *ciecha ignorāza j̄ tal modo chōduce*
a ⌡ *e chome ciecha ignjorāza ci chōduce*
che
o mjseri mortalj aprite liochj

Il tema della "vera luce" compare nei fogli del *Codice Atlantico* 187 r (ex 67 r-a) e 692 r (ex 257 r-b) entrambi contenenti una favola che ha per soggetto una farfalla e un lume. Nel foglio 187 r, il "vagabundo parpaglione", bruciatosi le ali su di una candela esclama: "O falsa luce, quanti come me debbi tu avere, ne' passati tempi, avere miseramente ingannati!". Nella favola del foglio 692 r il contenuto morale si fa esplicito e direttamente collegabile al commento poetico del foglio di Torino: "Andando il dipinto parpaglione vagabundo e discorrendo per la oscurata aria, li venne v[i]sto un lume, al quale subito si dirizzò e con vari circuli quello attorniando, forte si maravigliò di tanta splendida bellezza e non istando contento solamente al vederlo, si mise innanzi per fare di quello, come delli odoriferi fiori fare solia, e dirizzato suo volo, con ardito animo passò per esso lume, el quale gli consumò gli stremi delle alie e gambe e altri ornamenti" (Marinoni 1973-80, vol. III, p. 42; vol. VIII, p. 239. Si veda, per questi due fogli, Milan 2013, pp. 28-29, 34). La pagina torinese è ritenuta precedente agli esempi del *Codice Atlantico*, datati intorno al 1490 (Pedretti in Turin 1975), e costituisce pertanto una prima riflessione sul tema. Nel corso del Cinquecento l'allegoria si trasformerà in senso positivo, come desiderio di conoscenza, per acquistare la quale si può anche morire.

47

7

LEONARDO DA VINCI (1452–1519)

Nudes for the "Battle of Anghiari" and Other Figure Studies
Nudi per la "Battaglia di Anghiari" e altri studi di figura
ca. 1505

Pen and brown ink and traces of charcoal on paper
Penna e inchiostro bruno e tracce di carboncino su carta
254 x 197 mm (10 x 7 ³/₄ inches)
Turin, Biblioteca Reale
(15577 D.C. recto and verso)

Literature/Bibliografia: Müller-Walde 1897, pp. 140–42; Berenson 1903, vol. II, p. 61, no. 1089; Giglioli 1944, pp. 140–41, pl. CLIII; Bertini in Turin 1950, p. 16, cat. 28; Brunetti in Florence 1952, pp. 41–42, cat. 62; Bertini 1958, p. 36, no. 227; Clark 1968–69, vol. I, pp. 27, 34, 129, 137, 146, vol. III, pp. 15, 19; Pedretti in Turin 1975, pp. 17–20, cat. 7; Griseri 1978, no. 11; Keele and Pedretti 1979–80, vol. II, pp. 811, 826–27; Pedretti 1990, pp. 91–93, no. 7; Pedretti in Turin 1990, pp. 48–49, cat. 14; Nepi Sciré in Venice 1992, pp. 278–79, cat. 37; Turin 1998–99, pp. 86–87, cat. II.7; Bambach 2001; Bambach in New York 2003, pp. 550–53, cat. 103; Bambach in Paris 2003, pp. 291–93, cat. 102; Pedretti in Turin 2006, pp. 48–49, cat. I.8; Laurenza in Florence 2006–7b, p. 133, cat. VII.3.b; O'Grody in Birmingham and San Francisco 2008–9, pp. 36–37, cat. 6; Salvi in Venaria Reale (Turin) 2011–12, pp. 96–97, cat. 1.14; Taglialagamba in Pedretti 2012, pp. 182–83, no. 74.

This is one Leonardo's most fascinating sheets, in regard to both its layout and its relation to other works by the artist. Particular attention must be paid to the compositional rhythm: the figures start at the upper right corner, move across to the left, then down to the center, and then to the right and downward. Following this visual path, the figures become increasingly smaller and sketchier, while still preserving their individual characteristics. These small figures are dominated by the large truncated figure at top right, which can be traced to the *Battle of Anghiari* (Müller-Walde 1897), Leonardo's now lost large mural, planned for and in part carried out in the Sala del Gran Consiglio (Sala dei Cinquecento) in the Palazzo Vecchio in Florence (1504–6). This figure, repeated to the left, can also be found on an anatomical study at Windsor (RL 12625 recto, K/P 95 recto), dedicated to the study of human lower limbs, also in comparison with those of the horse. The date traditionally proposed for the present sheet is 1505, extended by some authors to 1508 (Nepi Sciré in Venice 1992 and Bambach in New York 2003). The year 1508 must be considered the latest possible date for this sheet, given that the figure second from top left is cited in Raphael's 1508 *Judgment of Solomon* in the Stanza della Segnatura (Loggia di Raffaello) at the Vatican.

Proceeding from top to bottom, the smaller sketches can be interpreted as follows: Venus and Cupid or a meditation on the classical theme of Hermes; to the left a study for *Leda*; below these a group of armed figures about to strike, related to the *Battle of Anghiari*. The last row is made up of studies of horses and riders, with a blank area beneath. A soldier similar to the small figure at center, who wears a flapping cloak and is about to strike, can be found on a ca. 1504 sheet at Windsor (RL 12340 recto); that sheet also includes a rider astride a galloping horse. Such a horse and rider also appear at the top left of a small sheet at the British Museum (1854, 0513.17). These sheets, like the present one, are without question studies for the *Battle of Anghiari*. They contain some visual thoughts not directly related to the painting, but even these are connected to research Leonardo carried out around 1505 or slightly later. On the verso is a sketch in charcoal of the central figure seen from the left, but its attribution is not certain.

Si tratta di uno dei fogli più affascinanti della produzione grafica di Leonardo, sia per l'impostazione della pagina, sia per i collegamenti con opere e altri studi dell'artista. Particolare attenzione va rivolta al ritmo compositivo, caratterizzato da una doppia obliquità, che muove dalla parte alta destra del foglio verso sinistra, e poi di nuovo verso destra e in basso. Seguendo questo percorso visivo, le figure si fanno più piccole e abbozzate, conservando tuttavia ognuna la propria evidenza, anche se secondarie rispetto alla grande figura tronca posta in alto a destra, riconducibile alla *Battaglia di Anghiari* (Müller-Walde 1897), il grande dipinto murale ora perduto progettato da Leonardo, e in parte eseguito, a Firenze, nella Sala del Gran Consiglio (Sala dei Cinquecento) di Palazzo Vecchio (1504-6). Tale figura viene ripresa, a sinistra, in veduta intera e, come in una citazione, nel foglio anatomico RL 12625 r, K/P 95 r di Windsor, dedicato allo studio degli arti inferiori umani anche in comparazione con quelli del cavallo. La datazione tradizionalmente proposta al 1505 è estesa da alcuni autori al 1508 (Nepi Sciré in Venice 1992, Bambach in New York 2003), data da considerarsi la più tarda, poiché una figura intera in analoga posa si trova, come una citazione, nel *Giudizio di Salomone* di Raffaello affrescato nella *Stanza della Segnatura* in Vaticano.

Procedendo dall'alto in basso, gli schizzi di più piccole dimensioni sono così riconducibili: il primo ad una Venere e Cupido, o ad una riflessione sul tema classico di Ermes; la figura estrema a sinistra a studi per la *Leda*; le figurine in atto di colpire, nuovamente alla *Battaglia di Anghiari*; le ultime in basso, che chiudono la porzione disegnata lasciando una balza bianca, al tema del cavallo e cavaliere. Lo stesso combattente con mantello svolazzante, intento a sferrare un colpo, si trova nel disegno di Windsor RL 12340 r (*c*. 1504), che contiene anche un cavallo e cavaliere lanciati al galoppo. Analogo schizzo di cavallo e cavaliere in corsa si trova nella parte alta sinistra di un piccolo foglio al British Museum (1854, 0513.17), rendendo inequivocabile come il disegno della Biblioteca Reale contenga temi e studi per la *Battaglia di Anghiari* e altri pensieri visivi riferibili alle ricerche intorno al 1505, o di poco successive. Al verso vi è uno schizzo a carboncino della figura centrale vista dal lato sinistro, di dubbia autografia.

PS

PS

8

LEONARDO DA VINCI (1452–1519)

Hercules with the Nemean Lion
Ercole con il leone nemeo
ca. 1505–8

Charcoal and metalpoint on paper, incised for transfer
Carboncino e punta metallica su carta, inciso per il trasferimento
280 x 190 mm (11 x 7 ½ inches)

Turin, Biblioteca Reale
(15630 D.C.)

Literature/Bibliografia: Berenson 1938, vol. II, p. 139, no. 1262A; Bertini in Turin 1950, p. 21, cat. 58; Bertini 1958, p. 61, no. 479; Pedretti 1958; Clark 1968–69, vol. I, pp. 116–17, vol. III, p. 19; Clark 1969, p. 21; Pedretti in Turin 1975, pp. 21–23, cat. 8; Keele and Pedretti 1979–80, vol. II, pp. 820, 827–28, 838–40; Pedretti 1990, pp. 93–94, no. 8; Marani 1997, pp. 176–77; Turin 1998–99, pp. 88–89, cat. II.8; Bambach 2001; Bambach in New York 2003, pp. 544–49, cat. 102; Pedretti 2005, pp. 117–21, no. 19a; Salvi in Turin 2006, pp. 50–51, cat. I.9; Laurenza in Florence 2006–7b, pp. 137–38, cat. VII.3.f; O'Grody in Birmingham and San Francisco 2008–9, pp. 38–39, cat. 7; Marani 2010, XIX, no. 33; Marani 2011a, p. 29; Salvi in Venaria Reale (Turin) 2011–12, pp. 98–99, cat. 1.15; Taglialagamba in Pedretti 2012, pp. 184–87, no. 75.

The figure on this sheet is the powerful and muscular mythological hero Hercules. Here he is seen from behind, holding a club in both hands, with a lion crouching quietly at his feet. The sheet is slightly damaged; it has been incised along the figure with a stylus in order to transfer the outline onto another sheet, which in some places has compromised the continuity and vigor of the soft charcoal strokes. Some authors (see, for example, Berenson 1938) have not considered it to be by Leonardo. However, Pedretti—like Frizzoni and Bodmer—has attributed it to Leonardo (see, for example, Pedretti 1958, Pedretti in Turin 1975, Pedretti 1990, and Pedretti 2005) and have dated it to 1505. On the occasion of the 2003 exhibition *Leonardo da Vinci: Master Draftsman* in New York—where the present sheet was seen alongside a small sheet from the Metropolitan Museum (2000.328) depicting Hercules with a club, seen from the front (recto) and the back (verso)—Bambach (in New York 2003) devoted an in-depth study to the Turin drawing, in which she emphasized the geometric tracing of the stylus. This tracing is invisible in reproductions, but was previously reported by Pedretti (in Turin 1975). The Metropolitan drawing (see also Bambach in Turin 2006, pp. 68–71, cat. 1.16) and another sheet at Windsor (RL 19043 verso, K/P 46 verso) suggest that the Turin *Hercules* must date to the period of the *Battle of Anghiari*.

By the fourteenth century, the heroic nude figure of the victorious Hercules had come to symbolize the civic virtues of Florence. This study can be regarded as part of a project for a statue that would have been placed adjacent to Michelangelo's *David*, at the entrance to the Palazzo Vecchio. (Leonardo had been part of the commission that decided, in 1504, where Michelangelo's statue should be located.) In the end, Baccio Bandinelli created the statue of Hercules, which preserves an echo of Leonardo's model.

Il soggetto mitologico di Ercole presuppone, come in questo disegno, la raffigurazione di un corpo muscoloso e dalla struttura possente. Qui l'eroe è visto di schiena, mentre regge una clava nelle mani e con il leone accovacciato ai piedi in atteggiamento mansueto. Il foglio ha avuto alterne fortune, poiché un intervento di ricalco a punta metallica, che ha ripassato il contorno della figura per trasferirne la sagoma su un altro foglio, ha corrotto in alcune parti l'unitarietà e il vigore del segno tenero del carbone. Alcuni autori (tra cui Berenson 1938) non lo hanno ritenuto un autografo di Leonardo, mentre Pedretti e altri (tra cui Frizzoni e Bodmer) ne hanno sostenuta l'autografia (si veda, ad esempio, Pedretti 1958, Pedretti in Turin 1975, Pedretti 1990 e Pedretti 2005) datandolo al 1505. Nell'occasione della sua esposizione a New York nel 2003 (nella mostra *Leonardo da Vinci: Master Draftsman*), a fianco del piccolo foglio acquistato dal Metropolitan Museum of Art (2000.328) raffigurante anch'esso un Ercole stante con clava, disegnato in veduta anteriore (al recto) e in veduta posteriore (al verso), Carmen Bambach (in New York 2003) ha dedicato a questo disegno un approfondito studio, evidenziando il diagramma geometrico tracciato a punta metallica, perciò invisibile in riproduzione, già segnalato da Pedretti nel 1975. Il disegno del Metropolitan (per il quale si veda anche Bambach in Turin 2006, pp. 68-71, cat. I.16) e quello a Windsor (RL 19043 v, K/P 46 v), di analogo soggetto erculeo, mantengono l'Ercole torinese ancorato cronologicamente agli anni della *Battaglia di Anghiari*.

Sul piano simbolico, il nudo eroico dell'Ercole vittorioso rappresentava le virtù civiche di Firenze già dal Trecento; questo studio può quindi essere considerato nell'orizzonte del progetto di una statua gemella a quella del *David* di Michelangelo, già collocata all'ingresso di Palazzo Vecchio (luogo deciso nel 1504 da una commissione di cui faceva parte anche Leonardo), che condurrà infine alla realizzazione della statua di Ercole da parte di Baccio Bandinelli, in cui si ritrova una eco del modello di Leonardo.

PS

PS

51

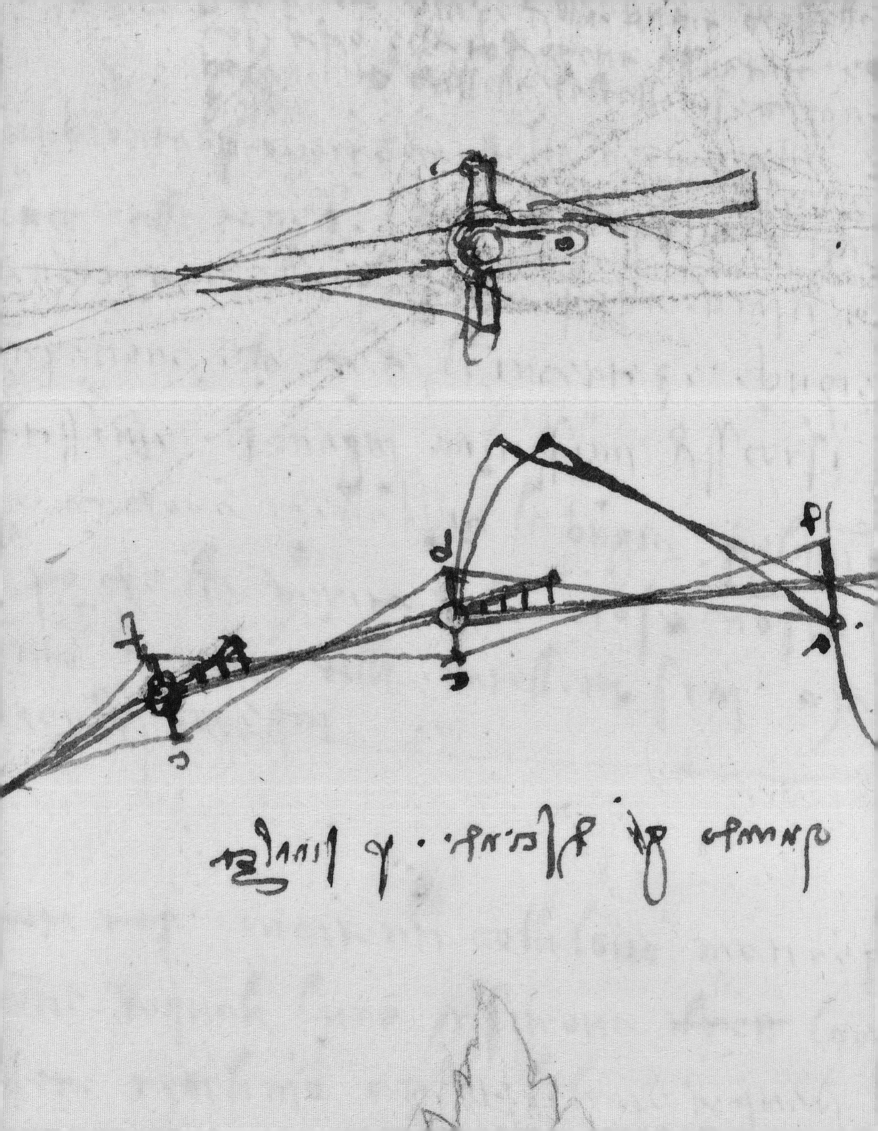

CODEX ON THE FLIGHT OF BIRDS
CODICE SUL VOLO DEGLI UCCELLI

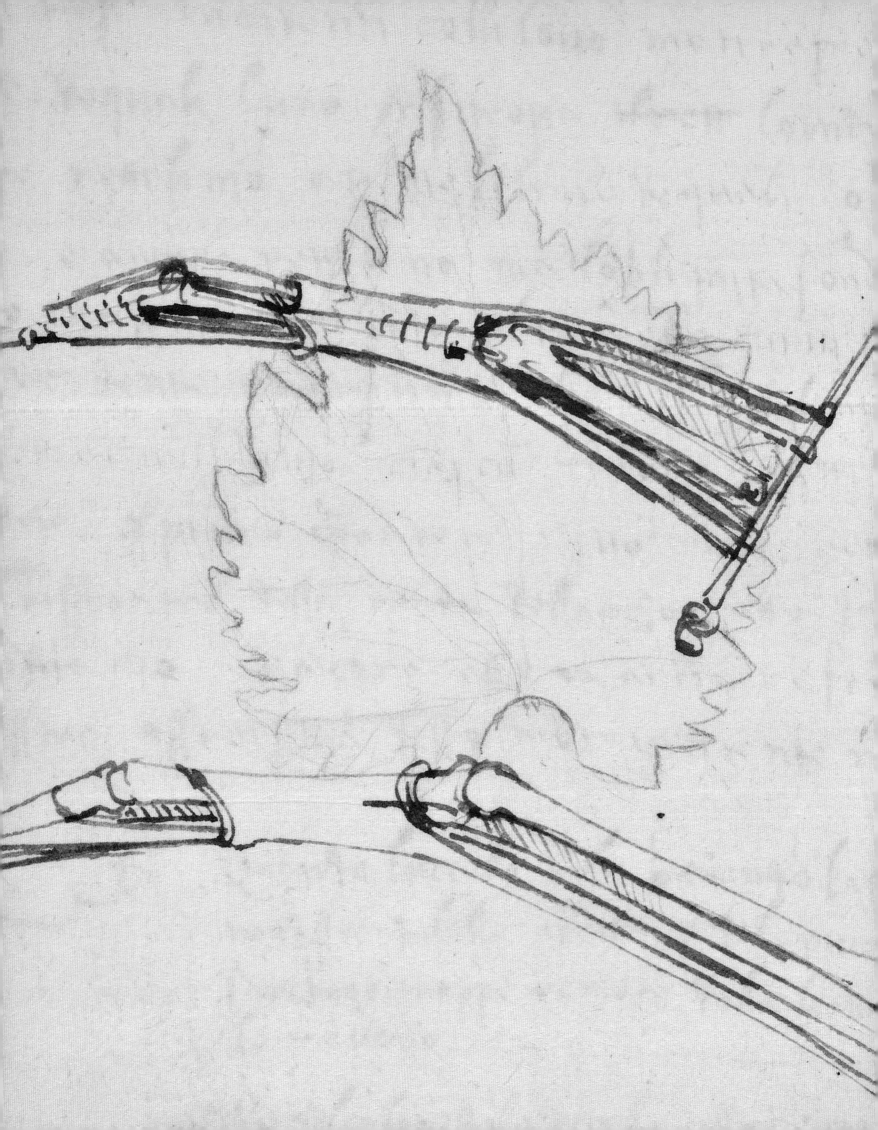

Leonardo da Vinci: "Birds and Other Things"

Leonardo da Vinci: "uccelli et altre cose"

Paola Salvi

The phrase *ucelli et altre cose* ("birds and other things") derives from an inscription, now visible only using specialized instruments,[1] found on the outer back cover of the manuscript by Leonardo at the Biblioteca Reale in Turin (Varia 95) that is known as the Codex on the Flight of Birds (cat. 9). The name given to the codex puts the focus on its principal topic, but other subjects are addressed as well. In this respect, the codex is like Leonardo's other manuscripts, which similarly include considerations, notes, and comments on questions totally diverse from the principal topic.

The brief description, *ucelli et altre cose*, attributed to Pompeo Leoni[2] (the title of the Italian essay uses the modern spelling of *uccelli*—birds—written with a double c), captures the miscellaneous nature of the Codex on the Flight of Birds, which has also guided the selection of drawings by Leonardo from the Biblioteca Reale. As I note elsewhere in this volume ("Treasures by Leonardo from the Biblioteca Reale, Turin," pp. 23–31), all the works in the exhibition at the Morgan Library & Museum are linked, in some way, to this precious codex.

The connective tissue of this project is a text that appears on fol. 16 recto of the codex:

> If you say that the nerves and the muscles of the bird are of incomparably greater power than those of man, since all the muscles and flesh of the breast are made for the benefit and increase of the movement of the wings, with that bone of the breast all in one piece, which provides the bird with great power, with the wings woven of thick nerves and other very strong ligaments of cartilage and skin [made] very strong with various muscles, here the reply is that so much strength is provided for power beyond the ordinary support of the wings, it needs in its place to double and triple the movement in order to flee from its predators or pursue its prey. Whence for that purpose it needs to double or triple its force

La dicitura "ucelli et altre cose" deriva da una iscrizione, ormai visibile solo con indagine strumentale,[1] già segnalata al verso della seconda coperta del manoscritto di Leonardo da Vinci conservato presso la Biblioteca Reale di Torino con la segnatura "Varia 95", e conosciuto come *Codice sul volo degli uccelli* (cat. 9). Quest'ultima definizione focalizza l'attenzione sull'argomento prevalente, ma esclude altri temi in esso contenuti. Anche questo codice risulta infatti dalla tipica redazione dei manoscritti di Leonardo, dove le materie si compongono in maniera non esclusiva, lasciando spazio a riflessioni, appunti e annotazioni di natura talvolta completamente diversa dal tema principale che viene trattato.

La sintetica descrizione "ucelli et altre cose", attribuita a Pompeo Leoni,[2] qui usata nella moderna dicitura "uccelli", è sembrata quindi significativa per comunicare sia la natura miscellanea del *Codice sul volo*, sia il filo conduttore che ha guidato la scelta dei disegni autografi di Leonardo da Vinci della Biblioteca Reale presentati alla Morgan Library & Museum, tutti in varie maniere collegabili, come si è visto nel mio saggio "Tesori leonardiani dalla Biblioteca Reale di Torino" in questo volume (pp. 23-31), al prezioso libretto.

Il 'tessuto connettivo' di questo percorso è costituito da un testo che compare nella carta 16 r del *Codice*:

> Se tu dirai che li nerbi e muscoli dell'uccello sanza comparazione essere di maggior potenzia che quelli dell'omo, con ciò sia che tutta la carnosità di tanti muscoli e polpe del petto essere fatti a benifizio e aumento del moto delle alie, con quello osso d'un pezzo nel petto, che apparecchia potenzia grandissima all'uccello, coll'alie tutte tessute di grossi nervi e altri fortissimi legamenti di cartilagini e pelle fortissima con vari muscoli, qui si risponde che tanta fortezza è apparecchiata per potere oltre all'ordinario suo sostenimento delle alie, gli bisogna a sua posta raddoppiare e triplicare il moto per fuggire dal suo predatore o seguitare la preda sua. Onde in tale effetto li bisogna raddoppiare o triplicare la forza sua e oltre a di questo portare tanto peso ne' sua piedi per l'aria, quanto è il peso di se

and beyond this to carry as much weight in its claws through the air as its own weight. As we see the falcon carrying the duck and the eagle the hare, by which thing it is very well demonstrated where such extreme strength is distributed. But it needs little strength to sustain itself and to balance itself on its wings and to oscillate them on the current of the wind, and to direct the rudder in its paths, and a little movement of the wings suffices, and is as much slower as the bird is larger.

Man too has a greater amount of strength in his legs than is required for his weight. And [to show] that this is true, place a man upright on fine sand and note how deep the print of his foot sinks. Then put another man on his back and you will see how much deeper he sinks. Then remove the man from his back and have him jump straight up as high as he can and you will find that the print of his feet has become deeper from jumping than from having the man on his back. Hence here it is proved in 2 ways that man has twice as much strength as is required to support himself.[3]

The themes and methods typical of Leonardo's research are evident in this reasoning, integrating anatomical study and functional observation with mechanical considerations, both static and dynamic, which he extends to man and animal. The intention to make a direct anatomical comparison between bird and man is set out in fol. 124 recto (ex 45 r-a) of the Codex Atlanticus, in which Leonardo writes:

You will make an anatomy of the wings of a bird together with the muscles of the breast which are the movers of these wings.
And you will do the same for a man, in order to show the possibility that there is in man who desires to sustain himself amid the air by the beating of wings.[4]

The comparison between man and animal is proposed on fol. 16 recto of the Codex on the Flight of Birds on the basis of a theory concerning the working of the body parts in the upper and lower limbs. These topics can be traced through a series of studies and notes, dating from the same period as the codex and following its completion (ca. 1505; see Appendix, 1. Dating), that pay particular attention to the power of man's lower limbs. These investigations involve

medesimo. Come si vede al falcon portare l'anitra e all'aquila la lepre, per la qual cosa assai bene si dimostra dove tal superchia forza si stribuisce. Ma poca forza li bisogna a sostener se medesimo e bilicarsi sulle sue alie e ventilarle sopra del corso de' venti, e dirizzare il temone alli sua cammini, e poco moto d'alie basta, e tanto di più tardi moto, quanto l'uccello è maggiore.

L'uomo ancor lui ha maggior somma di forza nelle gambe <ch>e non si richiede al peso suo. E che sie vero, posa in piedi l'omo sopra la lita [sabbia fine] e pon mente quanto la stampa del suo piedi si profonda. Di poi li metti un altro omo addosso e vedrai quanto più si profonda. Di poi li leva l'omo da dosso e fallo saltare in alto a dirittura quanto esso può e troverai essere la stampa del suo piodi ocsersi più profondata nel salto che coll'omo addosso. Adunque qui per 2 modi è provato l'omo aver più forza il doppio che non si richiede a sostenere se medesimo.[3]

In questa argomentazione compaiono temi e metodi propri della ricerca di Leonardo, che integra lo studio anatomico e l'osservazione funzionale con la valutazione meccanica, sia statica sia dinamica, che si estende all'uomo e agli animali. L'intenzione di un diretto confronto anatomico tra uccello e uomo è esplicitata nel foglio 124 r (ex 45 r-a) del Codice Atlantico, nel quale Leonardo scrive:

Farai la natomia dell'alie d'uno uccello insieme colli muscoli del petto, motori d'esse alie.
El simile farai dell'omo per mostrare la possibilità che è nell'omo a potersi sostenere infra l'aria con battimento d'alie.[4]

La comparazione uomo-animale è proposta nella carta 16 r del Codice sul volo sulla base di una teoria riguardante la funzionalità dei distretti corporei degli arti superiori e inferiori. A questi temi è riconducibile una serie di studi e riflessioni che coinvolge un ampio numero di disegni del periodo coevo e successivo alla stesura del volumetto (c. 1505, si veda al proposito l'Appendice, 1. Datazione), con particolare attenzione alla potenza degli arti inferiori dell'uomo. Si tratta di un argomento che trova significativi esempi nella Collezione della Biblioteca Reale di Torino, esposti in quest'occasione.
Più in generale, i filoni tematici che si riscontrano nel fascicolo torinese derivano anche dalla storia materiale del volume, a partire dalla sua costituzione come tale, che Leonardo operò recuperando fogli già parzialmente utilizzati per schizzi e disegni a sanguigna più o meno finiti.

a vast number of drawings; among them are sheets from the Turin collection, on display in this exhibition. More generally, the topics to be found in the Turin notebook also derive from the history of the volume itself, beginning with its compilation, since Leonardo reused sheets already partially used for more or less complete sketches and drawings in red chalk. These sketches and drawings either remain visible under the text or are framed by words when the overlap on the drawing would have made the text less legible, as in the case of fol. 17 verso, which includes a sketch of a lower limb (see p. 130). The binding of the codex shows the imperfect correspondence of the sequences of the folded folios, which arose from interventions during its preparation by Leonardo himself (see Appendix, 2. Collation, p. 86) and does not derive from Guglielmo Libri's mutilation of the folios when he stole the manuscript from Paris (see Appendix, 3. Historical Events, p. 91), where it was held together with Manuscript B.[5]

The "Bird" and Its Flight

Leonardo uses the word "bird" both ornithologically and aeronautically to describe the creature and the machine that he was designing to allow man to fly (which he also calls the "instrument.") The Codex on the Flight of Birds is replete with this double usage, as in this sentence, which begins the text on fol. 18 verso: "From the mountain, which bears the name of the great bird, the famous bird will take its flight, which will fill the world with its great fame."[6] On the inner back cover, Leonardo elaborates: "The great bird will take its first flight, from the back of the great Cecero, filling the universe with wonder, filling all writings with its fame, and eternal glory to the nest where it was born."[7] The mythic and emphatic tone of these declarations should not belie the systematic work that the artist-engineer carried out on flight. The Turin codex is an exemplar of that work, but it represents only part of Leonardo's studies on this topic, as we know from the numerous manuscripts and loose papers that survive.[8]

Leonardo's reflections and studies on the topic of flight—in relation both to the creatures that fly and to the flying machine he designed many times over—bring together anatomical, comparative, functional, and mechanical analyses in a unified way. These interact in a way of thinking not always understood by modern culture, which is accustomed to distinguishing among the various branches of knowledge. The

Questi sono rimasti visibili al disotto della scrittura o sono da essa contornati, laddove, come nel caso della carta 17 v (che contiene proprio un esempio di rappresentazione di arto inferiore, si veda p. 130), l'interferenza del disegno avrebbe confuso la leggibilità della scrittura. La fascicolazione del *Codice* rivela inoltre – al di là della mutilazione di pagine operata da Guglielmo Libri (si veda l'*Appendice*, 3. Vicende storiche, p. 91), quando il manoscritto fu sottratto a Parigi, dove era conservato insieme al *Ms. B* –[5] la non perfetta coincidenza delle sequenze di bifogli, che deriva da interventi in corso d'opera di Leonardo stesso (si veda l'*Appendice*, 2. Fascicolazione, p. 86).

L'uccello e il suo volo

Il termine 'uccello' trova negli scritti di Leonardo un duplice valore, sia nel senso ornitologico che aereonautico, per indicare tanto l'animale quanto la macchina che egli andava progettando per consentire all'uomo di volare (indicata altre volte come 'strumento'). Il *Codice sul volo degli uccelli* rivela a pieno questa duplicità, a partire dalla dicitura che compare nella carta 18 v: "Del monte, che tiene il nome del grande uccello, piglierà il volo il famoso uccello, ch'empierà il mondo di sua gran fama".[6] Il motivo è amplificato in una nota che si trova al recto della seconda coperta, dove Leonardo scrive: "Piglierà il primo volo il grande uccello, sopra del dosso del suo magno Cècero, empiendo l'universo di stupore, empiendo di sua fama tutte le scritture, e groria etterna al nido dove nacque".[7] Il valore mitico ed enfatico di queste dichiarazioni non deve far perdere di vista il lavoro sistematico che l'artista-ingegnere ha condotto sul volo; inoltre il codice torinese deve essere valutato come emblematico ma assolutamente parziale rispetto alla complessità degli studi condotti su questo tema da Leonardo nell'arco della sua vita, che ci sono giunti attraverso numerosi manoscritti e fogli sparsi.[8]

La riflessione e gli studi del Vinciano sul volo e sull'entità che lo compie, biologica – l'uccello vero e proprio – o artificiale – la più volte progettata macchina volante –, contemplano l'analisi anatomica, comparata, funzionale e meccanica secondo un procedimento unitario. Questi aspetti interagiscono infatti secondo una forma di pensiero non sempre compresa dalla cultura odierna, abituata a distinguere e separare le varie branche del sapere. L'annotazione che compare nel foglio 434 r (ex 161 r-a) del *Codice Atlantico* si rivela particolarmente significativa al riguardo:

> L'uccello è strumento operante per legge matematica, il quale strumento è in potestà dell'omo poterlo fare con tutti li sua moti, ma non con tanta potenzia, ma solo s'astende nella potenzia del

annotation that appears in fol. 434 recto (ex 161 r-a) of the Codex Atlanticus is particularly significant on this subject:

> A bird is an instrument working according to mathematical law, which instrument it is within the capacity of man to reproduce with all its movements, but not with a corresponding degree of strength, though it is [*sic*! is not] deficient only in the power of maintaining equilibrium. We may therefore say that such an instrument constructed by man is lacking in nothing except the life of the bird, and this life must needs be supplied from that of man.
>
> The life which resides in the bird's members will without doubt better conform to their needs than will that of man which is separated from them, and especially in the almost imperceptible movements which preserve equilibrium. But since we see that the bird is equipped for many obvious varieties of movements, we are able from this experience to declare that the most rudimentary of these movements will be capable of being comprehended by man's understanding; and that he will to a great extent be able to provide against the destruction of that instrument of which he has himself become the living principle and the propeller.[9]

This text, which dates from ca. 1505, the period when the Codex on the Flight of Birds was written, contains, in my opinion, the reasons for and the intentions of the evolution of Leonardo's studies on flight, which proceed from the mechanical design process for the construction of the flying machine to the in-depth study of the flight of birds.

In order to understand the meaning of this text, one should avoid the temptation to give it a metaphysical interpretation, despite the reference to an apparently external and extracorporeal order such as the soul. Rather, we should refer to Leonardo's observations on the soul in his anatomical studies, noting that, through the *senso comune* and the nerves ("the leaders of the soul"), the soul is directly involved in transmitting *sentimento* (that is sensory function) and, consequently, movement. Note II of an anatomical study at Windsor (RL 19019 recto, K/P 39 recto), in which the relationship between the soul and sensory transmission is established, remains emblematic:[10]

bilicarsi. Adunque diren che tale strumento composto per l'omo non li manca se non l'anima dello uccello, la quale anima bisogna che sia contra fatta dall'anima dell'omo.

L'anima alle membra delli uccelli sanza dubbio obbidirà meglio a' bisogni di quelle che a quelle non farebbe l'anima dell'omo da esse separato, e massimamente ne' moti di quasi insensibile bilicazioni; ma poi che alle molte sensibile varietà di moti noi vediamo l'uccello provvedere, noi possiamo per tale esperienza giudicare che le forte sensibili potranno essere note alla cognizione dell'omo, e che esso largamente potrà provvedere alla ruina di quello strumento, del quale lui s'è fatto anima e guida.[9]

Questo testo, riferibile al 1505 circa, cioè al periodo di stesura del *Codice sul volo degli uccelli*, contiene, a mio parere, i motivi e le intenzioni dell'evoluzione degli studi di Leonardo sul volo, che procedono dalla progettazione meccanica per la realizzazione della macchina volante all'approfondita analisi del volo degli uccelli. Per comprenderne il senso, bisognerà rifuggire qualunque tentazione d'interpretazione metafisica che il richiamo ad un'entità apparentemente d'ordine esterno ed extracorporeo come l'anima potrebbe suggerire. Vale invece la medesima riflessione che Leonardo ha compiuto sull'anima nei suoi studi anatomici, dove questa, attraverso il senso comune e i nervi ("condottieri dell'anima"), è direttamente coinvolta nella trasmissione del "sentimento", cioè della sensibilità, e di conseguenza anche del movimento. Resta emblematica a questo fine la Nota II del foglio anatomico di Windsor RL 19019 r, K/P 39 r, nella quale è stabilito il rapporto tra l'anima e la trasmissione sensoriale.[10]

Come i cinque sensi sono offiziali dell'anima

L'anima pare risiedere nella parte iudiziale, e la parte iudiziale pare essere nel loco dove concorrano tutti i sensi, il quale è detto senso comune; e non è tutta per tutto il corpo, come molti hanno creduto, anzi, tutta innella parte, imperò che s'ella fussi tutta per tutto e tutta in ogni parte non era necessario fare li strumenti de' sensi fare infra loro uno medesimo concorso a uno solo loco, anzi, bastava che l'occhio operassi l'uffizio del sentimento sulla sua supefizie e non mandare per la via delli nervi ottici la similitudine delle cose vedute al senso, che l'anima alla sopra detta ragione le poteva complendere in essa superfizie dell'occhio.

[…]

How the five senses are servants of the soul

The soul appears to reside in the seat of judgement, and the judicial part appears to be in that place where all the senses come together, which is called the 'senso comune'; and it is not all of it everywhere in the whole body, as many have believed, but all in this part. For if it was all in the whole and all in each part it would not have been necessary to make the instruments of the senses converge to one and the same concourse in one place only. On the contrary it would have sufficed for the eye to perform its sensory function on its surface and not transmit by way of the optic nerves the similitudes of the things seen to the 'senso comune', because the soul, for the aforesaid reason, would be able to comprehend them on the surface of the eye. […]

The perforated cords carry (*sensation*) command and sensation to the functioning parts (*and there it has little force which*). These nerves, entering between the muscles and sinews, command these to move, and these obey (*with the bones*). And such obedience is put into action by a swelling, for the reason that swelling shortens their length and pulls them back. The nerves which are interwoven amidst the particular parts of the limbs being infused into the ends of the digits, carry to the 'senso [comune]' the cause of their contact.

The tendons with their muscles serve the nerves just as soldiers serve their leaders; and the nerves serve the 'senso comune' just as the leaders their captain; and the 'senso comune' serves the soul just as the captain serves his lord.

(*Therefore the tendon serves the muscle and the muscle—*)
Therefore the joint between bones obeys the tendon, and the tendon the muscle, and the muscle the nerve, and the nerve the 'senso comune' and the 'senso comune' is the seat of the soul; memory is its store and the 'imprensiva' is its standard of reference (*and the heart is its …*)

How the sense gives to the soul, and not the soul to the sense; and where the sensory function is missing from the soul, the soul in this life lacks information from the function of that sense, as appears in a mute or one born blind.[11]

Le corde preforante portano il comandamento e sentimento alli membri offiziali; le quali corde, entrate infra i muscoli e lacerti, comandano a quelli il movimento, quelli obbediscano, e tale obbedienzia si mette in atto collo sconfiare, imperò che 'l gonfiare raccorta le loro lunghezze e tirasi dirietro i nervi, i quali si tessano per le particule de' membri essendo infusi nelli stremi de' diti, portano al senso la cagione del loro contatto.
I nervi coi loro muscoli serv<o>no alle corde come i soldati a' condottieri, e le corde servano al senso comune come i condottieri al capitano, e 'l senso comune serve all'anima come il capitano serve il suo signore.

Adunque la giuntura delli ossi obbedisce al nervo e 'l nervo al muscolo, e 'l muscolo alla corda, e la corda al senso comune, e 'l senso comune è sedia dell'anima, e la memoria è sua ammunizione, e la imprensiva è sua referendaria.

Come il senso dà all'anima e non l'anima al senso, e dove manca il senso, offiziale dell'anima, all'anima manca in questa vita la notizia dell'uffizio d'esso senso, come appare nel muto o nell'orbo nato.[11]

L'anima, quindi, che abita nel suo corpo,[12] e riceve dai sensi informazioni percettive, interviene nella trasmissione del movimento attraverso il senso comune, i nervi e i tendini.[13] Per rendere possibile il volo dell'uomo, Leonardo progetta una macchina azionata dalla propulsione umana e assimilabile ad una protesi, cioè ad uno strumento che, in un modo o nell'altro, viene condotto dall'uomo come propria estensione corporea, al fine di realizzare una funzione come il volo per la quale egli non possiede abilità. L'anima dell'uccello, che ne abita direttamente il corpo, è invece in contatto con le sollecitazioni esterne e più appropriatamente potrà rispondere ai bisogni delle sue membra. Nel caso della macchina per volare, "strumento operante per legge matematica", l'anima dell'uomo dovrà farsi guida dello strumento, che le resta comunque separato. L'uomo, per superare questo gap, non può che procedere per cognizione, cioè osservando e giudicando le "molte sensibili varietà di moti" cui l'uccello (animale) sa provvedere. Da questa consapevolezza muove quindi l'approfondito studio del volo degli uccelli, che coinvolge Leonardo nei primi anni del Cinquecento.
L'impegno nella progettazione della macchina volante aveva avuto un avvio di molto precedente, risalente agli ultimi anni fiorentini e ai primi del soggiorno milanese,[14] per continuare fino agli anni Novanta del Quattrocento. I problemi meccanici cui Leonardo attese riguardarono inizialmente la

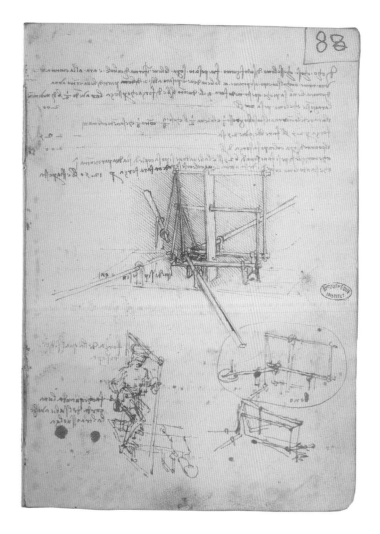

FIG. 6
LEONARDO DA VINCI
Manuscript B / *Ms. B*,
fol. 88 recto, ca. 1487–90
Pen and brown ink
on paper / Penna e
inchiostro bruno su carta
230 x 160 mm
Paris, Institut de France
(Ms 2173)

The soul, which lives in its body[12] and receives perceptual information from the senses, intervenes in the transmission of movement through the *senso comune*, nerves, and tendons.[13] In order to make flight by man possible, Leonardo designed a machine that, in one way or another, is operated by a man as an extension of his body so that he can perform a function like flight, of which he is not otherwise capable. The soul of the bird, which directly inhabits the body, is, in contrast, in contact with external stimuli and can respond more appropriately to the needs of its limbs. In the case of the flying machine, an "instrument operating according to mathematical law," the soul of man must guide the instrument, which remains separate. To overcome this gap, man can proceed only by knowledge, that is, by observing and assessing the "many considerably different types of movement" that the (biological) bird can make. From this awareness comes, therefore, the in-depth study of bird flight that occupied Leonardo in the early sixteenth century.

costruzione dell'ala, la propulsione (umana), le modalità di trasmissione del movimento e la posizione dell'uomo all'interno del meccanismo, che poteva essere disteso o posto in piedi, impegnato comunque a generare l'energia necessaria al moto attraverso i suoi arti inferiori, attivati mediante un sistema di spinta e sollevamento alternato. I numerosi meccanismi progettati, da quelli del periodo 1483-86 fino a quello che Luca Beltrami ha definito "l'aeroplano di Leonardo",[15] con una trasmissione del movimento a molle (foglio 863 r [ex 314 r-b] del *Codice Atlantico*), databile alla seconda metà degli anni Novanta del Quattrocento, sono ripercorribili attraverso numerosi fogli del *Codice Atlantico* e del *Ms. B*. Nell'ambito di questi studi, un'attenzione inevitabilmente ricorrente coinvolge la costruzione dell'ala, la sua portanza (si vedano al proposito, tra gli altri, il foglio 1058 v [ex 381 v-a] del *Codice Atlantico*, e il foglio 88 v del *Ms. B*), nonché le modalità del suo funzionamento, che devono prevedere il sollevamento del proprio peso e di quello dell'uomo che pilota la macchina. Per queste valutazioni quantitative Leonardo ricorre a calcoli del tipo espresso nel foglio 88 r del *Ms. B*, accompagnati dalle figure del meccanismo e dell'uomo in azione sullo stesso (fig. 6).

> Dico così che se l'omo di sotto figurato fia posato sopra le lieve in forma di calcole [pedali], e arà alla cintura uno tirare e col suo capo usi pontare, e la lieva, dove è posato, abbi 2 parti di lieva contro a una di contra lieva: sappi che questo modo farà mille ducento libbre di forza con prestezza, avendo $1/2$ braccio di movimento.
> La ragion si è che l'omo pesa libbre 200
> il tirare della cintura ha il suo subbio grosso $1/8$, e la lieva $1/2$ braccio, che son $9/8$ contra $1/8$, che facendo colle mani forza per 25 libbre, farebbe 9 via 25 fa 225
> il pontare di sopra col capo fa forza di libbre 200
> che tutti questi pesi fanno somma di 625 libbre, e la lieva dove si posa co' piedi, sia dua parti contra una, che stando l'omo co' piedi in testa a detta lieva colle cose sopra dette, farà forza per 1250 libbre, e fia presta.[16]

L'ala può quindi ottenere la sua battuta (alzata e abbassata) attraverso il rapido movimento di leve azionate dagli arti inferiori dell'uomo, sulla cui potenza Leonardo continuerà a ritornare.[17] Per altri due tipi di movimento, la flesso-estensione e la rotazione, risulta di fondamentale importanza il perfezionamento dei meccanismi articolari delle componenti che costituiscono l'ala stessa, studiata e progettata secondo il medesimo procedimento che Leonardo adotta nell'anatomia dell'apparato locomotore, cioè vestendo le ossa "a grado a grado" (foglio RL 19041 r, K/P 44 r).[18]

Well before he produced the codex, Leonardo committed himself to designing a flying machine. He began the process toward the end of his Florentine period and in the first years of his stay in Milan, and continued working on it until the 1490s.[14] The mechanical problems that Leonardo expected initially concerned the structure of the wing, (human) propulsion, the ways of transmitting motion, and the position of the man inside the mechanism. The operator could lie down or stand up, but he would always be employed in generating the necessary power by using his lower limbs in a system of alternate thrusting and lifting. The numerous mechanisms he designed included those dating from 1483–86 and what Luca Beltrami called "Leonardo's airplane,"[15] dating from the late 1490s, which transmitted movement through the use of springs (fol. 863 recto [ex 314 r-b] of the Codex Atlanticus). These studies can be traced through many folios of the Codex Atlanticus and Manuscript B. In them, recurrent questions involve the construction of the wing, its carrying capacity (see on this matter, among others, fol. 1058 verso [ex 381 v-a] of the Codex Atlanticus and fol. 88 verso of Manuscript B), and exactly how it would work, since it had to lift not only its own weight but also that of the operator. For these quantitative computations Leonardo used calculations of the type expressed in fol. 88 recto of Manuscript B, accompanied by sketches of the mechanism and of a man using it (fig. 6).

So, I say that if the man portrayed below were positioned above the shaped levers [pedals], having a strap attached round his waist, and if he pushed with his head, then the lever at the point where he pushes would enact a force 2 times stronger than the counterlever: then this would correspond to one thousand two hundred *libbre* of force applied rapidly, that is, half a *braccio* [unit of measurement] of movement. This is because the man weighs 200 *libbre*, the belt pull has a cylindrical element $1/8$ and the lever $1/2$ of one *braccio*, which is $9/8$ against $1/8$, therefore pushing with the hands to exert a force of 25 *libbre* would make 9 times 25, which equals 225, the aforementioned pushing with the pedals exerts a force of 200 *libbre*, so all these weights add up to 625 *libbre*, and the lever on which the foot is placed should be in two parts against one, so that when the man has his foot on the aforementioned lever with the aforementioned parts, he will exert a force of 1250 *libbre* and will move swiftly.[16]

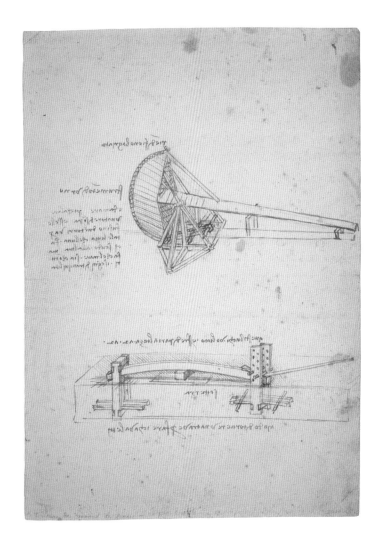

FIG. 7
LEONARDO DA VINCI
Designs for a Maritime Assault Mechanism and a Device for Bending Beams / Progetti per una macchina d'assalto dal mare e di un meccanismo per sagomare il legno, ca. 1487–90
Pen and brown ink over black chalk on paper / Penna, inchiostro bruno e pietra nera su carta
284 x 201 mm
New York, The Morgan Library & Museum
(1986.50)

In questo caso la similitudine tra lo scheletro e il sistema articolato di aste snodate che costituiscono la struttura portante dell'ala è immediato, come si può apprezzare nel foglio 843 r (ex 307 v-a) del *Codice Atlantico* (cronologicamente vicino al codice torinese; fig. 10). Una simile ma più rigida struttura, anni prima era stata innervata mediante un'armatura ventrale su cui era disteso il rivestimento, come risulta dal disegno del foglio 74 r del *Ms. B* (fig. 8), con la seguente didascalia:

The wing could, therefore, flap (be raised and lowered) thanks to the rapid movement of levers operated by the man's lower limbs, on whose power Leonardo frequently commented.[17]

For the other two types of movement, flexion-extension and rotation, Leonardo had to perfect the articular mechanisms of the components that constituted the wing itself, which he studied and designed according to the same procedure he adopted in visualising the anatomy of the locomotor apparatus, that is, covering the bones "step by step" (Windsor RL 19041, K/P 44 recto).[18] The similarity between the skeleton and the articulated system of jointed rods that made up the bearing structure of the wing is immediately evident, as we can see in fol. 843 recto (ex 307 v-a) of the Codex Atlanticus, which is chronologically close to the Turin codex (fig. 10). Some years earlier he had designed a similar but more rigid structure, with a ventral skeleton on which the membrane was stretched, as seen in the drawing on fol. 74 recto of Manuscript B (fig. 8), which has the following caption:

> A the struts should be of fir-wood, because it has a good grain and is lightweight
> B it should be of fustian pasted on so that it does not come off easily
> C should be starched taffeta, and as a test use thin pasteboard.[19]

Amongst the various types of wing, those of the spring-driven flying machine mentioned above were inspired by the wings "of the *pannicola* [insect, dragonfly] or *pesce rondine* [flying gurnard]" as can be seen on fol. 844 recto (ex 308 r-a) of the Codex Atlanticus (fig. 9).

Studies and designs of mechanisms to be made of wood, including means for shaping the material, are depicted in a rare autograph drawing by Leonardo, held at the Morgan Library (1986.50), on display in this exhibition. It comprises a siege tower for scaling a sea fort and a machine for bending wood which carries the note: "A way to bend a beam for making trestles"[20] (fig. 7).

The lengthy and intensive design procedure regarding mechanical flight is set out in the Codex on the Flight of Birds on the following folios, which run backward from the end of the notebook, for reasons that will be explained later:

Fol. 18 recto (cat. 9, pl. XXXVII) shows a detail of a mechanical wing.

> A sarà asse d'abete innerbata, che ha tiglio ed è leggere
> B sarà fustagno incollatovi piuma, acciò che l'aria di leggeri non fugga
> C sia taffetà innamidato, e per pruova torrai carte sottili.[19]

Tra le varie tipologie di ali, quella per la macchina volante con motore a molle sopracitata aveva avuto un'ispirazione dalle ali "di pannicola o di pesce rondine", come risulta nel foglio 844 r (ex 308 r-a) del *Codice Atlantico* (fig. 9).

Lo studio e la progettazione di meccanismi da realizzare in legno, provvedendo anche alla loro sagomatura, sono il soggetto in un prezioso autografo di Leonardo della Morgan Library (1986.50), esposto in mostra, contenente un meccanismo d'assalto per scalare una torre dal mare e un sistema di curvatura del legno, che contiene la seguente annotazione: "Modo di torciere una trave per fare i chavaletti"[20] (fig. 7).

L'intenso e lungo lavoro progettuale riguardante il volo meccanico è testimoniato nel *Codice sul volo degli uccelli* dalle seguenti pagine, che si ripercorrono dal fondo del fascicolo, per le ragioni che si diranno più avanti:

carta 18 r (cat. 9, tav. XXXVII), dove compare un particolare d'ala meccanica;

carta 17 r (cat. 9, tav. XXXV), con studi grafici di ala meccanica, dispositivi di rotazione e annotazioni sulla battuta (movimento di alzata e abbassata dell'ala);

carta 16 v (cat. 9, tav. XXXIV), dove, sia nel disegno sia nel testo, è analiticamente studiato il sistema di rotazione con la finalità di consentire all'ala di assumere una posizione di taglio rispetto all'aria;

carta 16 r (cat. 9, tav. XXXIII), con la comparazione tra uccello e uomo ai fini della potenza che occorre all'uomo per sostenersi in aria, nonché, nella nota e nei disegni in margine, con sistemi di sicurezza per limitare i danni nella eventuale caduta, già accennati nella carta precedente, 16 v;

carta 15 v (cat. 9, tav. XXXII), dove è schizzato lo strumento per calcolare il centro di gravità ai fini della costruzione della macchina volante;

carta 15 r (cat. 9, tav. XXXI), dove si raccomanda d'imitare l'ala del pipistrello;

carta 12 v (cat. 9, tav. XXVI), con note intitolate al "pericolo della ruina" della macchina volante (che ricorda un aliante ad ali mobili) e a valutazioni proporzionali tra la larghezza dello strumento e i centri di gravità dello stesso e "del grave da lui portato" (che devono essere sulla stessa verticale, con il centro di gravità del grave, in quanto più pesante, al di sotto di quello della macchina);

carta 11 v (cat. 9, tav. XXIV), con disegni di strutture per ala meccanica e schematizzazioni di tiranti per il movimento di flesso-estensione della stessa;

Fol. 17 recto (cat. 9, pl. XXXV) has sketches of a mechanical wing and of rotating devices, plus comments on flapping (the up-and-down movements of wings). Fol. 16 verso (cat. 9, pl. XXXIV) contains a detailed analysis, in text and drawing, of the system of rotation necessary to allow the wing to take an edgewise position with respect to the air.

Fol. 16 recto (cat. 9, pl. XXXIII) compares bird with man in regard to the power a man needs to stay aloft, and includes, in the notes and sketches in the margins, safety systems to limit damage from falls, a topic also mentioned on fol. 16 verso.

Fol. 15 verso (cat. 9, pl. XXXII) includes a sketch of an instrument for calculating the center of gravity for the purpose of constructing the flying machine.

Fol. 15 recto (cat. 9, pl. XXXI) contains a recommendation to imitate the wing of a bat.

Fol. 12 verso (cat. 9, pl. XXVI) contains notes on how to "avoid the danger of destruction" of the flying machine (which resembles a glider with maneuverable wings) and on the proportions of the width of the instrument and its center of gravity and "the center [of gravity] of the weight it carries" (which must be on the same vertical plane, with the center of gravity of the heaviest part being below that of the machine).

Fol. 11 verso (cat. 9, pl. XXIV) has sketches of the structure of a mechanical wing and diagrams of braces for the wing's flexion-extension.

Fol. 7 recto (cat. 9, pl. XV) includes another detailed drawing of, and comments on, the braces of the wings as well as comments on the articulation of parts and notes on methods for raising the mechanical bird to a great height and on avoiding the danger of falling. Here, as in his anatomical studies, Leonardo uses the word "nerve"; in the flying machine this is a strong, thick tie of leather tanned with alum without any iron parts.

Fol. 6 verso (cat. 9, pl. XIV) shows a detail of a mechanical joint with a "strong leather tie" and has notes on the flight conditions required, "so that the wings do not get wet."

Fol. 5 recto (cat. 9, pl. XI) contains a quick sketch of a man sitting in the flying machine, "free from the waist up in order to be able to balance himself, as he does in a boat, so as that his center of gravity and that of the instrument can balance and change as necessity demands, according to shifts in the center of his resistance."[21]

Before we deal with other topics in the codex, it is useful to recall the structure of the manuscript (see

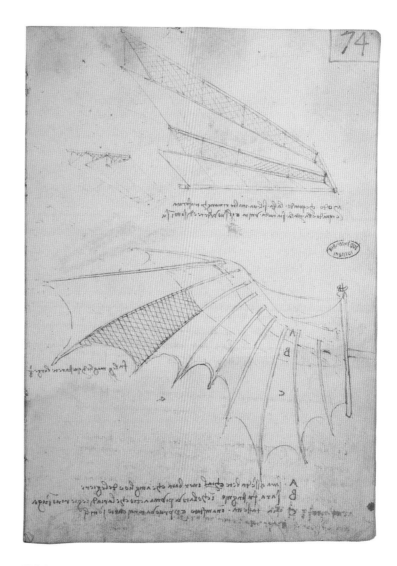

FIG. 8
LEONARDO DA VINCI
Manuscript B / *Ms. B*, fol. 74 recto, ca. 1487–90
Pen and brown ink on paper /
Penna e inchiostro bruno su carta
230 x 160 mm
Paris, Institut de France
(Ms 2173)

carta 7 r (cat. 9, tav. XV), con un altro disegno dettagliato e annotazioni sui tiranti dell'ala, sui punti di articolazioni tra le parti – per i quali, come negli studi anatomici, Leonardo usa il termine 'nervo', che, nella macchina volante "vole essere di grosso maschereccio" e senza alcuna ferramenta – e sui modi per levare l'uccello meccanico in grande altezza, fuggendo il pericolo di rovina;
carta 6 v (cat. 9, tav. XIV), nuovamente con il disegno di un particolare di articolazione meccanica con "maschereccio" e indicazioni sulle condizioni di volo, "acciò che l'alia non si bagni";

also Appendix, 2. Collation), in particular fol. 7 and fol. 8, which lack the part of the sheet corresponding to the second half of the notebook. Excluding the cover, fols. 1/18 and 2/17 are paired but cut in two, because they are four of the five folios removed following the theft by Guglielmo Libri. The pairs of fols. 3/16, 4/15, 5/14, 6/13 are complete, each including the corresponding left and right halves; fol. 7 and fol. 8, are both in the first half (left-hand side) of the book; they lack their corresponding pendant and are attached only by a tab. Following this anomaly, fols. 9/12 are once again complete, forming a single sheet that extends left and right, while fols. 10/11, between which lies the stitching, were rejoined during restoration, since fol. 10 is one of the five removed from the codex and sold separately.

With regard to the sequence of the folios, an important reference point is the handwritten numbering by Leonardo in the upper right-hand corner of the recto. It is absent on fol. 1 and fol. 2 (however, the latter has been trimmed at the top, probably to eliminate the numbering and allow it to be sold as a separate sheet). It is present without corrections on fol. 3 and fol. 4, and from fol. 5 to fol. 16 it is continuous (except for fol. 10, which is trimmed at the top like fol. 2), but with the omission of one number (from 6 to 17). The handwritten numbering returns to the correct sequence (from 5 to 16), thanks to a correction in another hand, probably that of Francesco Melzi.[22] It is widely considered that the omission of number 5 was an inadvertent mistake by the artist. The last two folios are not numbered; once again, they are among those removed from the notebook following the theft. That the extant folios of the codex are complete is confirmed by Leonardo himself, on fol. 17 recto (cat. 9, pl. XXXV), where, under the drawing of the complex device of the mechanical wing, he wrote, "On the nineteen folios of this [book] is demonstrated the cause of this."[23] There are, in fact, eighteen folios, but due to the omission of number 5, it appeared to Leonardo that there were nineteen.

The numbering of the folios proceeds normally, with the spine of the quires to the left. The order of the texts and the drawings, however, appears to start from the end, at fol. 18 recto, and proceed to the front of the notebook. It is never possible to attribute to Leonardo rigid respect for a sequence; he had a habit of returning to his writings, skipping from one page to another, after a considerable time. Nevertheless, in this case, the main topic follows a backward path that

carta 5 r (cat. 9, tav. XI), con lo schizzo abbreviato di un uomo collocato nella macchina volante, "libero dalla cintura in su per potersi bilicare, come fa in barca, acciò che 'l centro della gravità di lui e dello strumento si possa bilicare e strasmutarsi, dove necessità il dimanda, alla mutazione del centro della sua resistenzia".[21]

Prima di affrontare gli altri temi contenuti nel *Codice*, è utile richiamare la struttura del manoscritto (per la quale si veda anche l'*Appendice*, 2. Fascicolazione), soffermandoci sulle carte 7 e 8, che mancano della parte di foglio corrispondente nella seconda metà del libretto. Escludendo al momento la coperta, le carte 1/18 e 2/17 risultano appaiate ma divise tra loro, perché corrispondono a quattro delle cinque carte avulse dal codice a seguito del furto di Guglielmo Libri. Le coppie di carte 3/16, 4/15, 5/14, 6/13 risultano integre, come fogli unitari in continuità tra parte sinistra e destra. La carta 7 e la carta 8, entrambe collocate nella parte sinistra del fascicolo, sono scempie, senza la corrispondente a destra, ma solo supportate da un'aletta. Dopo questa anomalia, le carte 9/12 sono nuovamente in continuità, costituite da un unico foglio che si estende a sinistra e a destra, mentre le carte 10/11, tra le quali si trova la cucitura, sono ora riunite da un intervento di restauro, poiché la carta 10 è nuovamente una delle cinque che furono avulse dal *Codice* e vendute separatamente.

Per quanto riguarda la sequenza delle pagine, si ha un solido punto d'appoggio nella numerazione autografa di Leonardo posta all'angolo destro alto del recto. Essa è assente sulla carta 1 e sulla 2 (quest'ultima è stata però rifilata in alto, probabilmente proprio per eliminare la numerazione e poterla vendere come pagina autonoma). È presente senza correzioni nelle carte 3 e 4 e, dalla 5 alla 16, è in continuità (a parte la 10, rifilata in alto come la 2), ma con lo scarto di un numero (da 6 a 17). La numerazione autografa è ricondotta alla giusta sequenza (5-16) da una correzione sovrapposta d'altra mano, probabilmente di Francesco Melzi.[22] Al proposito, è opinione largamente condivisa che l'omissione del numero 5 sia stata una svista dell'artista, che lo avrebbe involontariamente saltato. Risultano senza numero le ultime due carte, nuovamente quelle che furono asportate dal volumetto dopo il furto. Che le carte siano ora tutte quelle ricomprese nella stesura finale del *Codice*, è confermato dallo stesso Leonardo, che nella 17 r (cat. 9, tav. XXXV), sotto il complesso congegno dell'ala meccanica, ha scritto: "Alle 19 carte di questo si dimostra la causa di questo".[23] La carte sono 18, ma considerando l'omissione del numero 5, a Leonardo risultavano 19.

La numerazione delle carte procede nel senso normale, con la costola del fascicolo a sinistra; la redazione dei testi e dei disegni sembra invece procedere dal fondo,

FIG. 9
LEONARDO DA VINCI
Codex Atlanticus /
Codice Atlantico,
fol. 844 recto
(ex 308 r-a),
ca. 1493–94
Black chalk, pen and brown ink on paper, with a note in red chalk / Pietra nera, penna e inchiostro bruno su carta, con una nota a sanguigna
290 x 218 mm
Milan, Biblioteca Ambrosiana

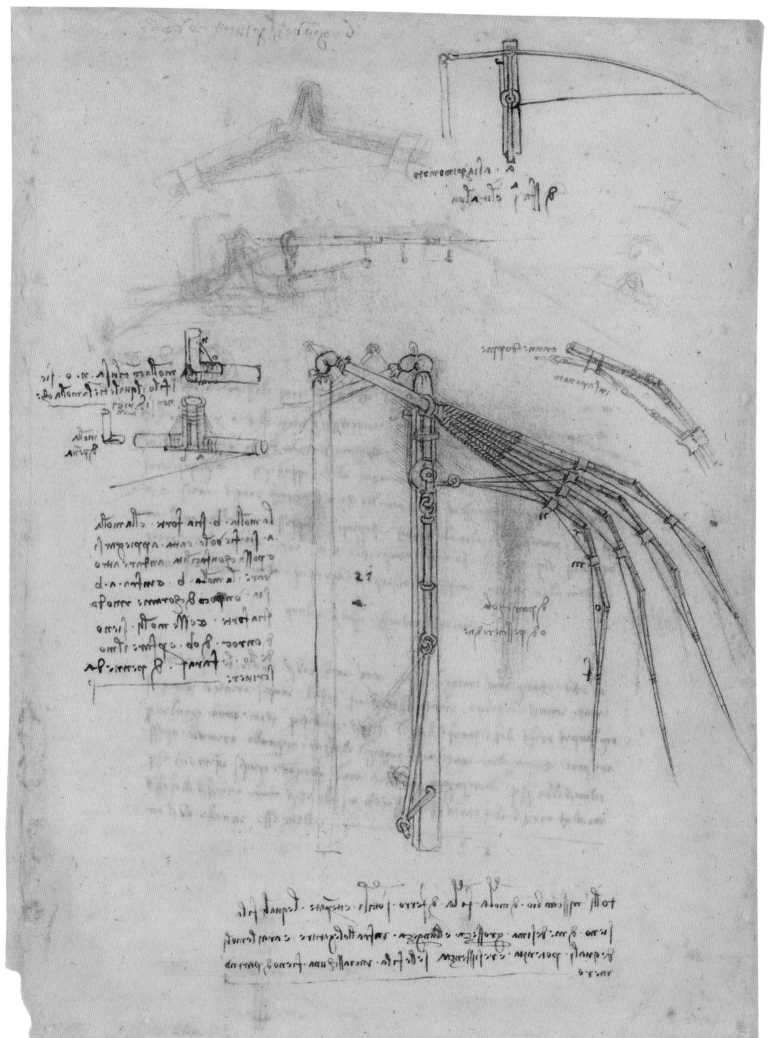

is confirmed not only by the passage from the recto of the folio to the verso of the previous one (which is on the left) but also from the verso to the recto of the same folio, as in the case of fol. 12.[24]

As for the content of the codex, it would seem that Leonardo, reviewing his studies from previous decades, began to write this notebook with equal attention to the flight of birds and mechanical flight, but gradually abandoned the latter topic to concentrate his attention on the former. He dedicated the first pages to mechanical studies on gravity and balances, integrating the notes on fol. 4 verso, which, being similar in reasoning, are certainly not extraneous. Between fol. 12 and fol. 13 there may have been folios in continuity with 7 and 8, which, as noted above, are loose and attached only by tabs. Even given the imperfect unity of topics dealt with in the volume, when we follow its backward path, we notice an especially large leap in content between fol. 13 recto and fol. 12 verso. Fol. 13 recto, apart from a riddle about "snow in summer," is entirely dedicated to the relation of the bird to the movements of the wind. Fol. 12 verso, dedicated to avoiding the risk of damage (*Per fuggire il pericolo della ruina*), begins with the words, "The destruction of such an instrument can happen in 2 ways, of which the first is breakage of the instrument."[25] This reference to "such an instrument" suggests that between fol. 12 and fol. 13 there may have been one or two others, presumably the folios that would correspond with fol. 7 and fol. 8, each of which now lacks a partner. Perhaps these folios contained drawings of the flying machine that did not satisfy Leonardo, who may have removed them before proceeding with the numbering of the folios. The theory of a rearrangement of the Turin codex with later eliminations and insertions of folios by Leonardo himself, and in any case prior to the numbering, has been advanced by Juliana Barone and Martin Kemp,[26] while Carlo Pedretti believes that fol. 7 and fol. 8 were both part of a single sheet folded over and tampered with, perhaps at the time of Guglielmo Libri (see Appendix, 2. Collation).[27] This is a question that deserves to be studied through careful analysis of the paper of all the sheets that make up the codex. A laboratory examination has found that neither the thickness nor the distribution of the chain lines is homogeneous.[28]
Between the writing of the codex from back to front and its final binding, normalized by Leonardo through the numbering from front to back, in the usual direction for a book, there is only one apparent

dalla carta 18 r, verso l'inizio. A Leonardo non si può mai attribuire il rigido rispetto di una sequenza, per l'abitudine di ritornare sui suoi scritti da una pagina all'altra, talvolta anche a distanza di tempo. Tuttavia, in questo caso, lo svolgimento principale degli argomenti segue un percorso a ritroso che trova conferma non solo nel passaggio dal recto di una carta al verso di quella precedente (posta a sinistra), ma anche dal verso al recto di una stessa carta, come nella carta 12.[24]

Tornando quindi al contenuto del *Codice*, sembrerebbe che, ricalcando il proprio percorso di studi, sviluppatosi nei decenni precedenti, Leonardo abbia avviato a scrivere questo libretto con attenzione parallela al volo degli uccelli e al volo meccanico, rarefacendo progressivamente quest'ultimo argomento per intensificare le annotazioni sul volo degli uccelli e dedicare a studi meccanici sulla gravità e sulle bilance le prime pagine, che si integrano alla carta 4 v con quelli sul volo, ai quali, per affinità di argomentazione, non sembrano certo estranei. Tra le carte 12 e 13 avrebbero potuto essere presenti le carte in continuità con la 7 e la 8, che, come si è detto, risultano scempie e supportate da una aletta ciascuna. In effetti, pur nella non perfetta organicità degli argomenti che interessa il volume, lungo il suo svolgersi a ritroso, tra le carte 13 r e 12 v si avverte un salto di contenuto particolare. La carta 13 r, a parte l'indovinello sulla "neve di state", è tutta dedicata al rapporto dell'uccello con il moto del vento; la carta 12 v, dedicata al pericolo di rovina ("Per fuggire il pericolo della ruina"), avvia con le seguenti parole: "Può accadere la ruina di tale strumento per 2 modi, de' quali il primo è del rompersi lo strumento…".[25] Il riferimento diretto a "tale strumento" induce ad ipotizzare che tra le carte 12 e 13 ci fossero le due corrispondenti alle 7 e 8 ora scempie, magari contenenti disegni sulla macchina volante che non convincevano del tutto l'autore, che potrebbe averle perciò eliminate prima di procedere con la numerazione del fascicolo. L'ipotesi di un rimaneggiamento del codice torinese con eliminazione e inserimenti successivi di carte da parte di Leonardo stesso, prima comunque della numerazione, è stata avanzata da Juliana Barone e Martin Kemp,[26] mentre Carlo Pedretti ha ritenuto che le carte 7 e 8 siano entrambe parte di un unico foglio ripiegato su se stesso e manomesso forse ai tempi del Libri (si veda l'*Appendice*, 2. Fascicolazione).[27] Si tratta di un problema che merita di essere approfondito mediante un'esaustiva analisi della carta di tutti i fogli che costituiscono il *Codice*, che ad un primo esame strumentale si è rivelata non omogenea per quanto riguarda gli spessori e la distribuzione dei filoni.[28]
Tra la stesura a ritroso del *Codice* e la sua confezione finale, normalizzata da Leonardo attraverso la numerazione

contradiction. The writing of the notebook reflects the course of Leonardo's studies on flight, beginning with mechanical flight and moving on to the flight of birds, but its final layout, established by the numbering, can be traced, although in a summary manner and not subdivided, to the project he described on fol. 3 recto of Manuscript K: "I have divided the treatise on birds into four books; of which the first treats of their flight by beating their wings; the second of flight without beating the wings and with the help of the wind; the third of flight in general, such as that of birds, bats, fishes, animals and insects; the last of the mechanism of this movement."[29]

In the final essay, therefore, discussion of mechanical motion would have followed the study of the flight of birds and other "flying animals," including fish, because there was thought to be a similarity, dating back to antiquity, between the elements of air and water. The inclusion of mechanical studies dedicated to the science of weights in the initial folios also follows a precise logic. On fol. 3 recto of the codex Leonardo writes:

> Instrumental or mechanical science is very noble and the most useful above all others, because by means of it all animated bodies, which have motion, carry out all their operations. Which motions are born from the center of their gravity, which is located in the middle of parts of unequal weights, and this has deficiency or abundance of muscles as well as lever and counterlever.[30]

In note V of an anatomical study at Windsor (RL 19009 recto, K/P 143 recto), dating from ca. 1509–10, Leonardo exhorts, in a similar manner:

> Arrange it so that the book On the Elements of Mechanics with its practice shall precede the demonstration of the movement and force of man and of other animals, and by means of these you will be able to prove all your propositions.[31]

The final organization of this small notebook thus reflects the general organization that Leonardo intended to give to his studies on the movement of animated beings, man and animal, with a view to publishing them in the form of essays. The theoretical portion of the argument was the section on abstract mechanics which demonstrated the laws of motion and formed a basis for the various specific demonstrations or il-

apposta nella direzione consueta di lettura di un testo, esiste una contraddizione solo apparente. La redazione del volumetto rispecchierebbe infatti il percorso dell'esperienza di studio di Leonardo, dal volo meccanico al volo degli uccelli, mentre l'impostazione finale data dalla numerazione è riconducibile, anche se in maniera sommaria e non suddivisa, al progetto che egli ha enunciato nel foglio 3 r del *Ms. K*: "Dividi il trattato delli uccelli in 4 libri, de' quali il pr<im>o sia del lor volare per battimento d'alie; il secondo del volo sanza batter alie per favor di vento; il terzo del volare in comune come d'uccelli, pipistrelli, pesci, animali, insetti; ultimo del moto strumentale".[29] Nel trattato finale, dunque, il moto strumentale avrebbe dovuto venire dopo aver preso cognizione dell'esperienza di volo degli uccelli e degli altri animali 'volanti', pesci compresi, per una similitudine tra il movimento nell'elemento aereo e in quello acqueo, che ha origini antiche.

Anche l'inserimento alle pagine iniziali di studi meccanici dedicati alla scienza dei pesi segue una precisa logica. Alla carta 3 r del *Codice* Leonardo scrive:

> La scienzia strumentale ovver machinale è nobilissima e sopra tutte l'altre utilissima, con ciò sia che mediante quella tutti li corpi animati, che hanno moto, fanno tutte loro operazioni. E quali moti nascano dal centro della lor gravità, che è posto in mezzo a parte di pesi disequali, e ha questo carestia o dovizia di muscoli ed etiam lieva e contra lieva.[30]

Nella Nota V del foglio anatomico di Windsor, RL 19009 r, K/P 143 r (*c.* 1509-10), parimenti Leonardo avverte

> Fa' che 'l libro delli elementi macchinali colla sua pratica vada innanzi alla dimostrazione del moto e forza dell'omo e altri animali, e mediante quelli tu potrai provare ogni tua proposizione.[31]

L'assetto finale del breve quaderno torinese rispecchia quindi l'impostazione generale che Leonardo intendeva dare ai suoi studi sul moto degli esseri animati, uomo e animali, nella prospettiva di pubblicarli in forma di trattati. Come base teorica egli poneva la parte "macchinale", fisico-meccanica, che può dimostrare le leggi del moto e dare fondamento alle varie dimostrazioni o raffigurazioni specifiche del soggetto studiato. Infine si può giungere all'aspetto artificiale. In questo caso si tratta del volo meccanico; nell'anatomia si tratta della costruzione di modelli, propri di una "anathomia artificialis", che fungano da compendio per evitare di dover tornare sempre all'esperienza (la dissezione, con tutte le oggettive difficoltà della stessa).[32] È da rilevare che nel foglio anatomico RL 19037 v, K/P 81 v,

lustrations of the subject under consideration. Finally, he intended to introduce the artificial aspect. In this case, that aspect is mechanical flight; in anatomy, it is the construction of models, belonging to an *anathomia artificialis*, which acted as a compendium of knowledge, so that one need not continually return to experimentation (that is, dissection, with all its difficulties).[32] We note that in another anatomical study at Windsor (RL 19037 verso, K/P 81 verso), dating from ca. 1508, Leonardo (in note II) defines a set of twenty-four illustrations of the parts of the human body as "the instrumental shape of man."[33]

In the Codex on the Flight of Birds, again reading backward from fol. 18 recto, we can identify two types of flight: "flight by flapping the wings" and flight "without flapping the wings and using the wind." Leonardo makes the same distinction in the Manuscript K, assigning to the two types of flight two distinct books of his planned treatise, which would have had further sections, each on the influence of external factors.

The Turin codex contains a number of studies on flight by means of the flapping of the wings, starting with fol. 18 recto, including theories on "impetus" and on the way the bird is supported by the air between flaps via a wedge effect (*fassi conio*) under its wings, which allows it to maintain its rise without flapping its wings.[34] Once again, Leonardo lingers on the ratio between the weight of the bird and its wingspan, and on the purpose of the rudder of the winglets (*alulae*), which he calls "the big finger, or rudder of the wing." He describes this rudder on fol. 13 verso (which includes a very clear sketch at top right) as:

> a bone of great strength, to which are joined very strong nerves and short feathers and of greater strength than the feathers that are on the wings of birds, because the bird supports itself with this above the already condensed air with all the force of the wing and its own power.[35]

He proceeds with an evocative and philologically precise comparison between a winglet and a claw (specifically, that of a cat climbing a tree). An anatomically correct study of the bone structure of the wing, including the bony projection of the winglet (sometimes called the bastard wing), is seen in a splendid drawing at Windsor (RL 12656 verso, K/P 187 recto), dating from ca. 1512–15 (fig. 11) which also includes an accurate series of ratios presumably referring to

Nota II (databile intorno al 1508), Leonardo definisce come "figura strumentale dell'omo" il corpo umano dimostrato attraverso il complesso delle illustrazioni delle sue parti (in ventiquattro figure).[33]

Per quanto riguarda il volo degli uccelli, si possono distinguere le tipologie di volo che egli individua nel *Codice*, partendo sempre, a ritroso, dalla carta 18 r. La divisione tra il "lor volare per battimento d'alie" e il volare "senza batter alie per favor di vento", operata nel *Ms. K* sopracitato, con l'assegnazione alle due tipologie di volo di due libri distinti del progettato trattato, rivela ulteriori articolazioni basate sull'incidenza dei fattori esterni.

Nel codice torinese troviamo vari studi relativi al volo battente, a partire dalla carta 18 r, dove compaiono le teorie relative all'impeto (*impetus*), alla sostentazione dell'uccello in aria tra una battuta d'ali e l'altra per un effetto di cuneo ("fassi conio") che l'aria stessa viene a creare sotto l'uccello, determinando il suo innalzamento senza battere le ali.[34] E, ancora, Leonardo si sofferma sul rapporto tra peso dell'uccello e apertura alare, nonché sulla funzione di timone delle alule, che definisce "dito grosso, ovver timone dell'alia" e alla cui descrizione dà ampio spazio nella carta 13 v (con l'efficace schizzo in alto a destra). Qui, "tal dito grosso" è indicato come

> un osso di tanta fortezza, al quale si congiugne nervi fortissimi e penne corte e di maggior fortezza che penne che sieno nelle alie delli uccelli, perché in essa s'appoggia l'uccello sopra la già condensata aria con tutta la potenzia dell'alia e della forza sua.[35]

Egli procede con un suggestivo, quanto filologicamente esatto, paragone dell'alula con un'unghia (nello specifico quella della gatta che sale sugli alberi). L'accurato studio della struttura ossea dell'ala, compresa la prominenza ossea dell'alula, è testimoniato dallo splendido disegno di Windsor RL 12656 v, K/P 187 r (fig. 11), datato al 1512-15 circa, dove compare pure un'accurata serie di rapporti proporzionali riferibili presumibilmente alle ali di rapaci.[36] Nei tre disegni principali, due della struttura ossea e miologica in veduta dorsale, il terzo in veduta ventrale, l'alula è indicata dalle lettere *a b*, richiamate nella Nota II: "*ab* è di grande importanz<ia>. Con ciò sia che tal membro è causa di tenere l'uccello fermo infra l'aria sopra al moto del vento".[37] Nel *Ms. E*, foglio 49 r, si trova un altro riferimento alla potenza delle alule: "Li timoni posti nelli omeri delle alie son di penne fortissime, perché sentan la massima fatica di tutte l'altre penne".[38]
Nelle carte 13 v, 11 r, 10 v del *Codice* compaiono, per descrivere manovre di volo, le definizioni "remare dell'alia", "rema indirieto", "remando l'alia indirieto", il cui valore non è solo figurato ma esprime un'analogia ricorrente (e di de-

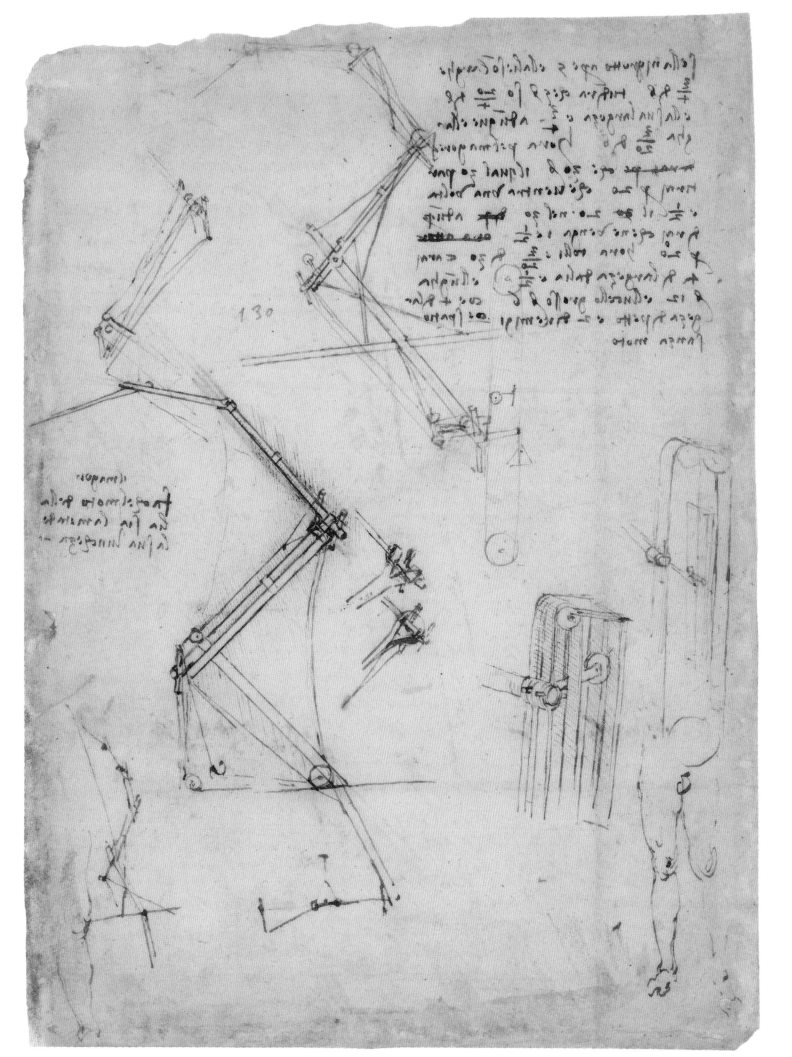

130

69

the wings of birds of prey.[36] In the three principal drawings, two of the bone and muscle structures in a dorsal view, the third from a ventral view, the winglet is indicated by the letters *a b*, mentioned in note II: "*ab* is of great importance because this part is the cause of keeping the bird steady in the air above the movement of the wind."[37] In Manuscript E, fol. 49 recto, we find another reference to the power of the winglet: "The rudders positioned in the humerus of the wings have very strong feathers, because they are subject to more stress than all the other feathers."[38] On fols. 13 verso, 11 recto, and 10 verso of the codex, Leonardo uses "rowing" to describe the motions of flight—a "rowing movement of the wings"; "the bird rows backwards with its wings"; "rowing the wing backwards"—reflecting the ancient analogy between the beating of wings and the movements of a swimmer or the rowing of a boat. Fol. 10 recto makes this comparison explicit: "The bird operates in the air with its wing and tail, as the swimmer does with his arms and legs in the water."[39] In the Codex Atlanticus, Leonardo writes: "swimming in the water teaches men how birds move through the air" (fol. 186 recto [ex 66 r-b]) and "Write of swimming under water and you will have the flight of the bird through the air"; "[First]—There is as much power of movement in the water or the air against an object as there is in this object against the air or the water. [Second]—The centre of gravity of the fish lying level in the water or of the bird lying level in the air is situated midway between the extremities which offer equal resistance" (fol. 571a recto [ex 214 r-d]).[40]

Manuscript L, fol. 62 recto, contains another nautical analogy, this time likening the bird's tail to the rudder of a ship:

> When the kite in descending turns itself right over and pierces the air head downwards, it is forced to bend the tail as far as it can in the opposite direction to that which it desires to follow; and then again bending the tail swiftly, according to the direction in which it wishes to turn, the change in the bird's course corresponds to the turn of the tail, like the rudder of a ship which when turned turns the ship, but in the opposite direction.[41]

On fol. 17 verso of the codex, in keeping with this analogy, Leonardo ponders the various movements of the tail during flight and the ratio between its size and that of the wingspan. On fol. 13 verso he calls the

rivazione antica) tra il volo e il nuoto, il battere delle ali e il movimento del nuotatore o del remare delle barche. Nella carta 10 r questo confronto è reso esplicito: "Tale offizio fa l'uccello coll'alie e coda infra l'aria, quale fa il notatore colle braccia e gambe infra l'acqua".[39] Al proposito, nel foglio 186 r (ex 66 r-b) del *Codice Atlantico*, Leonardo scrive: "Il notare sopra dell'acqua insegna alli omini come fanno li uccelli sopra dell'aria", e nel foglio 571a r (ex 214 r-d), "Scrivi del notare sotto l'acqua e arai il volare dell'uccello per l'aria". E ancora: "Prima – Tanto è a movere l'acqua o l'aria contro l'obbietto, quanto movere esso obbietto contro all'aria o l'acqua. Seconda – Il centro della gravità del pesce equigiacente nell'acqua o dell'uccello equigiacente nell'aria è posto in mezzo a stremi equalmente resistenti".[40] Un'altra analogia 'nautica' riguarda la funzione di timone assegnata alla coda, quale si trova nel foglio 62 r del *Ms. L*:

> Se 'l nibbio discende voltandosi e trivellando l'aria col capo di sotto, esso è constretto a torcere la coda quanto po in contrario moto a quello che lui vol poi seguire; e poi torcendo con velocità essa coda per quello verso che lui vole voltare; e tanto quanto fia la volta della coda, tanto fia quella dello uccello, a similitudine del timone della nave, il quale volta la nave secondo che lui si volta, ma in contrario moto.[41]

Coerentemente con questa definizione, nella carta 17 v del *Codice* Leonardo si sofferma sui vari movimenti della coda nell'azione del volo, segnalando anche il rapporto tra le sue dimensioni e l'apertura alare, mentre nella carta 13 v definisce la coda "secondo timone" (il primo sono le alule) ponendola in relazione con il centro di gravità dell'uccello e approfondendo le osservazioni sui suoi movimenti condizionati dall'incidenza del vento.

Il rapporto tra la direzione del volo e quella del vento, con i rischi di "arrovesciamento" cui è esposto il volatile e con la segnalazione dei movimenti che esso deve compiere con la testa, le ali e la coda in relazione al proprio centro di gravità, sono temi ricorrenti nel *Codice*, supportati da valutazioni di tipo teorico. Sia nel volo librato che in quello battente, l'uccello è esposto a colpi di vento che ne mettono continuamente a rischio l'equilibrio. Nella discesa, inoltre, sia essa sopra vento o sotto vento, il pericolo è sempre quello di essere "voltato sotto sopra" dalle raffiche, per cui occorre un 'appesantimento' ottenuto dallo stringere le ali contro il busto.[42] Le possibili casistiche e le manovre necessarie all'uccello per conservare l'equilibrio in aria, e mantenere il proprio moto, sono numerosissime e disseminate in vari manoscritti (*Codice Atlantico*, *Codice di Madrid II*, *Mss. E, F, K, L*, ecc.). Alcuni principi significativi

FIG. 11
LEONARDO DA VINCI
The Bones and the Muscles of a Bird's Wing / *Studio dello scheletro e dei muscoli dell'ala di un uccello*, ca. 1512–15
Pen and brown ink over black chalk on paper / Penna e inchiostro bruno, pietra nera su carta
222 x 204 mm
Windsor
(RL 12656 verso, K/P 187 recto)

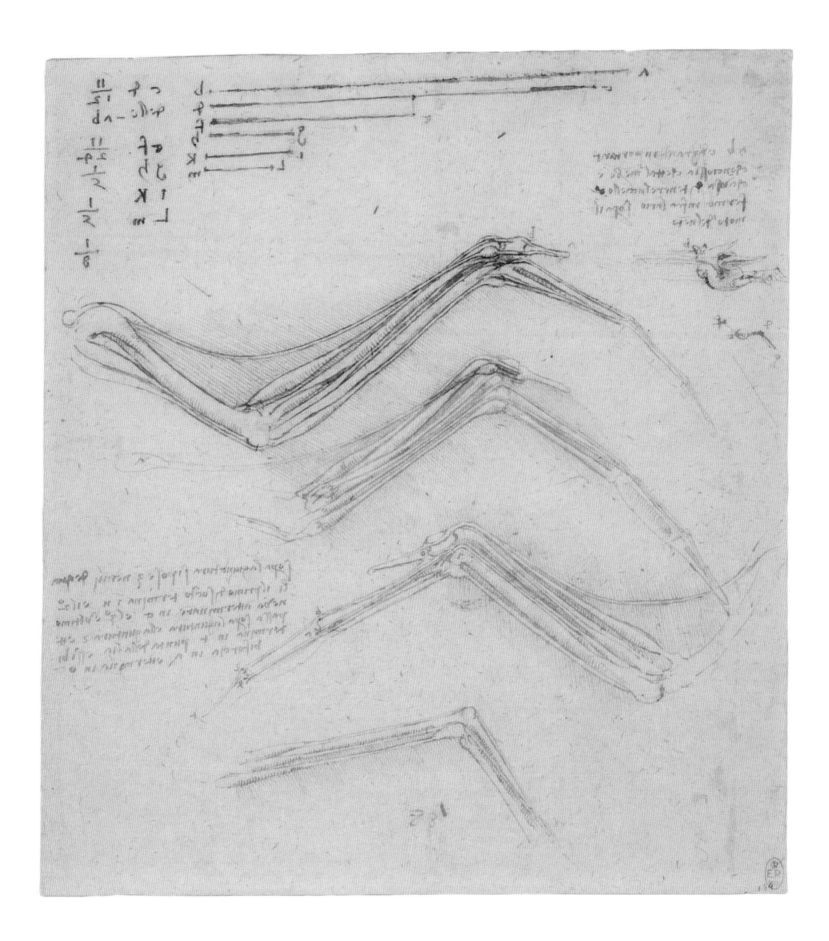

71

tail "the second rudder" (the first being the winglet), comparing it to the center of gravity of the bird and analyzing how it moves in relation to the direction of the wind.

The relationship between the direction of flight and that of the wind, with the risk of being overturned that the bird must face, is a recurrent topic in the codex, as is the relationship between the bird's center of gravity and the movements made by the head, wings and tail, all supported by theoretical assessments. When hovering or gliding and when flapping its wings, the bird is constantly subject to gusts of wind that affect its equilibrium. Likewise, when descending, whether it is above the wind or below the wind, the bird always risks being overturned by the gusts, so that it must "become heavier" by drawing its wings toward its body.[42] Scattered throughout various manuscripts (Codex Atlanticus, Codex Madrid II, Manuscripts E, F, K, L, etc.) are Leonardo's numerous comments on the possible reasons for the maneuvers that the bird must make in order to preserve its equilibrium in the air and continue advancing. Some important principles are to be found in the Turin codex, starting with fol. 17 verso, with the bird descending to the east "being above the southern wind." This type of movement is described on fol. 11 recto in four variations according to the rectilinear or curvilinear nature of the movement (incident movement or reflex movement) and obliquity. On fols. 9 verso, 9 recto, 8 verso, 8 recto, 7 verso, and 6 verso, Leonardo describes in detail the effects of gusts of wind on various flight positions, illustrating with delightful and precise explanatory sketches the initial conditions of flight and the corrections that the bird must make in order to avoid being overturned.

But when the bird is struck leeward under one of its wings, then it would be possible for the wind to overturn it, unless immediately upon being turned with its breast to the wind, it extended the opposite wing toward the earth and shortened the wing that was first struck by the wind, which remains higher and thus will return to a state of balance.[43]

If the wing and the tail are too far above the wind, lower half of the opposite wing and receive the percussion of the wind in it, and the bird will right itself.

And if the wing and the breast are above the wind, lower half of the opposite wing, which

si trovano tuttavia nel codice torinese, a partire dalla carta 17 v, con l'uccello che scende a levante stando "sopra il vento meridionale". La tipologia dei moti è descritta nella carta 11 r, in quattro varianti secondo la natura rettilinea o curvilinea del moto (incidente o riflesso) e il tipo di obliquità. Nelle carte 9 v, 9 r, 8 v, 8 r, 7 v, 6 v Leonardo si addentra in maniera particolareggiata nella descrizione dei casi di incidenza di colpi di vento su posizioni di volo diversificate, illustrando, anche con squisiti ed efficaci disegni esemplificativi, la condizione di volo di partenza e la correzione che l'uccello deve apportare per impedire di essere capovolto.

Ma quando l'uccello è percosso sotto vento sotto l'una delle sue alie, allora sarebbe possibile che 'l vento l'arroversciassi, se immediate che è volto col petto al vento, esso non astendessi inverso la terra la opposita alla e raccortassi l'alia che prima dal vento fu percossa, la qual resta superiore e così verrà a ritornare al sito della equalità.[43]

Se l'alia e la coda sarà troppo sopra vento, abbassa la metà dell'alia opposta e ricevivi dentro la percussione del vento, e si verrà a dirizzarsi.
[…]
E se l'alia e 'l petto sarà sopra a' vento, abbassisi la metà dell'alia opposta, la qual fia percossa dal vento e rigittata in alto e e' dirizzerà l'uccello.
Ma se l'alia e la schiena saran sotto vento, allor si debbe alzare l'alia opposta e mostrarla al vento, e subito l'uccel si dirizzerà.
E se l'uccello sarà dalla parte dirieto sopra vento, allora si debbe mettere la coda sotto vento, e verrassi a ragguagliare le potenzie.
Ma se l'uccello arà la sue parte dirieto sotto vento, entri colla coda sopra vento e dirizzerassi.[44]

Oltre a queste precise valutazioni, ve ne sono altre relative al volo librato come caratteristica propria di uccelli come il nibbio, "che battan poco le alie", o di quegli uccelli "che volano a scosse", che cioè "si levano in alto col lor battimento d'alie, e quando calano si vengano a riposarsi, perché nel lor calare non battano le alie".[45] Nel *Codice Madrid II*, foglio 101 v, Leonardo asserisce che il primo libro del progettato trattato sul volo avrebbe riguardato il volare "sanza moto d'alie".[46] La condizione principale di ogni tipo di volo è comunque il rapporto tra il centro di gravità dell'uccello e le manovre da effettuare per "bilicarsi", cioè per attuare il costante ritorno "al sito della equalità" (equilibrio),[47] che segue la legge fisica per cui "sempre la parte più grave de' corpi è quella che si fa guida del lor moto".[48] Peraltro, le riflessioni sul centro di gravità e sul mantenimento dell'equilibrio nell'avanzamento in condizioni di vento sono estese anche alla figura umana,

will be struck by the wind and tossed upward and will straighten the bird.

But if the wing and the back are below the wind, then the opposite wing must be raised and exposed to the wind, and the bird will quickly right itself.

And if the bird is so that hindquarters are above the wind, then the tail must be placed below the wind, and thus there will be an equalization of forces.

But if the bird has its hindquarters below the wind, it must enter with the tail above the wind and it will right itself.[44]

There are also descriptions of gliding flight as a characteristic of birds, such as the kite, "that move their wings little" or those that "fly in stops and starts," that is, birds that "raise themselves up by beating their wings, and when they descend they rest, because in descending they do not beat their wings."[45] In the Codex Madrid II, fol. 101 verso, Leonardo states that the first book of his planned treatise on flight would concern flying "without flapping the wings."[46] The main condition of all flight is, however, the relationship between the bird's center of gravity and the maneuvers necessary to maintain balance, that is, to always return to a position of equilibrium ("a state of balance").[47] The bird must obey the physical laws by which "the heaviest part of bodies is always that which becomes the guide of their movement."[48] In section 430 of the *Treatise on Painting*, "On a figure moving against the wind," which includes a drawing, Leonardo extends to the human figure his considerations on the center of gravity and the maintenance of equilibrium when moving against the wind: "A figure moving against the wind in any direction does not keep its center of gravity duly disposed upon the center of its support."[49] Section 435 of the *Treatise*, "On bodies that move by themselves, either quickly or slowly,"[50] describes the flight of birds. The Codex on the Flight of Birds includes many specific topics that must be neglected here so that we may concentrate our attention on Leonardo's constant pondering on the center of gravity, analyzed both in order to build the flying machine and to understand how a real bird moves. The first notes on fol. 15 verso, accompanied by explanatory drawings, deal with the relationship between the center of gravity and the center of resistance in a descending and ascending bird, and are also the first instance in the codex where Leonardo relates his theories on balance to bird flight. On fol. 14 recto, the morphological and

come risulta dal cap. 430 del *Libro di Pittura*, intitolato "Della figura che va contro vento", accompagnata da uno schizzo: "Sempre la figura che si move infra 'l vento per qualunque linea non osserverà il centro della sua gravità con debita disposizione sopra il centro del suo sostentaculo".[49] Nel *Libro di Pittura* si trova un altro capitolo (435) intitolato "De' corpi che per sé si movono o veloci o tardi", che ha per oggetto proprio il moto degli uccelli.[50]

Il *Codice sul volo degli uccelli* contiene, nelle maglie fini del discorso, molti altri argomenti specifici, che si debbono qui trascurare per concentrare l'attenzione sulla costante riflessione sul centro di gravità, studiato sia per la realizzazione della macchina volante, sia per comprendere le possibilità di movimento dell'uccello naturale. Si rinvia quindi alla lettura delle prime note della carta 15 v, con disegni esplicativi, per il rapporto tra centro di gravità e centro della resistenza in un uccello in moto discendente e ascendente, nonché per un primo raffronto con le bilance. Nella carta 14 r affiora invece la valutazione morfologica e funzionale: "sempre l'equal resistenzia dell'alie nel loro uccello è nata per essere equalmente remote co' loro extremi dal centro della gravità di tale uccello. Ma quando l'un delli stremi dell'alie si farà più vicino al centro della gravità dell'uccello che l'altro stremo, allora l'uccello discenderà da quella parte, dove lo stremo dell'alie è più vicino al centro della gravità".[51] Questo concetto è ripreso nella carta 9 v, dove Leonardo precisa come la natura abbia provveduto a dare il peso del corpo dell'uccello più basso del sito della "astensione dell'alie".[52] Sebbene le carte 1 r – 4 v siano dedicate ad argomenti più direttamente e squisitamente meccanici, possono essere naturalmente ricondotte al tema principale del *Codice* per gli approfonditi studi di Leonardo sul centro di gravità, sul mantenimento dell'equilibrio in volo, sulla potenza dell'uccello e sulla potenza del vento.

Altre cose

Tra le "altre cose", si può quindi assegnare il primo posto agli studi meccanici che occupano le pagine iniziali (secondo la numerazione) del *Codice*, dedicate alla forza di gravità e alla "ventilazione" (oscillazione) delle bilance. Secondo Paolo Galluzzi, nel "foglio 1 r del *Codice sul volo*, l'analisi delle interpolazioni tra i centri della gravità «matematico» e «accidentale» viene approfondita con il ricorso al consueto metodo della trasformazione di concetti astratti in illuminanti schematizzazioni geometriche".[53] Si tratta, anche in questo caso, di un metodo di visualizzazione di aspetti teorici che Leonardo sottopone alla verifica dell'esperienza, distinguendo la parte puramente speculativa e matematica della scienza *de ponderibus* dalla sua applicazione pratica, con l'interazione dei pesi degli oggetti che si trovano ad agire

functional appraisal resurfaces: "The equal resistance of the bird's wings always springs from [the fact that the wings] are equally distant at their extremities from the center of gravity of the bird. But when one of the ends of the wings is nearer to the center of gravity of the bird than the other end, then the bird will descend from that side, when the end of the wing is closer to the center of gravity."[51] This concept is also dealt with on fol. 9 verso, where Leonardo explains how nature has provided for the weight of the bird's body to be lower than the site of the "extension of the wings."[52]

Although fol. 1 recto to fol. 4 verso are dedicated to abstract mechanics, they relate directly to the notebook's in-depth studies on the center of gravity and maintaining equilibrium in flight, which requires continual adjustments in trim according to the force and direction of the wind and the speed of the bird.

Other Things

Primary among the "other things" included in the codex are the studies of abstract mechanics that occupy the initial folios (according to the numbering). These are dedicated to the force of gravity and the oscillation (*ventilazione*) of balances. According to Paolo Galluzzi, on "fol. 1 recto of the Codex on the Flight of Birds, the analysis of the interpolation between the 'mathematical' and the 'accidental' centers of gravity is studied in depth, using the usual method of transforming abstract concepts into instructive geometric schemas."[53] It is also, in this case, a method of visualisation of the theoretical aspects that Leonardo subjects to the test of experience, distinguishing the purely speculative and mathematical aspect of the *scientia de ponderibus* (the study of the behavior of weights) from practical application, exploring the interaction of the weight of the objects that act according to the laws formulated abstractly.

On fol. 108 recto of the Codex Madrid I, Leonardo writes, "The balances have real as well as potential arms. Real arms consist of some matter, such as wood, iron, and the like. Potential arms are those which take provision where matter is lacking, that is, where the line of the power of the weight is nearest to the center of the balance."[54] For this reason, in the left-hand column of fol. 1 recto of the Codex on the Flight of Birds, Leonardo reports:

> The smaller the fulcrum of a balance, the less the momentum of its oscillation.

secondo le leggi formulate in via astratta. Nel foglio 108 r del *Codice Madrid I* Leonardo scrive: "Hanno le bilance bracci reali e bracci potentiali. Bracci reali son quelli che son d'alcuna materia, come legnio, ferro e ssimili. E potentiali son quelli che ssoperiscano dove manca la materia, cioè dove la linia della potentia del peso più s'avicina al cientro di tal bilancia".[54] Per questo, nella colonna sinistra della carta 1 r del *Codice sul volo*, Leonardo segnala che

> Quanto il polo della bilancia sarà di minor grossezza, tanto la sua ventilazione fia di minor momento. Quanto la bilancia è più lunga, tanto è di minor momento, perché il polo a tanta lunghezza viene a essere più sottile che alla bilancia corta, essendo all'una e all'altra bilancia il polo d'una medesima grossezza.
> Sempre la cosa lieve sta sopra alla grave, essendo in libertà l'una e l'altra.[55]

E ancora, "Come se 'l centro matematico fussi suffiziente a esser polo de la bilancia, la ventilazione non accaderebbe mai in tal bilancia".[56] In queste poche dense pagine Leonardo si pone molti interrogativi, esponendo anche le formulazioni dell'"avversario", cioè quelle che intende confutare. Come evidenzia Galluzzi, Leonardo intende avanzare un'"ambiziosa riforma della *scientia de ponderibus*", destinata al progettato trattato degli *Elementi macchinali*.[57] Il codice torinese offre esempi significativi di questa intenzione di revisione. Si tratta di una materia che alcuni autori hanno voluto vedere come estranea al tema principale del *Codice*, riferendola anche a momenti diversi,[58] ma che è invece coerente con la necessità di trasferire le formulazioni teoriche, con cui egli si confronta, alle valutazioni derivanti dal complesso sistema di equilibri osservati nell'azione del volo, fino alle applicazioni pratiche che richiede la progettazione della macchina per volare.

Negli ampi orizzonti di riflessione di Leonardo, emerge pure, nell'ordinata carta 1 r, il problema della densità del ghiaccio e del suo galleggiamento: "Quel corpo che più si condensa, più si fa grave: come l'aria nelle palle a vento. Ma se così è, perché sta il diaccio a noto sull'acqua, ch'è più denso che essa acqua? Perché lui cresce nel risolversi".[59]

Ai tre nuclei di argomenti fin qui affrontati, il volo meccanico, il volo animale e gli studi meccanici, sono inframmezzati disegni o annotazioni di diverso contenuto.
Nella carta 3 r compare, in basso, uno studio di carro, con il disegno dettagliato della ruota raggiata e di altri congegni e particolari meccanici che ne consentono il funzionamento. La carta 18 v è attraversata dall'imponente disegno di un fiume, con sbarramenti che generano un impetuoso

The longer the balance, the less the momentum, because the fulcrum at such a length comes to be thinner than that of the short scale, the fulcrum of one and of the other balance being of equal thickness.

Always the lighter object is above the heavier one, both of them being free.[55]

He goes on to say, "If the mathematical center were sufficient to be the fulcrum of the balance, oscillation would never occur in such a balance."[56] In these few dense pages, Leonardo poses many questions, also setting out the formulations of "the adversary," that is, any attempt to confute his ideas. As Galluzzi points out, Leonardo proposes to advance an "ambitious reform of the *scientia de ponderibus*," intended for the planned treatise *Elementi macchinali*.[57] The Turin codex offers important examples of Leonardo's intention to do so. It is a topic that some authors have taken to be extraneous to the main theme of the codex, and it has sometimes been dated to different periods.[58] But in fact, it is consistent with the need to transfer his theoretical formulations to his evaluations of the complex system of equilibrium observed in the act of flying and to the practical applications that the design of a flying machine require.

Among Leonardo's wide-ranging ponderings, there appears, on the neat fol. 1 recto, the problem of the density of ice and its capacity to float: "That body which condenses most, becomes heavier: like the air in balloons. But if this is so, why does ice float on water, when it is denser than water? Because it increases in the process of becoming itself."[59]

The three topics dealt with so far—mechanical flight, animal flight, and abstract mechanics—are interspersed with drawings and comments on other topics. For example, on fol. 3 verso there is, at the bottom, a study of a cart, with a detailed drawing of the spoked wheel and of other devices and mechanical details that allow it to work. Fol. 18 verso is dominated by a drawing of a river, its dams and weirs causing an impetuous flow of water; this folio has been linked to the studies for the canalization of the Arno.[60] The sketch on the left is of a similar subject, while at the bottom there are technological studies for gearing mechanisms, later crossed out. On this page there are also two notes on daily life, with dates that are particularly important (like that on fol. 17 verso) in establishing a precise date for the Codex on the Flight of Birds (see Appendix, 1. Dating). The sketch of the river

scorrere dell'acqua, che è stato messo in relazione con gli studi per la canalizzazione dell'Arno.[60] Di analogo soggetto è lo schizzo a sinistra, mentre in basso vi sono studi tecnologici di rocche coniche, poi biffati. In questa pagina sono anche due note di vita quotidiana con alcune date, importantissime, come quella della carta 17 v, per collocare con più precisione cronologica il *Codice sul volo degli uccelli* (si veda l'*Appendice*, 1. Datazione). Nel recto della seconda coperta continua il disegno del decorso fluviale, a fianco di dettagliati disegni architettonici per i quali Carlo Pedretti ha proposto un riferimento al 1506, in rapporto con i progetti per la villa di Charles d'Amboise a Milano.[61] Oltre alla profezia sul 'grande uccello', che è vergata nella parte bassa, nell'angolo alto destro del cartoncino vi sono annotazioni di spese domestiche e calcoli in scrittura normale (da sinistra a destra), che rendono questo codice testimone di aspetti umili di vita quotidiana e insieme di grandi ambizioni.

La carta 11 r raccoglie invece una tra le riflessioni più profonde di Leonardo. Vi si trova infatti riassunta la sua concezione della verità come ricerca in tutto quanto può essere oggetto dell'esperienza, in contrasto con gli altisonanti e vaghi discorsi che riguardano quanto è, per definizione, inconoscibile. Questi argomenti occupano la porzione alta della pagina, suddivisi in tre note di cui la più estesa costituisce il nucleo del discorso, completato dalle due in margine.

> Sanza dubbio tal proporzione è dalla verità alla bugia, qual è da la luce alle tenebre. Ed è essa verità in sé di tanta eccellenzia, che ancora ch'ella s'astenda sopra umili e basse materie, sanza comparazione ella <e>ccede le incertezze e bugie estese sopra li magni e altissimi discorsi. Perché la mente nostra, ancora ch'ell'abbia la bugia pel quinto elemento, no<n> resta però che la verità delle cose non sia di sommo notrimento delli intelletti fini, ma non di vagabundi ingegni.
>
> [in alto] Ed è di tanto vilipendio la bugia che s'ella dicessi be<n> gran cose di Dio, ella to' di grazia a sua deità; ed è di tanta eccellenzia la verità che s'ella laldassi cose minime, elle si fanno nobili.
>
> [al margine destro] Ma tu che vivi di sogni, ti piace più le ragion soffistiche e barerie de' pa<r>lari nelle cose grandi e incerte, che delle certe, naturali e non di tanta altura.[62]

Nel foglio 327 v (ex 119 v-a) del *Codice Atlantico*, nel contesto dell'elogio dell'occhio e del senso della vista, il sapere degli antichi è sottoposto ad una critica analoga:

> Or guarda, lettore, quello che noi potremo credere ai nostri antichi, i quali hanno voluto difinire

75

continues on the inside back cover, alongside detailed architectural drawings—for which Pedretti proposed a date of 1506—that relate to the designs for the villa of Charles d'Amboise in Milan.[61] Apart from the "prophecy" about the "big bird," written in the lower part of the page, in the top right-hand corner there are some notes on domestic expenses and calculations in standard script (from left to right), all of which make this codex at once a witness both to the humble aspects of daily life and to great ambitions.

On fol. 11 recto, in contrast, we find one of Leonardo's most profound considerations. He summarizes his concept of truth as research into all matters pertaining to experience, unlike the usual pompous and vague sort of discourse on what is, by definition, unknowable. These comments occupy the upper portion of the page, divided into three notes, of which the longest is the nucleus of the discourse, completed by the two notes in the margin:

> Without doubt there is a similar proportion between truth and falsehood, as there is between light and darkness. And this truth is in itself of such excellence, that even if it is applied to humble and lowly matters, without comparison it exceeds the uncertainties and falsehoods applied to great and lofty subjects. Because our mind, even though it has falsehood as its quintessence, nevertheless it remains that the truth of things is the supreme nourishment of refined intellects, but not for idle minds.
>
> And falsehood is so contemptible, that if it said even great things of God, it would take grace away from the deity; and truth is of such excellence that if it praised trifles, they would become noble.
>
> But you who live on dreams, the sophistical reasoning and deceits of words in great and uncertain things please you more than certain things, natural and not so lofty.[62]

On fol. 327 verso (ex 119 v-a) of the Codex Atlanticus, in the context of praise of the eye and the sense of sight, the knowledge of the ancients is subjected to a similar criticism:

> Consider now, O Reader, what trust can we place in the ancients who have set out to define the nature of the soul and of life,—things

che cosa s\<ia\> \<a\>nima e vita, cose improvabili, q\<uando\> quelle che con isperienza ognora si possano chiaramente conoscere e provare, sono per tanti seculi ignorate e falsamente credute. L'occhio, che così chiaramente fa sperienza del suo ofizio, è insino ai mia tempi per infiniti altori stato difinito in un modo; trovo per isperienzia essere 'n un altro.[63]

Già nella prima nota dello stesso foglio, Leonardo rivela la sua contrapposizione al dogmatismo del sapere ufficiale fondato sugli *auctores*, dimostrandosi a favore dell'esperienza, che "è maestra vera" e solo fondamento nella distinzione del vero dal falso.

> Molti mi crederanno ragionevolmente potere riprendere, allegando le mie prove esser contro all'alturità d'alquanti omini di gran reverenza appresso de' loro inesperti iudizi, non considerando le mie cose essere nate sotto la semplice e mera sperienzia, la quale è maestra vera.
>
> Queste mie regole son cagione di farti conoscere il vero dal falso; la qual cosa fa che li omini si promettano le cose possibili e con più moderanza, e che tu non ti veli di ignoranza, che farebbe che, non avendo effetto, tu t'abbi con disperazione a darti malinconia.[64]

Le note sulla verità della carta 11 r del codice torinese sono state oggetto di un intervento di André Chastel, che ne ha ricondotto lo spirito alla filosofia di stampo positivista del XIX secolo e a quella, del secolo successivo, di Ludwig Wittgenstein.[65] Si tratta di salti cronologici forse eccessivi, con una ricerca di analogie che non aiuta a comprendere il pensiero di un autore, dato che le osservazioni di Leonardo sul ruolo dell'esperienza possono essere riconducibili a vari momenti della filosofia occidentale. Con ciò, siamo comunque di fronte ad un atteggiamento generale nei confronti della conoscenza orientato verso quella che Immanuel Kant ha definito, con un'espressione giustamente famosa, la "fertile bassura (*Bathos*) dell'esperienza", contrapposta alle "alte torri" della metafisica.[66]

Tra le annotazioni di soggetto diverso dal 'volo', resta da citare quella in margine alla carta 13 r:

> Porterassi neve di state ne' lochi caldi, tolta dell'alte cime de' monti, e si lascerà cadere nelle feste delle piazze nel tempo della state.[67]

Secondo vari interpreti, compreso Paul Valéry,[68] il breve testo riguarderebbe la possibilità, attraverso la macchina volante, di portare la neve dai monti nei caldi luoghi delle città in estate. Carlo Pedretti ha evidenziato la natura di in-

incapable of proof,—whilst those things which by experience may always be clearly known and proved have for so many centuries either remained unknown or have been wrongly interpreted.

The eye which thus clearly offers proof of its functions has even down to our own times been defined by countless writers in one way, but I find by experience that it acts in another.[63]

In the first note on the same folio, Leonardo expresses his opposition to the official dogma founded on the *auctores* (Authors). He shows himself to be in favor of experience, "the true master," the only basis for the distinction between what is true and what is false.

Many will believe that they have the right to criticize me, because my proofs contradict the arrogance of a number of great men with their inexpert opinions, not taking into account the fact that my statements are born of simple and plain experience, which is the true teacher.

These rules of mine are meant to show you the difference between true and false: which means that men will promise themselves things that are possible and with more moderation, and that you shall not be veiled in ignorance, which would, giving no results, mean that you would become desperate and fall into melancholy.[64]

Leonardo's notes on truth on fol. 11 recto of the Turin codex have been studied by André Chastel, who compared their essence to the positivist philosophy of the nineteenth century and to that of Ludwig Wittgenstein in the following century.[65] These are perhaps excessive chronological leaps, with a search for analogies that do not help us to understand the author's thinking; rather, Leonardo's observations on the role of experience can be traced through various moments in Western philosophy. In any case, his general attitude toward knowledge tends toward what Immanuel Kant called, in a rightly famous expression, the "fruitful bathos, the bottom-land, of experience," as opposed to the "high towers" of metaphysics.[66]

Comments in the codex on subjects other than flight include this one, found in the margin of fol. 13 recto: "Snow will be brought to warm places in summer, taken from the high peaks of the mountains, and will be let to fall in festivals in the squares in the summertime."[67] According to various interpreters, in-

dovinello del testo, che vuole sottintendere le fontane, che festosamente lasciano cadere l'acqua (proveniente dalle cime innevate dei monti) nelle piazze.[69]

Il verso della prima coperta contiene, infine, ricette per la lavorazione delle medaglie ("Dello improntare medaglie"), per la macinazione degli smalti e su varie tecniche di trattamento di materiali quali diamante, smeriglio, ottone. Si tratta di una nota avvicinabile a quella intitolata "A gittare medaglie" che compare nel foglio 141 r del *Codice Madrid II*. D'altra mano e in spagnolo, la coperta del libretto torinese è annotata in alto con la dicitura "Secretos de polvos materiales".[70]

Al verso di sette carte del *Codice sul volo* compaiono, infine, i disegni a sanguigna tracciati prima della stesura del testo, e raffiguranti soggetti diversi. Le carte che accolgono tali schizzi, più o meno finiti, sono 10 v, 11 v, 12 v, 13 v, 15 v, 16 v, 17 v. Tra queste, le centrali, da 11 v a 16 v, sono di soggetto naturalistico, caratterizzate da un segno analitico che ne ha consentita una ipotetica individuazione botanica. Nelle carte 11 v e 15 v (cat. 9, tavv. XXIV e XXXII) troviamo due esempi di foglia polimorfa di gelsomoro (*Morus*), nel primo caso solo abbozzata e nel secondo chiaroscurata e ripresa ad inchiostro lungo tutto il margine dentellato. Alcuni particolari della prima foglia, in alcuni punti di conduzione un po' rigida, hanno suscitato qualche perplessità sull'autografia di Leonardo. La campitura chiaroscurale della seconda foglia è inoltre condotta da destra a sinistra, fatto che tuttavia, secondo Pedretti, non costituisce motivo per credere che il disegno sia d'altra mano.[71] Le carte 12 v e 13 v (cat. 9, tavv. XXVI e XXVIII) contengono lo schizzo di una viola mammola, un po' più definita nella prima carta, più essenziale nella seconda, sempre comunque allo stato di abbozzo sapiente ed elegante. Più compiuta nel disegno e chiaroscurata è la fresca illustrazione (ora capovolta) di un piccolo rametto con germogli che compare nella c. 16 v (cat. 9, tav. XXXIV), identificato come un ramoscello d'acero allo spuntare primaverile delle foglie.[72]

Un discorso a parte meritano i disegni che occupano l'uno la carta 17 v (cat. 9, tav. XXXVI) e l'altro la 10 v (cat. 9, tav. XXII). Il primo, capovolto nell'attuale legatura del *Codice*, raffigura un arto inferiore sinistro condotto a sanguigna e ripreso ad inchiostro bruno nel profilo e nell'individuazione volumetrica dei muscoli (fig. 12). Si tratta di un inchiostro della stessa tonalità e intensità della scrittura, che a differenza degli altri casi, si mantiene esterna al disegno, sovrapponendovisi solo nelle parti più leggere del piede e della gamba. Lo studio degli arti inferiori e della loro potenza muscolare è ricorrente in Leonardo, che ne ripete frequentemente la postura e le parti anatomiche principali.[73]

FIG. 12

cat. 9, fol. 17 verso
(detail of the
straightening of the
leg / dettaglio
raddrizzato della
gamba)

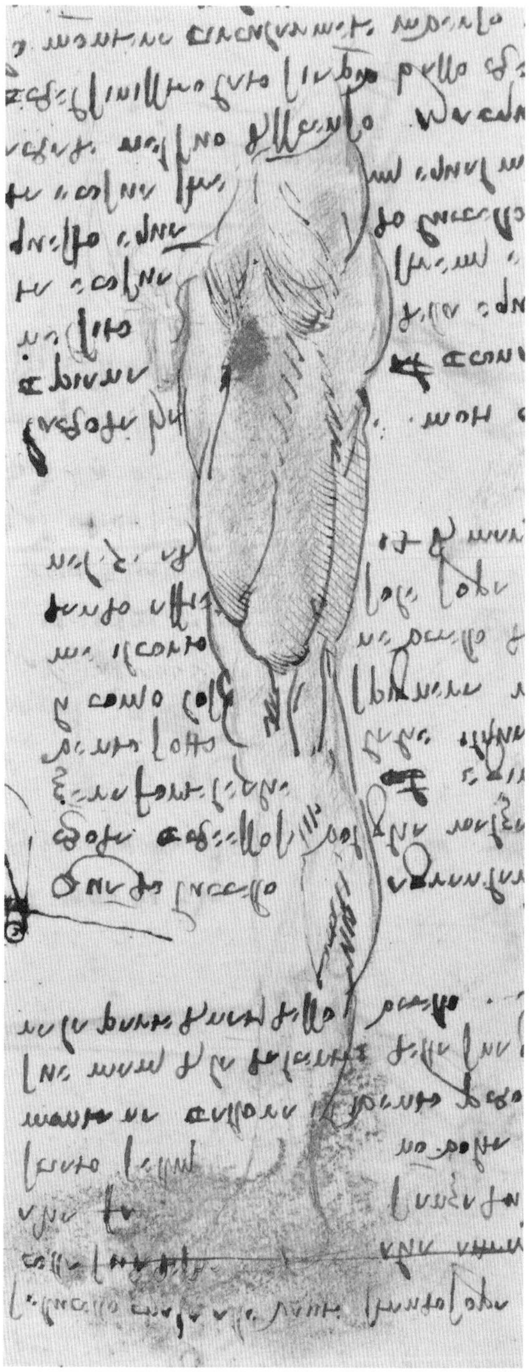

cluding Paul Valéry,[68] this brief text may concern the possibility that during the summer a flying machine could carry snow from the mountains to the towns. Pedretti has pointed out that the text is a riddle that refers to the fountains, with their gay cascades of water (which comes from the snowy mountain peaks) in the city squares.[69]

In addition, on the inside front cover there are instructions for forging medals (*Dello improntar medaglie*) and grinding enamels pigments and comments on various techniques for treating materials such as diamond, emery, and brass, along with a note similar to *gittare medaglie* on fol. 141 recto of the Codex Madrid II. Also, at the top of the inside front cover of the Turin codex there is a note, in Spanish and in another hand, that reads *Secretos de polvos materiales*.[70]

Finally, seven folios of the Codex on the Flight of Birds feature more or less complete red chalk drawings that were made prior to the writing of the text: fols. 10 verso, 11 verso, 12 verso, 13 verso, 15 verso, 16 verso, and 17 verso. The central ones from fol. 11 verso to fol. 16 verso are of subjects from nature and possess an analytical precision that has permitted their botanical identification. Fol. 11 verso and fol. 15 verso (cat. 9, pls. XXIV and XXXII) each contain a drawing of one of the polymorphous leaves of the mulberry (Morus), in the first case only sketched and in the second shaded and outlined in ink along the serrated edge of the leaf. The line in some parts of the first leaf is rather stiff, which has raised questions about its attribution to Leonardo. Also, the shading of the second leaf is from right to left; however, according to Pedretti, that is not a reason to believe that the drawing is by another hand.[71] Fol. 12 verso and fol. 13 verso (cat. 9, pls. XXVI and XXVIII) each carry a drawing of a violet. The flower is better defined on the first folio and sketchier on the second, but even that drawing is skilled and elegant. More complete in drawing and shading is the clearly executed illustration on fol. 16 verso (cat. 9, pl. XXXIV)—now upside down—which has been identified as a small twig of maple with spring buds.[72]

The drawings on fol. 17 verso (cat. 9, pl. XXXVI) and fol. 10 verso (cat. 9, pl. XXII) deserve particular attention. The former, upside down in the present collation of the codex, shows a volumetrically defined left leg in red chalk and brown ink (fig. 12). The ink is of the same color and intensity as in the writing and, unlike in other cases, remains outside the drawing, overlaying it only in the lighter parts of the foot and the leg.

In particolare questo disegno riprende con grande fedeltà, a parte la tecnica grafica, il disegno a destra nel foglio di Windsor RL 12637 r, K/P 9 r (fig. 13) realizzato a punta metallica (con rialzi di biacca) su carta preparata azzurra nel 1490-91 circa, nel contesto di uno studio miologico di un corpo virile in posizione eretta lateralizzata. Analogamente, è delineata la parte bassa del tronco, con la parte finale della muscolatura che lo chiude anteriormente e lateralmente. In entrambi i disegni sono abbozzati anche i genitali e sono messe in evidenza la muscolatura glutea,

The study of the lower limbs and their muscular power recurs in Leonardo's work; he frequently returns to this pose and its principal anatomical articultaions.[73] Apart from the difference in technique, this particular drawing faithfully reproduces a drawing at Windsor (RL 12637 recto, K/P 9 recto; fig. 13), which was drawn in metalpoint with white highlights on blue prepared paper, ca. 1490–91. The context is a myological study of the male body standing in the *contrapposto* position (a term used in the visual arts to describe a human figure standing with most of its weight on one foot, for example, Michelangelo's *David*). Similarly, in the lower part of the trunk, the terminal of the muscles is drawn from the front and from the side. In both drawings, the genitals are outlined and the gluteal muscles are emphasized with perfectly studied morphology, as are those of the thigh, while from the knee downward the muscular structure is merely suggested and disappears in the front part of the leg and toward the foot, which concludes with a mere profile. Given the close affinity with a sheet that is much earlier than the writing of the codex, the period of time in which this drawing was made extends from the period in which Leonardo began to use red chalk (the first half of the 1490s), as *terminus post quem*, and the writing of the codex, as *terminus ante quem*, without excluding the possibility that the red chalk sketch and the "finishing" in ink could be from two different periods.

Fol. 10 verso shows a male head, with a beard and a hat, turned three-quarters to the right (to the viewer) and completely overwritten. In 1975, Pedretti[74] isolated it from the writing using photo-mechanical procedures, "removing" the writing, and pointed out similarities to Turin's renowned *Self-Portrait* by Leonardo (15571 D.C.; fig. 1). Luigi Firpo, however, saw a resemblance to Turin's red chalk portrait (cat. 2) and rejected the idea that it could be a sketch for a self-portrait.[75] Nevertheless, recent examinations, using digital techniques that have made it possible to examine the face free of the lines of writing, have revealed that head and mouth of the red chalk sketch on fol. 10 verso are in fact similar to those in the *Self-Portrait*.[76] The head on fol. 10 verso also shares common traits with

secondo una morfologia perfettamente corrispondente, e quella della coscia, mentre dal ginocchio in giù la miologia è richiamata in modo sommario, per scomparire nella parte anteriore della gamba e verso il piede, che si conclude con il solo profilo. Per la stretta affinità con un foglio che è di molto precedente alla stesura del *Codice*, l'arco temporale a cui riferire la realizzazione di questo disegno si dilata tra il periodo in cui Leonardo ha iniziato ad usare la sanguigna (prima metà degli anni Novanta del Quattrocento), come *terminus post quem*, e la scrittura del *Codice*,

FIG. 13

LEONARDO DA VINCI
Studies of a Male Nude / Studi di figura maschile, ca. 1490
Metalpoint heightened with white on blue prepared paper / Punta metallica e lumeggiature di biacca su carta preparata azzurra
177 x 140 mm
Windsor (RL 12637 recto, K/P 9 recto)

a drawing at Windsor (RL 12726 recto), which I have recently indicated might be a "replacement copy" by Francesco Melzi (ca. 1518) of a possible self-portrait of Leonardo in profile (dating from the early 1500s and now lost).[77]

All in all, the Turin codex is a dense collection of topics on which Leonardo tended to concentrate his attention. His extended studies of flight are a significant part, but not the sole subject matter, of the notebook; it even includes a reference to the enigma of his face, which Paolo Giovio described as "extraordinarily handsome."[78]

come *terminus ante quem*, senza escludere che lo schizzo a sanguigna e la 'rifinitura' ad inchiostro possano appartenere a due momenti diversi.

La carta 10 v accoglie una testa maschile volta di tre quarti a destra (per chi osserva) completamente sovrascritta e raffigurante un uomo con barba e copricapo. Carlo Pedretti nel 1975[74] la enucleava liberandola dalla scrittura con procedimenti fotomeccanici, e la descriveva ponendola in relazione con il celebre *Autoritratto* conservato sempre a Torino (15571 D.C.; fig. 1). Luigi Firpo ne ha rilevato invece l'analogia con il triplice ritratto del foglio torinese a sanguigna 15573 D.C. (cat. 2), escludendo che possa trattarsi di un abbozzo di autoritratto.[75] Tuttavia, recenti elaborazioni con tecnologie digitali hanno consentito di mettere a fuoco il volto libero dalle righe di scrittura ed evidenziare similitudini di fisionomia con l'*Autoritratto*,[76] riscontrabili nella struttura del volto stesso, nella forma del naso, nella piega della bocca. Sono tratti comuni anche al disegno di Windsor RL 12726 r, che ho recentemente indicato come possibile *replacement copy* (c. 1518) di Francesco Melzi da un eventuale autoritratto di Leonardo in profilo (databile ai primi anni del Cinquecento), oggi perduto.[77]

Il breve libretto torinese si configura quindi, oltre che come una significativa parte dei suoi estesi studi sul volo, come una densa raccolta di temi sui quali Leonardo è solito concentrare le proprie attenzioni, e contiene pure un richiamo all'enigma del suo volto, che Paolo Giovio ci ha descritto come "straordinariamente bello".[78]

---

[1] Dondi 1991, p. XIII: "The title *Ucelli et altre cose*, now visible only using an ultraviolet lamp, is written on the second external page of the same cover, in the opposite sense to the direction of the text."

[2] Firpo 1991, p. XXI.

[3] Codex on the Flight of Birds, fol. 16 recto, Marinoni 1982, pp. 73–74.

[4] Codex Atlanticus, fol. 124 recto (ex 45 r-a), Marinoni 1973–80, vol. II, p. 33 (English translation MacCurdy 1955, p. 421). The annotation is in the top left-hand corner of the folio, once this has been turned upside down, as the final part of a paragraph written in a compact column and separate from the page; it is also written in different ink from the rest of the study dedicated to "recreational geometrical elements." Villata, in Milan 2012, considers the note on flight parallel with the anatomical studies of the Roman period because it is present on a folio dedicated to Leonardo's later ponderings. Nevertheless, the general content of the observation, which is transcribed here, dates it to a period very close, and presumably prior to the Turin codex, as Giacomelli 1936, p. 164 points out. At the beginning, Leonardo's text says: "Unless the bird beats its wings downwards with more rapidity than there would be in its natural descent with its wings extended in the same position, its movement will be downwards. But if the movement of the wings is swifter than the aforesaid natural descent then this movement will be upwards, with so much greater velocity in proportion as the downward stroke of the wings is more rapid. The bird descends on that side on which the extremity of the wing is nearer to the centre of its gravity. You will make an anatomy of the wings of a bird [etc.]" (English translation MacCurdy 1955, p. 421).

[5] Firpo 1991, p. XXI.

[6] The mountain that Leonardo refers to is Monte Ceceri, near Florence, in the municipality of Fiesole. At the time, Florentines called swans *ceceri*. The quotation is from Marinoni 1982, p. 80.

[7] *Ibid.*, p. 81.

[8] For Leonardo's writings on flight, scattered through various manuscripts, see Giacomelli 1936.

[9] Codex Atlanticus, fol. 434 recto (ex 161 r-a), Marinoni 1973–80, vol. V, p. 341 (English translation MacCurdy 1955, p. 493, it is evident to the author that is a mistranslation in the first paragraph). See also Villata in Milan 2012, p. 35, for the importance of this passage from an "ideological" point of view, which leads him to wonder "whether it would be excessive to read this mechanism in a precartesian sense?"

[10] Cf. Pedretti 2007, pp. 31–36.

[11] Keele and Pedretti 1979–80, vol. I, p. 88.

[12] On fol. 207 recto (ex 76 r-a) we read: "Whoever would see in what state the soul dwells within the body, let him mark how this body uses its daily habitation, for if this be confused and without order the body will be kept in disorder and confusion by the soul," ca. 1490, Marinoni 1973–80, vol. III, p. 142 (English

[1] Dondi 1991, p. XIII: "il titolo *Ucelli et altre cose*, ora visibile solo con la lampada a raggi ultravioletti, scritto sulla seconda facciata esterna della stessa copertina in senso opposto alla stesura del testo".

[2] Firpo 1991, p. XXI.

[3] *Codice sul volo…*, c. 16 r, Marinoni 1976, pp. 67-68.

[4] *Codice Atlantico*, f. 124 r (ex 45 r-a), Marinoni, 1973-80, vol. II, p. 33. L'annotazione si trova all'angolo superiore sinistro del foglio, una volta che questo sia stato capovolto, come parte finale di un brano composto in una colonna compatta e a se stante nella pagina, nonché vergato con un inchiostro diverso dal resto degli studi dedicati a "Elementi ludici geometrici". Villata, in Milan 2012, pone la nota sul volo in parallelo con gli studi anatomici del periodo romano per la sua presenza in un foglio dedicato a tarde speculazioni di Leonardo. Tuttavia il contenuto generale dell'osservazione, che qui si trascrive integralmente, la riporta ad un periodo molto prossimo, e presumibilmente anteriore (*c.* 1503-5), come già messo in evidenza da Giacomelli 1936, p. 164. Il testo di Leonardo recita dall'inizio: "Se l'uccel non batte in basso le sue alie con più velocità che non sarebbe il suo discenso naturale colla medesima astensione e situazione di tale alie, allora il suo moto sarà allo in giù. Ma se tal moto d'alie sarà più veloce che 'l predetto natural discenso, allora tal moto sarà allo in su con tanta maggiore velocità, quanto il discenso di tale alie sarà più veloce. L'uccello discende da quella parte, donde lo stremo dell'alia è più vicino al centro della sua gravità. Farai la natomia dell'alie d'uno uccello [ecc.]".

[5] Firpo 1991, p. XXI.

[6] Il monte cui si riferisce Leonardo è il monte Ceceri, vicino a Firen-

translation MacCurdy 1955, p. 63). On the anatomical drawing RL 19001 recto, K/P 136 recto we read: "And thou, man, who in this labour of mine considers the marvellous works of Nature, if thou judgest it to be a wicked thing to destroy it, think how very wicked a thing it is to take away the life of a man; and if this his composition appears to thee a marvellous construction remember that this is nothing compared with the soul that dwells within that structure. For truly whatever it may be, that is a thing divine. Leave it then to dwell in its work at its good pleasure," Keele and Pedretti 1979–80, vol. II, p. 486.

[13] It is necessary to recall that the term *nerve* used by Leonardo has the twofold meaning of a nerve in the true sense of the present word and also tendon, due to the etymological derivation and to the objective difficulty in distinguishing between the two anatomical parts until the eighteenth century.

[14] See also Villata in Milan 2012, pp. 10–11.

[15] Beltrami 1912, pp. 19–25.

[16] Manuscript B, fol. 88 recto, Marinoni 1986–90, *Il manoscritto B*, 1990, pp. 123–24 (English translation KMC).

[17] See Codex on the Flight of Birds, fol. 16 recto.

[18] Salvi 2013a, pp. 59–60, 85. Leonardo writes on K/P 44 recto (note I): "In the second demonstration you will put on these muscles the second motors of the fingers and you will do this step by step in order not to confuse. But first put on the bones those muscles which join the bones together without confusing them with other muscles," Keele and Pedretti 1979–80, vol. I, p. 110.

[19] Manuscript B, fol. 74 recto, Marinoni 1986-90, *Il manoscritto B*, 1990, p. 109 (English translation KMC).

[20] Pedretti 1993, p. 39 ; Galluzzi in Florence 1992, p. 200, cat. 9.20.

[21] Codex on the Flight of Birds, fol. 5 recto, Marinoni 1982, p. 40.

[22] Pedretti 1990, p. 110.

[23] Codex on the Flight of Birds, fol. 17 recto, Marinoni 1982, p. 76.

[24] *Ibid.*, pp. 60–63.

[25] *Ibid.*, p. 62.

[26] Barone and Kemp 2008, pp. 99–102; Marinoni 1982, pp. 15–16, deals with the problem of the numbering, citing the opinion of Nando De Toni regarding a hypothetical elimination by Leonardo of fol. 5, after he had numbered the pages.

[27] Pedretti 1990, pp. 110–11.

[28] The preliminary analysis was carried out by Mauro Missori of the Istituto dei Sistemi Complessi del CNR (ISC-CNR) and Lorenzo Teodonio, doctoral student at the Centro Interdipartimentale Nanoscienze & Nanotecnologie & Strumentazione (NAST) at the Università di Roma Tor Vergata, who used instruments made available *in situ* by Davide Manzini of the company Madatec, and we would like to thank them all. A complete analysis of the paper of the Codex on the Flight of Birds could be made possible by the partecipation of ICRCPAL (Istituto Centrale per il Restauro e la Conservazione del Patrimonio Archivistico e Librario) in Rome, where a complete diagnostic analysis of Leonardo's *Self Portrait*, also from Turin (fig. 1), was carried out.

[29] Manuscript K, fol. 3 recto, Marinoni 1986-90, *Il manoscritto K*, 1989, p. 7 (English translation MacCurdy 1955, p. 479). Manuscript K is considered to have been written prior to the Codex on the Flight of Birds. See, conclusively, Bambach 2009, pp. 38–39.

[30] Codex on the Flight of Birds, fol. 3 recto, Marinoni 1982, pp. 34–35.

[31] Keele and Pedretti 1979–80, vol. II, p. 530.

[32] See Salvi 2005a, p. 48 and Salvi 2013a, p. 102.

[33] "We shall demonstrate the instrumental shape of man in <twenty-four> figures of which the three first will be the ramification of the bones; that is one from the front which demonstrates the widths of the positions and shapes of the bones; the second will be seen in profile, and will show the depth of the whole and of the parts in position. The third figure is to demonstrate the bones from behind. Then we shall make three other figures from the same aspects with the bones sawn through, in which their thickness and their hollow cavities will be seen. Three other figures of the complete bones, and of the

ze, nel comune di Fiesole. Con il nome ceceri erano indicati dai fiorentini i cigni. La citazione da Marinoni 1976, p. 73.

[7] *Ibid.*, p. 74.

[8] Per gli scritti di Leonardo sul volo, diffusi in vari manoscritti, cfr. Giacomelli 1936.

[9] *Codice Atlantico*, f. 434 r (ex 161 r-a), Marinoni 1973-80, vol. V, p. 341. Cfr. anche Villata in Milan 2012, p. 35 per l'importanza di questo brano dal punto di vista "ideologico", che conduce l'autore a chiedersi se "sarà eccessivo leggere tale meccanicismo in senso precartesiano?".

[10] Cfr. Pedretti 2007, pp. 31-36.

[11] Keele and Pedretti 1980-84, vol. II, p. 88.

[12] Nel f. 207 r (ex 76 r-a) si legge: "Chi vole vedere come l'anima abita nel suo corpo, guardi come esso corpo usa la sua cotidiana abitazione; cioè se quella è sanza ordine e confusa, disordinato e confuso fia il corpo tenuto dalla su' anima", c. 1490, Marinoni 1973-80, vol. III, p. 142. Nel foglio anatomico 19001 r, K/P 136 r si legge: "E tu, omo, che consideri in questa mia fatica l'opere mirabili della natura, se g<i>udicherai esse<r> cosa nefanda il destruggerla, or pensa essere cosa nefandissima il torre la vita all'omo, del quale, se questa sua composizione ti pare di maraviglioso artifizio, pensa questa essere nulla rispetto all'anima che in tale architettura abita e, veramente, quale essa si sia, ella è cosa divina sicché lasciala abitare nella sua opera a suo beneplacito", Keele and Pedretti 1980-84, vol. III, p. 486.

[13] Occorre ricordare che il termine nervo è utilizzato da Leonardo nel doppio significato di nervo vero e proprio e tendine, sulla base della derivazione etimologica e per l'oggettiva difficoltà di distinguere, fino al XVIII sec., le due entità anatomiche.

[14] Cfr. anche Villata in Milan 2012, pp. 10-11.

[15] Beltrami 1912, pp. 19-25.

[16] *Ms. B*, f. 88 r, Marinoni 1986-90, *Il manoscritto B*, 1990, pp. 123-24.

[17] Cfr. *supra*, c. 16 r del *Codice sul volo degli uccelli*.

[18] Salvi 2013a, pp. 59-60, 85. Scrive Leonardo nel f. K/P 44 r (Nota I): "Nella seconda dimostrazione vestirai questi muscoli delli secondi motori de' diti, e così farai a grado a grado per non confondere; ma, primo, poni sopra dell'ossa quelli muscoli che con esse ossa si congiungano sanza altra confusione d'altri muscoli", Keele and Pedretti 1980-84, vol. II, p. 110.

[19] *Ms. B*, f. 74 r, Marinoni 1986-90, *Il manoscritto B*, 1990, p. 109.

[20] Pedretti 1993, p. 39 ; Galluzzi in Florence 1992, p. 200, cat. 9.20.

[21] *Codice sul volo…*, c. 5 r, Marinoni 1976, p. 37.

[22] Pedretti 1990, p. 110.

[23] *Codice sul volo…*, c. 17 r, Marinoni 1976, p. 69.

[24] *Ibid.*, pp. 55-58.

[25] *Ibid.*, p. 57.

[26] Barone and Kemp 2008, pp. 99-102; Marinoni 1976, pp. 12-13, affronta il problema della cartulazione riportando in nota l'opinione di Nando De Toni circa una ipotetica eliminazione da parte di Leonardo della c. 5, dopo la numerazione.

[27] Pedretti 1990, pp. 110-11.

[28] Gli esami preliminari sono avvenuti grazie al dottor Mauro Missori dell'Istituto dei Sistemi Complessi del CNR (ISC-CNR) e al dottor Lorenzo Teodonio, dottorando presso il Centro interdipartimentale Nanoscienze & Nanotecnologie & Strumentazione (NAST) dell'Università di Roma Tor Vergata, che si sono avvalsi di strumentazione messa a disposizione in loco da Davide Manzini della ditta Madatec, che si ringraziano. Un esame completo della carta del *Codice sul volo* potrebbe avvenire per intervento dell'ICRCPAL (Istituto Centrale per il Restauro e la Conservazione del Patrimonio Archivistico e Librario) di Roma, che ha già eseguito una completa indagine diagnostica sull'*Autoritratto* di Leonardo, conservato anch'esso presso la Biblioteca Reale di Torino (fig. 1).

[29] *Ms. K*, f. 3 r, Marinoni 1986-90, *Il manoscritto K*, 1989, p. 7. Il *Ms. K* è ritenuto precedente al *Codice sul volo*. Si veda, conclusivamente, Bambach 2009, pp. 38-39.

[30] *Codice sul volo…*, c. 3 r, Marinoni 1976, p. 32.

[31] Keele and Pedretti 1980-84, vol. III, p. 530.

[32] Cfr. Salvi 2005a, p. 48 e Salvi 2013a, p. 102.

[33] "Questa figura strumentale dell'omo dimonsterreno in <ventiquattro> figure, delle quali le tre prime saranno la ramificazione

nerves which arise from the spinal cord, and in which limbs they ramify. Then three others of the bones and vessels and where they ramify. Then three with muscles; and three with the skin, proportionally drawn." Keele and Pedretti 1979–80, vol. I, p. 272.

[34] See Giacomelli 1936, pp. 206–7.

[35] Codex on the Flight of Birds, fol. 13 verso, Marinoni 1982, p. 66.

[36] Clayton and Philo write in London 2012, p. 216, cat. 76: "The lines at the top of the page are a proportional analysis of the different sections of the bird's wing. In the absence of a scale, the species dissected by Leonardo cannot be identified, but the length of the 'hand' suggests that it was a bird capable of strong soaring flight, such as a raptor."

[37] Keele and Pedretti 1979–80, vol. II, pp. 750–51. Of no less importance is the quality of the drawing of a wing on fol. 184 recto, with relative note [I], on a page with architectural subjects. The drawing shows the two antagonistic muscles in the flexion-extension of the radial-ulnar portion of the wing. The note [I] explains its action: "the tendon *ab* moves all the tips of the feathers towards the elbow of the wings; and it does this in flexing the wings; but in extending [the wing] by means of the pull of the muscle *nm* these feathers direct their lengths towards the point of the wing." *Ibid.*, vol. II, p. 738.

[38] Manuscript E, fol. 49 r, Marinoni 1986–90, *Il manoscritto E*, 1989, p. 95–96 (English translation KMC).

[39] Codex on the Flight of Birds, fol. 10 recto, Marinoni 1982, p. 54.

[40] Codex Atlanticus, fol. 186 recto (ex 66 r-b), Marinoni 1973–80, vol. III, p. 39 (English translation KMC); fol. 571a recto (ex 214 r-d), *ibid.*, vol. VII, p. 113–14 (English translation MacCurdy 1955, p. 431).

[41] Manuscript L, fol. 62 recto, Marinoni 1986–90, *Il manoscritto L*, 1987, p. 56–57 (English translation MacCurdy 1955, p. 489).

[42] Codex Atlanticus, fol. 185 recto (ex 66 r-a), Marinoni 1973–80, vol. III, p. 33 (English translation MacCurdy 1955, p. 421): "The bird which descends above or below the wind keeps its wings closed in order not to be held up or checked by the air; it keeps them well above its body, so that it may not be turned upside down by the impetus."

[43] Codex on the Flight of Birds, fol. 9 recto, Marinoni 1982, pp. 51–52.

[44] *Ibid.*, fol. 8 recto, pp. 48–49.

[45] *Ibid.*, fol. 5 verso, p. 42.

[46] Madrid II, fol. 101 verso: "The first book deals with flying without motion of the wings." This folio contains numerous notes on the topic, many of them are very close to those of the Turin codex. Here are some of them: "The bird which desires to descend lowers its wings from its middle down, at the side it wants to descend, and this steers it, along the line *a b*. Afterwards, it turns round, in the face of site *a b*, and descends with the same obliquity, turning on itself until facing the place where it desires to land." "When the north wind blows and the bird faces the east, with its tail leeward, this means that the bird desires to rise in circles, by the favor of the wind, which helps the bird's motion by holding down its tail and aiding it above obliquely; the wind makes the bird partially rotate, as a result of the resistance of the wind's streams breaking at the upper part of the tail. And this occurs until the bird turns facing the wind. Afterwards, when it turns towards the west the bird is struck from beneath by the wind and it is made to turn and to continue its circular motion." "When the kite, in its circling motion, rises and returning presents the upper wing to the onrush of the wind, it would often be overturned were it not for the fact that it immediately changes the position of the upper wing, which was windward, by letting it down and placing it, from its middle on, leeward," Reti 1974a, vol. V, p. 210.

[47] Codex on the Flight of Birds, fol. 9 recto, Marinoni 1982, p. 51.

[48] *Ibid.*, fol. 15 recto, p. 71.

[49] Pedretti 1995, vol. II, p. 310 (English translation KMC).

[50] *Ibid.*, p. 312 (English translation KMC).

[51] Codex on the Flight of Birds, fol. 14 recto, Marinoni 1982, p. 68.

delle ossa, cioè una dinanzi che dimostri la latitudine de' siti e figure delli ossi; la seconda sarà veduta in profilo e mosterrà la profondità del tutto e delle parti e loro sito; la terza figura fia dimostratrice delle ossa dalla parte dirieto. Dipoi faren tre altre figure ne' simili aspetti, colle ossa segate, nelle quali si vedrà le lor grossezze e vacuità. Tre altre figure faremo dell'ossa intere e de' nervi che nascan della nuca e in che membra ramifichino. E tre altre de ossa e vene, e dove ramifichino. Poi tre con muscoli e tre con pelle e figure proporzionate". Keele and Pedretti 1980-84, vol. II, p. 272.

[34] Cfr. Giacomelli 1936, pp. 206-7.

[35] Codice sul volo..., c. 13 v, Marinoni 1976, p. 60.

[36] Clayton and Philo, in London 2012, p. 216, cat. 76, scrivono: "The lines at the top of the page are a proportional analysis of the different sections of the bird's wing. In the absence of a scale, the species dissected by Leonardo cannot be identified, but the lenght of the 'hand' suggest that it was a bird capable of strong soaring flight, such as a raptor".

[37] Keele and Pedretti 1980-84, vol. III, pp. 750-51. Di non minore qualità il disegno di ala del f. 184 r, con relativa Nota [I], in un foglio di soggetto architettonico. Il disegno evidenzia i due muscoli antagonisti che agiscono nella flesso-estensione della porzione radio-ulnare dell'ala. La Nota [I] ne esplicita l'azione: "*ab*, corda, muove tutte le cime delle penne in verso il gomito dell'alie. E questo fa nel ripiegare dell'alie; ma, nell'astendersi mediante il tirare del muscolo *nm*, esse penne dirizzan le lunghezze delle lor penne verso la punta dell'alie", *ibid.*, vol. III, p. 738.

[38] Ms. E, f. 49 r, Marinoni 1986-90, *Il manoscritto E*, 1989, pp. 95-96.

[39] Codice sul volo..., c. 10 r, Marinoni 1976, p. 50.

[40] Codice Atlantico, f. 186 r (ex 66 r-b), Marinoni 1973-80, vol. III, p. 39; f. 571a r (ex 214 r-d), *ibid.*, vol. VII, pp. 113-14.

[41] Ms. L, f. 62 r, Marinoni 1986-90, *Il manoscritto L*, 1987, pp. 56-57.

[42] Codice Atlantico, f. 185 r (ex 66 r-a), Marinoni 1973-80, vol. III, p. 33: "L'uccello che discende sopra o sotto al vento, tiene l'alie stretto per non esser sostenuto o impedito dall'aria. Tielle forte sopra del suo busto, acciò non sia dall'impito voltato sotto sopra".

[43] Codice sul volo..., c. 9 r, Marinoni 1976, p. 47.

[44] *Ibid.*, c. 8 r, pp. 44-45.

[45] *Ibid.*, c. 5 v, p. 39.

[46] Md. II, f. 101 v: "El primo libro tratt<a> <d>e volar sanza moto d'alie". Questo foglio contiene molte note sull'argomento, molto vicine a quelle del codice torinese. Se ne trascrivono alcune: "L'uccello che vol calare, abassa l'alia dal mezo inanzi, da cquel <l>ato che esso voi disscendere, la quale fa timone a esso moto, per la linia *a b*. E poi si volta in faccia a esso sito *a b*, e cala per la medesima obbliquità, trivellando insin che ssi volti col viso al loco ove vol prodare". "Quando tramontana spira e ll'ucello stia con la fronte a llevante, la coda stando sotto vento, colla bassezza del suo lato a ttramontana, fa che questo è ssegnio che ll'ucello vol montare a circuli per favor di vento, il quale lo favorisce nel moto tenendoli bassa la coda, e lla percote di sopra per obliquo, e parte lo gira, per la resistentia de' ronpimenti de' razi del vento che 'n tal disopra della coda percote. E cque<sto> fa insino che si volta col viso al vento. Di poi, quando si volta a ponente, è percossa di sotto e ffallo girare e seguitare il moto circulare". "Quando il nibi<o> nel suo moto circulare si leva in alto, e che nel ritornare coll'alia superiore all'avenimento del vento, spesso sarebe aroversciato se llui non mutassi immediate l'alia superiore, che era sopra il vento, e lla abassassi e mettessi, dal mezo in là, sotto vento", Reti 1974b, vol. V, p. 209.

[47] Codice sul volo..., c. 9 r, Marinoni 1976, p. 47.

[48] *Ibid.*, c. 15 r, p. 65.

[49] Pedretti 1995, vol. II, p. 310.

[50] *Ibid.*, p. 312.

[51] Codice sul volo..., c. 14 r, Marinoni 1976, pp. 62-63.

[52] *Ibid.*, c. 9 v, p. 49.

[53] Galluzzi 2006, p. 21.

[54] Madrid I, f. 108 r, Reti 1974b, vol. IV, p. 269.

[55] Codice sul volo..., c. 1 r, Marinoni 1976, pp. 26-27. Al proposito, Galluzzi 2006, p. 21, scrive: "Nel caso infatti che l'asta della

[52] *Ibid*., fol. 9 verso, p. 54.

[53] Galluzzi 2006, p. 21 (English translation KMC).

[54] Madrid I, fol. 108 recto, Reti 1974a, vol. IV, p. 270.

[55] Codex on the Flight of Birds, fol. 1 recto, Marinoni 1982, p. 28. See also Galluzzi 2006, p. 21: "In fact if the rod of the balance is extremely thin (tending that is to correspond to the demate-rialization considered by the authors (*de ponderibus*) the math-ematical center and the effective center of balance will be so close as to be almost indistinguishable." See also Galluzzi 1989.

[56] Codex on the Flight of Birds, fol. 1 recto, Marinoni 1982, p. 29.

[57] Galluzzi 2006, p. 21.

[58] Pedretti 1990, p. 111, points out "the *ductus* characteristic of the notes from 1504–5 of Madrid Manuscript II," considering it probable that, when the pages on flight were written, these first pages already bore mechanical notes. Firpo 1991, p. XXIX suggests that these notes were written later, at an unknown time: "The small codex, which had been promoted from sketch book to 'book', accompanied him on his last journey to Lom-bardy, but was again demoted to a mere draft of notes and taken up again only to use the last pages not yet invaded by writing, that is pages 1 to 4 […]. It would be useless, however, to attempt to find some connection with his studies on flight in this last series of notes." According to Marinoni 1982, p. 16, "the first four folios dedicated to the science of weights (the 'Mathematical figures' mentioned in the deed of Arconati's donation), constitute an appendix to the main theme of the Co-dex, the flight of birds, which forms a coherent unit."

[59] Codex on the Flight of Birds, fol. 1 recto, Marinoni 1982, p. 30.

[60] See Pedretti 1990, p. 114.

[61] *Ibid*.

[62] Codex on the Flight of Birds, fol. 11 recto, Marinoni 1982, p. 58.

[63] Codex Atlanticus, fol. 327 verso (ex 119 v-a), Marinoni 1973–80, vol. IV, p. 199 (English translation MacCurdy 1955, p. 232).

[64] *Ibid*., p. 196 (English translation KMC).

[65] Chastel 1982, p. 8.

[66] Kant (1783) 1982, p. 146.

[67] Codex on the Flight of Birds, fol. 13 recto, Marinoni 1982, p. 65.

[68] Valéry (1894) 1996, p. 39: "His joy is to be found in decorations for fêtes, in enchanting inventions, and when he had the idea of constructing a *flying man*, he imagined it taking flight to seek the snow on the peaks of the mountains, returning to scatter it in the streets of the cities, quivering in the summer heat" (English translation KMC).

[69] Pedretti 1977, vol. I, § 705, p. 400; Pedretti in Turin 2006, p. 14.

[70] Another note in Spanish is to be found on fol. 12 verso: "para ujr el peligro dela ruina."

[71] Pedretti 1990, p. 112, with reference to Windsor RL 12422 recto.

[72] *Ibid*.

[73] See Salvi 2005a, pp. xxviii–xxx; Salvi 2006, pp. 23–25 and Salvi 2013a, pp. 77–84 and *passim*.

[74] Pedretti in Turin 1975, cat. 25.

[75] Firpo 1991, pp. XXII–XXIII.

[76] The digital procedure was given considerable attention in the work by the broadcaster Piero Angela, who also devoted a pro-gram in the television series *Ulisse* to the topic (January 2009).

[77] See also Salvi in Venaria Reale (Turin) 2011–12, pp. 36–37 and pp. 106–11, cats 1.19, 1.20.

[78] Maffei 1999, pp. 234–35: "Fuit ingenio valde comi, nitido, liberali, vultu autem longe venustissimo."

bilancia sia estremamente sottile (tenda cioè a corrispondere a quella smaterializzata considerata dagli autori *de ponderibus*), il centro matematico e quello effettivo di ponderazione risulteranno talmente prossimi da essere praticamente indistinguibili". Si veda anche Galluzzi 1989.

[56] *Codice sul volo*…, c. 1 r, Marinoni 1976, p. 27.

[57] Galluzzi 2006, p. 21.

[58] Pedretti 1990, p. 111, evidenzia "il *ductus* caratteristico delle note del 1504-5 nel Ms. II di Madrid", ritenendo probabile che, al momento della scrittura delle pagine sul volo, queste prime carte fossero già occupate dalle note di meccanica. Firpo 1991, p. XXIX, indica queste note come scritte per ultime in un tempo impreci-sato: "Il codicetto, che da quaderno di schizzi era stato promosso a 'libro', lo accompagnò nel nuovo soggiorno lombardo, ma daccapo degradato a mero brogliaccio di appunti e ripreso tra mano solo per utilizzarne le ultime facciate non ancora invase dal-la scrittura, cioè le carte 1-4. […] Vano sarebbe tuttavia tentar di rintracciare un qualche nesso con gli studi sul volo in quest'ultima serie di appunti". Per Marinoni 1976, p. 13, "i primi quattro fogli dedicati alla scienza dei pesi (le «figure Mathematiche» nomina-te nella donazione Arconati) costituiscono un'appendice al tema principale del codice, il Volo degli Uccelli, che forma un blocco compatto".

[59] *Codice sul volo*…, c. 1 r, Marinoni 1976, p. 28.

[60] Cfr. Pedretti 1990, p. 114.

[61] *Ibid*.

[62] *Codice sul volo*…, c. 11 r, Marinoni 1976, pp. 53-54.

[63] *Codice Atlantico*, f. 327 v (ex 119 v-a), Marinoni 1973-80, vol. IV, p. 199.

[64] *Ibid*., p. 196.

[65] Chastel 1982, p. 8.

[66] Kant (1783) 1982, p. 146.

[67] *Codice sul volo*…, c. 13 r, Marinoni 1976, p. 60.

[68] Valéry (1894) 1996, p. 39: "La sua gioia si placa in decorazioni di feste, in invenzioni incantevoli, e quando avrà l'idea di costruire un *uomo volante*, egli lo immaginerà spiccare il volo per andare a cercare la neve sulla cima delle montagne e tornare a spargerla nelle vie delle città, vibranti per il calore estivo".

[69] Pedretti 1977, vol. I, § 705, p. 400; Pedretti in Turin 2006, p. 14.

[70] Un'altra nota in spagnolo si trova alla c. 12 v: "para ujr el peligro dela ruina".

[71] Pedretti 1990, p. 112, con richiamo al f. RL 12422 r a Windsor.

[72] *Ibid*.

[73] Cfr. Salvi 2005a, pp. xxviii-xxx; Salvi 2006, pp. 23-25 e Salvi 2013a, pp. 77-84 e *passim*.

[74] Pedretti in Turin 1975, cat. 25.

[75] Firpo 1991, pp. XXII-XXIII.

[76] La realizzazione ha avuto grande eco ad opera del divulgatore scientifico Piero Angela, che ha dedicato all'argomento una pun-tata del suo programma televisivo *Ulisse* (gennaio 2009).

[77] Salvi in Venaria Reale (Turin) 2011-12, pp. 36-37 e le schede 1.19 e, soprattutto, 1.20, pp. 106-11.

[78] Maffei 1999, pp. 234-35: "Fuit ingenio valde comi, nitido, liberali, vultu autem longe venustissimo".

Appendix

Appendice

1. Dating

The Codex on the Flight of Birds includes the following biographical notes:

> Fol. 18 verso:
> 1505, Tuesday evening, on the 14th day of April, Lorenzo came to stay with me. He said he was 17 years old.
> And on the 15th day of the said April I had 25 gold ducats from the chamberlain of Santa Maria Nova;[1]

> Fol. 17 verso:
> When the bird has a large wingspan and a short tail and it wishes to ascend, then it will strongly raise its wings and turning it will receive the wind under its wings. Which wind, forming a wedge, will quickly push it upward, like the *cortone* [kite], a bird of prey, that I saw on my way to Fiesole, above the site of Barbiga, in '5 on the 14th day of March.[2]

These dates, although detailed, have given rise to debate about whether the year in question is 1505 or 1506. This ambiguity derives mainly from two factors:
a) March 14, 1505, could refer to two different years, according to whether it is interpreted under the Florentine *ab incarnatione* formula (1506), or under the *a nativitate* formula (1505). In the first case (which places the start of the year on March 25), the date corresponds to the last days of 1505, but under the *a nativitate* formula it would coincide with the year 1506.
b) The April dates refer to the year 1505, under both formulas (*ab incarnatione* and *a nativitate*). According to Giuseppe Dondi, however, the day Tuesday, April 14, 1505, is "an incorrect date that acquires value, in the chronological limits of Leonardo's life, only in 1506,"[3] since in 1505, April 14 would have fallen on a Monday. Therefore, Leonardo could have been mistaken in writing the year, a common error at the start of a new year, when people continue to write the old

1. Datazione

Il *Codice sul volo degli uccelli* presenta le seguenti annotazioni biografiche:

> c. 18 v
> 1505, martedì sera addì 14 aprile venne Lorenzo a stare con meco. Disse essere d'età d'anni 17;
> E addi 15 del detto aprile ebbi ducati 25 d'oro dal camarlingo di Santa Maria Nova;[1]

> c. 17 v
> Quando l'uccello ha gran larghezza d'alie e poca coda e che esso si voglia inalzare, allora esso alzerà forte le alie e girando riceverà il vento sotto l'alie. Il quale vento, facendoseli conio, lo spignerà in alto con prestezza, come il cortone, uccello di rapina, ch'io vidi andando a Fiesole, sopra il loco del Barbiga nel '5 a dì 14 di marzo.[2]

Queste date, seppur circostanziate, hanno dato luogo ad interpretazioni che oscillano tra l'accettazione dell'anno 1505 e il suo spostamento al 1506. Questa ambiguità deriva sostanzialmente da due ragioni:
a) il 14 di marzo del 1505 può essere riferito a due anni diversi, a seconda se interpretato con lo stile *ab incarnatione* (1506), fiorentino, o *a nativitate* (1505). Nel primo caso (che fa iniziare l'anno il 25 marzo), la data corrisponderebbe ai giorni finali del 1505, ma in realtà coinciderebbe con l'anno 1506 secondo il computo dello stile *a nativitate*;
b) le date di aprile sono, con entrambi gli stili (*ab incarnatione* e *a nativitate*), riferite all'anno 1505. Secondo Giuseppe Dondi, tuttavia, il giorno *martedì* 14 aprile 1505 è "una data errata che acquista valore, nei limiti cronologici della vita di Leonardo, solo nel 1506",[3] poiché nel 1505 il 14 di aprile cadde di lunedì. Leonardo avrebbe pertanto sbagliato a scrivere l'anno, come accade a molti che all'inizio di un nuovo anno, continuano per un po' a confondersi scrivendo l'anno vecchio. Secondo altri autori, invece, l'anno sarebbe quello esatto, mentre l'errore starebbe nel giorno: Leonardo avrebbe quindi erroneamente scritto martedì invece di lunedì.

year. According to other authors, the year is correct, but Leonardo made an error in the day of the week, writing Tuesday instead of Monday.

This debate leads to the following observations:

1. With regard to the notes on fol. 18 verso, it should be pointed out that the second note, concerning the withdrawal of twenty-five gold ducats from the depository of Santa Maria Nova, is confirmed by documents, held in the state archives in Florence, that are dated April 15, 1505.[4] These documents consequently validate the year 1505 in the first biographical note, owing to its close link to the second. It is important to pay attention to the graphic arrangement of the first note: "1505 daprile" is a heading; on the line below is the text "martedì addì 14 venne Lorenzo a stare con meco. Disse essere d'anni 17" ("Tuesday, this 14th April, Lorenzo came to stay with me. He said he was 17 years old.") The word "evening" was added just above and between the words "Tuesday" and "this day," specifying when the young man arrived.

A particularly important date is that of the death of Leonardo's father, which he notes twice, both times in normal writing (that is, proceeding from left to right). The first instance is on fol. 196 verso (ex 71 v-b) of the Codex Atlanticus: "Wednesday at seven o'clock, Ser Piero da Vinci died on the day 9 of July 1504 / Wednesday at almost seven o'clock."[5] The second instance appears on fol. 272 recto of the Codex Arundel: "This day 9 July 1504 on Wednesday at seven o'clock died Ser Piero da Vinci public notary at the Palazzo del Podesta, my father, at seven o'clock; he was aged eighty and left ten male children and two female."[6] I would like to draw attention here to the fact that in both instances Leonardo erred in indicating July 9 as a Wednesday; in 1504 it fell on a Tuesday.[7]

Some of the accounting references for 1504 on fol. 196 verso of the Codex Atlanticus also include specific dates. On June 29, the feast of Saint Peter, Leonardo writes that he gave a ducat to Tomaso, his "servant, to spend." He sometimes adds the day of the week: "Friday morning of 19 July one ducat, less six *soldi*. There remain seven ducats and twenty-two *soldi* in the cashbox"; "Tuesday 23 July one ducat to Tomaso"; "Thursday morning this first day of August one ducat to Tomaso"; "Sunday 4 August one ducat [to Tomaso]"; "Friday this day 9 August I take ten ducats from the cashbox."[8] All these dates are correct with regard to the day of the week. The only exception is the date of his father's death, which to coincide with these references, should in fact be a Tuesday.

Questo dibattito merita le seguenti osservazioni.

1. Per quanto riguarda le annotazioni della c. 18 v, è da segnalare che la seconda, riferita al prelievo di 25 ducati d'oro dal deposito di Santa Maria Nova, è attestata dai documenti conservati presso l'Archivio di Stato di Firenze esattamente nel giorno 15 aprile 1505.[4]

Ne consegue che anche la prima annotazione, cui la seconda è strettamente collegata, è valida per l'anno 1505. Sembra importante osservare la scrittura di questa nota, che è così composta: in intestazione sta "1505 daprile"; sulla riga continua sottostante sta il testo "martedì addì 14 venne Lorenzo a stare con meco. Disse essere d'anni 17". La parola "sera" è aggiunta appena sopra tra le parole "martedì" e "addì", come una precisazione che indica il momento della giornata dell'arrivo del giovane.

Mi preme richiamare una data importante, quella della morte del padre, che Leonardo annota due volte, entrambe in scrittura normale, vergata cioè da sinistra a destra, una nel *Codice Atlantico*, foglio 196 v (ex 71 v-b) "Mercoledì a ore 7 morì ser Piero da Vinci a dì 9 di luglio 1504 / Mercoledì vicino alle 7 ore",[5] l'altra nel foglio 272 r, P 79 r del *Codice Arundel*: "Addì 9 di luglio 1504, in mercoledì a ore 7, morì ser Piero da Vinci, notaio al palagio del podestà, mio padre, a ore 7. Era d'età d'anni 80. Lasciò 10 figlioli masschi e 2 femmine".[6] Anche in questo caso è stato rilevato che Leonardo sarebbe incorso in un errore, indicando il giorno 9 luglio come mercoledì, mentre nel 1504 cadde di martedì.[7]

In effetti, nel foglio 196 v del *Codice Atlantico* sono riportate alcune date, con riferimenti contabili, relative all'anno 1504, a cominciare dal 29 giugno, giorno di S. Pietro, nel quale Leonardo scrive di aver dato un ducato a Tomaso, suo "famiglio, per ispendere". Tra le varie annotazioni, alcune portano il riferimento al giorno della settimana: "Venerdì mattina a dì 19 di luglio ducati uno manco soldi 6. Restommi ducati 7 e 22 in cassa"; "Martedì a dì 23 di luglio ducati uno a Tomaso"; "Giovedì mattina addì primo d'agosto ducati uno a Tomaso"; "Domenica d<ì> 4 d'agosto ducati uno [a Tomaso]"; "Venerdì addì 9 d'agosto 1504 tolgo ducati 10 dalla cassa".[8] Tutte queste date coincidono perfettamente tra loro per quanto riguarda il giorno della settimana, tranne la data della morte del padre, che, per coerenza con questi riferimenti, dovrebbe effettivamente essere di martedì.

Pare davvero strano che Leonardo sia caduto per ben due volte nello stesso errore nell'arco di meno di un anno (tra il 9 luglio 1504 e il 14 aprile 1505 vi sono nove mesi di distanza), e soprattutto in due date per le quali egli manifesta la volontà di massima precisione (per l'alto valore biografico nel caso della morte del padre, e per l'intento di specificazione che rivela nella integrazione della parola

It seems odd that Leonardo should make the same error twice in less than a year (in the nine months between July 9 and April 14, 1505), especially since he shows a desire to express himself with maximum precision—for example, by the addition of "evening" in his note on Lorenzo's arrival at his home—and also because of the personal importance of his father's death. Moreover, the error would have been of a similar nature: writing the day of the week following the day on which the event occurred. All this leads to the conclusion that the error Leonardo made in the codex was in the day of the week, not the year. Nevertheless, given the objective strangeness, and the reiteration, of these two hypothetical errors, I believe that the calculation of days of the week and the year has yet to be verified conclusively (but this is not the place to do so), and perhaps also compared with the calculation of the hours, which at that time began with the Ave Maria, in the ancient manner.

2. With regard to the note on fol. 17 verso, because Leonardo was in Florence at the time, it has been taken for granted that he used the formula for calculating the years employed in that city, which was also his birthplace. Nevertheless, Augusto Marinoni has pointed out that on fol. 211 recto (ex 77 r-b) of the Codex Atlanticus (a folio that carries, among other things, important notes on the flight of birds), Leonardo notes that he withdrew fifty gold ducats from the Spedale di Santa Maria Nova "sabato a dì 5 marzo" (Saturday, March 5) with the year given as 1503. In the records of the Spedale, the withdrawal is registered for the year 1502 (obviously *ab incarnatione*). Therefore, Marinoni stresses, "the Florentine Leonardo did not follow the Florentine style, but the *a nativitate*."[9]

What is more, since the dates on fol. 18 verso, written on a page left blank (as a protective folio for the start of the codex) undeniably refer to April 1505, it would be very strange if the date of one of the initial folios (such as fol. 17 verso, given the backward progress of the collation), were to refer to the following year. Consequently, the date of March 14, 1505, is to be considered *a nativitate*, that is referring to the year 1505. Therefore, we may surmise that the Codex on the Flight of Birds was written in the spring of 1505 without particular temporal fluctuation.

2. Collation

Another question that remains open and that has been subject to various interpretations by scholars

"sera" nella data che segnala l'arrivo in casa di Lorenzo). Inoltre l'errore sarebbe stato della medesima natura: scrivere il giorno della settimana successivo invece di quello in cui l'evento sarebbe avvenuto. Tutto ciò porta a considerare come possibile l'errore rispetto al giorno della settimana nella data del *Codice sul volo degli uccelli*, eliminando qualunque ipotesi di errore rispetto all'anno. Tuttavia, più in generale, per l'oggettiva stranezza e la reiterazione di questi due ipotetici errori, credo si debba aprire una verifica (che non è qui luogo di affrontare) sul computo dei giorni della settimana e dell'anno, magari con riferimento anche al computo delle ore, che nella maniera antica iniziava dall'Avemaria.

2. Per l'annotazione della carta 17 v, il riferimento allo stile fiorentino deriva da un'interpretazione basata sul fatto che Leonardo era a Firenze, e quindi è dato per scontato che aderisse al computo degli anni della città che era anche la sua patria. Tuttavia Augusto Marinoni ha messo in evidenza che nel foglio 211 r (ex 77 r-b) del *Codice Atlantico* (foglio che riporta, tra l'altro, importantissime note sul volo degli uccelli), Leonardo annota di aver ritirato 50 ducati d'oro dallo Spedale di Santa Maria Nova "sabato a dì 5 di marzo" con l'anno 1503. Nei registri dello Spedale l'operazione è invece registrata all'anno 1502 (ovviamente *ab incarnatione*). Ne consegue, sottolinea Marinoni, "che il fiorentino Leonardo non segue lo stile fiorentino, ma quello a «nativitate»".[9]

Peraltro, poiché le date della carta 18 v, scritte su una pagina lasciata vuota (come foglio di protezione all'inizio della stesura del *Codice*), risultano a questo punto inequivocabilmente da riferire all'aprile del 1505, sarebbe molto strano che la data di uno dei fogli compilati per primi (come il 17 v), per la scrittura a ritroso del fascicolo, si riferisse ad un anno dopo. Ne consegue che la data del 14 marzo 1505 è da considerare *a nativitate*, cioè da riferire proprio all'anno 1505 e il *Codice sul volo degli uccelli* potrebbe quindi aver avuto stesura nella primavera del 1505, senza grandi sconfinamenti temporali.

2. Fascicolazione

Un'altra questione aperta, soggetta a diverse interpretazioni degli studiosi, è la fascicolazione del *Codice*, che ad oggi si presenta nella condizione del sottostante schema (fig. a), dove si segnalano le carte divise a seguito del furto del Guglielmo Libri con il centro tratteggiato.

La numerazione autografa di Leonardo è presente alle carte 3 e 4 (figg. 14-15) e dalla 5 alla 16, con omissione del numero 5. Si determina pertanto la seguente sequenza: [1], [2], 3, 4, 6, 7, 8, 9, 10, [11], 12, 13, 14, 15, 16, 17,

FIG. 14

cat. 9, fol. 3 recto, viewed using a stereoscopic microscope / ripresa con il microscopio stereoscopico (detail of the numbering / dettaglio della numerazione)

FIG. 15

cat. 9, fol. 4 recto, viewed using a stereoscopic microscope / ripresa con il microscopio stereoscopico (detail of the numbering / dettaglio della numerazione)

concerns the collation of the codex as it exists today. The diagram below shows the pages as they are currently arranged, after the theft by Guglielmo Libri, with the center line dotted (fig. a).

Leonardo's handwritten numbering is present on fols. 3 and 4 (figs. 14–15) and fols. 5 to 16, although he omitted number 5, resulting in the following sequence: [1], [2], 3, 4, 6, 7, 8, 9, 10, [11], 12, 13, 14, 15, 16, 17, [18], [19]. This sequence was subsequently corrected by another hand (presumably that of Francesco Melzi) to become: [1], [2], 3, 4, 5, 6, 7, 8, 9, [10], 11, 12, 13, 14, 15, 16, [17], [18] (figs. 16–17). The numbers in brackets indicate the folios that carry neither the handwritten numbering nor the subsequent correction; these folios are the ones removed from the codex by Libri. In the case of fols. 2 and 10, trimming on the upper part is evident, a mutilation presumably inflicted to eliminate the numbering and allow the pages to be sold as independent folios. Fols. 1, 17, and 18 were not trimmed; only an analysis of the paper will show without doubt whether the numbering was present and later erased. On fol. 17 recto, just below a detail of the mechanical wing, Leonardo wrote: "Alle 19 carte di questo si dimostra la causa di questo." (On the nineteen folios of this [book] the cause for this is demonstrated.) This notation confirms that today's Codex on the Flight of Birds consists of all the folios he collated, which were eighteen in number, just as there are today. Because of Leonardo's accidental omission of number 5, it appeared to him that there were nineteen.

The skipping of number 5 has been subject to various interpretations. The most commonly accepted is that Leonardo left it out by mistake. Pedretti has suggested that the artist, at a certain point, noticed that the inside front cover, with its numerous notes,

[18], [19], successivamente corretta da altra mano (presumibilmente da Francesco Melzi) e così risultante: [1], [2], 3, 4, 5, 6, 7, 8, 9, [10], 11, 12, 13, 14, 15, 16, [17], [18] (figg. 16-17). I numeri che ho qui posto tra parentesi quadra indicano le carte che non portano né la numerazione autografa né la conseguente correzione. Si tratta di tutte le carte distaccate dal *Codice* da Libri. Nel caso delle carte 2 e 10 è evidente la rifilatura della parte alta, mutilazione evidentemente inflitta per eliminare proprio la numerazione e poter vendere la pagina come foglio autonomo. Nel caso della prima carta e delle ultime due, le pagine sono integre dal punto di vista dimensionale; solo un'analisi dello stato della carta ci potrà dire con sicurezza se la numerazione era esistente ed è stata poi abrasa. Nella carta 17 r, appena sotto la struttura dell'ala meccanica, Leonardo ha annotato: "Alle 19 carte di questo si dimostra la causa di questo". Ciò ci conferma che le carte costituenti il *Codice sul volo degli uccelli* sono ad oggi tutte quelle da lui riunite,

FIG. a

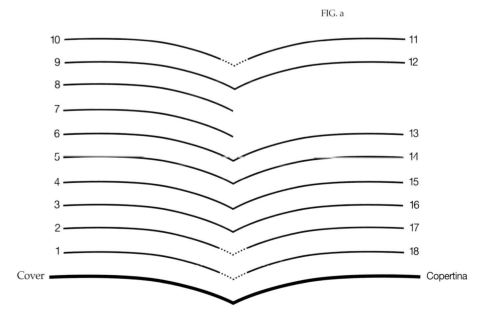

FIG. 16

cat. 9, fol. 6 recto, viewed
using a stereoscopic
microscope / ripresa con il
microscopio stereoscopico
(detail of the numbering /
dettaglio della numerazione)

FIG. 17

cat. 9, fol. 12 recto, viewed
using a stereoscopic
microscope / ripresa con il
microscopio stereoscopico
(detail of the numbering /
dettaglio della numerazione)

could also be considered part of the notebook, and
deliberately skipped number 5 in order to include the
cover in the numbering, but then did not correct the
numbers he had already written (1 to 4).[10]

There have also been various interpretations of the
lack of symmetry between the number of folios on
the left of the stitching (ten) and those on the right
(eight). This is due to the absence of the two right-
hand folios in continuity with folios 7 and 8. As
previously mentioned, fols. 1/18 and 2/17 are split
because they correspond to four of the five folios removed from the codex when it was stolen by Libri.
The pairs of fols. 3/16, 4/15, 5/14, 6/13 are complete
bifolios; fols. 7 and 8, both positioned in the left half
of the collation (fig. 18), are loose, without their corresponding right-hand folios, and are supported by
a tab (figs. 19–20). The pair of fols. 9/12 is a single
bifolio, and of fols. 10/11, with the stitching falling
in between, were joined during restoration. (Fol. 10
was one of those removed from the codex to be sold
separately.)

Carlo Pedretti stated that fols. 7 and 8 derived from
a single, folded folio, now separated because it was
tampered with, perhaps at the time of Libri.[11] Marinoni also appears to tend toward this interpretation,
although he leaves open the question of the separa-
tion of the two folios.[12]

More recently, Barone and Kemp have suggested a
more complex interpretation, involving interpolation
of the codex, once again by Leonardo.[13] Their theory
takes into account the absence of the number 5 and
presupposes the insertion of another folio (or bifolio)
between the present 13 and 14:

> Let us suppose that Leonardo's codex at one
> stage comprised more pages than in its pres-
> ent form. If we consider that there was indeed

poiché se è vero che le carte in nostro possesso sono 18,
è anche vero che per l'omissione del numero 5 a Leonardo
risultavano 19.

Tale salto di numerazione ha dato luogo a diverse interpretazioni. La più comunemente accettata è che Leonardo
abbia saltato il numero 5 per una banale svista. Pedretti
ha formulato l'ipotesi che l'artista, ad un certo punto, si
sia reso conto che anche la coperta, fittamente annotata,
poteva a ben titolo far parte del fascicolo, quindi avrebbe
intenzionalmente saltato il numero 5 per ricomprenderla
nella numerazione, senza però provvedere alla correzione
dei numeri già apposti (fino al 4).[10]

La mancanza di simmetria tra la quantità della parte a sinistra della cucitura (10 carte) e quella a destra (8 carte) per
l'assenza delle carte in continuità destra con la 7 e la 8, è
oggetto anch'essa di diverse interpretazioni.

Come già anticipato, ed evidenziato dallo schema sopra
riportato, le carte 1/18 e 2/17 sono divise tra loro perché
corrispondono a quattro delle cinque avulse dal Codice
a seguito del furto di Guglielmo Libri. Le coppie di carte
3/16, 4/15, 5/14, 6/13 risultano bifogli integri; la carta 7
e la carta 8, entrambe collocate nella parte sinistra del fascicolo (fig. 18), sono scempie, senza la corrispondente a
destra, ove sono supportate da un'aletta (figg. 19-20); le
carte 9/12 risultano da un unico bifoglio; le carte 10/11, tra
le quali si trova la cucitura, sono riunite da un intervento di
restauro, poiché la carta 10 è l'altra delle cinque che furono
staccate dal Codice per essere vendute separatamente.

Carlo Pedretti ha ritenuto che le carte 7 e 8 derivino da un
unico bifoglio ripiegato e oggi separato poiché manomesso, forse ai tempi del Libri.[11] Anche Marinoni sembra fosse
orientato in questo senso, seppure mantenendo aperto
l'interrogativo circa la separazione delle due carte.[12]

Più recentemente Juliana Barone e Martin Kemp hanno
ipotizzato un più complesso sistema di interpolazioni del
Codice, sempre da parte di Leonardo,[13] che coinvolge an-

a page 5 (or an entire double sheet), and, as we have seen, another page (or another double sheet), which produced the red chalk "imprint" on page 14 recto, Leonardo's insertion of the ninth sheet (now pages 7 and 8) takes place exactly where expected: on top of the group of eight. That this sheet is unlikely to have been part of the original structure of the Codex is suggested by the fact that the cross-references on page 7 recto were written after the text of page 6 verso, developing its original content. It is possible that Leonardo also added others (folios 9–12, 10–11), and then, during the process of numbering them, he further separated, removed, and reordered pages. As we have indicated, nothing with Leonardo is ever easy to follow![14]

This theory is debatable for the following reasons. The existence of a fol. 5 or of an entire double sheet, which would have been positioned to the right of the present fols. 14 and 15, that is, between Leonardo's fols. 15 and 16, is based only on the omission of the number 5 in the handwritten numbering, because there are no noticeable leaps in content between the present fols. 15 recto and 14 verso. With regard to the possible existence of a folio between the present fols. 13 and 14, Barone and Kemp suggest that

Leonardo's manipulations are of several types. Evidence of his removal of pages is found when we look at what are (in the current structure of the Codex) two adjacent pages [13 verso and 14 recto]. Both show traces of red chalk. Oddly, though, the red chalk drawing of a flower on the verso of page 13 cannot have originated the "offprint" that appears on the

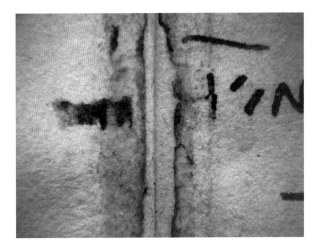

FIG. 18

cat. 9, fols. 7 verso–8 recto, viewed using a stereoscopic microscope / ripresa con il microscopio stereoscopico (detail of the stitching / dettaglio della legatura)

che l'assenza del numero 5 e presuppone l'inserimento di un'altra carta (o bifoglio) tra le attuali 13 e 14.

Let us suppose that Leonardo's Codex at one stage comprised more pages than in its present form. If we consider that there was indeed a page 5 (or an entire double sheet), and, as we have seen, another page (or another double sheet), which produced the red chalk "imprint" on page 14 recto, Leonardo's insertion of the ninth sheet (now pages 7 and 8) takes place exactly where expected: on top of the group of eight. That this sheet is unlikely to have been part of the original structure of the Codex is suggested by the fact that the cross-references on page 7 recto were written after the text of page 6 verso, developing its original content. It is possible that Leonardo also added others (folios 9-12, 10-11), and then, during the process of numbering them, he further separated, removed, and reordered pages. As we have indicated, nothing with Leonardo is ever easy to follow![14]

Questa ipotesi è da discutere per le seguenti ragioni. L'esistenza di una carta 5, o di un intero bifoglio che si sarebbe

FIG. 19

cat. 9, fol. 12 verso with the tabs of fols. 7 and 8 / c. 12 verso con le alette delle cc. 7 e 8, viewed using a stereoscopic microscope / ripresa con il microscopio stereoscopico (detail of the stitching / dettaglio della legatura)

FIG. 20

cat. 9, fols. 12 verso–13 recto with the tabs of fols. 7 and 8 / cc. 12 verso–13 recto con le alette delle carte 7 e 8, viewed using a stereoscopic microscope / ripresa con il microscopio stereoscopico (detail of the stitching / dettaglio della legatura)

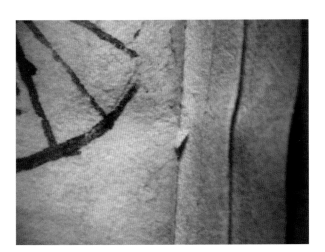

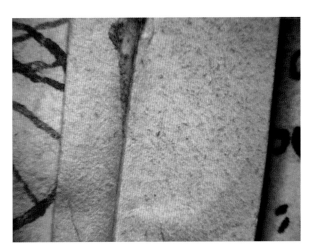

FIG. 21

cat. 9, fol. 14 recto, viewed under oblique light / ripresa a luce radente (detail of the area that might seem to be an "offprint" / dettaglio della zona che sembra un "offprint")

FIG. 22

cat. 9, fol. 14 recto, viewed under oblique light / ripresa a luce radente (detail of the area that might seem to be an "offprint" / dettaglio della zona che sembra un "offprint")

recto of page 14. This "offprint" is considerably lower down the page. It does not relate to the drawing on page 13, or to any other in the Codex. The "offprint" must have been produced by a drawing on a page that Leonardo removed during the process of reworking the Codex. After the exclusion of that page, Leonardo seems to have added two new passages at the bottom of page 14 recto, and running out of space, finished the lower one across page 13 verso.[15]

It is necessary to point out that the anomaly of the reddish traces on fol. 14 recto involves not only its position, lower than the small sketch on 13 verso, but also its nature, which is quite different from the trace that red chalk drawings leave on their facing folios. Observation of the original folio allows us to see that the surface of the paper in the area that might seem to be an "offprint" differs in texture from the rest of the folio. We can also see wrinkling in this area of the kind found when paper comes into contact with water or another damp substance. These observations were confirmed by using a stereoscopic microscope, which verified that surface of the paper in what could seem to be an "offprint" area was less compact than the rest of the sheet, and by oblique light, which enabled us to see the wrinkles more clearly (figs. 21–22). Thus, it is possible to suppose that water dripped onto that part of the page and was immediately wiped off, so that the stains typical of soaking did not form. What remains is a very slight abrasion of the surface and wrinkling typical of a dampened area. Furthermore, the drawing on fol. 13 verso is so delicate that without more thorough instrumental analysis it is not possible to obtain any significant additional information regarding its possible imprint on

collocato a destra tra le attuali carte 14 e 15, ossia le 15 e 16 di Leonardo, si basa solo sull'omissione del numero 5 nella numerazione autografa, non essendovi particolari salti di contenuto tra l'attuale carta 15 r e la 14 v. Per quanto riguarda la possibile esistenza di una carta tra le attuali 13 e 14, Barone e Kemp suggeriscono quanto segue:

> Leonardo's manipulations are of several types. Evidence of his removal of pages is found when we look at what are (in the current structure of the Codex) two adjacent pages [13 v and 14 r]. Both show traces of red chalk. Oddly, though, the red chalk drawing of a flower on the verso of page 13 cannot have originated the "offprint" that appears on the recto of page 14. This "offprint" is considerably lower down the page. It does not relate to the drawing on page 13, or to any other in the Codex. The "offprint" must have been produced by a drawing on a page that Leonardo removed during the process of reworking the Codex. After the exclusion of that page, Leonardo seems to have added two new passages at the bottom of page 14 recto, and running out of space, finished the lower one across page 13 verso.[15]

Al proposito, bisognerà segnalare, però, che l'anomalia che riguarda le tracce rosate sulla carta 14 r non coinvolge solo la sua posizione, più bassa del piccolo disegnino presente nella 13 v, ma anche la sua natura, affatto diversa dalle impronte che si trovano affrontate alle carte che contengono disegni a sanguigna. L'osservazione dell'originale permette di apprezzare una diversa consistenza superficiale del materiale cartaceo nell'area che potrebbe sembrare un "offprint" e una irradiazione di piccole pieghe, come si verificano intorno a zone interessate da contatto con l'acqua o altra sostanza umida. Tali rilevazioni sono state confermate dall'osservazione che ho potuto effettuare al microscopio stereoscopico (per quanto concerne la minore compattezza dello strato superficiale della carta), e

the facing page. Only such an analysis could give further clues as to whether fols. 7 and 8 are two parts of a single bifolio or belong to two different bifolios, removed from the right-hand part of the notebook by Leonardo before he numbered the pages, as the leap in content between fols. 13 recto and 12 verso allows us to hypothesize.

In addition to the handwritten numbering and the subsequent correction in another hand, the folios of the codex show other numbering in pencil, placed in the top corners on both the recto and the verso. These numbers mark different moments in the life of the manuscript, which was split up and reassembled to include the five folios removed from the notebook by Libri. One series of numbers is on the recto and verso of the folios and proceeds from 1 to 26, beginning with the present 3 recto, missing out the present 10 recto and verso, and terminating with the present 16 verso. (Therefore, all five of the pages removed and sold separately were missing when this numbering took place.) The other series is somewhat irregular and only numbers the folio starting from the present fol. 1 recto; the present fol. 2 is numbered on the verso; and the present fol. 3 recto is numbered as 4. After that, the numbering becomes regular up to number 9, which appears on the present fol. 8 recto, and then becomes irregular. It reaches 19 on the present fol. 18 recto. (It has probably been affected by the reinsertion of the lost pages.)

3. Historical Events

The Codex on the Flight of Birds was inherited by Francesco Melzi and on his death passed, like Leonardo's other codices, to the sculptor Pompeo Leoni. From 1622 to 1637, it belonged to the Milanese nobleman Galeazzo Arconati, who donated it to the Biblioteca Ambrosiana in Milan, where it remained until 1796, when it was taken to Paris on the orders of Napoleon Bonaparte, together with other manuscripts by Leonardo from the Biblioteca Ambrosiana, including the Codex Atlanticus.

The Codex on the Flight of Birds was stitched together with another manuscript, now identified as Manuscript B, which is held in Paris at the Institut de France. The codex was studied by Giambattista Venturi in 1797 and around 1830 by the scientific historian Libri, who stole it. Using the infallible method of placing threads soaked in acid between the pages and waiting for the corrosion to detach them, he was able to carry out numerous thefts (including the last

dall'osservazione a luce radente (per quanto riguarda l'irradiazione delle pieghe; figg. 21-22). Da questi elementi si può ipotizzare che in quel punto sia caduta dell'acqua prontamente asciugata, così che non si sono formati gli aloni tipici delle gore ma si è avuta una lievissima abrasione superficiale della carta e la tipica irradiazione circolare di pieghe intorno alla zona interessata dall'inumidimento. Peraltro il disegno della carta 13 v è talmente flebile da non poter dare esiti significativi circa la sua impronta sulla pagina a fronte, se non nel contesto di più ampie e auspicabili indagini strumentali.

Solo queste, infine, ci potranno dare ulteriori elementi per provare a risolvere l'interrogativo che resta aperto sulle carte 7 e 8, se cioè esse siano i due elementi di un unico bifoglio o se, invece, siano carte appartenenti a due bifogli diversi, elisi nella parte destra da Leonardo prima della numerazione del Codice, come il salto di contenuto tra la carta 13 r e la 12 v permette d'ipotizzare.

Oltre a quella autografa e alla successiva correzione d'altra mano, le carte del Codice presentano altre numerazioni a matita, apposte agli angoli alti sia del recto sia del verso. Rispecchiano momenti diversi del manoscritto, mutilo e reintegrato delle cinque carte avulse dal Libri. Una numerazione interessa recto e verso delle carte e procede da 1 a 26, a partire dalla attuale 3 r, saltando l'attuale 10 r e v, per terminare all'attuale 16 v (mancavano quindi tutte e cinque le carte distaccate e vendute separatamente). L'altra è piuttosto irregolare e numera solo la carta a partire dall'attuale 1 r; la seconda carta è numerata al verso; all'attuale carta 3 r è apposto il numero 4; la numerazione diviene regolare fino al numero 9 sull'attuale 8 r, poi perde di regolarità e giunge al numero 19 sull'attuale 18 r (risente probabilmente del progressivo reinserimento delle carte perdute).

3. Vicende storiche

Il Codice sul volo degli uccelli fu ereditato da Francesco Melzi e passò, alla sua morte, come altri codici di Leonardo, allo scultore Pompeo Leoni. Dal 1622 al 1637 appartenne al milanese conte Galeazzo Arconati, che lo donò alla Biblioteca Ambrosiana di Milano, dove restò fino al 1796, quando fu portato a Parigi per volontà di Napoleone Bonaparte, insieme agli altri manoscritti di Leonardo conservati presso l'Ambrosiana, compreso il Codice Atlantico.

Il Codice sul volo era cucito insieme ad un altro manoscritto, oggi indicato come Ms. B, rimasto a Parigi all'Institut de France. Qui fu studiato da Giambattista Venturi nel 1797 e, intorno al 1830, dallo storico della scienza Guglielmo Libri, il quale se ne appropriò. Attraverso l'infallibile metodo di collocare fili intrisi d'acido fra le pagine dei codici, atten-

pages of Manuscript E from the Institut de France, as mentioned in the essay by Carlo Pedretti in this volume),[16] and the entire Codex on the Flight of Birds, which he detached from Manuscript B by destroying the stitching that held the two together.

After the theft had been discovered, Libri went to England, taking with him a considerable amount of plunder, which he began to sell. In the case of the Codex on the Flight of Birds, he removed five pages to sell separately. Then, in 1868, he sold the mutilated notebook to Count Giacomo Manzoni of Lugo in Romagna. On Manzoni's death, in April 1892, it was sold to the Russian patron Theodore Sabachnikoff. In 1893, Sabachnikoff, together with the Leonardo scholar Giovanni Piumati, published the first facsimile edition, also managing to recover one of the missing folios (fol. 18). In December of the same year, Sabachnikoff made the munificent gesture of donating the manuscript to King Umberto I in Rome on December 31, 1893, and by early January it had reached Turin, along with a letter from General Ponzio Vaglio, Regent of the Ministry of the Royal House, addressed to Baron Domenico Carutti di Cantogno, the librarian of the Biblioteca Reale.[17] Thanks to Giovanni Piumati, through Senator Luigi Roux, fol. 17 was reintegrated in 1903, while the other three were found in England by Seymour De Ricci in 1913 and purchased by Enrico Fatio of Geneva. In 1920, Fatio donated them to King Vittorio Emanuele III, so that they could complete the Codex on the Flight of Birds at the Biblioteca Reale in Turin, where it is still held today.

[1] Marinoni 1982, p. 80.
[2] *Ibid.*, p. 77.
[3] Dondi 1991, p. XIII.
[4] Beltrami 1919, p. 99; Florence 2005, pp. 246–47, cat. IX.117.
[5] Marinoni 1973–80, vol. III, p. 95.
[6] Pedretti 1998, p. 271.
[7] Villata in Florence 2005, p. 202, cat. VI.82.
[8] Marinoni 1973–80, vol. III, p. 95.
[9] Marinoni 1982, p. 18: "On folio 211 r (formerly 77 recto-b) of the Codex Atlanticus, Leonardo recorded that he had collected fifty ducats from Santa Maria Nova on 'Saturday the fifth day of March'. On the verso of the folio the same date, invisible before restoration, reappears in complete form: '5 of March 1503'. The financial transaction was recorded differently in the registers of the hospital of Santa Maria Nova in Florence: 'on the IIII day of March 1502' (evidently according to the calendar *ab incarnatione*. Thus it appears that Leonardo, a Florentine, did not follow the Florentine calendar but rather the *a nativitate* tradition, and there seems to be a discordance between the fourth and fifth day of the month, more easily attributable to an error on Leonardo's part than to the hospital's accounts." Cf. also Beltrami 1919, p. 78; Florence 2005, pp. 246–47, cat. IX.117.
[10] Pedretti 1990, p. 110.
[11] *Ibid.*, p. 111: "The double folios are organised as a notebook, that is one on top of the other and then folded in half and

dendo che la corrosione operasse il distacco della pagina, egli compì numerosi furti (comprese le ultime pagine del *Ms. E* dell'Institut de France, per il quale si veda qui il testo di Carlo Pedretti),[16] tra cui l'intero codicetto oggi a Torino, per il quale bastò agire sulla cucitura con il *Ms. B* per ottenere il facile distacco di tutto il fascicolo.

Compiuto il furto e ormai scoperto, il Libri si rifugiò in Inghilterra con un'imponente refurtiva, cominciò a vendere i fogli di cui si era appropriato e, nel caso del *Codice sul volo*, asportò 5 carte per venderle alla spicciolata, mentre il fascicolo mutilo fu venduto nel 1868 al conte Giacomo Manzoni di Lugo di Romagna, alla morte del quale fu venduto (aprile 1892) al mecenate russo Teodoro Sabachnikoff. Questi ne pubblicava nel 1893, insieme al leonardista Giovanni Piumati, la prima edizione facsimilare, riuscendo anche a recuperare una delle carte mancanti (c. 18). Nello stesso anno il Sabachnikoff compiva il munifico gesto della donazione dell'autografo vinciano al Re d'Italia Umberto I (Roma, 31 dicembre 1893), e già agli inizi di gennaio il prezioso libretto giungeva a Torino, con la lettera del Reggente del Ministero della Real Casa, il generale Ponzio Vaglio, indirizzata al bibliotecario della Biblioteca Reale, barone Domenico Carutti di Cantogno.[17] Ad opera di Giovanni Piumati, tramite il senatore Luigi Roux, era reintegrata nel 1903 la c. 17, mentre le altre tre furono ritrovate in Inghilterra da Symour De Ricci nel 1913 e acquistate da Enrico Fatio di Ginevra. Questi, nel 1920, le donava al Re Vittorio Emanuele III, perché potessero andare a completare il *Codice sul volo degli uccelli* conservato nella Biblioteca Reale di Torino, dove ad oggi ancora si trova.

[1] Marinoni 1976, p. 73.
[2] *Ibid.*, p. 70.
[3] Dondi 1991, p. XIII.
[4] Beltrami 1919, p. 99; Florence 2005, pp. 246-47, cat. IX.117.
[5] Marinoni 1973-80, vol. III, p. 95.
[6] Pedretti 1998, p. 271.
[7] Villata in Florence 2005, p. 202, cat. VI.82.
[8] Marinoni 1973-80, vol. III, p. 95.
[9] Marinoni 1976, p. 15: "Nel f. 211 r (già 77 r. b) del codice Atlantico Leonardo registra di aver incassato 50 ducati da S. Maria Nova «sabato a dì 5 di marzo». Nel verso del foglio la stessa data, invisibile prima del restauro, riappare in forma completa «5 di marzo 1503». Nei registri dello Spedale di S. Maria Nova in Firenze l'operazione finanziaria è invece registrata «a dì IIII di marzo 1502» (evidentemente «ab incarnatione»). Appare dunque che il fiorentino Leonardo non segue lo stile fiorentino, ma quello «a nativitate» e che c'è una discordanza tra il giorno 4 e il 5, più facilmente imputabile a una confusione di Leonardo che ai contabili dello Spedale". Cfr. anche Beltrami 1919, p. 78; Marinoni 1973-80, vol. III, pp. 158, 163; Florence 2005, pp. 246-47, cat. IX.117.
[10] Pedretti 1990, p. 110.
[11] *Ibid.*, p. 111: "I doppi fogli sono disposti a quaderno, cioè uno sopra l'altro e quindi piegati a metà e tenuti insieme da una cucitura unica, per cui un numero uguale di carte dovrebbe

held together by a single stitching, so that there should be the same number of pages before and after the stitching. Instead, a double folio, probably halved at the time of Gugliemo Libri's tampering, had been added by Leonardo himself during the compilation and numbered by him 8 and 9, later corrected to 7 and 8 [...]. There is no doubt that the anomaly can be traced to Leonardo."

[12] Marinoni 1982, p. 14: "Leonardo was in the habit of writing on loose folios usually joined together in groups of eight and folded in half to form a series of sixteen sheets. In some cases additional folios could be added by placing them on top of the first eight as the book was spread open. In the present case, however, it seems that the ninth folio was not placed on top of the first eight, so as to be in a central position when the sheets were folded, but rather was folded first and inserted between sheets 6 and 9, forming sheets 7 and 8 of the series. The original double sheet that formed sheets 7 and 8 has been cut in half, however."

[13] Barone and Kemp 2008, pp. 99–102.

[14] Ibid., p. 102.

[15] Ibid., p. 99.

[16] Cf. pp. 151–67 in this volume.

[17] "Rome, January 5, 1894. Messrs Theodore Sabachnikoff and Giovanni Piumati have donated to our August Sovereign during a private audience, the handwritten manuscript herewith on the flight of birds and other topics by Leonardo da Vinci. It is not necessary for me to point out to your most honorable person the scientific and literary importance of this precious manuscript, which therefore I commend particularly to your well-known competence and I pray you to give it a suitable place in the Biblioteca Reale and to preserve it with the care it deserves. I take this occasion to thank you most honorable Baron, and to pay my homage. The Regent of the Ministry of the Royal House, General E. Ponzio Vaglio." Cf. Biblioteca Reale in Turin, Historical Archives, letter from the Ministry of the Royal Household, Secretariat of His Majesty the King, protocol 89, Rome, January 5, 1894 (English translation KMC).

trovarsi prima e dopo la cucitura. E invece un doppio foglio, dimezzato probabilmente al tempo delle manomissioni del Libri, era stato aggiunto da Leonardo stesso durante la compilazione e da lui numerato 8 e 9, poi corretto in 7 e 8. [...] Non c'è dubbio che l'anomalia risalga a Leonardo".

[12] Marinoni 1976, p. 12: "Leonardo aveva l'abitudine di scrivere su fogli sciolti, solitamente riuniti in gruppi di otto, piegati a metà e formanti una serie di 16 carte. In qualche caso altri fogli supplementari potevano essere aggiunti collocandoli sopra gli otto primitivi a fascicolo aperto. Nel caso presente sembra tuttavia che il nono foglio non sia stato posto sopra gli otto e quindi in posizione centrale, ma che sia stato singolarmente piegato e collocato tra le carte 6 e 9, formando le carte 7 ed 8 della serie. Tali carte o fogli 7 ed 8 risultano però divise l'una dall'altra".

[13] Barone and Kemp 2008, pp. 99-102.

[14] Ibid., p. 102.

[15] Ibid., p. 99.

[16] Cfr. pp. 151-67, infra.

[17] "Roma, li 5 gennaio 1894. I signori Teodoro Sabachnikoff e Giovanni Piumati hanno rassegnato in dono al nostro Augusto Sovrano, in particolare udienza, il qui unito autografo di Leonardo da Vinci sul volo degli uccelli e su varie altre materie. Non fa d'uopo che io faccia rilevare alla Signoria Vostra Onorevolissima la grande importanza scientifica e letteraria di questo prezioso manoscritto, che perciò io raccomando in particolare modo alla ben nota competenza di V.S., onde si compiaccia, come ne La prego, dargli un conveniente collocamento in codesta Reale Biblioteca e farlo custodire con quella speciale cura che merita. Con anticipate grazie Le rioffro, Onorevolissimo Signor Barone, gli atti della mia distintissima osservanza. Il Reggente il Ministero della R. Casa Generale E. Ponzio Vaglio". Cfr. Biblioteca Reale di Torino, Archivio Storico, lettera del Ministero della R. Casa, Segreteria di S.M. Il Re, prot. 89, Roma 5 gennaio 1894.

9

LEONARDO DA VINCI (1452–1519)

Codex on the Flight of Birds
Codice sul volo degli uccelli
ca. 1505

Pen and brown ink on paper (some pages include traces of black chalk and red chalk)
Penna e inchiostro bruno su carta (alcune pagine includono tracce di pietra nera e sanguigna)
213 x 153 mm (8 ⅜ x 6 inches)
Turin, Biblioteca Reale
(Cod. Varia 95)

Literature / Bibliografia: Uzielli 1884, pp. 389–412; Sabachnikoff and Piumati 1893; Carusi 1926; Giacomelli 1936, *passim*; Piantanida in Milan 1939, pp. 347–61; da Badia Polesine 1946; Uccelli and Zammattio 1952, pp. XXXII, 47, *passim*; Luporini 1953, pp. 107–9, pl. I; Pedretti in Turin 1975, pp. 41–50, cats. 24–25; Dondi 1975a and 1975b; Marinoni 1976; Firpo 1978; Galluzzi 1979, pp. 80–81; Marinoni 1982; Pedretti 1990, pp. 109–14, Appendix 1; Dondi in Giacobello Bernard 1990, pp. 108–13, pls. LII–LVI; Dondi 1991; Firpo 1991; Turin 1998–99, pp. 60–73, cat. II.2; Laurenza in Turin 2003–4, pp. 70–73, cat. 21; Laurenza 2004; Baselica 2005; Ancona 2005–6, pp. 70–74, cat. 22; Turin 2006, pp. 30–37, cat. I.2; Laurenza in Florence 2006–7b, pp. 156–65, cat. VII.5; Barone and Kemp 2008; Prum 2008; O'Grody in Birmingham and San Francisco 2008–9, pp. 56–96, cat. 12; Zanon 2009; Bambach 2009, pp. 38–39; Salvi in Venaria Reale (Turin) 2011–12, pp. 114–17, cat. 1.22; Moscow 2012–13.

The manuscript is composed of a hard cover and eighteen folios. The folios are bound in an asymmetrical arrangement, that is, with ten folios on the left-hand side and eight on the right-hand side. The outer front cover and the outer back cover include notes in another hand. On the outer front cover we find, centered at the top, the words LEONARDO DA VINCI. On the outer back cover there are some notes and numbers in various hands, including, at top center, the note in ink "sono folie 18" ("there are 18 folios"). More or less halfway down the outer back cover is the note "N d P," by Francesco Melzi, the compiler of the *Treatise on Painting*. These letters stand for "Nulla di Pittura" ("nothing on painting"), that is, nothing to be copied into the *Treatise*. Both the inner front and inner back cover are annotated. The codex was written backward and from right to left, starting from fol. 18 recto. Fol. 18 verso was at first left as a protective page but was later drawn and written on by Leonardo, either during the writing of the notebook or after it was full. Some of the sheets of the codex already contained sketches in red chalk on a variety of subjects. The folios were numbered by Leonardo himself, and he did so in the normal direction, that is, from the front to the last page. Leonardo's numbering, which omitted number 5, has been corrected in another hand. Flicking through the codex according to the numbering, it is clear that topics are organized more or less homogeneously. On the inner front cover we find notes and formulas for making medals and for treating enamels and similar materials. Fol. 1 recto to fol. 4 recto are devoted to notes and drawings on mechanics. Fol. 4 verso to fol. 18 recto are filled with notes and sketches on the flight of birds and on artificial flight. On fol. 18 verso we find biographical notes, sketches of mechanisms, one of the two "prophesies" on the "great bird" (the flying machine), and an important sketch of waterworks on a river. The river continues on the adjacent inner back cover, which also contains architectural drawings, notes on household expenses, and a second version of the "great bird" prophecy. Whereas sketches accompanying the writings on bird flight are fitted into the margins or within the text itself, drawings of the mechanical components for the flying machine's wing occupy larger areas of the sheets.

Il manoscritto è composto da una copertina di cartoncino e da 18 carte legate in maniera non simmetrica, cioè 10 dalla parte sinistra e 8 dalla parte destra. Il recto della prima coperta e il verso della seconda contengono annotazioni d'altra mano. Nella prima di coperta troviamo, centrata in alto, la scritta LEONARDO DA VINCI. Nell'ultima di coperta sono varie annotazioni e numeri di mani diverse, tra cui, in alto, centrata, si riconosce la scritta ad inchiostro "sono folie 18". Più o meno a metà è la sigla "N d P", del compilatore del *Libro di Pittura* (Francesco Melzi), ad indicare che vi è "Nulla di Pittura", vale a dire niente da riportare nel trattato sulla pittura. Le due pagine interne della coperta sono entrambe annotate. Il fascicolo è stato redatto a ritroso e da destra a sinistra, a partire dalla c. 18 r. La c. 18 v fu lasciata inizialmente come foglio di protezione e poi disegnata e annotata da Leonardo nel corso, o a ultimazione, della stesura del fascicolo. Questo è stato composto riunendo fogli già parzialmente utilizzati in momenti diversi, contenenti schizzi a sanguigna di soggetto vario. Le carte sono state numerate da Leonardo stesso nel senso normale di lettura di un testo, cioè tenendolo con la costola a sinistra.

La numerazione di Leonardo, che aveva saltato il numero 5, è stata corretta da un'altra mano. Percorrendo il fascicolo nel senso della numerazione, possiamo trovare le diverse materie organizzate più o meno omogeneamente. Nella pagina interna della prima coperta troviamo note e ricette sulla realizzazione di medaglie e il trattamento di smalti e materiali simili. Nelle carte 1-4 r vi sono esclusivamente note di meccanica. Le carte 4 v-18 r contengono le note sul volo degli uccelli e sul volo artificiale. Nella c. 18 v troviamo note biografiche, schizzi di meccanismi, una delle due 'profezie' sul "grande uccello" (la macchina per volare) e un'imponente schizzo di decorso fluviale incanalato, che continua nella contigua coperta interna. Quest'ultima accoglie un altro schizzo di decorso fluviale, disegni d'architettura, note di spese e una seconda versione della 'profezia' sul volo del "grande uccello". I testi sul volo degli uccelli sono organizzati con corredo di disegni disposti a margine della pagina o trasversalmente; i componenti meccanici per la realizzazione dell'ala per la macchina per volare occupano invece più ampie porzioni di foglio.

PS

PS

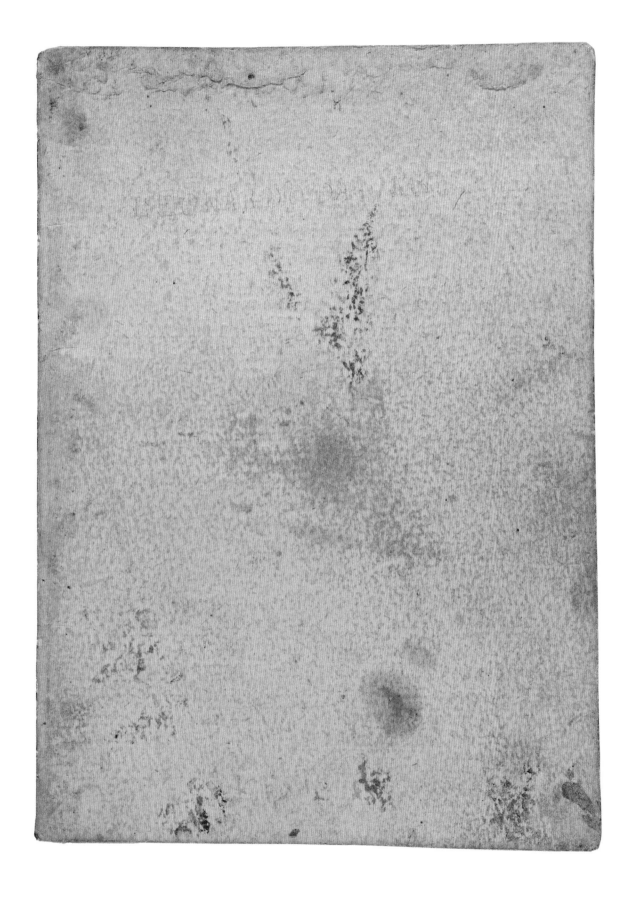

l, outer front cover /
prima coperta esterna

II, inner front cover /
prima coperta interna

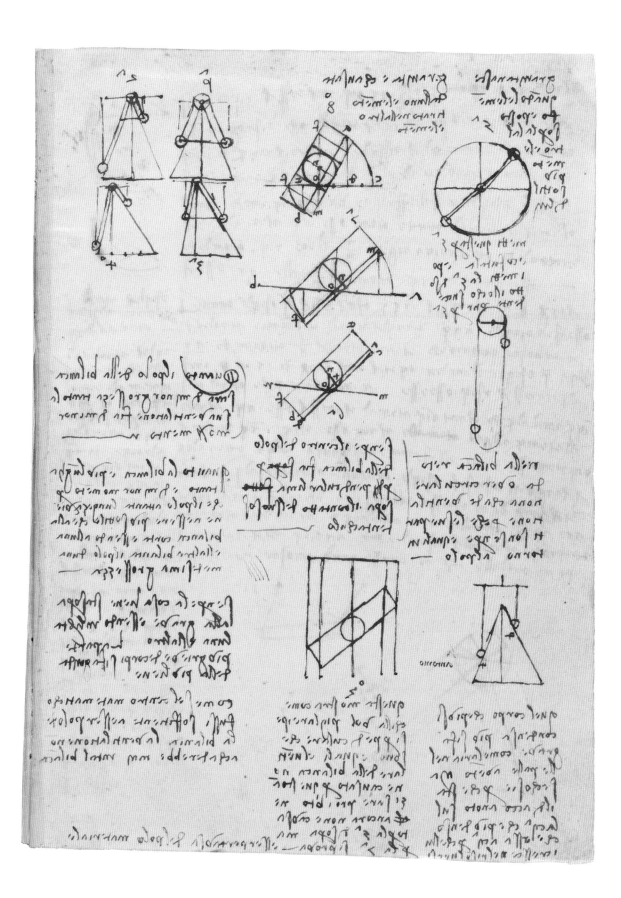

IV, fol. 1 verso

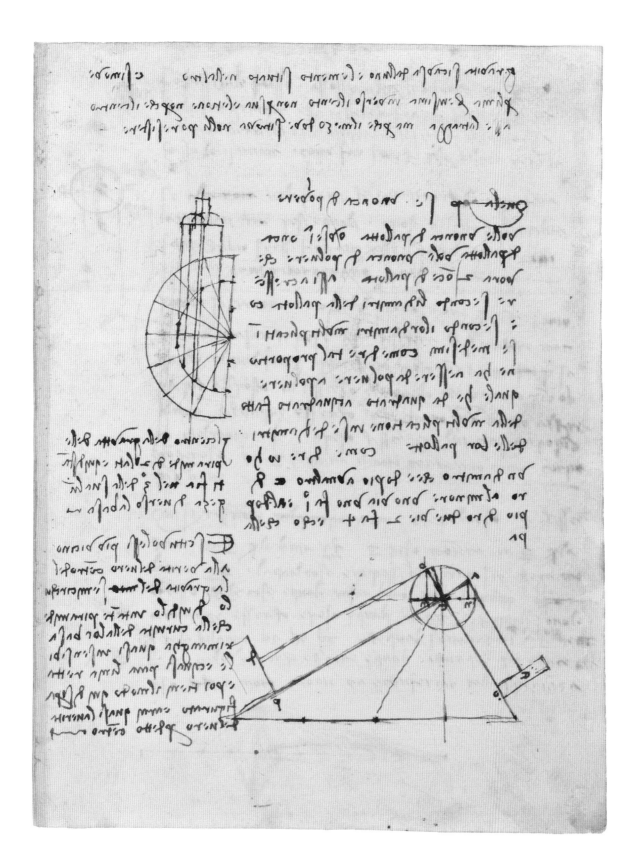

VI, fol. 2 verso

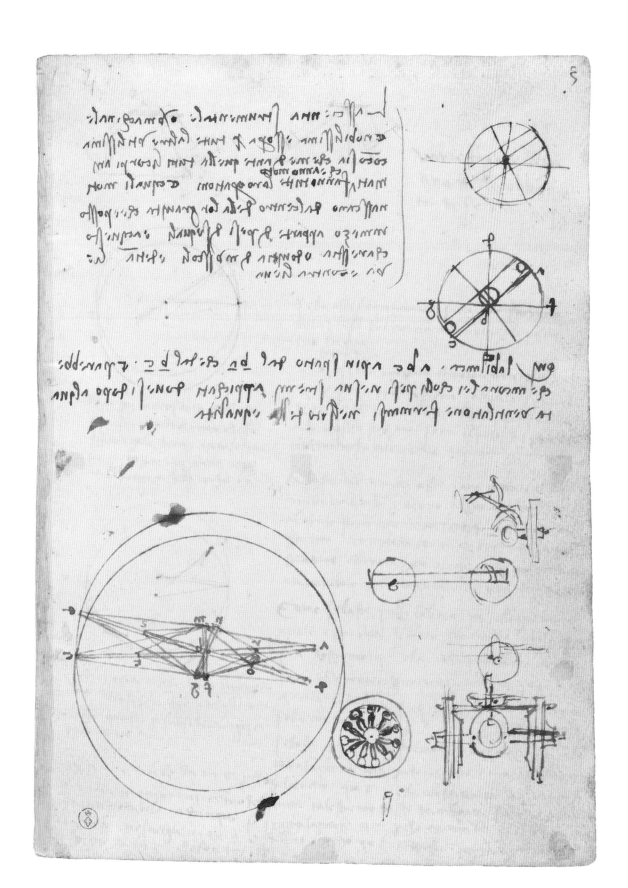

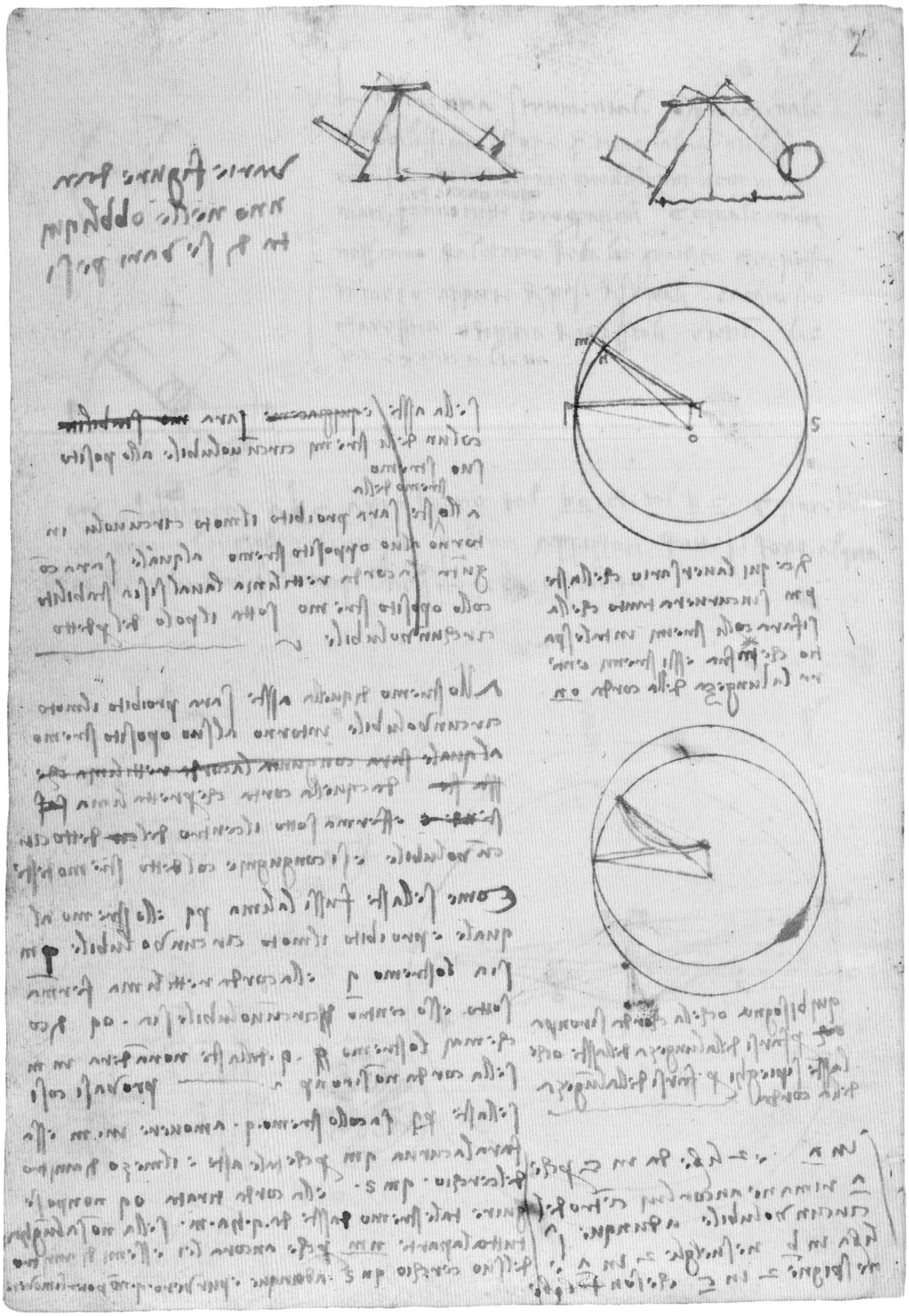

VIII, fol. 3 verso

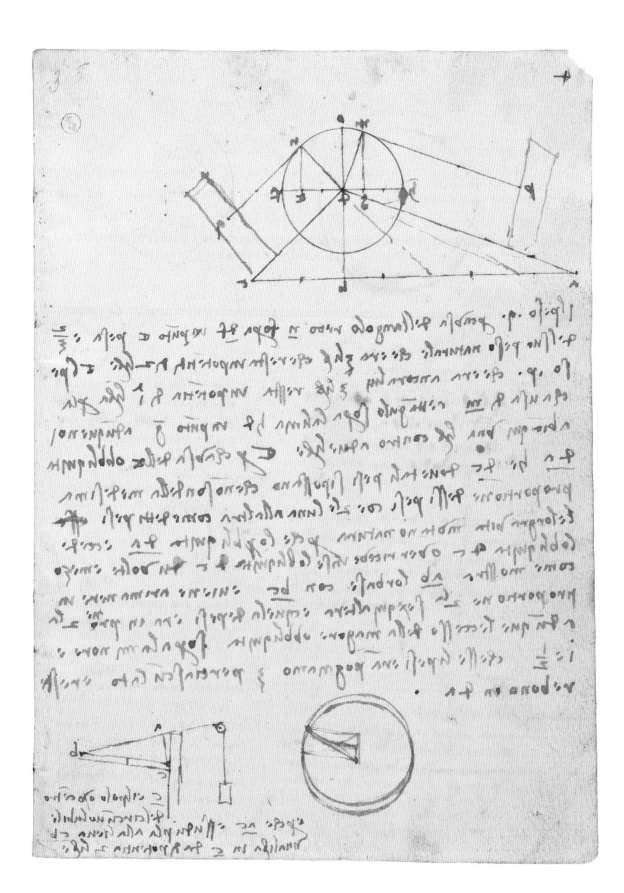

IX, fol. 4 recto

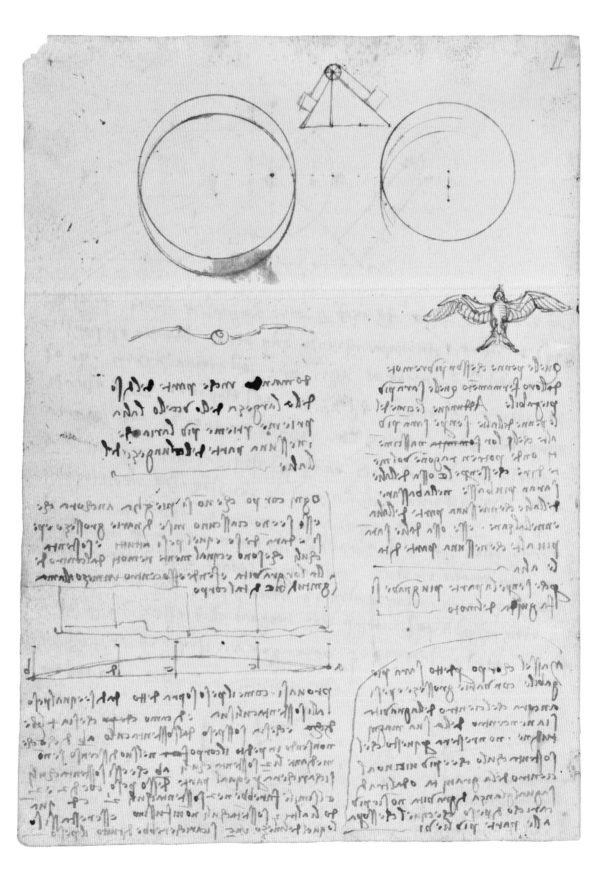

X, fol. 4 verso

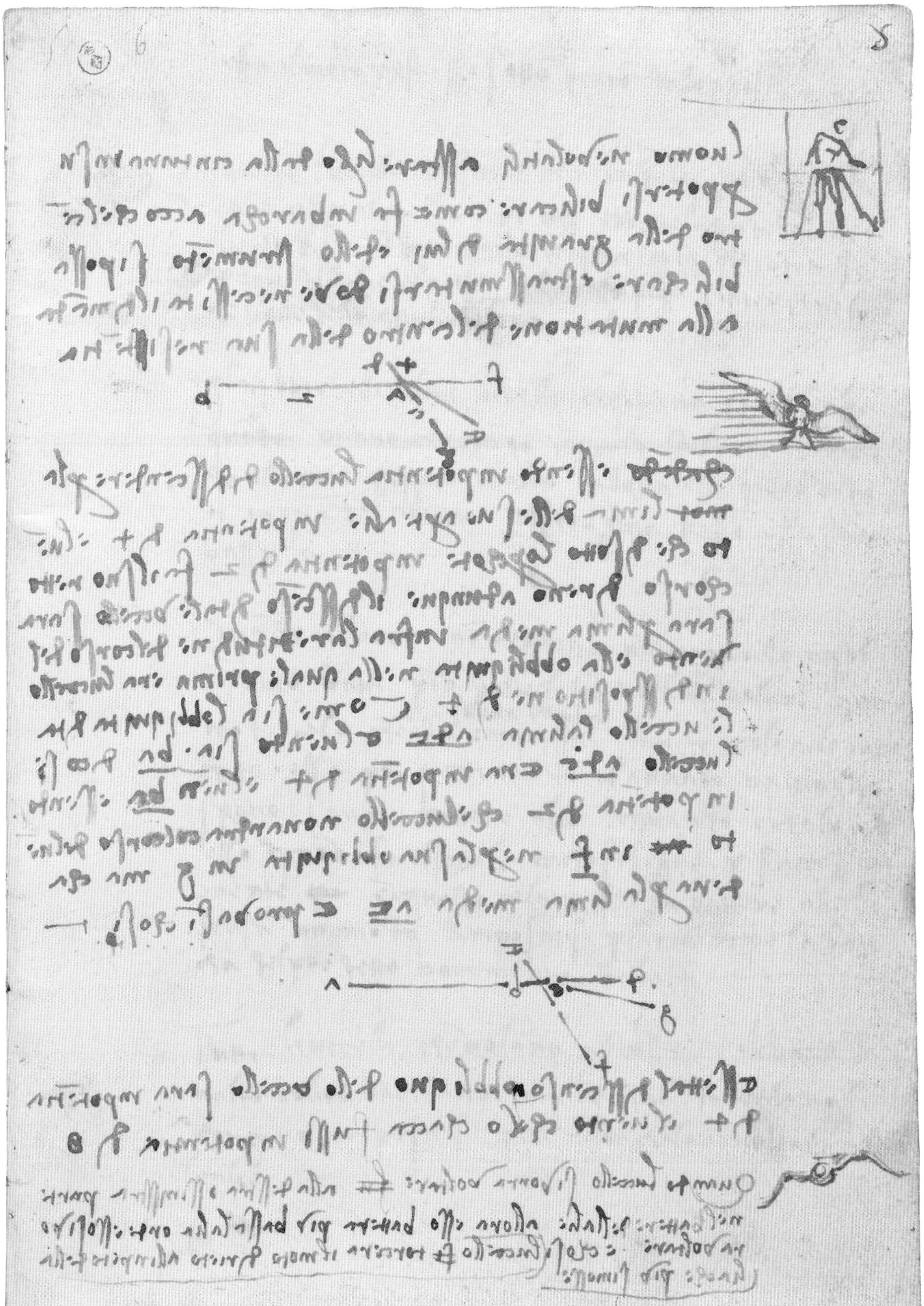

XI, fol. 5 recto

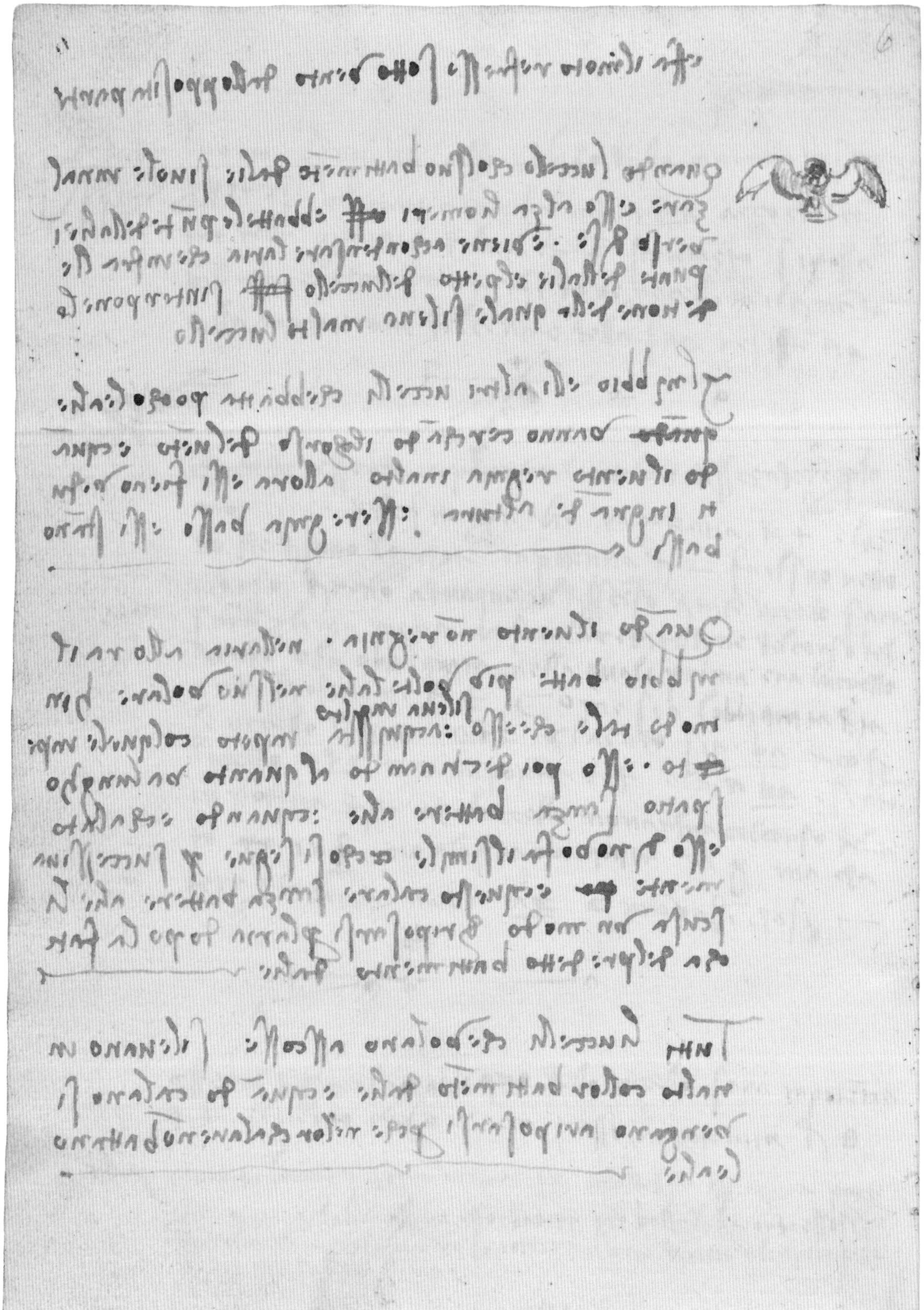

XII, fol. 5 verso

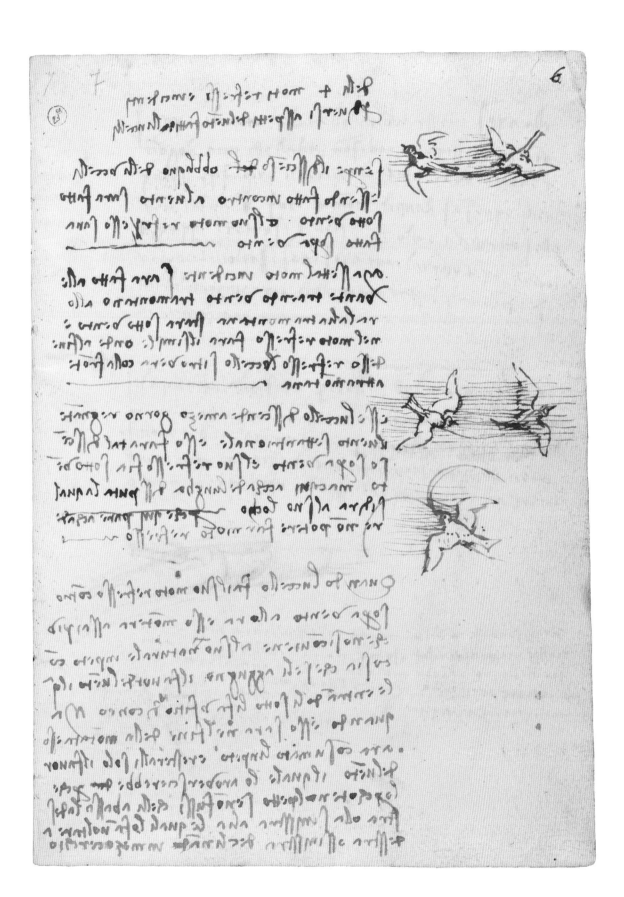

XVI, fol. 7 verso

XVII, fol. 8 recto

XVIII, fol. 8 verso

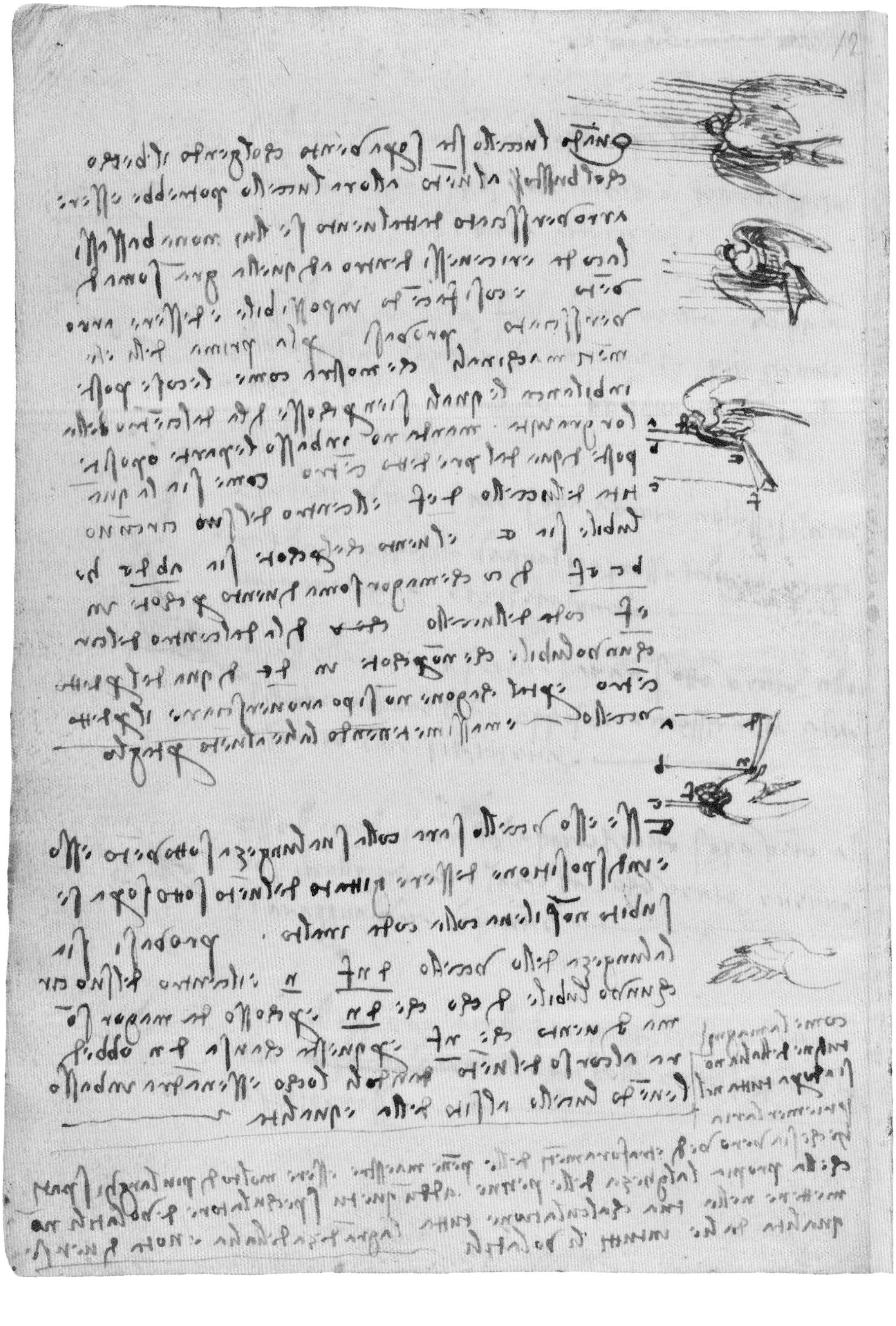

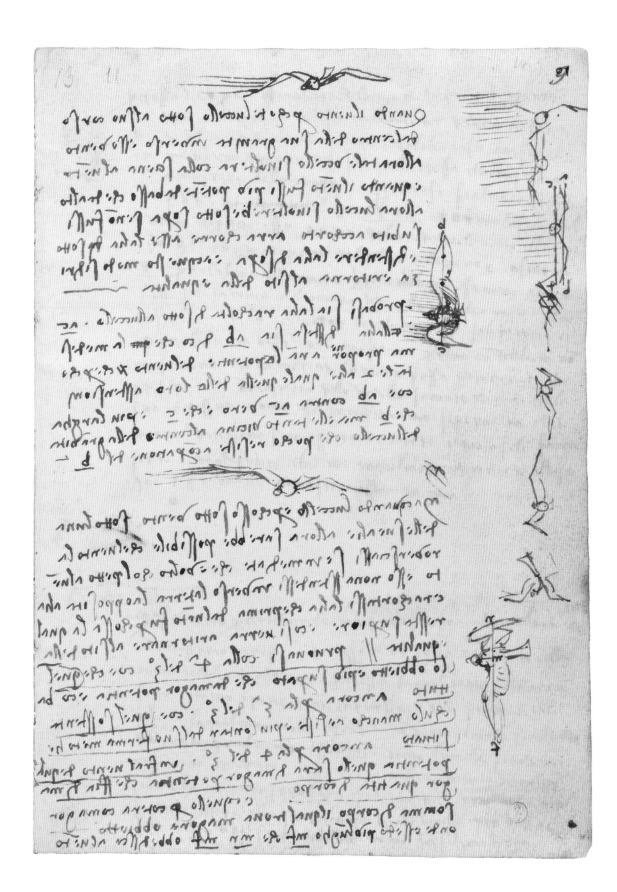

XXII, fol. 10 verso

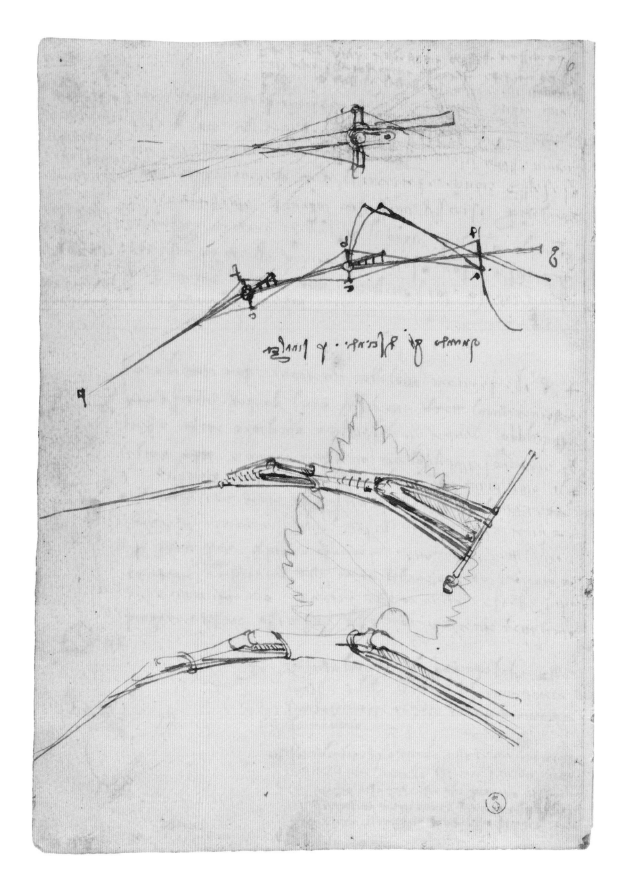

XXIV, fol. 11 verso

XXV, fol. 12 recto

XXVII, fol. 13 recto

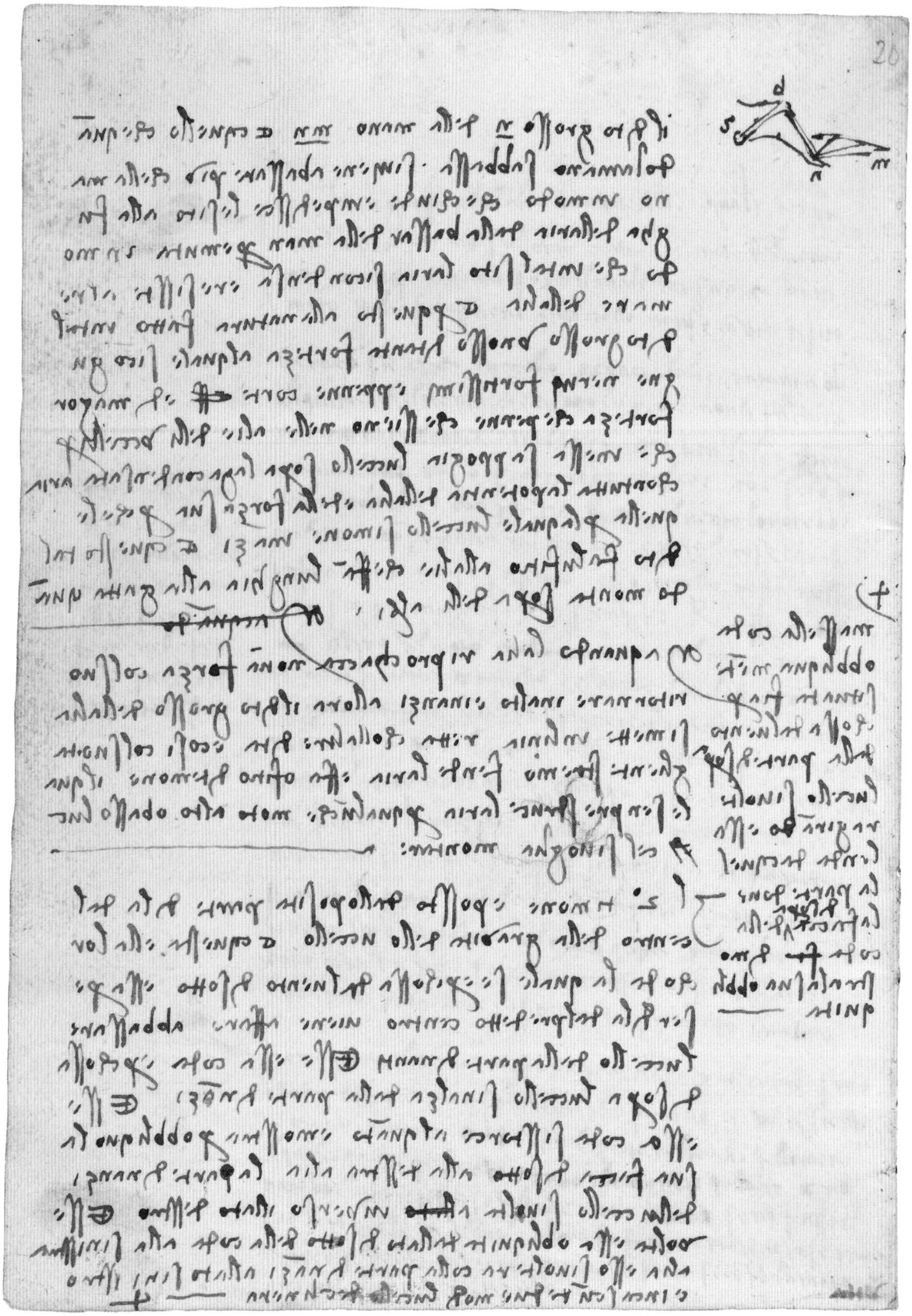

XXVIII, fol. 13 verso

XXIX, fol. 14 recto

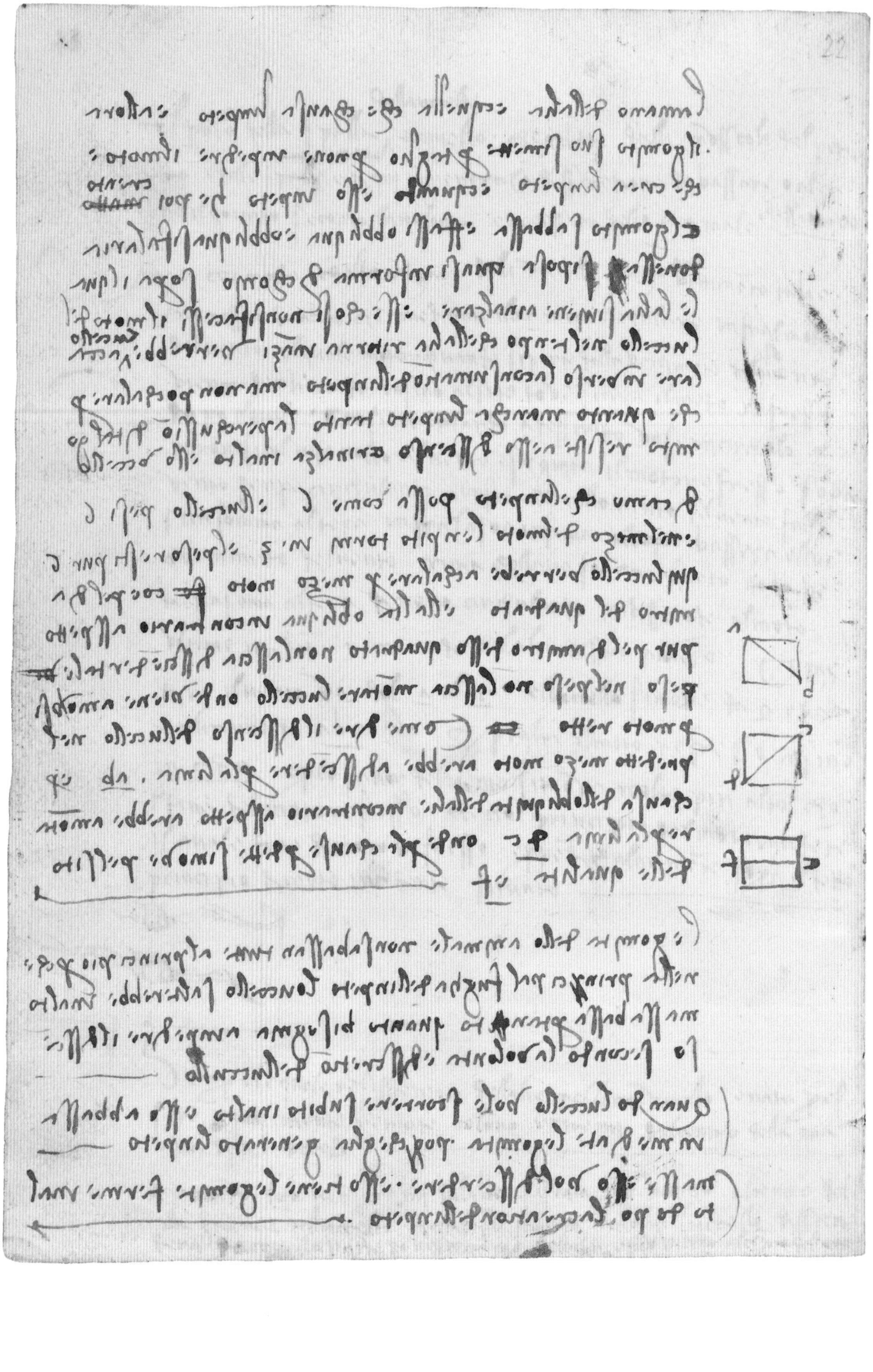

XXX, fol. 14 verso

XXXI, fol. 15 recto

XXXII, fol. 15 verso

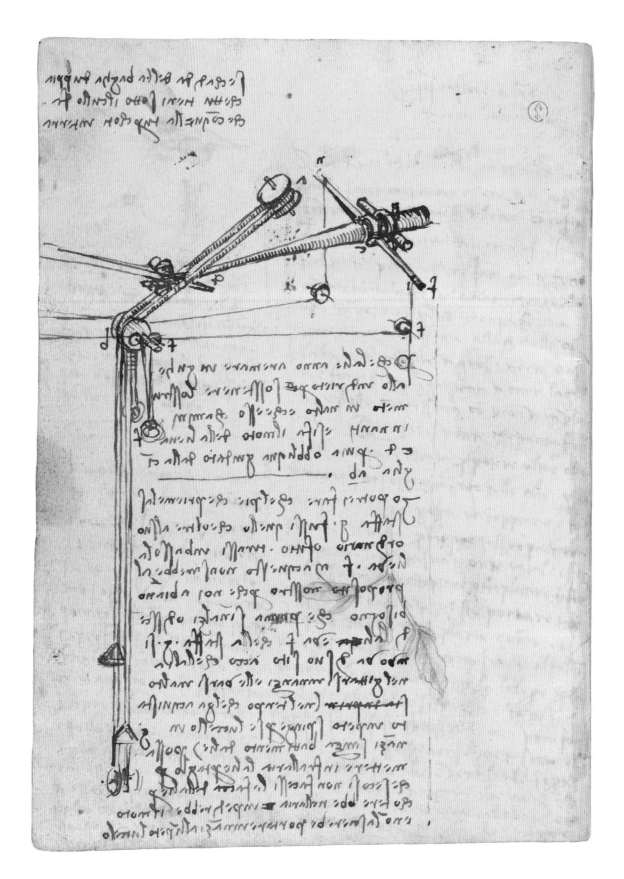

XXXIV, fol. 16 verso

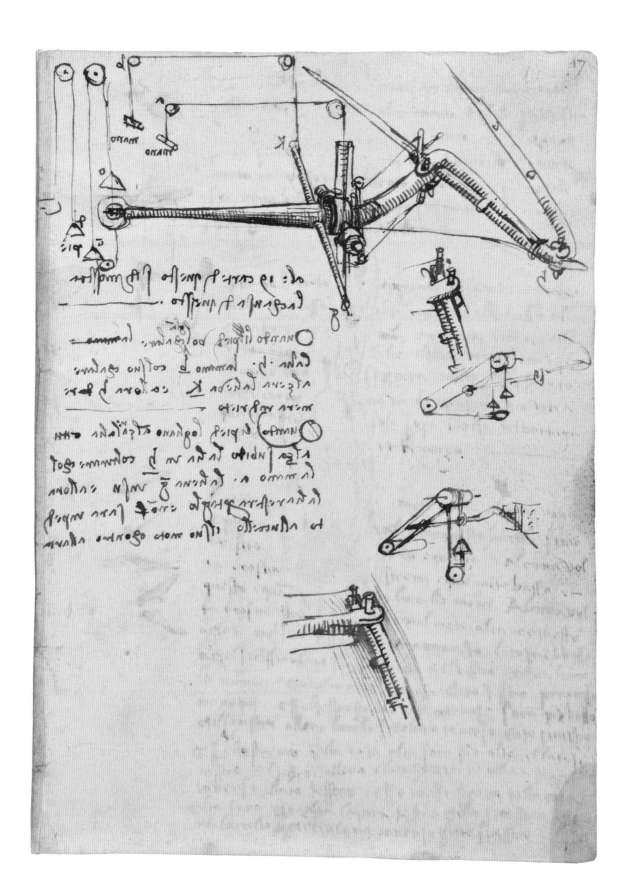

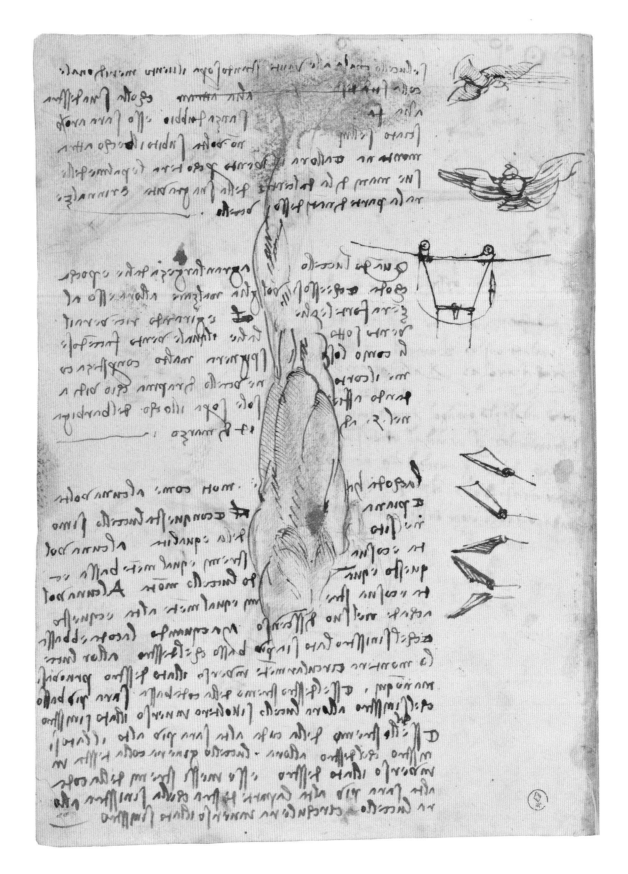

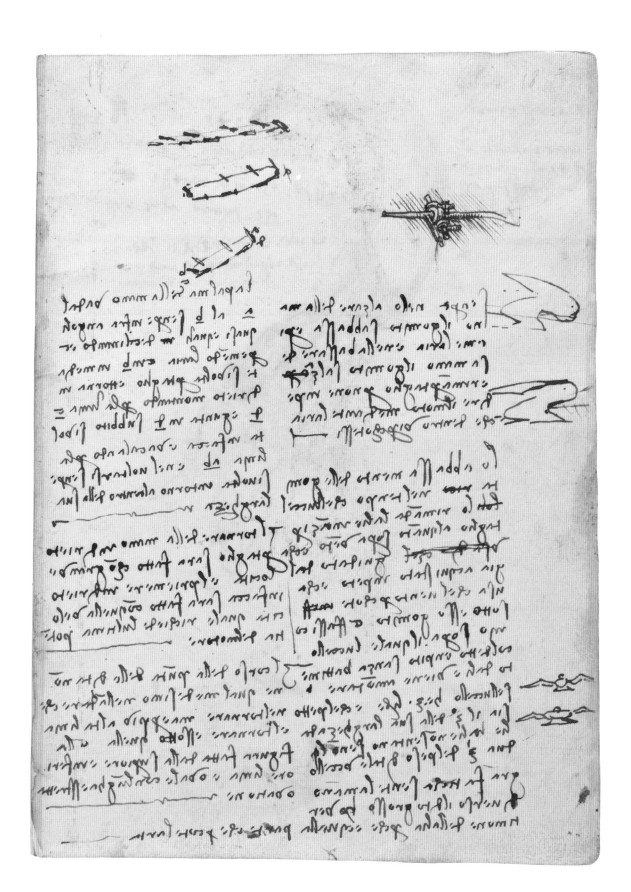

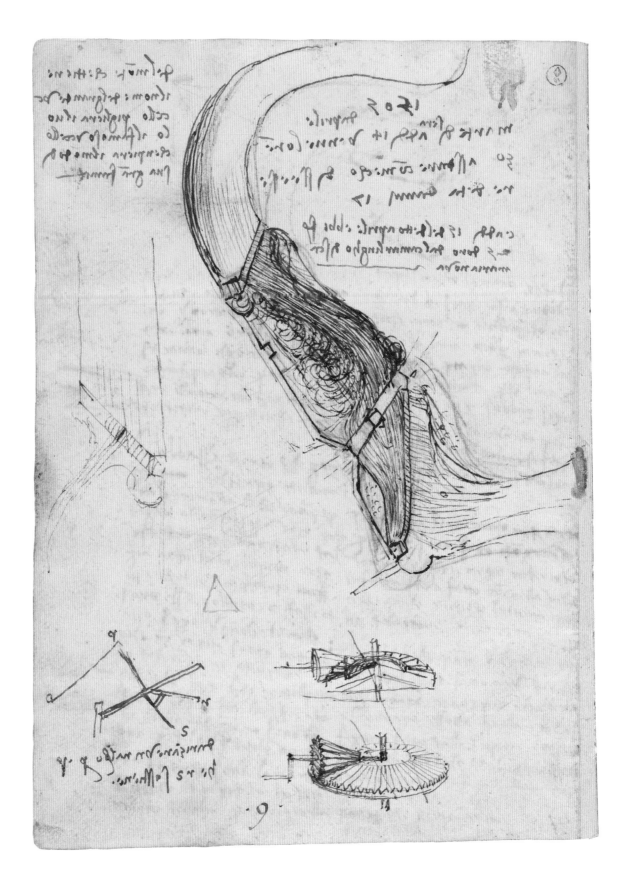

XXXVIII, fol. 18 verso

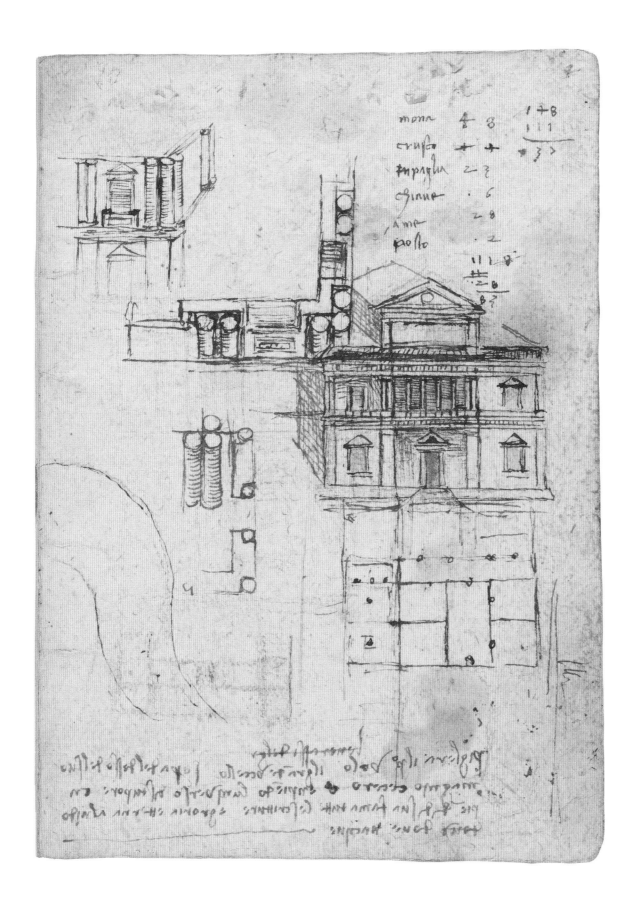

XXXIX, inner back cover /
seconda coperta interna

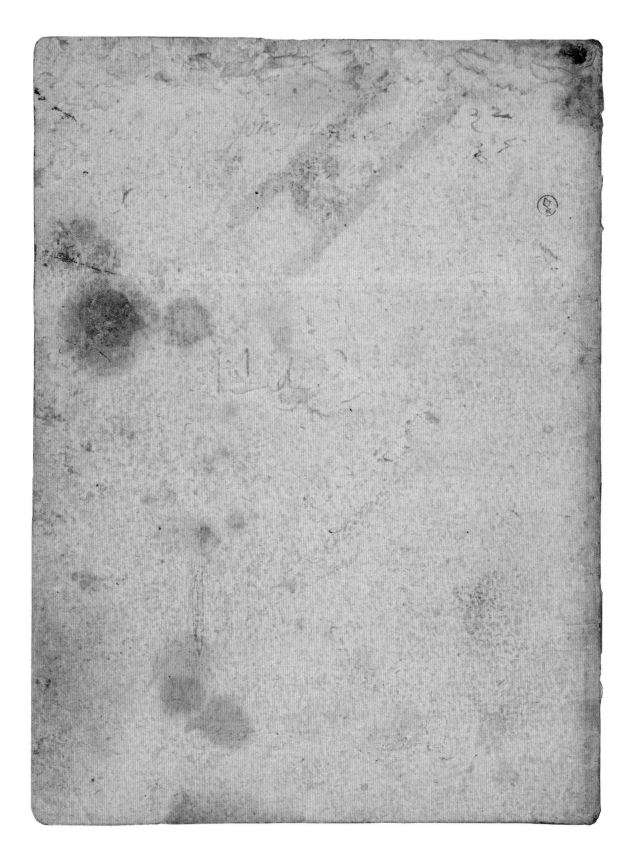

XL, outer back cover /
seconda coperta esterna

Codex on the Flight of Birds

Translated by Katherine M. Clifton from the transcription by Augusto Marinoni (Marinoni 1976).

Inner Front Cover

On striking medals. Mush of emery mixed with *acqua vite* or flakes of iron with vinegar, or ashes of walnut leaves, or ashes of finely chopped straw.

The diamond is crushed wrapped in lead, and pounded with a hammer, and this lead is rolled out several times and doubled. And it is kept wrapped in paper so that the powder does not spill out. And then you melt the lead, and the powder lies on the surface of the melted lead; it is then rubbed between two sheets of steel, so that it is finely pulverized. Then you wash it with nitric acid and the blackness of the iron will dissolve, leaving the powder clean.

Emery in large pieces is broken by putting it on many layers of cloth and hitting it from the side with a hammer; and in this manner it will break into scales little by little, and then it can be pounded easily. And if you put it on an anvil, you would never break it, because it is so big.

Anyone who grinds enamels must do so on plates of tempered steel with a steel grinder, and then add nitric acid, which dissolves all the steel that has rubbed off and mixed with the enamel, making it black, then it will be purified and clean. And if you grind on porphyry, the porphyry disintegrates and mixes with the enamel and spoils it; and the nitric acid will never remove it, because it cannot dissolve porphyry.

If you want to make a beautiful sky-blue color, dissolve the enamel with tartar, and then remove the salt from it.

Vitrified brass makes a fine red.

Fol. 1 recto

[top right]

Gravity is born when the element is placed above another element lighter than itself.

Gravity is caused by one element being drawn towards another element.

[left column]

Four sketches of weights on inclined planes, marked:
1st – 2nd – 3rd – 4th

The smaller the fulcrum of a balance, the lesser the momentum of its oscillation.

The longer the balance, the less the momentum, because the fulcrum at such a length comes to be thinner than that of the short scale, since the fulcrum of one and of the other balance are of the same thickness.

The lighter object is always above the heavier one, both of them being free. The heaviest part of a body will guide the lighter one.

For example, if the mathematical center were sufficient to be the fulcrum of the balance, it would never oscillate.

[central column]

Sketch of an inclined balance, marked:
8th – f a – n – f e o d c – b m

Similar sketch, marked: 7th – m – n – b o a – f

Similar sketch, marked: 6th – e – a – c - n – t – r o m – f – b – d

The center of the fulcrum of the balance should always be perpendicular above the attachment of its support.

Sketch of an inclined balance, marked: 5th

This shows that when we want to consider equal perpendicular weights, the oscillation of the balance is not caused by this, indeed it would be prevented, nor is it caused by the 5th above, but by the 7th and it can be proved that this happens because of the fulcrum itself.

[right column]

Sketch of an inclined balance, marked: 5th

Put this as 5th and confute it; and then put the 5th below it, in the next place also as 5th.

Sketch of a pulley

In the round or circular balance there is no oscillation, because its parts are always equal around the fulcrum.

Sketch of weights on an inclined plane, marked: 4 – 4; Antonio

The body that is most compressed is heavier: like the air in a balloon. But if this is so, why does ice float on water, if it is denser than water? Because it grows in forming itself.

Fol. 1 verso

Sketch of an arc and chords, marked:
v p – 14 7 – m – 14 r – 8 – n

The weight p will descend faster by the arc than by the chord, and the reason is that to the middle of the arc, it falls from p to r by a perpendicular line, and the remainder of the course is by reflex motion, which has a velocity of $7/8$ of the velocity of the incident motion, as proven in the 5th. And if you let this weight descend by the chord

p n, its speed is an entire half slower than the motion *p r*, that is $^4/_8$ and we already said that the reflex motion *r n* is $^7/_8$ of the motion *p r*.

Let us say weight *p*, descending by *p r*, descends in eight units of speed and has traveled half the arc *p r n*, and the reflex motion *r n* is diminished $^1/_8$ of the incident motion, which come to be in total 8 and 7. 15 units of time, during which *p* has passed the arc and reached *n*.

And if this weight falls by chord *p n*, it falls at half the speed than it would have if it fell by the perpendicular line *p r*, because that chord cuts the right angle *r p v* in half. Therefore it is evident that it is slower by half; so that, when the weight has descended half the arc in 8 units of time, it has descended half the chord in 16 units of time; and then the other half of the arc is made up of 7 units of power and the rest of the chord is still made up of 16, that is, in total one is made up of 32 and the other of 15.

[margin]

Sketch of an arc and chord

The velocity of the weight along the arc, that is 8 and 7 units of velocity.

The velocity of the weight, descending along the chord, is half the speed, because the chord cuts the right angle *r p v* in half, and therefore it has half the speed it would have descending by the perpendicular line *p r*. So, it will be the slower by half, and for this reason we say that the weight descends by the chord in 4 and 4 units of velocity and by the arc in 8 and 7 units of velocity, which makes 15 units of velocity by the arc and 8 by the chord. Thus it is faster by the arc than by the chord as much as 15 is greater than 8, which is 7; that is the $^7/_8$ faster.

Fol. 2 recto

Gravity is caused by one element situated in the other, and it moves along a very short line towards the center, not by choice, nor because the center itself attracts it, but because the medium in which it exists cannot resist it.

If an ounce of powder requires a one-ounce ball, or if a one-ounce ball requires an ounce of powder, how much powder will a two-ounce ball require? It must increase according to the diameters of the ball, that is according to the diameters multiplied by themselves, that is to say: this proportion must be powder to powder, which is square to square made by multiplying by itself the diameter of the balls. That is to say, if I have a diameter that is double another one, and I will say of the smaller: one times one equals one, and of the double one I will say two times two makes four; so that the ball …

Diagram of a steelyard balance linked to a double semicircle divided into sections

Let the center of gravity of the pyramid with two equidistant sides be in the third of its length towards the base.

And if you want to be closer to the true center of gravity of the semicircle, divide it into so many pyramids that the curvature of their bases is almost imperceptible and almost appears to be a straight line, and then you will have the example shown here, and you will almost have the truth of the aforesaid true center.

Sketch of a pulley with two weights on inclined planes, marked: b a – m c n – d e – p o

Fol. 2 verso

If it were possible to suspend the steelyard balance at its center of gravity, it would always remain still without any oscillation, in whatever slanted position it were situated, as can be seen in a round balance.

Sketch of a pulley, marked: a – e b d – c – f – 4 – 4

If two equal weights are attached to the circumference of a wheel and placed in equilibrium, undoubtedly, if they are taken away from that equilibrium, they will never return to it on their own.

It can be proven, contrary to the proposition of the adversary. I say that each of the weights *a c* wants to descend, but the one that can move on a straighter course will descend faster than one on a more oblique course. Therefore, since the movement *a d* is straighter than the movement *c f*, it will descend as if it were a heavier object, and *c* will follow the opposite motion as a lighter body.

Here I will answer that, if the weight *a* descends to *d* by the line *a d*, the weight *c* will rise to *e* by the line *c e*. This is impossible, because I have already established that things which are equal do not overtake each other. Therefore, the weights *a* and *c* being equal and the arms of the steelyard balance *b a* and *b c*, being equal, and the arcs of the movements *a d* and *c e* with their chords and segments being equal, there is no reason for movement here, as confirmed by experience.

Fol. 3 recto

Instrumental or mechanical science is very noble and above all very useful, because it is thanks to this [science] that all animated bodies, which are capable of movement, perform all their operations. These movements are born from their center of gravity, which is positioned between parts of unequal weight, and has a deficiency or sufficiency of muscles as well as lever and cantilever.

Two diagrams of steelyard balances, marked: d – a – g b f – c – e

Here the steelyard balance *a b c* has more space from *b a* than from *b c* and it would seem that with the weights attached to its ends it would stop on a horizontal line after a number of oscillations.

[bottom left]

Sketch of a system of rods tied with ropes, marked:
e S m n – c b r a – t o – g f d

[bottom right]

Sketches of a wheel and a cart (and its parts)

Fol. 3 verso

Two sketches of weights on inclined planes

Varying figures give varying weights in their obliquities.

[left column]

Sketch of a rod tied with a rope, marked: m – n – q p – o S

If one of the ends of the rod can rotate around its opposite end …

The end of the rod will be prevented from rotating around its opposite end, which will be tied to a rectilinear rope, which will be tied at the other end below the fulcrum of said rotational movement.

The end of the rod will be prevented from rotating around its opposite end by the rope, which is fixed in a straight line below said rotational movement and is tied to the end of the rod.

If the rod were the line *p q*, and the end, which is prevented from making a circular movement *q m*, were *q*, and the rectilinear rope fixed below the rotational center were *o q*. I say that the end *q* of the rod will not reach *m*, unless the rope breaks.

It can be proven thus: if the rod *p q* has to move the end *q* to *m*, it will trace a curve *q m*, because the rod is half the diameter of the circle *q m S*, and the taut rope *o q* cannot follow the end of the rod from *q* to *m*, unless the entire part *n m* is lengthened, because it too is half the diameter of its circle *q n S*. So, it is true that *q* cannot move.

[right column]

Here the adversary says that the rod *p m* will bend sufficiently for its ends to fit within that space, and the length of the rope *o n* will fit between those ends.

Similar sketch, with curved rod

Here it is necessary for either the rope to break in order to become the length of the rod, or for the rod to bend in order to become the length of the rope.

[bottom right]

[continued from fol. 4 recto] at *a* and 2 pounds at *c* because *a* remains the fulcrum of the rotation. Therefore 1 pound at point *b* pulls 2 pounds at *a* and pushes 2 pounds at *c*, which makes 4 pounds.

Fol. 4 recto

Sketch of a pulley with weights on inclined planes, marked:
o – m – n – f e d g h p – q – c b a

Weight *q*, because of the right angle *n* above *d f* at point *e*, weighs $2/3$ of its natural weight, which was 3 pounds, which retains the power of 2 pounds. Weight *p*, which was also 3 pounds, has a potential of one pound because of the right angle *m* above the line *h d* at point *g*. So, here we have one pound against two pounds. And on account of the obliquities *d a* and *d c*, where the weights rest, which are not of the same proportion as these weights, that is one double the other like the said weights, their gravities change in value, because the obliquity *d a* exceeds the obliquity *d c*, or rather contains in itself the obliquity *d c* two and a half times, as shown by their base *a b* with *b c*, and turns out to be in double sesquialtera proportion, and that of the weights was in double proportion. Hence the difference between the greater obliquity and the lesser is $1^1/2$; so that if the weights were, let us say, 3 on each side, they would rest on *d a*

Sketch of a pulley supporting a pole, marked: a – b c

c is the fulcrum or center of the rotation, and since *a c* is equal to half the lever *c b*, one pound at *c* gives a force of 2 pounds [continued on fol. 3 verso]

Fol. 4 verso

Three sketches similar to those on fol. 4 recto

[right column]

Sketch of a bird seen from below

The [part of] the feathers that is farthest from the root will be more flexible. Therefore the wing feathers will always be wider at the tips than at the roots; so that we can reasonably say that the bones of the wings will always be lower than any other part when the wings are lowered, and when the wings are raised the wing bones will be higher than any other part of the wing. Because the heaviest part always guides the movement.

[left column]

Sketch of a bird seen from the front

I wonder in what part of the underside of the width of the bird the wing compresses the air more than in any other part of the length of the wings.

All bodies that do not bend, even if they are all of varying sizes and weights, will exert identical force on all the supports that are equally distant from their center of gravity, because it is centered in the middle of the magnitude of the body.

Two sketches of a wing, marked: b d e c a

It can be proven that the aforesaid weight exerts equal force on its supports. And let us say that it is 4 pounds and that it is borne by the supports *a b*. I say that if the body is not impeded in its descent, except for the 2 supports *a b*, that these supports will bear the load equally, that is 2 and 2; and the same would happen for the two secondary supports *c d*, even when the other 3 supports were not present: and if only the middle one *c* remained, it would bear all the weight.

But if the said body were flexible with varying thicknesses and weights, and the center of gravity were at its center of magnitude, this would not mean that the support closest to the center of gravity, or to inequalities in gravity, would not bear more weight than that which is above the lighter parts.

Fol. 5 recto

Sketch of a man inside a machine

A man in a flying machine must be free from the waist up so that he can keep his balance, as he would in a boat, so that his center of gravity and that of the instrument can balance and shift as necessary, according to the shifts in the center of his resistance.

Sketch of a bird

Diagram, marked: d 4 – b 2 a f – c – e – g

The bird, being capable of descending by the line of its open wings with a force of 4, with the wind striking it from below a force of 2, will move in a straight line, we will say then that the descent of said bird will be by the median line between the straight course of the wind and the obliquity of the bird under force 4. For example: let the obliquity of the bird be the line *a d c* and the wind be *b a*. I say that if the bird *a d c* had a force of 4 and the wind *b a* had a force of 2, the bird will not follow the course of the wind to *f*, nor by its own obliquity to *g* but will descend by the median line *a e*. It can be proven thus:

Similar diagram, marked: e – a b c d – g – f

And if this oblique descent of the bird has a force of 4 and the wind driving it has a force of 8 …

Sketch of a bird

When the bird wants to turn to the right or to the left it begins by flapping its wings, then it will flap the wing on the side to which it wants to turn lower

down, and so the bird will twist the movement behind the impetus of the wing that moved most.

Fol. 5 verso

[continued from fol. 6 recto] and it makes the reflex movement under the wind on the opposite side.

Sketch of a bird

When the bird wants to ascend by flapping its wings, it raises its humeri and flaps the tips of the wings towards itself and this compresses the air, which is interposed between the wings of the bird and the breast, this compression is what raises the bird.

The kite and other birds of prey that flap their wings only a little, seek out the currents of wind, and when the wind blows high up, they can be seen at great heights, and if it blows low down, they remain low.

When the wind is not blowing, then the kite flaps its wings more often when flying, so that it rises to a great height and gains impetus, with which it then descends somewhat and travels for long distances without flapping its wings. And when it has descended, then it does the same again, and so it continues. And this descending without flapping their wings allows them to rest in the air after the effort of flapping their wings.

All the birds that fly in stops and starts, rise by flapping their wings, and when they descend they can rest, because they do not flap their wings when descending.

Fol. 6 recto

On the 4 reflex and incident motions of birds in varying directions of the wind

Double sketch of a bird

The oblique descent of the birds, being made against the wind, will always be made under the wind, and its reflex motion will be made above the wind.

But if this incident motion is made towards the east when the wind is blowing from the north, then the wing turned towards the north will be below the wind and in the reflex motion it will do the same, so that at the end of this reflex motion the bird will find itself facing north.

Double sketch of a bird

And if the bird descends to the south, in a prevailing north wind, it will make its descent above the wind and its reflex motion under the wind. But here begins a long debate, which will be set out in the appropriate

place, because here it seems that the bird would not be able to make a reflex motion.

Sketch of a bird

When the bird makes its reflex motion against and above the wind, then it will rise much more than it should from its natural impetus, being also favored by the wind, which, entering below it, acts as a wedge. But when it is at the end of its ascent, it will have used up the impetus and will remain there only supported by the wind, which could overturn it, because it strikes the breast, if it did not lower the right or left wing, which will make it turn to the right or the left, descending in a half circle [continued on fol. 5 verso]

Fol. 6 verso

The movement of the bird must always be above the clouds, so that the wings do not get wet and to look over more towns and to escape the danger of the whirling of the winds among the mountain passes, which are always full of gusts and eddies of wind. And apart from this, if the bird should overturn, you have sufficient time to turn it back with the instructions already given, before it falls to the ground.

Sketch of a bird

If the tip of the wing is struck by the wind and this wind enters under said tip, then the bird will be in a situation where it can be overturned, if the bird does not use one of two remedies, that is either it enters immediately with the tip under the wind, or it lowers the opposite wing from the middle outwards.

Sketch of the joints of an artificial wing, marked:
leather tanned with alum

Sketch system of braces for an artificial wing, marked:
a b c d – e f g h

a b c d are four upper nerves for raising the wing, and they are as powerful as the lower nerves *e f g h* should the bird overturn, and they resist this above as below, although only one thick and wide tanned leather tie, might by chance be sufficient, but after all we will judge from experience.

Fol. 7 recto

The aforesaid bird must with the help of the wind rise to a great height, and this for its safety, because, even if all the aforesaid revolutions happened, it would have time to return to the state of equilibrium, providing its limbs are very strong, so that they can resist the fury and impetus of the descent with the aforesaid solutions, and its joints must be of strong tanned leather and its nerves of very strong raw silk rope. And it must not be hampered by any iron fittings, be-

cause they will soon snap as they twist or wear out, so it is not wise to burden yourself with them.

Sketch of a wing with a single brace, marked: a

The nerve *a*, used to extend the wing, must be made of thick tanned leather so that, if the bird overturns, it can overcome the fury of the air that strikes the wing and would close it, because this would be fatal for the bird. But for greater safety, you will make exactly the same nerve outside and inside, and you will be beyond all fear and danger.

Detail of the attachment of the brace, marked: a b c d

a b c are the places where the nerves of the three joints of the fingers of the wings are attached; *d* is where the motor of the lever *a d*, which moves the wing, is located.

Fol. 7 verso

When the edge of the tip of the wing is against the edge of the wind, a small movement will be sufficient to place it below or above the edge of the wind and the same happens with the tip and the sides of the tail and similarly to the rudders of the humeri of the wings.

The bird's descent will always be by the end that is closest to its center of gravity.

The heaviest part of the descending bird will always be in front of the center of its magnitude.

3rd — When the bird hovers in the air, without the favor of the wind and without flapping its wings, in a state of equilibrium, this shows that the center of gravity is concentric with the center of its magnitude.

Sketch of a bird

4th — The heaviest part of the bird descending with its head down, will never be higher than or on a level with its lighter parts.

Sketch of a bird

If the bird falls tail first by throwing its tail back, it will bring itself to a state of equilibrium, and if it were to throw it forward, it would overturn.

Sketch of a bird

1st — When the bird is in a state of equilibrium, it will throw the center of resistance of the wings behind its center of gravity, then the bird will descend headfirst.

Two sketches of birds

2nd — And the bird that is in a state of equilibrium, will have its center of resistance of the wings in front of its center of gravity. Then this bird will descend with its tail turned towards the ground.

Fol. 8 recto

Sketch of a bird

If the wing and the tail are too far above the wind, lower half of the opposite wing and take the force of the wind on it, and you will regain balance.

Sketch of a bird in flight

And if the wing and the tail were under the wind, raise the opposite wing and you will regain balance, providing the wing that is raised is less slanted than the opposite one.

Sketch of a bird in flight

And if the wing and the breast are above the wind, half the opposite wing must be lowered until the wind strikes it and thrusts it upwards and balances the bird

Sketch of a bird in flight

But if the wing and the back are under the wind, then the opposite wing must be raised and presented to the wind, and the bird will regain balance immediately.

Sketch of a bird in flight

And if the bird has its rump above the wind, then it must put its tail under the wind, and the forces will be adjusted.

Sketch of a bird in flight

But if the bird has its rump under the wind, it must enter with its tail above the wind and it will regain balance.

Fol. 8 verso

Three sketches of a bird, marked: a d – b e – c f

When the bird is above the wind, with its beak and its breast to the wind, then the bird could be overturned by said wind, if it did not lower its tail and gather a great quantity of wind under it; and then it is impossible for it to be overturned. This can be proven by the first of the *elementi machinali*, which shows how things in equilibrium, which are struck on one side of their center of gravity, lower the opposing parts situated on this side of said center of gravity. For example, let the volume of the bird be *d e f*, and its center of rotation be *e* and the wind that strikes it *a b d e* and *b c e f*, I say that a greater quantity of wind strikes the tail of the bird at *e f*, beyond the center of rotation, than at *d e* this side of said center; and for that reason it is not possible to overturn said bird, and particularly when it is holding its wings edgewise to the wind.

Sketch of a bird, marked: a d – b n – c f

And if this bird is positioned with its length below the wind, it is likely to be overturned by the wind, unless it immediately raises its tail. To prove it: let the length of the bird be *d n f*, while *n* is its center of rotation. I say that *d n* is struck by more wind than *n f*, and for this reason *d n* will obey the course of the wind, giving way to it, and it will move downwards, raising the bird to a state of equilibrium.

Sketch of the wing of a bird

How the volume of the wing is not used in compressing the air. And if it is true, see how the spaces between the primary feathers are much wider than the width of the feathers themselves. So you, who study birds, do not base your calculation on the size of the wing, but observe the different types of wings of all birds.

Fol. 9 recto

[margin]

Sketches showing a bird struck by wind, marked: c a – d b

[column]

Sketch of a bird

When the wind strikes the bird below its path with its center of gravity towards this wind, then the bird will turn its back to the wind. And if the wind were stronger from below than from on top, then the bird would turn upside down, if it were not careful to immediately draw in the lower wing and extend the upper wing. In this way it would straighten up and return to a state of equilibrium.

Sketch of a bird, marked: b – a – c

To prove it: Let the wing withdrawn under the bird be *a c* and the extended wing *a b*. I say that the forces of the wind striking the two wings are equal, whatever their extension, that is *a b* against *a c*. It is true that *c* is larger than *b*, but it is so much closer to the bird's center of gravity that it offers little resistance, compared to *b*.

Sketch of a horizontal bird

But when the bird is struck under the wind below one of its wings, then it might be possible for the wind to overturn it, if it did not, as soon as its breast turned to the wind, extend towards the ground the opposite wing, withdrawing the wing previously struck by the wind, which will remain higher and will thus return to a state of equilibrium.

Sketch of a bird, marked: n m f

This is proven by the 4th of the 3rd, that is to say, "the object that is attacked by a greater force is more overcome." And by the 5th of the 3rd, that is to say, "the rump support that is located farthest from the point of attachment

will be less resistant." Again, by the 4th of the 3rd: "of winds that have equal force, the one with greater volume will be of greater power," and it will strike with a greater volume when it finds a larger object, so that *m f* being longer than *m n*, *m f* will obey the wind.

Fol. 9 verso

[continued from fol. 10 recto] struck from above, the force of the wind, striking from above, is not at its full power, so that the wedge of wind which splits from the middle of the humerus down, raises the wing with the same force as the upper wind that presses down on the wing.

Sketch of the profile of a wing, marked: e f – a b – c d

To prove it, let the humerus of the wing be *f b d,* and *e f c d* the sum of the wind striking the humerus of the wing, of this wind half is *a b c d,* which strikes from the top of the humerus *b* to *d*. And because the line of this humerus *b d* is oblique, the wind *a b c d* forms a wedge at the point of contact *b d* raising it, and the upper wind *a b e f* that strikes the obliquity *b f*, makes a wedge and pushes the wing down. So these two opposing forces do not allow the humerus to immediately enter below or above the course of the bird, according to its need. So this necessity has been met by placing a rudder above the round humerus, which acts as a shield and immediately cuts the wind in the manner required by the bird, as shown in *m n*.

Sketch of the tip of a wing, marked: rudder – n m

Sketch of a wing, marked: a n

But if the wind strikes the bird on the right or the left wing, then it is necessary that it enter above or below this wind with the tip of the wing struck by the wind, this change is equal to the thickness of the tips of the wings. If this change is below the wind, the bird turns its beak to the wind, and if this change is above the wind, the bird will turn its tail to the wind. And this is where the danger arises of the bird overturning, had nature not placed the weight of the bird's body below the place of the full extension of the wings, as shown here.

Fol. 10 recto

The bird performs in the air with its wings and tail, as the swimmer does with his arms and legs in the water.

If a man swims with his arms equally towards the east and his body points east, said swimmer will move towards the east. But if the northern arm makes a longer stroke than the southern arm, then the movement of his body will be north-easterly. And if the right arm makes a longer stroke than the left, the man's movement will be south-easterly.

Sketch of a bird banking

The impetus of one of the wings thrust edgewise towards the tail will immediately cause the bird to make a circular movement, following the impetus of said wing.

Sketch of a bird in spiral movement

When the bird ascends in a spiral movement above the wind, without flapping its wings, using the force of the wind, the wind will carry it away from the area it wants to return to, even without flapping its wings. So it turns into the wind, entering with its obliquity under the wind, descending somewhat until it is above the place it wants to return to.

Three sketches of the "rudder" of the wing, marked: a b; b a – d c – f e

The edge *a* of the rudder of the wing, that is the big finger of the bird's hand *b a* is that which immediately places the humerus of the wing above or below the wind. And if this humerus were not sharp, with a narrow, strong edge, the wing could not immediately enter above or below the wind when necessary, therefore, if this humerus were rounded and the wind *f e* struck the wing from below and the wing were immediately [continued on fol. 9 verso]

Fol. 10 verso

If the bird wants to turn quickly to one side and continue its circular movement, it will flap the wing on that side twice, rowing the wing backwards, while keeping the opposite wing still, or giving a single beat versus the two of the opposite wing.

Since the wings compress the air faster than it can escape from under them, the air is condensed and resists the movement of the wings. The motor of said wings, overcoming the resistance of the air, raises itself in opposition to the movement of the wings.

Sketch of a bird descending

This bird will descend at higher speed and the descent will show less obliquity. The descent of the bird with the tips of the wings and their humeri close together will show less obliquity.

Double sketch of a bird ascending

The lines of the movements of ascending birds are of two kinds, one twists like a screw, and the other is rectilinear and curvilinear.

The bird that ascends using a spiral movement like a screw will use reflex motion against the thrust of the wind and against the outrush of the wind, always turning to the right or to the left.

As if the north wind were blowing and you above the wind using a reflex motion were flying into said wind, and the impetus of this wind tends to overturn you as you make your straight ascent, then you are free to lower your right or your left wing, and with the inner wing lowered you will follow a curved path, with the help of the tail you bend towards the lower wing, always descending and bending towards the lower wing, until you gain altitude on the current of air in the direction of the wind. And when you are about to overturn, the same lowered wing will curve the movement and you will return against and under the wind, until you have acquired impetus. And then it will raise you above the wind, in its direction and by the impetus already acquired you will make the reflex motion greater than the incident motion.

[margin]

Sketch of an ascending bird, seen from the front

The ascending bird always keeps its wings above the wind without flapping them, and it always moves in a circular movement.

And if you want to move to the west without flapping your wings, with the north wind blowing, make the incident motion straight and under the north wind and the reflex motion above the north wind.

[underneath, in red chalk]

Sketch of the head of a man

Fol. 11 recto

Undoubtedly there is a similar proportion between truth and falsehood, as there is between light and darkness. And this truth is in itself of such excellence, that even if it is applied to humble and lowly matters, it unquestionably exceeds the uncertainties and falsehoods applied to grand and lofty subjects. Because although falsehood is the quintessence of our mind, nevertheless the truth of things must be the supreme nourishment of refined intellects, but not of wandering minds.

And falsehood is so contemptible that even if it said great things of God, it would take away grace from the deity; and truth is so excellent that even if it praised trivialities, it would ennoble them.

But you who live in dreams, you prefer the sophistry and duplicity in talking of great and uncertain things to certain, natural and more lowly things.

Sketch of two geometrical figures

Sketch of a geometrical figure, marked: a b

Sketch of a geometrical figure, marked: c d

Sketch of a geometrical figure, marked: e f

Sketch of a bird, marked: g h

The incident motions with their reflex motions are of 4 different kinds, of which one - the incident and the reflex - is found to be rectilinear, having lines of equal obliquity; the other is also rectilinear but the obliquity varies; the third has rectilinear incident motion and the reflex curvilinear; the fourth has curvilinear incident motion and rectilinear reflex motion. Each of these rectilinear and curvilinear lines is divided into two parts, because the first may have its rectilinear incident motion directly opposite the chord of the arc made by the curvilinear reflex motion, and also the reflex arc can curve right or left of this rectilinear incident motion.

Sketch of a bird

When the bird flies by flapping its wings, it does not extend its wings at all, because the tips of the wings would be too far from the lever and the nerves that move them.

Sketch of a bird banking

If the bird rows backwards with its wings when descending, it will move swiftly. And this happens because the wings beat the air, which then flows behind the bird to fill the vacuum it has left behind it.

Fol. 11 verso

Sketch of crossed braces or tie rods for a mechanical wing

Similar sketch, marked: f b d g – c e a – p

When g descends, p rises.

Two further sketches of a mechanical wing

[underneath, in red chalk]

Sketch of a leaf

Fol. 12 recto

Sketch of a sinuous line

[continued from fol. 12 verso] would curve the movement forming a semicircle, then, at the end of this movement, the bird would find itself with its beak turned to the place where the reflex began. If it were made against the direction of the wind, the end of the reflex motion would be much higher than the beginning of the incident motion; and this is the way that the bird rises without flapping its wings and by circling. The remainder of said circumference is completed in the direction of the wind by incident motion always with one of the wings and one side of the tail lowered; the bird then makes a reflex mo-

tion toward the outrush of the wind and finally remains with its beak turned toward the outrush of the wind, and then it repeats incident and reflex motions against the wind, always circling.

Sketch of a bird

When the bird wants to turn suddenly on its side, it quickly pushes the tip of the wing on that side towards its tail, and since "every movement tends to persist, or rather every moving body will continue to move as long as the momentum of its motor persists," this wing thrust violently towards the tail, still reserving at the end part of said momentum, not being able by itself continue the movement already started, will move the entire bird until the impetus of the moved air is consumed.

Sketch of a bird

The tail pressed on its surface and struck by the wind, immediately moves the bird in the opposite direction.

Sketch of a bird, marked: c o m a – d n b

When the bird is in the position *a n c* and it wants to rise, it will raise the humeri *m o* and will then find itself in the position shown in the sketch *b m n o d* and the air will be pressed between the ribs and the tip of the wings, so that it will be compressed and will push the bird upwards, generating impetus in the air, this impetus of the air will push the bird upwards by its compression.

Fol. 12 verso

To avoid the risk of damage

Such an instrument can be damaged in 2 ways, of which the first way is the breakage of the instrument, the second is when the instrument turns edgewise or near that edge, because it should always descend at a great slant and keeping an almost horizontal course.

Sketch of a bird within a circle divided into sections

As to protecting the instrument from breakage, this can be avoided by making it very strong, for whatever way it might turn: that is edgewise, descending headfirst or tail first, or with the tip of the right or the left wing, or by the halves or quarters of said lines, as the drawing shows.

Sketch of a bird

As to turning edgewise in any way, this must be prevented from the start by building the instrument so that in descending, in whatever direction this can be done, the solution has already been found. And this will be done by placing the center of gravity above the center of the weight it carries always in a straight line and with some distance between one center and the other. That is, in an instrument 30 *braccia* wide, the centers should be 4 *brac-*

cia apart, and one, as has been said, should be below the other and the heavier should be underneath, because in descending the heavier part can in part guide the movement. Apart from this, if the bird wants to descend with its head down and a slant that would cause it to overturn, this cannot happen, because the lighter part would be below the heavier part and would descend before the heavy one, which is impossible in a long descent, as is proven in the 4th of the *elementi machinali*.

Three sketches of birds falling

And if the bird should fall with its head down with part of the obliquity of the body turned towards the earth, then the undersides of the wings must turn level with the ground and the tail must be raised toward the loins, and the head, or rather the throat, must also be turned towards the ground, so that the bird's reflex motion will begin immediately, thrusting it back towards the sky; thus, at the end of that reflex, the bird would fall backwards, if in rising it did not lower somewhat one of the wings, which [continued on fol. 12 recto]

[underneath, in red chalk]

Sketch of a flower

Fol. 13 recto

Sketch of a bird

Here the big fingers of the bird are what keep the bird still in the air against the movement of the wind. That is, the wind moves and the bird supports itself on it without flapping its wings, and the bird stays in one place.

The reason is that the bird holds its wings at such an angle that the wind striking on them from below does not form a wedge of the kind that would raise it, but rather lifts it only as much as it weight would cause it to descend. That is, if the bird would fall with a force of 2, the wind would raise it with another force of 2; and because things that are equal do not overcome one another, the bird remains in one place without ascending or descending. It remains to speak of the movement that does not thrust either forwards or backwards; and this is, if the wind were to accompany it or push it out of its place with a force 4 and the bird with the same force failing due to said obliquity against the wind, once again, the forces being equal, the bird will not move forwards nor will it be driven back, if the wind remains equal. But, since the movements and forces of the winds are variable, this slant of the wings must not change, because if the wind increases and destroys the obliquity, the bird could be pushed upwards by the wind.

Sketch of the "alula", marked: a

In the aforesaid cases the wind does not enter like a wedge under the slanted wings, but only strikes the wing on the edge that tends to descend against the wind. Then

it strikes the edge of the humerus and said humerus shields the rest of the wing and the wing would have no protection if it were not for the big finger *a*, which then faces forwards and takes upon itself the entire force of the wind directly or less directly, according to the strength of the wind.

[margin]

Snow could be carried to hot places from the highest peaks of the mountains, and dropped on the fêtes held in the squares in the summer.

Fol. 13 verso

Diagram of a wing, marked: b – S – n m

The big finger *n* of the hand *m n* is that which, when the hand is lowered, will be lowered more than the hand, so that it closes and prevents the air compressed by the lowering of the hand from escaping, so that in this place the air is condensed and resists the rowing movement of the wing. And that is why nature has made the big finger such a strong bone, joined to very strong nerves and short feathers, with greater strength than the feathers on the wings of the bird, because using them, the bird can support itself on the already compressed air with all the force of the wing and its own power, because this is how the bird moves forward. And this finger serves the same purpose for the wings as the claws of a cat when it climbs a tree.

But when the wing recaptures new power with its movement upwards and forwards, then the big finger of the wing aligns with the other fingers, and thus its cutting edge fends the air and acts as a rudder, which always cuts the air according to the upwards or downwards distance that the bird wants to move.

The second rudder is positioned in an opposing position, beyond the bird's center of gravity; and this is the tail, which, if it is struck from underneath by the wind, being beyond said center of gravity, lowers the frontward part of the bird. And if the tail is struck from above, the frontward part of the bird is raised. And if the tail is twisted somewhat and shows its underside obliquely to the right wing, the front part of the bird turns to the right. And if it turns the slant of the underside of the tail towards the left wing, it will turn with its frontward part to the left side, and both ways the bird will descend.

But if the slanted tail is struck by the wind on the upper surface, the bird will turn, circling and ascending on the side where the upper surface of the tail shows its obliquity.

[underneath, in red chalk]

Sketch of a flower

Fol. 14 recto

The fulcrum of the bird's shoulder is that which is turned by the muscles of the breast and the back. It is here that the discretion of lowering or raising the elbows according to the will or the need of the moving animal is generated.

Two sketches of flight lines, marked: d – c a – b

I conclude that the ascent of birds without flapping of their wings derives from nothing other than their circular motion, within the movement of the wind; this movement, when it originates in the direction of the wind, declines to where a reflex motion is created; after which, thus circling, it has described a semicircle and finds itself with its face to the wind; and it repeats the reflex motion above the wind, always circling, until with the help of the wind it reaches the greatest height between its lowest position and the direction of the wind, and remaining with its left wing to the wind; and from this greatest height again circling, it descends to the last position, always with the right wing to the wind. As if to say: the wind goes from *a* to *c* while the bird moves from *a* descends from *a b c*, and at *c* it takes the reflex motion to *c d a* and supported by the wind it finds itself much higher at the end of the reflex motion than with the incident motion; the end of the reflex motion is situated perpendicularly above the said beginning of the incident motion.

Double sketch of a bird

Again, the equal resistance of the bird's wings is designed so that they are equally distant at their tips from the center of gravity of the bird.

But when one of the tips of the wings moves closer to the center of gravity of the bird than the other, then the bird will descend from the side on which the tip of the wing is closer to the center of gravity.

Fol. 14 verso

The hand of the wing is that which gives impetus. And so the elbow is placed edgewise in order to avoid impeding the movement that creates the impetus, and when this impetus is created, the elbow is lowered and slanted and the air on which it rests slants, almost forming a wedge, on which the wing rises, and if this did not happen, the movement of the bird, in the time it takes for the wing to move forward again, would descend towards the source of the impetus. But it cannot descend because, when the impetus is lacking, the percussion of the elbow resists the descent and thrusts the bird upwards.

Three sketches of squares, marked: a b; c d; e f

Let us say that the impetus is force 6 and the bird weighs 6 and in the midst of the movement the impetus reverts to 3 and the weight remains 6. Here the bird would descend by half the distance, that is the diameter of the square, and the slanted wing lying in the opposite direction, also

by the diameter of the square will not allow the weight to sink, nor will the weight allow the bird to rise; so it moves horizontally. That is to say: the descent of the bird in this half distance would descend by the line $a\,b$, and due to the slant of the wings in the opposite direction it would ascend on the line $d\,c$; so, for said reasons it moves on the horizontal line $e\,f$.

The elbows of the animal are not lowered completely at first, because in the first thrust of the impetus the bird would leap upwards, but they are lowered just enough to prevent the descent, according to the will and the discretion of the bird.

When the bird wants to suddenly move upwards, it immediately lowers its elbows after generating the impetus.

But if it wants to descend, it keeps its elbows upwords following the creation of the impetus.

Fol. 15 recto

Sketch of a bat

Remember that your bird must only imitate the bat because the membranes form an armor, or the joints of the armor, that is the mainsails of the wings.

Sketch of a bird

And if you were to imitate the wings of the feathered birds, they are made of more powerful bone and nerves, because they are pierced; that is their feathers are not joined together and air can pass through them. But the bat is helped by the membrane that is all one and is not pierced.

Sketch of a bird

On the way of balancing oneself.

Sketch of a bird, almost upturned, marked: b a

The heaviest part of a body is always that which guides its movement.

Therefore, the bird, finding itself in the position $a\,b$, and a being lighter than b, where the motor is, a will always be above b; so it will never happen that a goes before b, except by accident, but it will not be for long.

Sketch of a bird

The bird that wants to rise without flapping its wings, sets itself on a slant against the wind, presenting its wings to the wind with its elbows towards its face, with the center of gravity more towards the wind than towards the center of the wings. So it happens that, if the obliquity of the bird wants to descend with a force of 2 and the wind strikes it with a force of 3, its movement will obey 3 and not 2.

Fol. 15 verso

Sketch of an instrument for determining the center of gravity

This is done to find the center of gravity of the bird, without this instrument the machine would be of little use.

Double sketch of a bird, marked: a c – b d; e f – h g

When the bird descends, the center of gravity of the bird is outside its center of resistance: as if the center of gravity were above the line $a\,b$ and the center of resistance were above the line $c\,d$.

And if the bird wants to rise, then its center of gravity will remain behind the center of resistance.

As if in $f\,g$ there was the aforesaid center of gravity, and in $e\,h$ there were the center of resistance.

Double sketch of a bird

The bird can stay in the air without keeping its wings in the horizontal position, because its center of gravity is not in the center of its body, as it is in a steelyard balance, it is not forced to keep its wings at the same height, like a steelyard. But if the wings are not horizontal, then the bird will descend on a slanting path according to the obliquity of its wings. And if the obliquity is composite, that is double, for example: the obliquity of the wings declines to the south and the obliquity of the head and the tail declines to the east, so the bird will descend with the obliquity to the southeast. And if the obliquity of the bird is double the obliquity of its wings, then the bird will descend in the middle, south-south east, and the obliquity of its movement will be between the two aforesaid obliquities.

[underneath, in red chalk]

Sketch of a flower

Fol. 16 recto

Sketch of a bird

Encouragement to attempt the undertaking, overcoming the objections

If you say that the nerves and the muscles of a bird are undoubtedly more powerful than those of man, both because the meatiness of so many muscles and the flesh of the breast are made to assist and increase the movement of the wings, with that single bone in the breast, which gives great power to the bird, with the wings all woven with great nerves and other strong ligaments of cartilage and strong skin with various muscles, I would answer that such strength is designed not merely to support the wings; when nec-

essary it can double and triple the movement in order to flee from a predator, or to follow its own prey. So at times it must double or triple its strength and also carry its own weight in its talons while flying. It is so when we see the falcon carry a duck and the eagle a hare, and this clearly shows where the extra strength is distributed. But little force is needed to support the bird itself and balance it on its wings, and hover on the currents of air, and straighten the rudder to give direction to its course, just a few flaps of the wings are sufficient, and the larger the bird, the slower the movement.

Man has greater strength in his legs than is required to support his weight. And to show that this is true, stand a man on the sand and see how deep his footprint is. Then put another man on his shoulders and you will see how much more he sinks. Then take the man off his shoulders and have him jump straight upwards as high as he can and you will find that his footprint has sunk more with the jump than with the man on his shoulders. So here are two ways to prove that man has double the strength needed to support his own weight.

[margin]

Sketches of wineskins

Wineskins so that a man falling from 6 *braccia* in height, will not hurt himself, whether he falls in the water or on the ground. And these wineskins, tied together like rosary beads, must be wrapped around him.

Fol. 16 verso

If you fall with the double wineskin under your rump, make sure that you hit the ground with it.

Sketch of a device for rotating the wing, marked:
n – a – d c – f – b f f – f – g

In order for the wings to row down and backwards to support the instrument in the air and for it to move forwards, the lever *c d* moves on a slant, guided by the belt *a b*. I could make it so that the foot pressed on the stirrup *g*, in addition to its usual function, pulled down the lever *f*. But this would not be useful, because we need the lever *f* to rise or descend first, before the stirrup *g* moves from its position, so that the wing, in thrusting forwards and rising (having already acquired impetus, lifts the bird without flapping of the wings) can turn the wings edgewise to the air, because if it did not do so, the face of the wings would strike the air, impeding movement, and preventing the bird from moving forwards.

[underneath, in red chalk, upside down]

Sketch of a twig with leaves

Fol. 17 recto

Sketch of a wing and a rotation device with various details, marked: b – a – hand – hand K – o – d – foot c – h – g

On the 19th page of this work the reason for this is shown.

When the feet want to lower the wing *h*, the hand *b* in lowering will raise the lever *k*, and then *h* will row backwards.

When the feet want to raise the wing, and you immediately raise the wing in *h* by pulling the lever *g* upwards with the hand *a*, and then the wing will remain edgewise and the bird will not be impeded in its movement against the air.

Fol. 17 verso

Two sketches of a bird

If the bird descends to the east, remaining above the south wind with the right wing, it will undoubtedly be overturned, if it does not immediately turn its beak to the north winds; and then the wind will beat the palms of its hands beyond the center of gravity and will raise the forward part of the bird.

Sketch

When the bird has a large wingspan and a short tail and it wants to rise, then it will thrust its wings upwards and will receive the wind under its wings. The wind forms a wedge and soon thrusts it upwards, like the kite, the bird of prey that I saw when I was going to Fiesole, above the site of Barbiga, in the year '5 [1505] on the 14th day of March.

Sketch of bird's tail in five different positions

The tail has movements; at times it is flat and then the bird moves horizontally; at times the tips are equally low, and this is when the bird is rising; at other times the tips are equally high, and this happens in descent. But when the tail is low and the left side is lower than the right, then the bird will rise with a circular motion turning to the right. This can be proven, but not here. And if the right tip of the lowered tail is lower than the left, then the bird will turn instead to the left. And if the tips of the raised tail are higher on the left side than on the right; then the bird will turn its head to the right; and if the tips of the raised tail are higher on the right than on the left, then the bird will turn instead to the left.

[underneath, in pen and ink and red chalk, upside down]

Sketch of a leg

Fol. 18 recto

[right column]

Sketch of a detail of a mechanical wing

Two sketches of the wing of a bird and two sketches of a bird

In raising the hand the elbow is always lowered and compresses the air, and in lowering the hand the elbow rises and remains sideways so as not to prevent the movement through the air that strikes it.

The lowering of the elbows, when the bird thrusts the wings forward somewhat edgewise above the wind, is guided by the impetus already acquired, this is because the wind strikes the elbow and forms a wedge, on which the bird rises, using said impetus and without flapping its wings. And if the bird weighs 3 pounds and the body is $^1/_3$ of the length of the wings, the wings, do not bear more than two-thirds of the weight of that bird.

Great effort is made by the hand towards the big finger, or rudder of the wing, because that is the part that beats the air.

[left column]

Three elliptical sketches describing the movement of the wing, marked: a d – b c

The palm of the hand goes from *a* to *b* always within almost equal angles lowering and compressing the air and in *b* it immediately turns edgewise and moves back again, rising on the line *c d*, and when it reaches *d*, it immediately turns over and moves down the line *a b*, and in turning it always turns around the center of its length.

The hand will turn edgewise at great speed; when it pushes back, flat, it will be at the speed that the ultimate power of the motor requires.

The course of the tips of the fingers is not the same when moving forwards and backwards, but is on a higher plane; the return is below it; and the figure traced by the upper and the lower lines, is oval, with a long and narrow ovality.

Fol. 18 verso

Sketches of a dam in a river

[top right]

1505, Tuesday evening, this 14th April, Lorenzo came to stay with me. He said he is 17.

And this day 15th of said April I had 25 gold ducats from the churchwarden of Santa Maria Nova.

[top left]

From the mountain that bears the name of the great bird, the famous bird will take flight, it will fill the world with its great fame.

[bottom left]

Diagram, marked: p – r – s

To raise a mast by *p*, and *r S* supports.

[bottom right]

Two sketches of a bevel gear with crank handle

Inner Back Cover

Architectural elevations, floorplan, river [continued from fol. 18 verso]

[top right]

Notes on expenses:

mona [= mia donna probably his housekeeper]	48	148
bran	4	111
straw	23	37
key	.6	
to me	28	
chicken	.2	
	111	
	.28	
	83	

[bottom of the page]

The great bird will make its first flight from the peak of Mount Cècero, filling the universe with wonder, filling all literature with its fame, and with eternal glory the nest in which it was born.

Prima figura del moto.

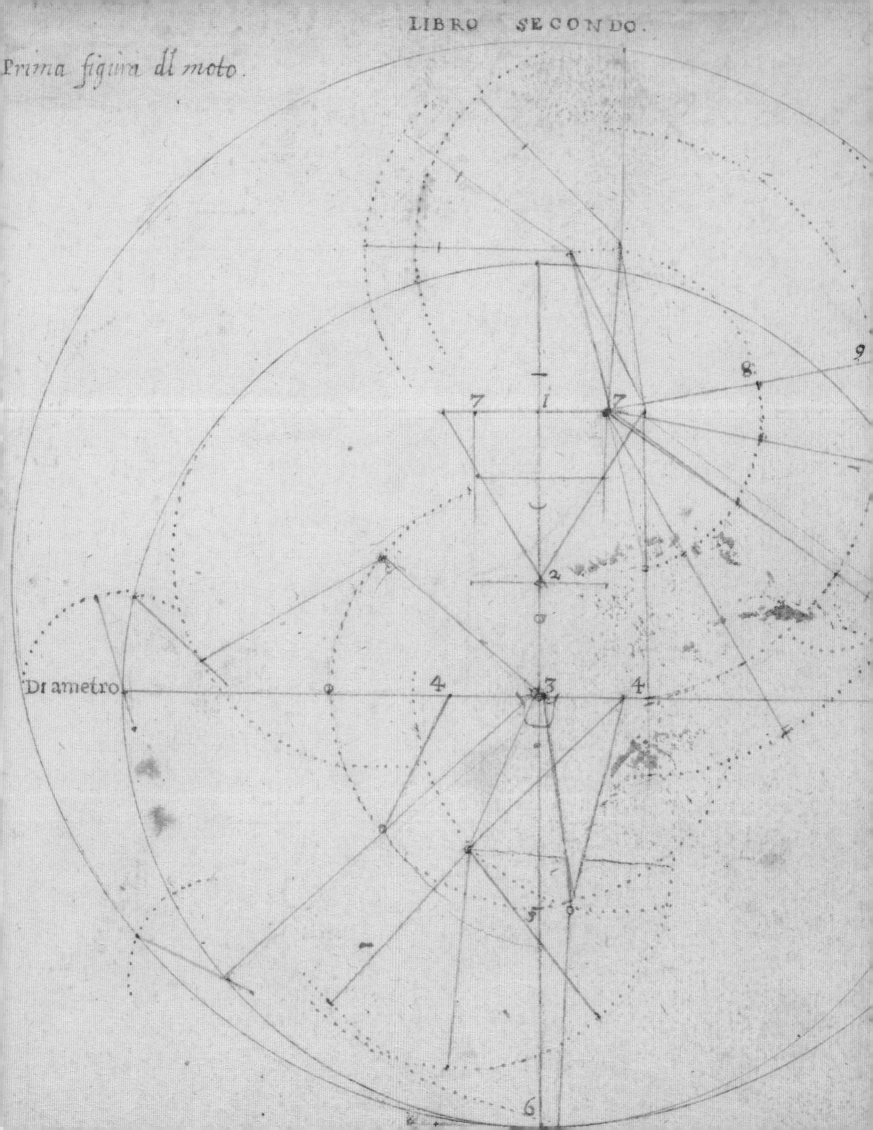

Diametro

CODEX HUYGENS
CODICE HUYGENS

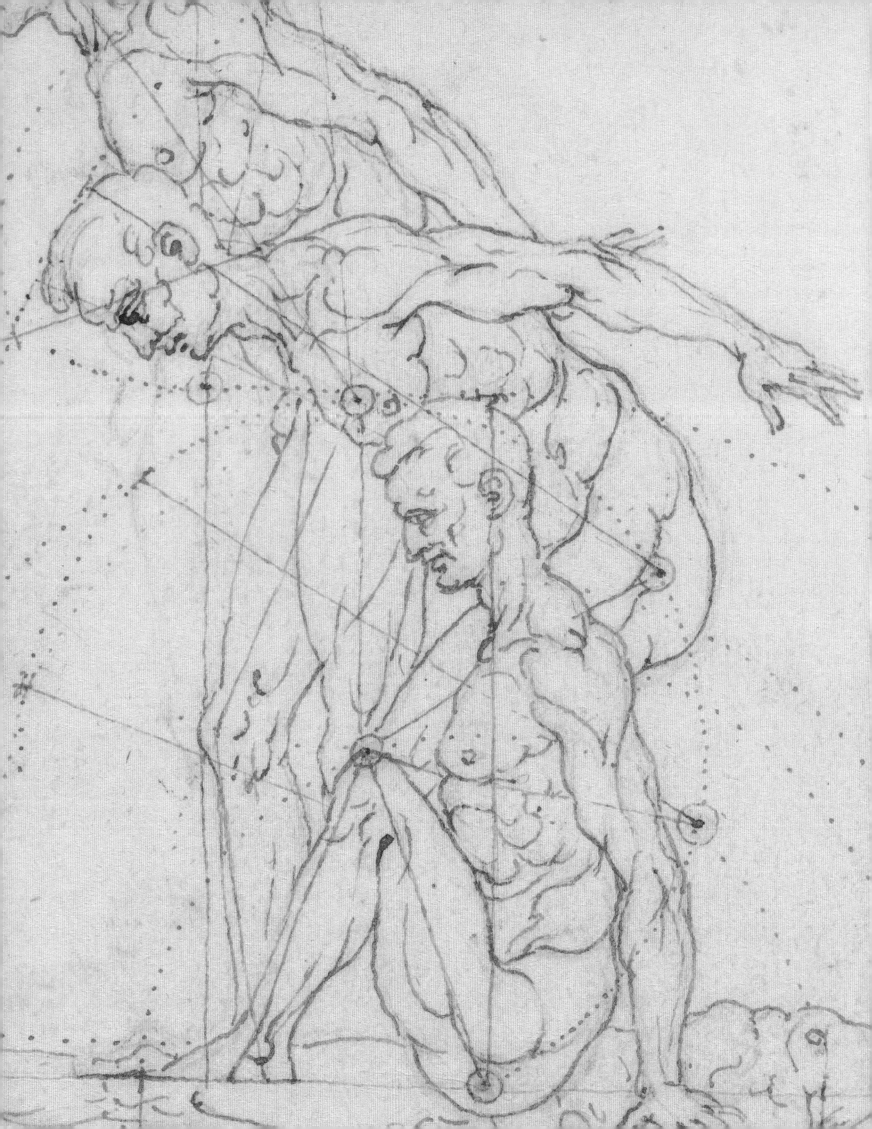

Proem to the Codex Huygens

Proemio al *Codice Huygens*

Carlo Pedretti

The sixth entry in the 1637 deed of donation with which Count Galeazzo Arconati (d. 1648) presented the Biblioteca Ambrosiana in Milan with twelve Leonardo manuscripts of various sizes—from the Codex Atlanticus to pocket-size notebooks—describes one of medium size as having 96 folios (i.e. 192 pages), the verso of the first folio (p. 2) containing "cinque figure mathematiche, parte quadrate, parte tonde" ("five diverse mathematical figures, some square, some circular"), while on the last sheet, namely the verso of fol. 96 (p. 192), there are "due figure humane con diuerse linee, che le circondano" ("two human figures with various lines that encircle them"). As the early inscription on the cardboard cover specifying the number of the sheets as being 96 is followed by the letter "B", it has been shown that this is the manuscript designated as Libro B in the list of the original sources that the compiler of Leonardo's *Treatise on Painting*, the Codex Vaticanus Urbinas lat. 1270, was able to use as he had inherited them directly from the master in 1519. That was Francesco Melzi, Leonardo's latest assistant and friend, who in turn had one or two assistants as helpers in carrying out the compilation task. This is shown, for instance, by the way each text excerpted from one of two of the notebooks used, either Libro A or Libro B, shows the added folio reference to its source by a hand different from that of the compiler, thus suggesting that the same method was to be applied to the whole apograph, only to be abandoned all too soon. And if Libro A could not be identified with any of the existing Leonardo notebooks, Libro B was recognized as the one known today as Manuscript E, in the library of the Institut de France in Paris: everything corresponds perfectly, except that its last signature of sixteen sheets (fols. 81 to 96) is missing as the result of a theft perpetrated by the notorious kleptomaniac Guglielmo Libri in the 1830s. Hence the importance of the brief description of the last page of that notebook in the Arconati deed of donation of 1637: *due figure humane con diuerse linee, che le circondano.* (two human figures with various lines that encircle them.)

Con un atto di donazione del 1637 a favore della Biblioteca Ambrosiana di Milano, il conte Galeazzo Arconati (morto nel 1648) disponeva un lascito di dodici manoscritti di Leonardo di varie misure e dimensioni, dal *Codice Atlantico* a taccuini di formato tascabile. Il sesto punto di questa donazione riguarda un codice di formato medio, composto da 96 fogli (e quindi 192 pagine) che mostrava al verso del primo foglio (pagina 2) "cinque figure mathematiche, parte quadrate, parte tonde", mentre nell'ultimo foglio, e cioè al verso del foglio 96 (pagina 192), "vi sono due figure humane con diuerse linee, che le circondano". Poiché un'antica iscrizione posta sulla coperta cartonata specificava che il numero dei fogli – 96 appunto – era seguito dalla lettera "B", quel manoscritto poteva essere identificato con il cosiddetto Libro B nell'elenco delle fonti originali che il compilatore del *Libro della pittura* di Leonardo, ovvero il Codice Vaticano Urbinate lat.1270, poteva usare perché lo aveva ereditato direttamente dal maestro nel 1519. Si tratta cioè di Francesco Melzi, l'ultimo assistente e amico di Leonardo, che a sua volta aveva uno o due assistenti come aiutanti nel lavoro di compilazione. È stato dimostrato, per esempio, che ogni brano scelto da uno dei due taccuini utilizzati, ossia il Libro A e il Libro B, mostra il riferimento al foglio della fonte da cui deriva, precisazione da parte di una mano diversa rispetto a quella del compilatore. Questo potrebbe suggerire che lo stesso metodo avrebbe potuto essere applicato all'intero apografo, ma fu poi ben presto abbandonato. Se il Libro A non è stato ancora identificato con alcuno dei taccuini conosciuti di Leonardo, il Libro B è invece il *Ms. E* conservato nella biblioteca dell'Institut de France a Parigi: tutto corrisponde perfettamente, eccezione fatta per l'assenza dell'ultimo sedicesimo (dal foglio 81 al 96) sottratto, come noto, dal cleptomane Guglielmo Libri attorno al 1830. Da qui la grande importanza della breve descrizione nell'ultima pagina del taccuino incluso nella donazione Arconati del 1637: *due figure humane con diuerse linee, che le circondano.*

Desidero porre una speciale enfasi su questa precisazione poiché se questa avesse ricevuto la dovuta attenzione da parte degli studiosi di Leonardo dell'era moderna a partire dal diciottesimo secolo – (in particolare Baldassare

I am deliberately placing special emphasis on this specification because if the Leonardo scholarship of the modern era, since the end of the eighteenth century—particularly that of Baldassare Oltrocchi (1714–97), Giambattista Venturi (1746–1822) and Giuseppe Bossi (1777–1815)—had paid proper attention to it, one of the most fascinating problems in the study of Leonardo's approach to art theory would have been understood sooner—long before Erwin Panofsky's seminal 1940 edition of the so-called Codex Huygens in the Morgan Library. Today, this manuscript is understood as containing Leonardo's most innovative views on every form of movement in man and animals, approached as a scientific discipline combining both Mechanics and Optics. Leonardo's method may be said to have paved the way to the idea, if not the advent, of the motion picture.

As the librarian of the Biblioteca Ambrosiana in Milan, Oltrocchi had direct access to the Leonardo manuscripts, which had entered the library in 1637 as a donation of Count Galeazzo Arconati and were therefore still intact, including the last signature of Manuscript E, in which he notes, without specifying on which sheet, a dated drawing of an "orrido" (ravine, steep gorge): "Trovo un disegno d'un orrido con matita nera, e sotto questa avvertenza: 'sulla riva del Po assanto Angiolo nel mille 500 quattordici, addí 22 settembre.'" ("I find a black chalk drawing of a ravine and below it the record 'By the banks of the Po River next to Santo Angiolo on September 22, 1514.'") Oltrocchi failed to note on the last page the drawings of human figures encircled by lines, as mentioned in the 1637 act of donation. Nor did Venturi notice them when he examined the same intact notebook in Paris for his 1797 Essay. He records the same date as being on fol. 96, possibly on the recto of it because on the verso there were the drawings of human figures that he does not mention. In the section on Les Ouvrages de Léonard de Vinci, on p. 52 of his 1797 Essay, he includes the entry:

> Edw. Cooper grava vers 1720, en Angleterre, le fragment d'un Traité de Vinci sur les mouvements du corps humain; et sur la manière de dessiner les figures suivant les règles géometriques. (Dix planches in-fol. y compris le frontispice.) (Around 1720, Edw. Cooper engraved, in England, fragment of a Treatise by da Vinci on the movements of the human body and the method for drawing figures according to geometric rules. [Ten plates in-folio, including the title-page.])

Oltrocchi (1714-1797), Giambattista Venturi (1746-1822) e Giuseppe Bossi (1777-1815) – uno dei più affascinanti problemi dello studio dell'approccio di Leonardo alla teoria artistica sarebbe stato affrontato molto tempo prima della svolta propulsiva rappresentata dall'edizione di Erwin Panofsky del 1940 del cosiddetto Codice Huygens della Morgan Library. Questo manoscritto contiene le considerazioni più innovative elaborate da Leonardo sul movimento degli uomini e degli animali. Lo studio del movimento umano è trattato come se fosse una disciplina scientifica che fa capo alla Meccanica e all'Ottica, in modo da aprire la strada all'idea, se non all'avvento stesso, del Cinema.

In qualità di bibliotecario dell'Ambrosiana a Milano, l'Oltrocchi ebbe diretto accesso ai manoscritti di Leonardo a partire dal 1637, quando questi fecero il loro ingresso in quella biblioteca a seguito della donazione Arconati, e quindi anche allo stesso Ms. E che, ancora intatto, comprendeva anche l'ultimo sedicesimo. L'Oltrocchi esaminando il manoscritto nota l'esistenza, senza specificare su quale foglio, di un disegno datato rappresentante un "orrido" (gola, dirupo spaventoso): "Trovo un disegno d'un orrido con matita nera, e sotto questa avvertenza: «sulla riva del Po assanto Angiolo nel mille 500 quattordici, addí 22 settembre»". L'Oltrocchi non menziona i disegni delle figure umane circondate da linee poste nell'ultima pagina e già menzionate nell'atto di donazione del 1637. Queste non sono prese in esame neppure dal Venturi quando esamina nel suo Essay del 1797 lo stesso taccuino, da poco pervenuto ancora intatto a Parigi. Tuttavia prende nota della stessa data menzionata al foglio 96, forse osservata al recto perché al verso si trovavano appunto i disegni delle figure umane che lui non menziona. Nelle pagine di Les Ouvrages de Léonard de Vinci, a p. 52 dello stesso Essay, egli riporta l'annotazione:

> Edw. Cooper grava vers 1720, en Angleterre, le fragment d'un Traité de Vinci sur les mouvements du corps humain; et sur la manière de dessiner les figures suivant les règles géometriques. (Dix planches in-fol. y compris le frontispice).

È possibile accertare che Venturi avesse tratto questa importante informazione da alcune bibliografie a stampa, ma non è accertabile se avesse pensato di controllare le biblioteche francesi per trovare una copia di quella pubblicazione, che soltanto nei nostri tempi è stata identificata come una selezione di fogli del Codice Huygens. Venturi non aveva neppure pensato alla possibilità di porre quel codice in rapporto all'informazione del 1637, circa le figure umane geometriche schizzate da Leonardo sull'ultimo foglio del Ms. E. Non esistono tracce di tale eventualità

The Rule of the Defign of Natural Motion.

I fay that ẏ Action or Motion of Human Members is to be confider'd by ẏ exterior Action, which ẏ Members make, or ẏ Body turning with its Arms & Legs, according to Nature: becaufe the Force so moving confifts in ẏ Bones & Nerves: & our common faying is very proper, when wee fay, that ẏ Whole is mov'd by Vertue of ẏ Soul, which is the Center & life of all: fince ẏ Fingers are mov'd by Vertue of ẏ Hand, & that by Vertue of ẏ Arm & that by Vertue of ẏ Body & Vital or animal Spirits. So it happens in our Scheme, that ẏ Motion which is attributed to the Members, will be found to be ẏ first Caufe & it's proper Center, which turning in ẏ form of a Circle, the Compas will trace ẏ Stability of what Actions one will, of Natural Motion, alloting to feveral one and diverfified Lines in one, turning to its Center according to our first Order of ẏ Heavenly Bodies, conftituting this Body form'd upon ẏ Natural Plan of our Great Mafterpiece, whereby we raife up & turn our felves: this is Demonftrated upon ẏ first Figure, and the Whole Scheme with all it's variety, by a fingle Line.

The Schemes & Geometrick Circles gives ẏ Intelligence of the Motions of ẏ first Figure by ẏ Demonftration of ẏ Mathematical Rules.

Libro del Difegno delli Moti Naturali.

Dico ch'il Moto, ò l'Azione delli Membri Humani si deve confiderare fecondo le Azioni esteriori, ch'il Corpo, ò li Membri fanno, torciendo, e movendo le Braccia, e le Gambe, come la Natura l'addita, Perche la Forza di questo Moto viene prodotta dalle Ossa, e nervi, ed il nostro commune Affioma è molto bene appropriato à questo, Perche noi diciamo, ch'il tutto si move per virtù, ò forza dello Spirito, che è il Centro e Vita del Tutto Mentre le Dita sono mosse per virtù della mano, Questa per quella del Braccio, e Questo per quello del Corpo, e Spiriti Anima li, Cosi accade nel nostro Disegno, dove il moto, che si attribuisce alle Membra si troverà esser la prima Causa, ed il proprio Centro che girando in forma di Circolo, il Compaffo troverà la stabilità di qualsivoglia Azione del Moto Naturale, permettendo a ciaschuna Linea di tornare al suo Centro, Conforme al nostro primo Ordine delli Corpi Celesti, costituendo questo Corpo formato conforme al Natural' Ordine del nostro Grand Disegno, Dove noi ci rivoltiam da noi Medesimi. Questo è dimostrato nella prima figura con tutt' il Disegno, da una sola Linea.

It can be ascertained that Venturi drew this important information from printed bibliographies, and there is no evidence that he had thought of checking French libraries for a copy of that publication, which only in our time could be shown to be a selection of sheets of the Codex Huygens; nor was he aware of the possibility of relating its contents to the 1637 information on the geometrical human figures drawn by Leonardo on the last sheet of Manuscript E. Furthermore, there is no mention of such a possibility in his correspondence with Bossi, who as a painter and a scholarly bibliophile was well prepared to value the importance of the Cooper engravings (figs. 23–32, from Pedretti 1977). Indeed, I have ascertained beyond any doubt that they remained unknown to Leonardo scholars and even to bibliographers and bibliophiles for more than two centuries. So far, the only known copy is still the one that I found in the library of the Duke of Devonshire in England in 1970 and that I reproduce in full in my 1977 Richter *Commentary* after a first account in the *Journal of the Warburg and Courtauld Institutes* in 1965 outlin-

neppure nella sua corrispondenza col Bossi, che sia come pittore sia come erudito bibliofilo era ben preparato a cogliere il valore dell'importanza delle incisioni Cooper (figg. 23-32, da Pedretti 1977). Ho riscontrato senza ombra di dubbio che queste rimasero sconosciute non soltanto agli studiosi di Leonardo ma anche ai bibliografi e bibliofili per più di due secoli. Fino a questo momento, l'unica copia conosciuta è quella che ho trovato nella biblioteca del duca di Devonshire in Inghilterra nel 1970 e che ho interamente pubblicato nel 1977 nel mio *Commentary* al Richter, dopo un primo resoconto offerto nel *Journal of the Warburg and Courtauld Institutes* nel 1965, nel quale descrivo la mia ricerca sistematica intrapresa in quasi tutte le biblioteche pubbliche in Europa e in America. Sapevo esattamente che cosa cercare, vale a dire quello che gli studiosi dall'Ottocento fino ai nostri giorni potevano e avrebbero dovuto aver fatto. Alla storia del *Codice Huygens* non manca più il suo significativo punto di svolta.

Il *Codice Huygens* conservato alla Morgan Library di New York (2006.14 [ex M.A. 1139]), prende il suo nome dal suo primo possessore, Constantine Huygens, fratello del

FIG. 23
Cooper Engravings,
Title-page / Frontespizio

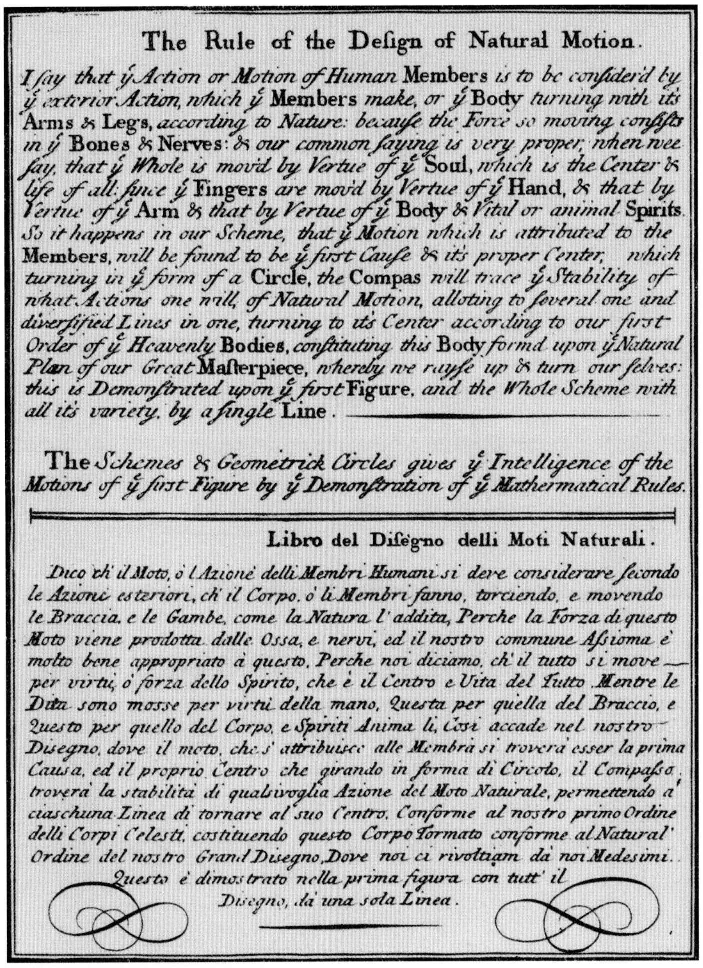

FIG. 24
Cooper Engravings,
pl. I; Codex Huygens,
fol. 11 recto

FIG. 25

Cooper Engravings,
pl. I; Codex Huygens,
fol. 12 recto

FIG. 26

Cooper Engravings,
pl. III; Codex
Huygens, fol. 26 recto

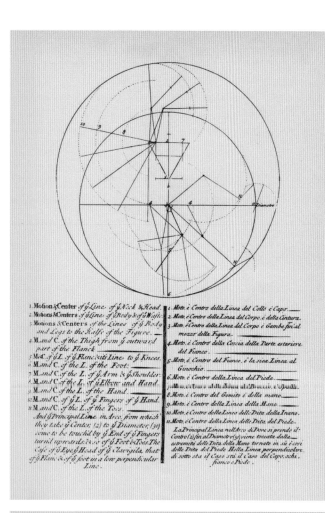

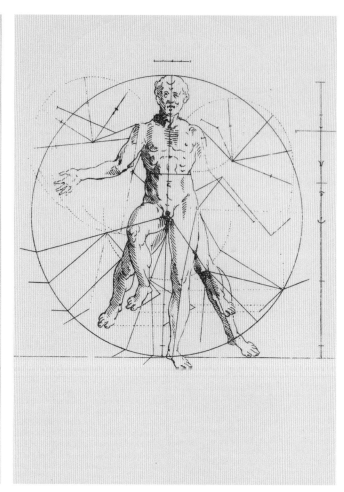

FIG. 27

Cooper Engravings,
pl. IV; Codex Huygens,
fols. 27 recto
and 14 recto

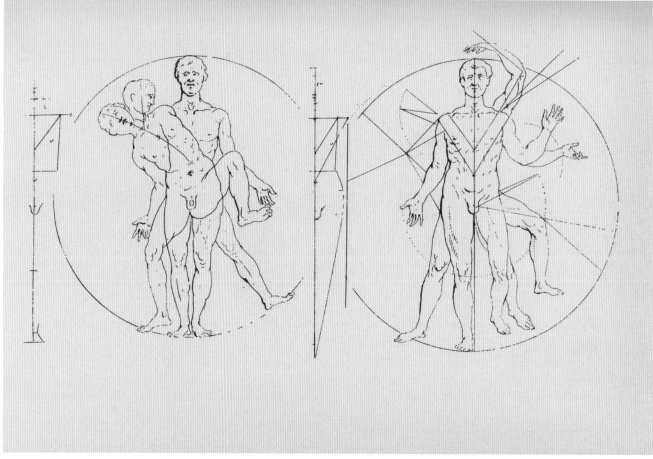

154

ing my systematic search in nearly every great public library in Europe and America. I knew then exactly what to look for, namely what scholars from the eighteenth century to our time could and should have done. Once the Cooper engravings were found, the history of the Codex Huygens was no longer missing its meaningful turning point.

The Codex Huygens at the Morgan Library (2006.14 [ex M.A. 1139]), takes its name from its former owner, Constantine Huygens, the brother of the famous physicist Christian and the secretary to King William III of England. Huygens records having acquired the book on March 2, 1690, from Mrs. Remy, a woman from Brabant whose husband had been a painter at the time of van Dyck. She has been identified with the widow of the Flemish painter Remy (Remigius) van Leemput, called "Remy" or "Remee." As Panofsky has shown in the introduction to his edition of the codex, Remy was born in Antwerp, and had come to London during the reign of Charles I. He is best known for his collection of prints and drawings, which was sold by his heirs in 1677, the year of his death.

The first description of the contents of the codex is in a letter that Constantine Huygens wrote to his brother Christian on March 3, 1690. He says that the book is in quarto and is written and drawn by Leonardo da Vinci: "It deals with the design of nude figures of men, females and infants, and contains also something about horses and perspective. The figures are for the greater part simply outlined, the muscles are lightly indicated, but these figures are extremely beautiful, as one may expect from a great hand. The purpose of the author is to explain all the proportions of members and parts of the body. I have paid 3½ guineas for it, but I would not sell it for four times that price."

An entry in Huygens' diary, under the date September 1, 1690, records that the Queen had sent for him in order to show him the books of drawings of Leonardo and Holbein. This is undoubtedly the first mention of the Leonardo drawings in the Royal Collection, not of the Codex Huygens, as Panofsky erroneously suggests with his paraphrase of the entry ("the Queen sent for him in order to be shown the precious volume"). The Leoni volume, which was acquired by Charles I about 1630, was described for the first time by Rogers in 1778, but Queen Mary was fully aware of its existence nearly a century earlier. The Codex Huygens reappeared about 1915 and was

famoso fisico Christian e segretario di re Guglielmo III di Inghilterra. Huygens segnala di avere acquistato il libro il 2 Marzo 1690 dalla signora Remy, una donna proveniente dal Brabante il cui marito era stato un pittore al tempo di van Dyck. La vecchia proprietaria del codice è stata identificata con la vedova del pittore fiammingo Remy (Remigius) van Leemput, detto "Remy" o "Remee". Come Panofsky ha dimostrato nella sua introduzione, Remy nacque ad Anversa e giunse a Londra sotto il regno di Carlo I. Questi è più noto per la sua collezione di disegni e stampe, che fu venduta dai suoi eredi nel 1677, anno della sua morte.

La prima descrizione del contenuto del codice si trova in una lettera che Constantine Huygens scrive a suo fratello Christian il 3 Marzo 1690. Egli afferma che il libro è *in quarto* e che è scritto e illustrato da Leonardo da Vinci: "Questo riproduce i disegni di figure nude di uomini, donne e infanti, e contiene anche qualcosa riguardo ai cavalli e alla prospettiva. Le figure sono per la maggior parte semplicemente ripassate, i muscoli sono appena indicati, ma queste sono estremamente belle, proprio come uno si aspetta da una mano talentuosa. L'autore vuole spiegare la proporzione delle membra e delle parti del corpo. Per quello ho speso 3½ ghinee, ma non lo venderei mai, neppure per quattro volte il suo prezzo".

Un'annotazione del diario di Huygens, datata 1 settembre 1690, ricorda che la Regina lo aveva mandato a chiamare per mostrargli i libri dei disegni di Leonardo e Holbein. Questa è senza dubbio la prima menzione dei disegni di Leonardo nella Collezione Reale, e non quella del *Codice Huygens*, come invece erroneamente Panofsky suggerisce con la frase: "the Queen sent for him in order to be shown the precious volume" ("La regina lo mandò a chiamare affinché gli fosse mostrato il prezioso volume"). Infatti, il volume di Leoni, acquistato da Carlo I attorno al 1630, fu descritto per la prima volta da Rogers nel 1778, anche se quasi un secolo prima la regina Mary sapeva della sua esistenza.

Il *Codice Huygens* riapparse attorno al 1915 e fu acquistato dalla Morgan Library negli anni Trenta dello stesso secolo. È questa la prima volta che una considerevole parte dei suoi fogli è esposta in una mostra. È da aggiungere che tutti i 128 fogli del *Codice Huygens* sono adesso disponibili online a colori e in alta risoluzione.

Le incisioni Cooper

Dal diario di Huygens si sa che tra il 26 novembre e il 27 dicembre 1690 il codice in suo possesso veniva smontato in modo da restaurare alcuni fogli e montarli tra le pagine di un volume di fogli bianchi. Sappiamo che i fogli sciolti furono affidati a uno stampatore chiamato Cooper che do-

FIG. 28

Cooper Engravings,
pl. V; Codex Huygens,
fols. 68 recto
and 16 recto

FIG. 29

Cooper Engravings,
pl. VI; Codex Huygens,
fols. 69 recto, 22 recto,
13 recto and 23 recto

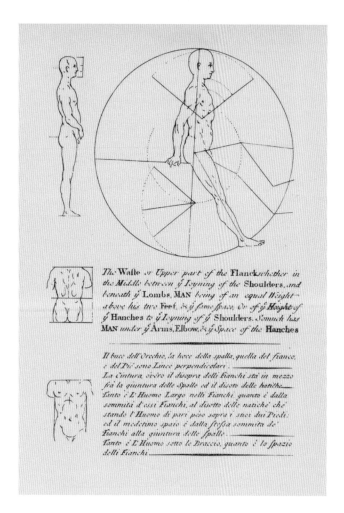

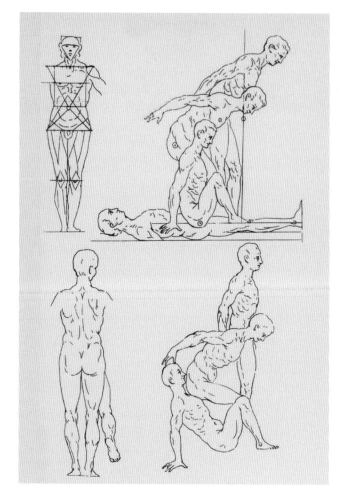

acquired by the Morgan Library in the 1930s. This is the first time that a considerable number of sheets is exhibited. What is more, all 128 sheets of the Codex Huygens are now finally available online, in high resolution and in color.

The Cooper Engravings

We know from Huygens' diary that between November 26 and December 27, 1690, he had taken apart the codex in his possession in order to have its sheets carefully restored and inserted between the pages of a volume of blank folios. Then we are told that he gave the loose sheets to a dealer in prints called Cooper for mending and mounting, and examined Cooper's work on December 27. In Verga's *Bibliografia vinciana* of 1931, under the date "1720 circa," is mentioned a set of nine engravings after Leonardo's drawings on human movement, published in London by the print dealer Edward Cooper. (It is reasonable to assume that this was the same print dealer who restored the Codex Huygens in 1690.) As we have seen, the engravings were so rare that they were known only

veva ripararli e montarli, il cui lavoro fu esaminato proprio il 27 dicembre. Nella *Bibliografia vinciana* del Verga nel 1931, sotto la data "1720 circa", è menzionato un gruppo di nove incisioni che rappresentano alcuni disegni sul movimento del corpo umano tratte da Leonardo e pubblicate a Londra dall'antiquario di stampe Edward Cooper. (Non sarebbe fuori luogo pensare che questi fosse lo stesso antiquario che restaurò il *Codice Huygens* nel 1690). Come si è visto, le incisioni erano talmente rare da essere conosciute soltanto grazie a tarde descrizioni ottocentesche. Infatti, la fonte del Verga era la famosa lettera del Mariette al Conte de Caylus, da cui tra poco sarà citato un piccolo estratto. La sua ricerca nelle varie biblioteche d'Europa fu senza successo e fu costretto ad ammettere senza esitazioni che neppure il British Museum ne fosse in possesso.

Lo strano mistero fu discusso da Gustavo Uzielli nel 1884. Egli riportò l'ipotesi erroneamente sostenuta dall'Amoretti per cui le incisioni fossero le riproduzioni degli originali allora in possesso del Cardinale Silvio Valenti. Scartata questa ipotesi, Uzielli credeva invece che i disegni riprodotti da Cooper fossero probabilmente quelli che appartenevano alla raccolta reale del Castello di Windsor.

through eighteenth-century descriptions. In fact, Verga's source is the well known long letter of Mariette to Count de Caylus, a brief excerpt of which will be quoted shortly. His search for the engravings in various libraries of Europe was unsuccessful, and he had to admit reluctantly that not even the British Museum had a set of them. This curious mystery was discussed by Gustavo Uzielli in 1884. He reported Amoretti's hypothesis that the Cooper engravings were reproductions of originals in the possession of Cardinal Silvio Valenti. This hypothesis proved to be wrong. Uzielli suggested that the drawings reproduced by Cooper were probably those in the Royal Collection at Windsor Castle.

For some unknown reason the Cooper engravings went out of circulation quite soon. As we have seen, in 1797 Gian Battista Venturi mentioned them in his *Essay*, but it does not seem that he had ever seen them, as we can infer from one of his letters to Giuseppe Bossi. In fact for two centuries no one has been able to see them, otherwise the texts of the Leonardo notes, which were even translated into English, would have been reproduced in some later publication. On the other hand, there are indications that the Cooper engravings were not reproductions of drawings in the Royal Collection. In fact, in 1730, Mariette described them on p. 23 as follows:

> Fragment d'un Traité sur les mouvemens du corps humain & la maniere de dessiner les figures suivant des regles geometriques. Cet ouvrage qui a été mis au jour à Londres depuis quelques années par E. Cooper, ne consiste qu'en neuf planches sans le titre. Quelquesunes sont de démonstrations avec des explications en Italien, données par Leonard, auxquelles on a joint la traduction Angloise. D'autres représentent des figures d'hommes & des femmes au trait. Elles sont executées avec esprit, & forment un très-petit cahier in-folio. (Fragment of a Treatise on the movements of the human body and the method for drawing figures according to geometric rules. This work, which was published in London a few years ago by E. Cooper, comprises just nine plates, except the title-page. Some of these plates have explanations in Italian provided by Leonardo, with English translations. Others represent male and female figures outlined. They are carried out with talent and form a very little book in-folio.)

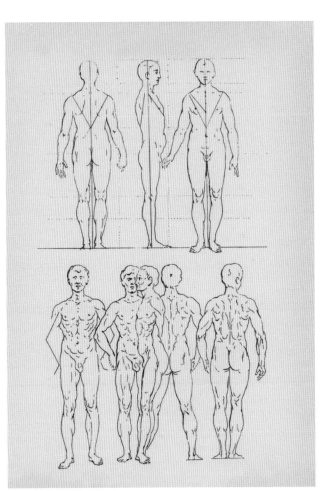

FIG. 30
Cooper Engravings,
pl. VII; Codex Huygens,
fols. 3 recto and 33 recto

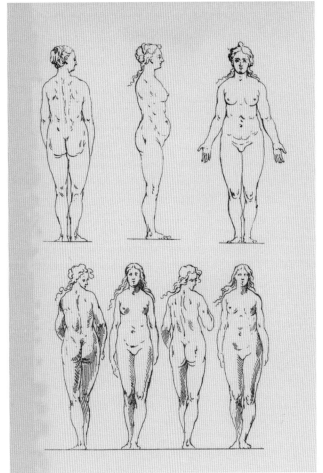

FIG. 31
Cooper Engravings,
pl. VIII; Codex Huygens,
fols. 4 recto and 46 recto

This description precisely corresponds with the type of figures and notes in the first part of the Codex Huygens. No original drawing by Leonardo, explaining the "maniere de dessiner les figures suivant des regles geometriques," was ever reported in England, and only Federico Zuccaro (1539–1609) seems to have seen some of them in Italy. On p. 31 of his *L'Idea de' pittori, scultori et architetti,* published in Turin in 1607 (a book not included in Verga's *Bibliografia vinciana)* he sharply criticizes the top art theoreticians of earlier times, from Dürer to Leonardo, though Leonardo is not mentioned by name. This text is quoted by Giovanni Bottari on p. 135 in vol. VI of his *Raccolta di lettere sulla pittura,* published in Rome in 1768. In Zuccaro's original edition of 1607 the matter is introduced by a lively preamble to an extraordinary source, surprisingly ignored by the Leonardo scholars of the last two centuries:

> Si sa che il Durero per quella fatica che non fu poca, credo ch'egli ascherzo, a passa tempo, e per dare trattenimento a quelli intelletti che stanno più su la contemplazione, che su le operationi, ciò facesse, e per mostrare che il Disegno, e lo spirito del Pittore sa, e può tutto ciò che si presuppone fare. Parimente di poco frutto fu, e di poca sostanza, altra regola che lasciò disegnata con scritti alla rouescia altro pur valent'huomo di professione, ma troppo sofistico anch'egli, in lasciare precetti pur mathematici a muouere e torcere la figura, con linee perpendicolari, con squadra e compassi: cose tutte d'ingegno sì, ma fantastico, & senza frutto di sostanza: pur come altri se la intendino, ciascuno può a suo gusto operare. Dirò bene che queste regole mathematiche si deuono lasciare a quelle scienze, e professioni speculatiue della Geometria, Astrologia, Arithmetica, e simili, che con le proue loro acquietano l'intelletto: ma noi altri professori del Disegno non habbiamo bisogno di altre regole, che quelle che la natura stessane dà, per quella imitare.
> [...]

Here Leonardo is unequivocally referred to as the author of drawings of the Codex Huygens type and who writes backwards: "Equally fruitless and lacking in substance [as those of Dürer] was the other rule about drawing, together with writings in mirror script, left by another man of our profession, but he also was too sophistic, relying on merely mathematical precepts

Per una ragione ancora da accertare, le incisioni Cooper uscirono ben presto dalla circolazione. Come abbiamo visto, nel 1797 il Venturi le menzionava nei suoi *Essay,* ma non sembra che avesse avuto modo di vederle come possiamo constatare da quello che scrive in una delle sue lettere al Bossi. Infatti, per due secoli a nessuno è stato possibile vederle, altrimenti i testi delle note di Leonardo da esse riportate perfino tradotte in inglese, sarebbero state riprodotte in qualche pubblicazione più tarda. D'altro canto, alcune indicazioni farebbero pensare che le incisioni Cooper non fossero riproduzioni tratte dai disegni appartenenti alla collezione reale. Infatti, nel 1730 Mariette a p. 23 le descrive in questo modo:

> Fragment d'un Traité sur les mouvemens du corps humain & la maniere de dessiner les figures suivant des regles geometriques. Cet ouvrage qui a été mis au jour à Londres depuis quelques années par E. Cooper, ne consiste qu'en neuf planches sans le titre. Quelques-unes sont de démonstrations avec des explications en Italien, données par Leonard, auxquelles on a joint la traduction Angloise. D'autres representent des figures d'hommes & des femmes au trait. Elles sont executées avec esprit, & forment un très-petit cahier in-folio.

Questa descrizione corrisponde precisamente al tipo delle figure e alle annotazioni poste nella prima parte del *Codice Huygens.* Nessun disegno autografo di Leonardo, che spieghi la "maniere de dessiner les figures suivant des regles geometriques", fu mai visto in Inghilterra, e solo Federico Zuccaro (1539-1609) sembra averne visti in Italia. A p. 31 del suo testo *L'Idea de' pittori, scultori et architetti* pubblicato a Torino nel 1607, libro non presente nella *Bibliografia vinciana* del Verga, critica aspramente i più rinomati teorici d'arte dei primi tempi da Dürer a Leonardo, anche se Leonardo non è menzionato per nome, e questo con un testo riportato da Giovanni Bottari a p. 135 nel vol. VI della sua *Raccolta di lettere sulla pittura* pubblicata a Roma nel 1768. Col libro di Zuccaro del 1607 il caso è introdotto da un vivace preambolo a una fonte straordinaria, sorprendentemente ignorata dagli studiosi di Leonardo negli ultimi due secoli:

> Si sa che il Durero per quella fatica che non fu poca, credo ch'egli ascherzo, a passa tempo, e per dare trattenimento a quelli intelletti che stanno più su la contemplazione, che su le operationi, ciò facesse, e per mostrare che il Disegno, e lo spirito del Pittore sa, e può tutto ciò che si presuppone fare. Parimente di poco frutto fu, e di poca sostanza, altra regola che lasciò disegnata con scritti alla rouescia altro pur

for the motion and twisting of the human figure, using perpendicular lines, square and compass; certainly these were ingenious things but fantastic, fruitless and insubstantial [...] I say that these mathematical rules should be left to such sciences and speculative disciplines as geometry, astrology, arithmetic, and the like, which, by giving proof, satisfy the mind. But we teachers of drawing do not need such rules, but only those which Nature herself gives us in order to imitate her." Zuccaro must have seen a lost book on human motion written by Leonardo himself. If the Codex Huygens were what he had in mind, he would not have mentioned "writings in mirror script."

In 1767 a second edition, not recorded by Verga, of Caylus, *Recueil de testes de caràctere et de charges dessinées par Léonard de Vinci florentin* (Mariette 1730; Verga 48) was issued in Paris. Mariette's introductory letter was printed according to the revisions of the author. This too has passed unnoticed to Leonardo scholars. The paragraph concerning the Cooper engravings is somewhat expanded. Mariette now describes figures that are unquestionably those of the Codex Huygens. On pp. 34–35, he also specifies that the plates are nine plus the title-page (before he had said "neuf planches sans le titre," and it was not clear whether the title-page was also a plate or whether the nine plates came without any title-page); and finally that the publication date was "vers l'année 1720":

> Fragment d'un traité sur les mouvemens du corps humain & la maniere de dessiner les figures humaines suivant des regles géométriques. Cet ouvrage qui a été mis au jour à Londres vers l'année 1720, par E. Cooper, ne consiste qu'en dix planc. y compris celle du frontispice, dont les plus importantes sont des démonstrations d'un système, à l'aide duquel on voit que Léonard prétendoit assujettir à des regles invariables les mouvemens des membres qui entrent dans la composition du corps humain. Dans d'autres planches sont représentées des figures d'hommes & de femmes de différentes proportions: tout cela est entremêlé de quelques écrits italiens, tels qu'ils étoient sur les desseins, suivis de la traduction en anglois; ce petit cahier *in-folio* est curieux. Celui qui a gravé les planches y a mis de l'esprit. (Fragment of a treatise on the movements of the human body and the method for drawing figures according

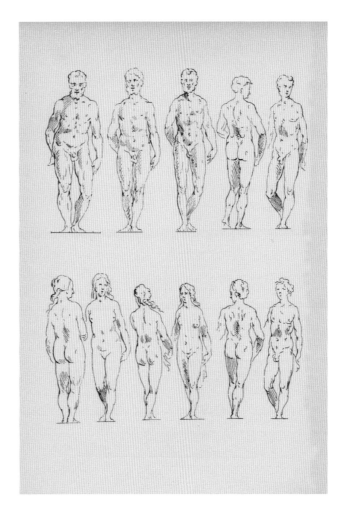

FIG. 32
Cooper Engravings, pl. IX; Codex Huygens, fols. 43 recto, 41 recto and 41 verso

valent'huomo di professione, ma troppo sofistico anch'egli, in lasciare precetti pur mathematici a muouere e torcere la figura, con linee perpendicolari, con squadra e compassi: cose tutte d'ingegno sì, ma fantastico, & senza frutto di sostanza: pur come altri se la intendino, ciascuno può a suo gusto operare. Dirò bene che queste regole mathematiche si deuono lasciare a quelle scienze, e professioni speculatiue della Geometria, Astrologia, Arithmetica, e simili, che con le proue loro acquietano l'intelletto: ma noi altri professori del Disegno non habbiamo bisogno di altre regole, che quelle che la natura stessane dà, per quolla imitaro.
[...]

Qui Leonardo è inequivocabilmente menzionato come autore dei disegni tipologicamente affini al *Codex Huygens* e con scrittura speculare: "Parimenti di poco frutto fu, e di poca sostanza, l'altra [regola] che lasciò disegnata con scritti alla rovescia altro pur valent'huomo di professione, ma troppo sofistico anch'egli, in lasciare precetti pur mathematici a muouere e torcere

to geometric rules. This work, which was published in London around the year 1720, by E. Cooper, comprises only ten plates and this is including the title-page, of which the most important are the demonstrations of a system, thanks to which Leonardo also claimed to have set consistent rules regarding the movements of the limbs which are part of the composition of the human body. In other plates he portrays male and female figures of varying proportions: they are all alternating with notes in Italian like in the drawings, followed by the translation into English; this little book in-folio is unusual. The author engraved the plates with talent.)

A set of Cooper's engravings reached Italy as early as 1732. In 1757, Bottari said on pp. 228 and 266 that it was Mariette himself who sent them, in 1731, to his friend Niccolò Gaburri in Florence:

Io ho il libro che ha dato alla luce Cooper da' disegni di Leonardo, e fate già conto, che sia vostro, ed averlo in vostro potere, perché ve lo manderò per la prima occasione. (I have the book published by Cooper with engravings after Leonardo's drawings. Consider it already yours, because I am planning to send it to you at the first occasion.)

In another letter, on January 28, 1732, Mariette announced that the book was on its way to Florence. On the following October 4, Gaburri acknowledged receipt of it, adding another interesting piece of information :

[…] Per ultimo mi son riservato a discorrervi del libro di Leonardo da Vinci delle proporzioni del corpo umano, per dirvi, che questo mi è stato caro al segno maggiore; principalmente perché è rarissimo, ed io non l'aveva mai veduto; in secondo luogo perché voi ne parlate in quella vostra lettera, che va avanti alle teste di caricature di Leonardo intagliate dal suddetto signor Conte [of Caylus]. La medesima lettera mi diede lume, che un disegno, che io posseggo già da gran tempo di quello autore, attenente alle sopradette proporzioni, potesse essere un foglio di quel libro stesso, che fu venduto alla spicciolata da chi non ne conosceva punto nè poco il merito; ed avendo confrontato il disegno istesso colle stampe del

la figura, con linee perpendicolari, con squadra e compassi: cose tutte d'ingegno sì, ma fantastico, & senza frutto di sostanza: pur come altri se la intendino, ciascuno può a suo gusto operare. Dirò bene che queste regole mathematiche si deuono lasciare a quelle scienze, e professioni speculatiue della Geometria, Astrologia, Arithmetica, e simili, che con le proue loro acquietano l'intelletto: ma noi altri professori del Disegno non habbiamo bisogno di altre regole, che quelle che la natura stessane dà, per quella imitare". Zuccaro doveva pertanto aver visto un libro sul movimento umano scritto da Leonardo ma andato poi perduto. Infatti, se il *Codice Huygens* fosse stato proprio il manoscritto a cui faceva riferimento, non lo avrebbe menzionato come "scritti alla rovescia".

Nel 1767 una seconda edizione del Caylus e intitolata *Recueil de testes de caràctere et de charges dessinées par Léonard de Vinci florentin* (Mariette 1730; Verga 48), non citata dal Verga, fu data alle stampe a Parigi e la lettera introduttiva del Mariette fu data in base a un testo riveduto dall'autore. Anche questa opera a stampa è passata inosservata agli studiosi di Leonardo. Il paragrafo dedicato alle incisioni è piuttosto esteso. Alle pp. 34 e 35, Mariette descrive tali figure che, in modo indiscutibile, appartengono al *Codice Huygens*. Egli specifica che le tavole sono nove, più il frontespizio (prima aveva detto "neuf planches sans le titre", e non era chiaro se la copertina fosse anch'essa una tavola oppure se le nove tavole non la comprendessero); e infine annota pure che la data di pubblicazione era "vers l'année 1720":

Fragment d'un traité sur les mouvemens du corps humain & la maniere de dessiner les figures humaines suivant des regles géométriques. Cet ouvrage qui a été mis au jour à Londres vers l'année 1720, par E. Cooper, ne consiste qu'en dix planc. y compris celle du frontispice, dont les plus importantes sont des démonstrations d'un systême, à l'aide duquel on voit que Léonard prétendoit assujettir à des regles invariables les mouvemens des membres qui entrent dans la composition du corps humain. Dans d'autres planches sont représentées des figures d'hommes & de femmes de différentes proportions: tout cela est entremêlé de quelques écrits italiens, tels qu'ils étoient sur les desseins, suivis de la traduction en anglois; ce petit cahier *in-folio* est curieux. Celui qui a gravé les planches y a mis de l'esprit.

libro mandatomi, ho trovato, che è della stessa misura tanto per l'altezza, che per la larghezza. Io ne ho fatto fare una copia più esatta, che è stato possibile da un giovane diligente, e che disegna bene, e questa mi fo ardito di mandarvela […]. ([…] I have left it til last to mention the book by Leonardo da Vinci on the proportions of the human body, as I want you to know that I consider this the most precious gift you sent me; first because it is extremely rare, for I have never seen it before; second, because you mentioned it in that letter you published as an introduction to the series of Leonardo's caricatures engraved by the above mentioned signor Conte [of Caylus]. That letter gave me the idea that a Leonardo drawing on proportions, which I possessed for a long time, could have been a sheet of the same book, since that book might have been sold sheet by sheet by someone unaware of its value. Now, comparing this drawing with the engravings you sent me I find that their measurements are exactly the same, both in height and width. I have had a copy of it made by a talented youth, who draws well, and this I am now eagerly sending to you […].)

In the edition of Leonardo's *Treatise on Painting*, published by Francesco Fontani in Florence in 1792, the statement that Leonardo had composed *un'opera sulla Meccanica del corpo umano* (note on p. xvi) is based on the information that a fragment of it had been published by Cooper in London. But it is doubtful that the engravings were known in Florence. The set that belonged to Gaburri, as well as the drawing owned by him—probably a missing sheet of the Codex Huygens—were apparently already out of reach. In fact they must have been unknown even to the well informed Monsignor Giovanni Bottari, if he could suggest (*Lettere sulla pittura*, vol. II [1757], pp. 179–80) that the Cooper engravings were probably after the codex that a "signore Inglese" brought to Florence in 1717, that is, Lord Leicester. It is true that the title-page of the Cooper engravings shows the dedication to a Thomas Coke, Vice Chamberlain to King George. But this is a different person with the same name as the Earl of Leicester, that is, Thomas Coke of Melbourne Hall.

After several years of search, following my first note in the *Journal of the Warburg and Courtauld Institutes* of 1965, and when my Richter *Commentary* was about to

Un gruppo di incisioni Cooper arrivò in Italia già a partire dal 1732. Come riporta Bottari nel 1757, alle pp. 228 e 266, fu lo stesso Mariette a inviarle in dono, nel 1731, al suo amico Niccolò Gaburri a Firenze:

> Io ho il libro che ha dato alla luce Cooper da' disegni di Leonardo, e fate già conto, che sia vostro, ed averlo in vostro potere, perché ve lo manderò per la prima occasione.

In un'altra lettera scritta in data 28 Gennaio 1732, Mariette annunciava che il libro era stato inviato. Il successivo 4 Ottobre, Gaburri dava notizia della sua ricezione, aggiungendo alcune interessanti informazioni:

> […] Per ultimo mi son riservato a discorrervi del libro di Leonardo da Vinci delle proporzioni del corpo umano, per dirvi, che questo mi è stato caro al segno maggiore; principalmente perché è rarissimo, ed io non l'aveva mai veduto; in secondo luogo perché voi ne parlate in quella vostra lettera, che va avanti alle teste di caricature di Leonardo intagliate dal suddetto signor Conte [di Caylus]. La medesima lettera mi diede lume, che un disegno, che io posseggo già da gran tempo di quello autore, attenente alle sopradette proporzioni, potesse essere un foglio di quel libro stesso, che fu venduto alla spicciolata da chi non ne conosceva punto nè poco il merito; ed avendo confrontato il disegno istesso colle stampe del libro mandatomi, ho trovato, che è della stessa misura tanto per l'altezza, che per la larghezza. Io ne ho fatto fare una copia più esatta, che è stato possibile da un giovane diligente, e che disegna bene, e questa mi fo ardito di mandarvela […].

Nell'edizione del *Trattato della pittura* pubblicato a Firenze nel 1792 a cura di Francesco Fontani, l'asserzione per cui Leonardo aveva composto "un'opera sulla Meccanica del corpo umano" (nota a p. xvi) si basa sulla notizia che un frammento di questa fosse stato appunto pubblicato da Cooper a Londra. È comunque improbabile che le incisioni fossero conosciute in ambiente fiorentino. L'esemplare che appartenne a Gaburri, così come il disegno in suo possesso identificato probabilmente come uno dei fogli mancanti del *Codice Huygens*, non erano facilmente accessibili. Infatti, dovevano essere sconosciuti anche all'informatissimo Monsignor Giovanni Bottari, se egli suggeriva (*Lettere sulla pittura*, vol. II [1757], pp. 179-80) che le incisioni Cooper dovevano essere ricercate probabilmente in un codice che un "signore Inglese" – identificato in Lord Leicester – comprò a Firenze nel 1717. È pur vero che il frontespizio delle incisioni Cooper mostra la dedica a

go to press in the Fall of 1970, I was able to locate a set of the Cooper engravings in the library of the Duke of Devonshire at Chatsworth. This is listed in J.P. Lacaita's *Catalogue of the Library of the Duke of Devonshire at Chatsworth* (London 1879) under Cooper, but not under Leonardo. It measures 225 x 357 mm, and it is composed of nine plates plus the title-page, which is also engraved. With their reproduction in my Richter *Commentary* of 1977, pp. 53–62, I gave a concordance with the corresponding selected sheets of the Codex Huygens.

Erwin Panofsky's scholarly edition of the Codex Huygens was published in London by the Warburg Institute in 1940. It is certainly only a matter of bibliographic curiosity that a selection of folios of the Codex Huygens was published also in London two centuries before. In a way, the story is like an open circle that has finally come to a close, again in England, with my Richter *Commentary* of 1977.

The First Exhibition

More than thirty years later, well into the new millennium, a selection of sheets from the Codex Huygens is exhibited at the Morgan Library for the first time, together with Leonardo's Codex on the Flight of Birds from the Biblioteca Reale in Turin.

The codex consists of 128 loose sheets inserted between the blank pages of a book bound in red morocco. Huygens himself informs us that he personally took the book apart in order to have it arranged as it is today, that is, as a collection of loose sheets. These measure about 130–135 x 180 mm, except for four bifolios. Huygens gives no information as to the original structure of the book, but states that he had the print dealer Cooper restore the sheets, "on op te placken"— namely, "mending and mounting." Panofsky points out that all the small sheets, as well as the individual sheets of the bifolios are reinforced at the edges by narrow strips of paper, and states that this was obviously done by Cooper in order to prevent the edges from fraying. I have reason to suspect that Cooper's work was less elaborate, and that the narrow strips of paper are the leftover of the margins of a previous mount that Cooper might in fact have tried to remove. This would be comparable to the way the loose sheets of the Codex Atlanticus were originally mounted by Pompeo Leoni. And as in the Codex Atlanticus, the double sheets of the Codex Huygens were mounted with a portion hanging loose and folded back as a flap-hence the presence of a strip of mount across the

Thomas Coke, da identificarsi non con il Vice Ciambellano di re Giorgio, come si era soliti credere, ma, per un caso di omonimia, con Thomas Coke di Melbourne Hall.

Dopo vari anni di ricerca, su istigazione della mia prima nota edita nel *Journal of the Warburg and Courtauld Institutes* nel 1965, e quando il mio *Commentary* al Richter stava per andare in stampa nell'autunno del 1970, riuscii a trovare l'esemplare delle incisioni Cooper nella biblioteca del duca del Devonshire a Chatsworth. Questo era stato inventariato in J.P. Lacaita, *Catalogue of the Library of the Duke of Devonshire at Chatsworth* (Londra 1879) sotto il nome Cooper, ma non sotto quello di Leonardo. Ogni incisione misura 225 x 357 mm e l'esemplare è costituito da nove tavole più il frontespizio, anch'esso inciso. Con la loro riproduzione alle pp. 53-62 del mio *Commentary* al Richter del 1977, ebbi modo di dare anche una concordanza tra queste e i corrispondenti fogli del *Codice Huygens*.

L'edizione critica del *Codice Huygens* a cura di Erwin Panofsky fu pubblicata a Londra nel 1940 dal Warburg Institute. È certamente una circostanza di mera curiosità bibliografica se una selezione di fogli appartenenti al *Codice Huygens* veniva pubblicata anch'essa a Londra due secoli prima. In un certo senso, la storia del codice è come un cerchio aperto che viene a chiudersi, sempre in Inghilterra, con il mio *Commentary* al Richter nel 1977.

La prima mostra

Più di trenta anni dopo, già da tempo entrati nel Nuovo Millennio, una selezione di fogli tratti dal *Codice Huygens* viene esposta alla Morgan Library a New York, insieme al *Codice del volo degli uccelli* di Leonardo conservato alla Biblioteca Reale di Torino.

Il *Codice Huygens* consiste di 128 fogli sciolti inseriti tra le pagine bianche di un libro rilegato in marocchino rosso. Huygens in persona ci informa che smontò il libro per disporlo come si può ammirare oggi, dunque come una collezione di fogli sciolti. I fogli misurano dai 130 ai 135 mm per 180 circa, ad eccezione di quattro fogli doppi. Huygens non fornisce alcuna informazione circa l'originale struttura del libro, ma afferma che fu l'antiquario Cooper a restaurare i fogli, "on op te placken"– vale a dire "riparandoli e montandoli". Panofsky sottolineava che i fogli piccoli, come pure quelli a metà dei più grandi furono rinforzati agli angoli da striscioline di carta, operazione effettuata da Cooper per evitare che i margini si danneggiassero. Ho motivo di credere che l'intervento di Cooper fosse meno elaborato e che le striscioline di carta fossero i resti dei margini di una precedente montatura che forse Cooper provò a rimuovere. Questo procedimento potrebbe essere paragonabile a quello effettuato anche sul *Codice Atlan-*

FIG. 33
CARLO URBINO
(ca. 1510/20–after 1585)
The Proportions of the Human Figure: A Nude Man Full Face, Arm Outstretched / Le proporzioni del corpo umano: un nudo virile in veduta frontale con un braccio disteso,
16th cent. / XVI sec.
Pen and brown ink over black chalk on paper / Penna, inchiostro bruno e pietra nera su carta
385 x 255 mm
Oxford, Christ Church (0012)

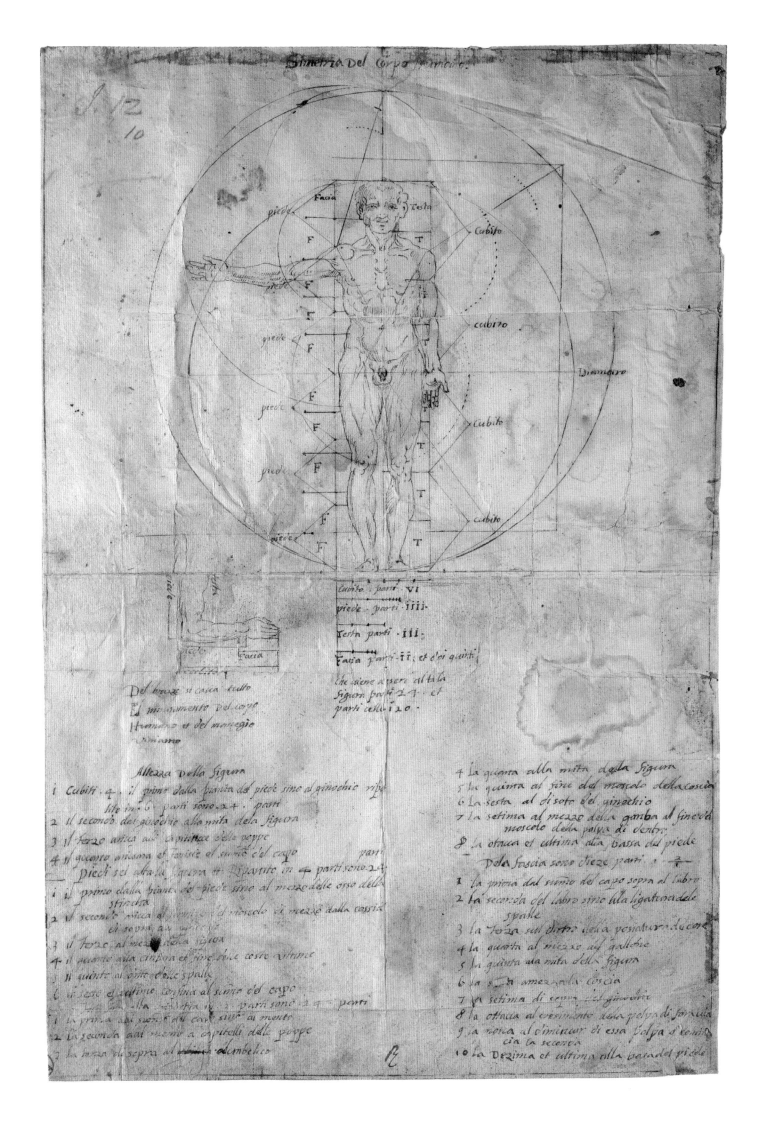

Facia · Testa
piede · Cubito
F · T
piede · F
F · cubito
piede · F
F · Diametro
piede · Cubito
F · T
piede · T
F · cubito
piede · T
F

Cubito · parti · VI
piede · parti · iiii
Testa · parti · iii
Facia parti · ii · et di quinti

Che viene a essere al tuta
figura parti 2 4 · et
parti delli · 1 2 o ·

Del braze si casca tutto
El movimento del corpo
Humano et del maneggio
umano

Alteza della figura
1 Cubiti · 4 · il primo dalla pianta del piede sino al ginochio ripa
      lite in · 6 · parti sono · 2 4 · parti
2 Il secondo dal ginochio alla mita dela figura
3 Il terzo arica al la pistrice della peppe
4 Il quarto ancora et finisce al summo d'el capo   parti
      Piedi sei alta la figura et dipartito in 4 parti sono 2 4
1 Il primo dalla pianta del piede sino al mezzo delle osso della
      stinetta
2 Il secondo nica al venire del moscolo di mezzo dalla cossia
      di sopra au orechie
3 Il terzo al mezzo della figura
4 Il quarto alla cinta et fine delle coste ultime
5 Il quinto al oste delle spalle
6 Il sesto el ultimo confina al summo d'el capo
      la alla faccia in parti sono 2 4 parti
1 la prima dal summo d'el capo sine al mento
2 la seconda dal mento a capitelli delle peppe
3 la terza di sopra al umbelico

4 la quarta alla mita della figura
5 la quinta al fine del moscolo della coscia
6 La sesta al di soto del ginochio
7 La setima al mezzo della gamba al fine del
      moscolo della palpa di dentro
8 la otaua et ultima alla bassa del piede
      Dela fascia sono dieze parti · 7
1 la prima dal summo del capo sopra al labro
2 La seconda del labro sino lila ligatura dele
      spalle
3 la terza sul dirto della pesiatura di core
4 la quarta al mezzo del gallone
5 la quinta ala mita della figura
6 la sesta di mezza la coscia
7 la setima di copra del ginochio
8 la otaua al cresinento dela polpa di fomula
9 la nona al siminuir di essa polpa a conti
      cia la secenta
10 La Dezima et ultima alla bacca del piede

middle of a double sheet. Thus the sheets of the Codex Huygens must have been mounted originally on the sheets of a larger book, and in fact Huygens refers to such a book as being in quarto, whereas the individual sheets can be more properly designated as being in octavo. A codex with its sheets kept loose turns out to offer the ideal conditions to display several of its sheets simultaneously, and also greatly facilitates their photographic reproductions.

There is no doubt that the 128 sheets represent only a fragment of a larger work. The way they were mounted originally may even suggest that they had been kept loose until they came into the hands of a collector, probably Pompeo Leoni himself. It is only conjectural but quite probable that they had come from the same source as the bulk of the Leonardo manuscripts, that is, from the Melzi estate.

Huygens does not question the attribution of the book to Leonardo, yet drawings and handwriting are unlike anything produced by Leonardo. Probably the previous binding or mounts included some information about a traditional attribution to Leonardo, in the sense of a compilation based on Leonardo material. As we have seen, there seems to be no doubt that Federico Zuccaro had seen an original manuscript from which much of the Codex Huygens was copied. Not only does he speak of a manuscript as being in mirror script, but he identifies it as Leonardo's "regola del disegno," which is the same title of the Codex Huygens (*Le Regole del Disegno*). It may be surmised that Zuccaro had seen it in Rome—probably the book brought there by the anonymous Milanese painter who visited Vasari shortly before 1564. (Vasari refers to that painter as the owner of "alcuni scritti di Leonardo, pur di caratteri scritti con la mancina a rovescio, che trattano della pittura e de' *modi del disegno*, e colorire.") This may explain why a copy was made in Milan, so that it could remain there, probably in Melzi's hands. A reexamination of the Codex Huygens, as suggested by Irma A. Richter in a seminal article in *The Art Bulletin*, 23 (1941), pp. 335–38, may reveal that the material is much closer to Leonardo than one may be inclined to believe. And one may add that even the structure, although it is the mere fragment of a greater work, probably reflects a Leonardo plan.

The codex is un an unfinished treatise on *disegno* by a Milanese painter active in the second half of the sixteenth century, recently identified as Carlo Urbino (ca. 1510/20-after 1585) as shown by a large en-

tico i cui fogli furono in origine montati da Pompeo Leoni. Così come per il *Codice Atlantico*, i fogli doppi del *Codice Huygens* erano montati con una parte sciolta e ripiegata all'indietro come una bandella – di qui la presenza di una strisciolina di supporto nel mezzo di un foglio doppio. Ne consegue che i fogli del *Codice Huygens* dovevano essere montati in origine sui fogli di un libro più grande, e infatti Huygens menziona un libro *in quarto*, mentre i fogli singoli possono essere più propriamente designati *in ottavo*. Un codice composto da fogli sciolti in modo da offrire le condizioni ideali per mostrare più fogli simultaneamente e per favorire notevolmente la riproduzione fotografica.

Non c'è dubbio che i 128 fogli rappresentino la parte frammentaria di un lavoro più ampio. Il modo in cui questi furono montati in origine potrebbe suggerire che i fogli rimasero sciolti fino a quando non arrivarono nelle mani di un collezionista, probabilmente lo stesso Pompeo Leoni. È soltanto in via congetturale, ma tuttavia altamente probabile, che questi provenissero dalla stessa fonte dalla quale provengono la grande quantità dei manoscritti di Leonardo, e cioè dall'eredità Melzi.

Huygens non mette in discussione l'attribuzione del libro a Leonardo, eppure i disegni e la scrittura non sono gli stessi di quelli prodotti dal maestro. Probabilmente la precedente legatura e montatura includeva alcune informazioni circa la tradizionale attribuzione a Leonardo da intendere come una compilazione basata su materiale di Leonardo. Come abbiamo visto, sembra non esserci alcun dubbio sul fatto che Federico Zuccaro avrebbe avuto modo di osservare il manoscritto originale dal quale il *Codice Huygens* fu copiato. Non solo egli parla di un manoscritto con una scrittura speculare ma non manca di identificarlo come la "regola del disegno" di Leonardo, che risulta essere lo stesso titolo del *Codice Huygens* (*Le Regole del Disegno*). Si potrebbe ipotizzare che Zuccaro avesse visto il manoscritto autografo a Roma, probabilmente identificabile con lo stesso libro portato da un pittore milanese anonimo che visitò Vasari subito prima del 1564. (Vasari parla di un pittore che possedeva "alcuni scritti di Leonardo, pur di caratteri scritti con la mancina a rovescio, che trattano della pittura e de' *modi del disegno*, e colorire"). Questo potrebbe suggerire la ragione per cui fu richiesta una copia, perché questo rimanesse a Milano probabilmente nelle mani del Melzi. Un accurato riesame del *Codice Huygens*, come già suggerito da Irma A. Richter in un suo fondamentale articolo del 1941 (*The Art Bulletin*, XXIII, pp. 335-38), potrebbe rilevare che il materiale è più vicino a Leonardo di quanto si possa credere. Si potrebbe perfino osservare che anche la struttura, anche se risultato frammentario di un lavoro più esteso, riflette probabilmente la stessa organizzazione data da Leonardo.

graving (345 x 505 mm) produced by the workshop of the Bolognese printmaker Gaspare dall'Olio, who inscribed it with the information: "Tauola | cauata dal quinto libro | della Prospettiva | delle Regole del Disegno | di Carlo Vrbini Pittore | V?A . V?B | .F." ("Plate taken from the Fifth Book on Perspective of the Rules of Design by Carlo Urbino Painter […].") The only known extant copy of this print is kept in the Museo di Castelvecchio in Verona (2556 3B 779) and was shown for the first time in the 2001 exhibition *Nel segno di Masaccio: L'invenzione della prospettiva* at the Uffizi in Florence, curated by Filippo Camerota (Cremante in Florence 2001, p. 177, cat. VIII.1.6).

The paper has watermarks pointing to a date around 1560–70. Thus the compiler had access to Leonardo's original material when it was still all together in one place, at Vaprio d'Adda before Melzi's death in 1570. In fact, the originals identified as sources are now at Windsor, Paris and Venice. The large compilation, as planned, was to include fourteen "regole [rules]" or "libri [books]," of which only the first five are included in the codex, and these, almost all on the human figure, are in an uneven and confused form. Their sequence is as follows:

The first book deals with the form and structure of the human body.
The second with its movements.
The third with methods of transforming the profile elevation of the human figure into front and rear elevations.
The fourth with proportions of the human figure and of the horse.
The fifth with perspective.

The sheets from the Codex Huygens that correspond to the plates of the Cooper engravings of ca. 1720 merit particular attention. In this context, one should also consider two sheets in the drawings collection of Christ Church at Oxford, which I published in 1977 in the first volume of my Richter *Commentary*. One of the two (0012; fig. 33) is in large format, 385 x 255 mm, about four times the size of a regular sheet of the Codex Huygens. It is of stronger paper, with a watermark (scales in a circle) that Briquet dates later than 1555. It is neatly drawn and compiled, with orderly notations and reference letters. It is a study of human proportions that betrays a Leonardo model such as the celebrated *Vitruvian Man* in Venice. As such it is very possibly an accurate copy of a Leonardo drawing now lost. The other sheet at Oxford (0671;

Il codice è dunque un trattato non finito sul disegno realizzato da un pittore milanese attivo nella seconda metà del sedicesimo secolo, recentemente identificato in Carlo Urbino (1510/20-post 1585) come mostra una grande incisione (345 x 505 mm) prodotta dalla bottega dello stampatore bolognese Gaspare dall'Olio che incise sulla tavola queste preziose informazioni: "Tauola | cauata dal quinto libro | della Prospettiva | delle Regole del Disegno | di Carlo Vrbini Pittore | V?A . V?B | .F. ". L'unica copia nota fino ad ora di questa stampa, quella conservata al Museo di Castelvecchio a Verona (2556 3B 779), fu esposta per la prima volta nella mostra del 2001 *Nel segno di Masaccio. L'invenzione della prospettiva* a cura di Filippo Camerota (Cremante in Florence 2001, p. 177, cat. VIII.1.6).

Il foglio mostra una filigrana databile attorno al 1560-70. Si può dunque pensare che il compilatore avesse accesso al materiale originale di Leonardo, magari proprio a Vaprio d'Adda, prima che questo fosse disperso a seguito della morte di Melzi avvenuta nel 1570. Infatti, le fonti originali si trovano oggi a Windsor, Parigi e Venezia. La grande raccolta doveva pertanto includere quattordici "regole" o "libri", dei quali soltanto i primi cinque furono inclusi nel codice. Questi tuttavia, quasi tutti sulla figura umana, sono redatti in una forma irregolare e confusa. La loro sequenza è come segue:

Il primo libro si occupa della forma e della struttura del corpo umano.
Il secondo dei suoi movimenti.
Il terzo dei metodi di trasformazione di una sezione della figura umana nella rappresentazione della figura vista di fronte e da dietro.
Il quarto delle proporzioni della figura umana e del cavallo.
Il quinto della prospettiva.

Il numero di fogli che corrisponde alle tavole delle incisioni Cooper del 1720 merita la dovuta attenzione. Si aggiunga che non sarebbe fuori luogo includere i due fogli conservati nella raccolta dei disegni alla Christ Church a Oxford, che ho pubblicato nel 1977 nel primo volume del mio *Commentary* al Richter. Uno di questi (0012; fig. 33) ha un grande formato, 385 x 255 mm, corrispondente a circa quattro volte le dimensioni di un foglio appartenente al *Codice Huygens* ed è realizzato utilizzando una carta più forte con una filigrana (una scala inscritta in un cerchio) che Briquet data post 1555. Questo è disegnato con la massima cura e compilato con citazioni ben ordinate e lettere di riferimento. Si tratta dello studio di proporzioni umane che fa pensare a un modello di Leonardo come l'*Uomo vitruviano* a Venezia. In quanto tale, potrebbe essere una copia accurata di un disegno di Leonardo andato perduto. L'altro foglio conservato a Oxford (0671; fig. 34) è piuttosto simile a quelli del codice.

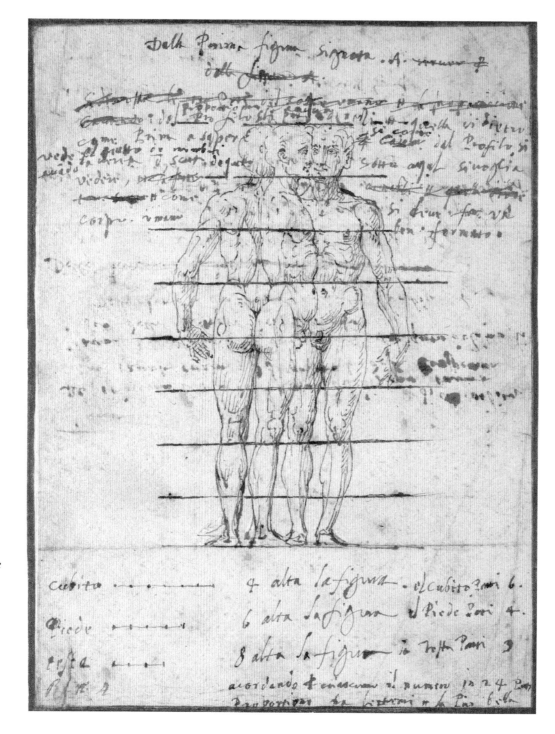

FIG. 34
CARLO URBINO
(ca. 1510/20–after 1585)
*Three Male Nude
Figures, Juxtaposed for
"Transformation"* /
*Tre vedute di una figura virile
in successione,*
16th cent. / XVI sec.
Pen and brown ink over
black chalk on paper /
Penna, inchiostro bruno e
pietra nera su carta
184 x 138 mm
Oxford, Christ Church
(0671)

fig. 34) is more similar to those of the codex. It measures 184 x 138 mm and is backed by heavier paper on which is written an old attribution to Raphael. Its verso is therefore only visible by holding it against a strong light, which reveals just a few words in the same cursive writing as the recto: *della Prospettiva* […] *delle Regole del Disegno*. Drawings and writing on the recto are as untidy as certain pages of the codex. The standing male figure, which is rapidly shown in three views merging one into the other, pertains to the subject of "Transformation" treated in the Third Book of the Codex Huygens. A note to it, albeit sketchy, is sufficiently clear in its reference to the principle of taking the side view of the human body as containing the data necessary for the representation of back and front views.

This is a principle applied time and again in the section on Perspective in the Codex Huygens, e.g., in the case of the "Rule to obtain from the profile of a body the front and back views of it" on fol. 100 verso. Also interesting in this context is a small drawing at Windsor (RL 12605), which Panofsky, following Berenson, Richter and others, considered an original Leonardo, while Kenneth Clark in 1935 had already identified it as a very feeble copy. Of course it is still a very important drawing as an example of parallel projection; furthermore, there should be no hesitation in ascribing it to the author of the Codex Huygens. Of course, Leonardo was certainly acquainted with the system, as adopted by Piero della Francesca and by such Milanese theoreticians as Foppa and Bramantino, and eventually by Dürer. This is shown by small diagrammatic sketches on a beautiful drawing at Windsor (RL 12603 verso) of about 1490, comparable in subject and style to a drawing at Turin now reconstructed from two fragments (15574 D.C.–15576 D.C.; fig. 4).

On a much later sheet of the Codex Atlanticus, fol. 318 ii verso (ex 115 v-b), ca. 1515, Leonardo again shows his debt to Piero della Francesca. A light profile of a head is projected into a three-quarter view of the same head by means of parallel lines. This is the same procedure adopted in the drawings on the recto with a diagram of perspective, showing the geometrical process involved in foreshortening a circle into an oval or ellipse, precisely as on Codex Atlanticus, fol. 602 recto (ex 223 r-a), where the same drawing in the same scale, shows the plan for an architectural structure that prefigures Michelangelo's oval design for the piazza of the Campidoglio (see my *Leonardo architetto* of 1978, pp. 302–3).

Questo misura 184 x 138 mm ed è realizzato su una carta più pesante sulla quale è appuntata una errata attribuzione a Raffaello. Al verso, visibile solo se visto in controluce, si leggono poche parole scritte nella stessa grafia corsiva del recto: *della Prospettiva* […] *delle Regole del Disegno*. I disegni e la scrittura sul recto sono disordinati proprio come in certe pagine del codice. La figura di uomo stante che è mostrata in successione in tre diverse vedute che sembrano originarsi l'una dall'altra, appartiene al tema della "trasformazione" trattato nel terzo libro del *Codice Huygens*. Una annotazione, anche se piuttosto abbozzata, è un chiaro riferimento al principio secondo il quale è sufficiente prendere la veduta in sezione di un corpo umano per ottenere i dati necessari per la riproduzione della visione frontale e posteriore.

Questo principio è applicato di tanto in tanto nella parte del *Codice Huygens* che tratta di Prospettiva, per esempio al foglio 100 v dove si legge la "Regola per ottenere dal profilo di un corpo la sua prospettiva frontale e posteriore". A questo riguardo si potrebbe considerare il piccolo disegno conservato a Windsor (RL 12605) che Panofsky, seguendo l'opinione di Berenson, Richter e altri, considera un originale di Leonardo mentre Kenneth Clark nel 1935 lo aveva già riconosciuto come una debole copia. Al di là dei dubbi attributivi, è comunque un disegno importante in quanto può essere considerato come un esempio di proiezione parallela e stilisticamente è ascrivibile senza esitazioni all'autore del *Codice Huygens*. Sicuramente Leonardo conosceva il sistema adottato da Piero della Francesca e dai teorici milanesi come Foppa e Bramantino, e infine da Dürer. Lo dimostra il piccolo diagramma schizzato accanto a un bellissimo disegno di Windsor (RL 12603 v) databile circa al 1490, e avvicinabile per soggetto e per stile al disegno di Torino, adesso ricostruito grazie all'unione di due frammenti (15574 D.C.-15576 D.C.; fig. 4).

In un foglio più tardo del *Codice Atlantico*, foglio 318 ii v (ex 115 v-b), *c.* 1515, Leonardo mostra ancora di essere debitore a Piero della Francesca. Il lieve profilo è realizzato in una veduta a tre quarti della stessa testa per mezzo di linee parallele, la stessa procedura è adottata nei disegni al recto con un diagramma prospettico che mostra il procedimento geometrico utilizzato nella rappresentazione in scorcio di un cerchio come ovale o ellisse, proprio come nel *Codice Atlantico*, al foglio 602 r (ex 223 r-a), dove lo stesso disegno nella stessa scala mostra il progetto per una struttura architettonica che prefigura il disegno ovale concepito da Michelangelo per la piazza del Campidoglio (rimando al mio *Leonardo architetto* del 1978, pp. 302-3).

Codex Huygens

Codice Huygens

Folios chosen by / Fogli scelti da *Paola Salvi*

This selection illustrates the principal topics into which the 128 folios of the Codex Huygens can be grouped, concerning:
The form, the structure and the anatomy of the human body;
The movements of the human body, portrayed in a circular motion that derives from the Aristotelian notion of *quantità continua* ("continuous quantity"), to which Leonardo refers in both his anatomical studies and the *Treatise on Painting;*
The projection of the body in various views, presented simultaneously, according to the principle that Leonardo expresses on anatomical fol. RL 19061 recto, K/P 154 recto ("Therefore through my plan you will come to know every part and every whole through the demonstration of three different aspects of each part", Keele and Pedretti 1979–80, vol. II, p. 594);
The proportional studies of the human body and the body of the horse;
The studies of the theory of shadow ("Del sole et l'ombra");
The perspective studies applied to the human body, with the explanation of rules for foreshortening.

Fol. 3 recto (fig. 35) shows three views (frontal, side and rear) of a standing male body, with references to the proportions of the principal external parts of the body;
Fol. 7 recto (fig. 36) carries the fifth and last figure of the first book on the "principles of motion." The drawing is directly related to the *Vitruvian Man* and appears to be a study that envisages a single center (the umbilicus), juxtaposing the circle and the square, which in the *Vitruvian Man* in Venice have different centers;
Fol. 12 recto (fig. 37) shows a schematic drawing in which the limbs are indicated by lines arranged along the principle directions of movement (those permitted by the joints);
Fols. 6 recto, 29 recto, 21 recto and 22 recto (figs. 38–41) show, in cinematic progression, the various stages of movement of a human body;
Fols. 54 recto and 53 recto (figs. 42–43) are copies of the proportional studies of the face, of which the originals by Leonardo are held respectively in Venice, Gallerie dell'Accademia (236 recto), and at Windsor (RL 12607 recto, K/P 21 recto);
Fols. 77 recto and 80 recto (figs. 44–45) are copies of proportional studies of the horse (the noble Sicilian breed "Ciciliano"), of which the originals by Leonardo are held at Windsor (RL 12294 and others);
Fol. 88 recto (fig. 46) shows the "first demonstration" of the theory of shadows applied to the human body;
Fols. 95 recto and 108 recto (figs. 47–48) are dedicated to the theoretical and figurative principles of perspective and foreshortening.

PS

Si propone qui una selezione che illustra gli argomenti principali in cui possono essere raggruppati i 128 fogli del *Codice Huygens*, che riguardano:
la forma, la struttura e l'anatomia del corpo umano;
il moto del corpo umano, raffigurato secondo un andamento circolare che deriva dalla nozione aristotelica di "quantità continua", cui Leonardo fa riferimento sia nei suoi studi anatomici sia nel *Libro di Pittura*;
la proiezione del corpo in diverse vedute proposte simultaneamente, secondo il principio che Leonardo esprime nel foglio anatomico RL 19061 r, K/P 154 r ("Adunque per il mio disegno ti fia noto ogni parte e ogni tutto mediante la dimostrazione di tre diversi aspetti di ciascuna parte", Keele and Pedretti 1980-84, vol. III, p. 594);
gli studi proporzionali del corpo umano e del corpo del cavallo;
gli studi di teoria delle ombre ("Del sole et l'ombra");
gli studi di prospettiva applicata ai corpi umani, con la definizione delle regole per lo scorcio.

Il foglio 3 r (fig. 35) raffigura le tre vedute (anteriore, laterale e posteriore) di un corpo virile in piedi, con riferimento anche alle quote delle principali parti esterne della figura;
il foglio 7 r (fig. 36) costituisce la quinta e ultima figura del primo libro sul "principio di moto". Il disegno ha diretta relazione con l'*Uomo vitruviano* e appare come uno studio che contempla un unico centro (l'ombelico), ponendo in diverso rapporto il cerchio e il quadrato, che nell'*Uomo* di Venezia hanno diverso centro;
il foglio 12 r (fig. 37) rappresenta una schematizzazione in cui le membra mobili del corpo sono sintetizzate come linee disposte secondo le principali direzioni di movimento (consentite dalle articolazioni);
i fogli 6 r, 29 r, 21 r, 22 r (figg. 38-41) raffigurano, secondo progressione cinematica, i vari stadi di moto di un corpo umano;
i fogli 54 r e 53 r (figg. 42-43) sono copie degli studi proporzionali del volto, di cui si conservano gli originali di Leonardo rispettivamente a Venezia, Gallerie dell'Accademia (236 r), e a Windsor (RL 12607 r, K/P 21 r);
i fogli 77 r e 80 r (figg. 44-45) sono copie di studi proporzionali del cavallo (di razza "ciciliano"), di cui si conservano gli originali di Leonardo a Windsor (RL 12294 e altri);
il foglio 88 r (fig. 46) raffigura la "prima dimostrazione" di teoria delle ombre applicata ai corpi umani;
i fogli 95 r e 108 r (figg. 47-48) sono dedicati ai principi teorici e figurativi della prospettiva e dello scorcio.

PS

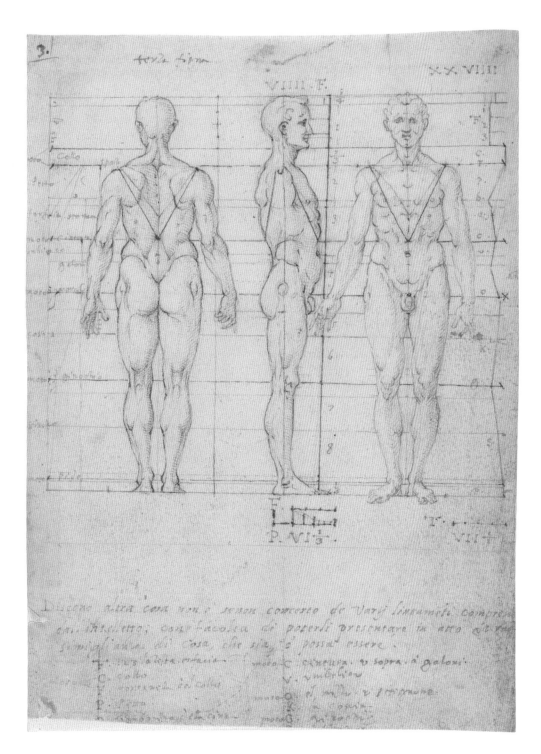

FIG. 35

CARLO URBINO
(ca. 1510/20–after 1585)
Codex Huygens,
fol. 3 recto
Pen and brown ink, red
ink and black chalk on laid
paper / Penna, inchiostro
bruno, inchiostro rosso,
pietra nera su carta vergata
185 x 134 mm
New York, Morgan Library
& Museum
(2006.14)

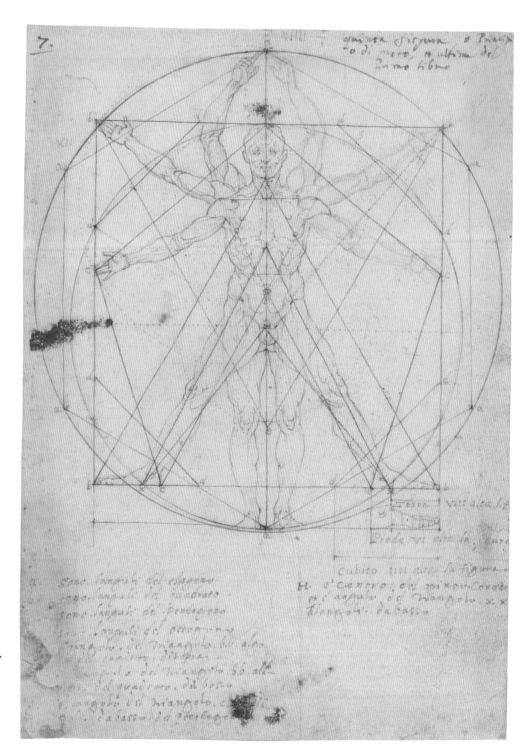

FIG. 36
CARLO URBINO
(ca. 1510/20–after 1585)
Codex Huygens,
fol. 7 recto
Pen and brown ink, black
chalk and red chalk,
inscribed with compass
on laid paper / Penna,
inchiostro bruno, pietra nera
e sanguigna su carta vergata,
incisa con compasso
188 x 133 mm
New York, Morgan Library
& Museum
(2006.14)

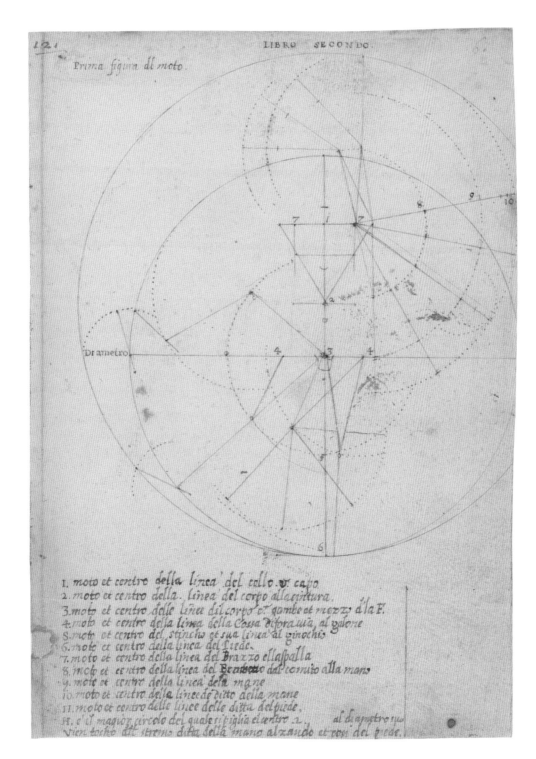

FIG. 37
CARLO URBINO
(ca. 1510/20–after 1585)
Codex Huygens,
fol. 12 recto
Pen and brown ink and
black chalk, inscribed with
stylus and compass on laid
paper / Penna e inchiostro
bruno, pietra nera su carta
vergata, incisa con stilo e
compasso
187 x 132 mm
New York, Morgan
Library & Museum
(2006.14)

FIG. 38
CARLO URBINO
(ca. 1510/20–after 1585)
Codex Huygens,
fol. 6 recto
Pen and brown ink and
black chalk, inscribed with
compass on laid paper /
Penna e inchiostro bruno,
pietra nera su carta
vergata, incisa con
compasso
184 x 131 mm
New York, Morgan Library
& Museum
(2006.14)

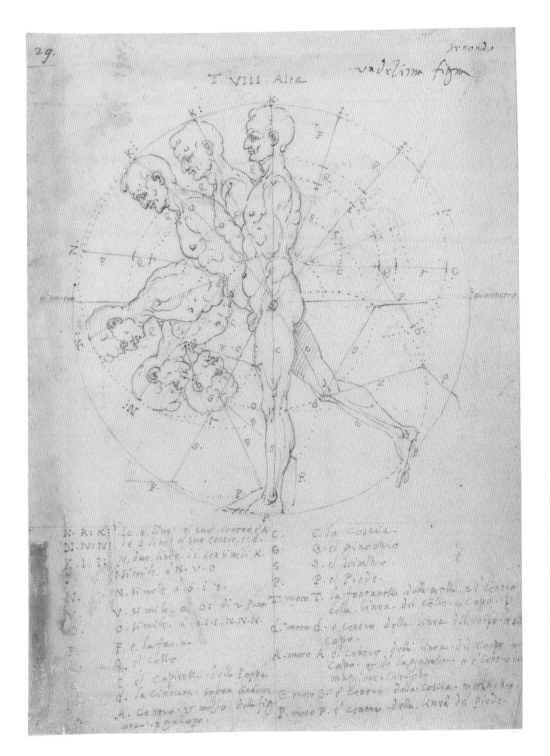

FIG. 39
CARLO URBINO
(ca. 1510/20–after 1585)
Codex Huygens,
fol. 29 recto
Pen and brown ink and
black chalk, inscribed with
stylus and compass on laid
paper / Penna e inchiostro
bruno, pietra nera su carta
vergata, incisa con stilo e
compasso
185 x 135 mm
New York, Morgan Library
& Museum
(2006.14)

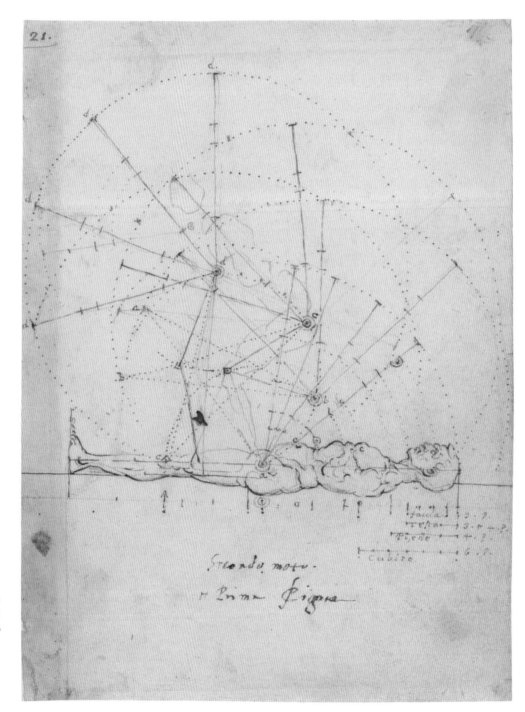

FIG. 40
CARLO URBINO
(ca. 1510/20–after 1585)
Codex Huygens,
fol. 21 recto
Pen and brown ink and red
chalk, traces of black chalk,
inscribed with compass on
laid paper / Penna e
inchiostro bruno, sanguigna,
tracce di pietra nera, su carta
vergata, incisa con compasso
181 x 135 mm
New York, Morgan Library
& Museum
(2006.14)

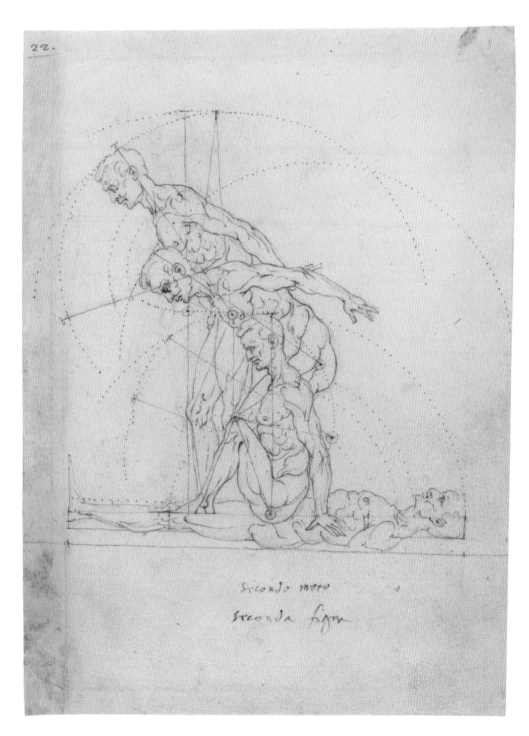

FIG. 41
CARLO URBINO
(ca. 1510/20–after 1585)
Codex Huygens,
fol. 22 recto
Pen and brown ink and
black chalk, inscribed with
stylus and compass on laid
paper / Penna e inchiostro
bruno, pietra nera su carta
vergata, incisa con stilo e
compasso
181 x 133 mm
New York, Morgan Library
& Museum
(2006.14)

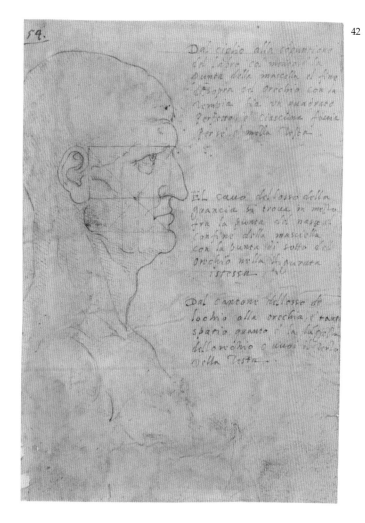

Dai ciglio alla congiuntione
del labro col mento, e fino
di sopra all'orecchia con la
tempia, fa un quadrato
perfetto, e ciascuna forma
per se, e nella Testa.

El cauo dell'osso della
guancia si troua in mezzo
fra la punta di nasce(?)
confine della mascella
con la punta di sotto d'l
orecchio nella figurata
istessa.

Dal cantone dell'osso d'l
lochio alla orecchia, è tanto
spatio quanto è la lughezza
dell'orechio e nuoi itteria
nella Testa.

a.b.c.d.e.f.g.h.ik. infra loro hanno
similitudine di grandezza: saluo ch. d. f. co

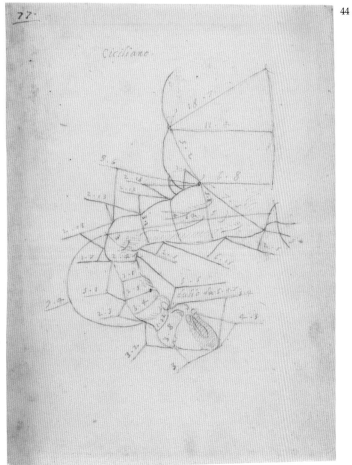

Ciciliano.

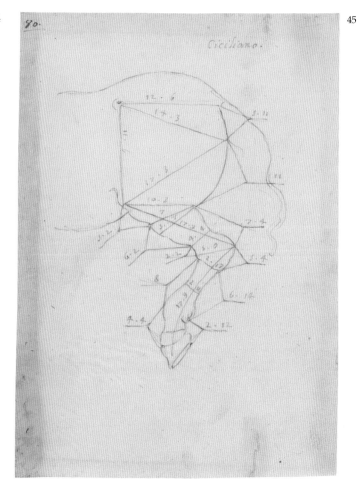

Ciciliano.

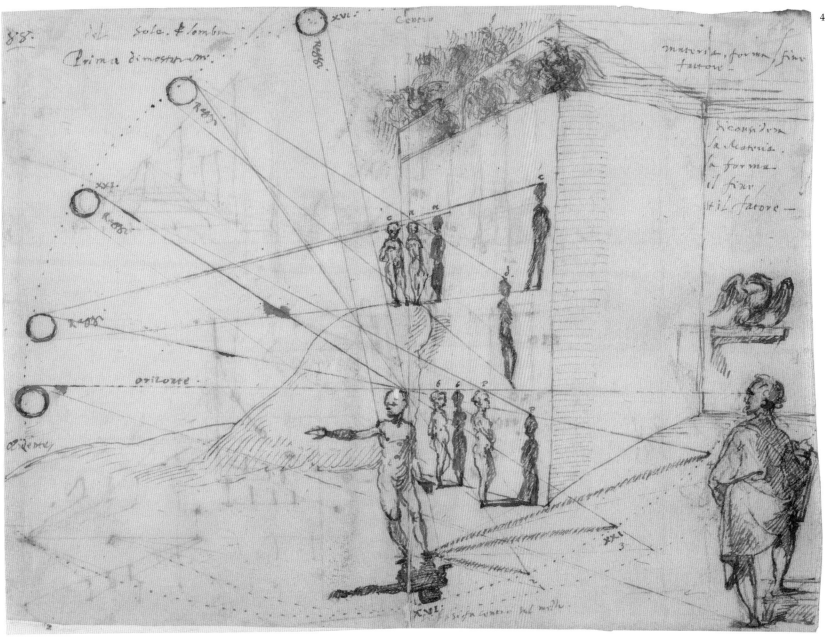

FIG. 42
CARLO URBINO
(ca. 1510/20–after 1585)
Codex Huygens,
fol. 54 recto
Pen and brown ink and
black chalk, inscribed with
stylus and compass on laid
paper / Penna e inchiostro
bruno, pietra nera su carta
vergata, incisa con stilo e
compasso
174 x 120 mm
New York, Morgan
Library & Museum
(2006.14)

FIG. 43
CARLO URBINO
(ca. 1510/20–after 1585)
Codex Huygens,
fol. 53 recto
Pen and brown ink and
black chalk on laid paper /
Penna e inchiostro bruno,
pietra nera su carta vergata
179 x 124 mm
New York, Morgan
Library & Museum
(2006.14)

FIG. 44
CARLO URBINO
(ca. 1510/20–after 1585)
Codex Huygens,
fol. 77 recto
Pen and brown ink and
black chalk, inscribed with
stylus on laid paper /
Penna e inchiostro bruno,
pietra nera su carta vergata,
incisa con stilo
176 x 131 mm
New York, Morgan
Library & Museum
(2006.14)

FIG. 45
CARLO URBINO
(ca. 1510/20–after 1585)
Codex Huygens,
fol. 80 recto
Pen and brown ink and
black chalk, inscribed with
stylus on laid paper /
Penna e inchiostro bruno,
pietra nera su carta vergata,
incisa con stilo
181 x 130 mm
New York, Morgan
Library & Museum
(2006.14)

FIG. 46
CARLO URBINO
(ca. 1510/20–after 1585)
Codex Huygens,
fol. 88 recto
Pen and brown ink, black ink,
black chalk, traces of red chalk
and opaque white, inscribed
with stylus on laid paper /
Penna e inchiostro bruno,
inchiostro nero, pietra nera,
tracce di sanguigna e biacca su
carta vergata, incisa con stilo
167 x 224 mm
New York, Morgan
Library & Museum
(2006.14)

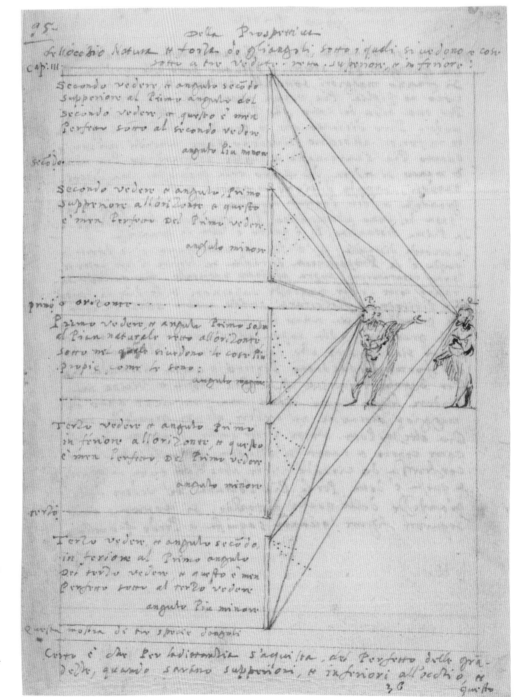

FIG. 47
CARLO URBINO
(ca. 1510/20–after 1585)
Codex Huygens,
fol. 95 recto
Pen and brown ink and
black chalk, inscribed with
stylus and compass on laid
paper / Penna e inchiostro
bruno, pietra nera su carta
vergata, incisa con stilo
e compasso
183 x 134 mm
New York, Morgan Library
& Museum
(2006.14)

FIG. 48

CARLO URBINO
(ca. 1510/20–after 1585)
Codex Huygens,
fol. 108 recto
Pen and brown ink and
black chalk, inscribed with
stylus and compass on laid
paper / Penna e inchiostro
bruno, pietra nera su carta
vergata, incisa con stilo e
compasso
181 x 134 mm
New York, Morgan Library
& Museum
(2006.14)

THE LEONARDESCHI
I LEONARDESCHI

Leonardo and his School:
The Importance of Drawing

Leonardo e la sua scuola.
Il primato del disegno

Annalisa Perissa Torrini

During the last years of Leonardo's life, which he spent in France, he dedicated some time to teaching. After visiting Leonardo's workshop in the Château du Clos Lucé, in Amboise, Cardinal Luigi d'Aragona's secretary wrote, in a letter dated October 10, 1517: "And although Messer Leonardo can no longer paint as sweetly as he was wont to, he can still draw and teach others."[1] And as we read in a 1501 letter from Fra' Pietro da Novellara to Isabella d'Este, Leonardo himself admits that he has helpers and pupils and more than once mentions them by name.[2]

In his ca. 1490 journal (Manuscript C, fol. 15 verso), Leonardo wrote that he had no fewer than four pupils—Giovanni Antonio Boltraffio, Marco d'Oggiono, Andrea Solario, and Salai—and that Salai, who had lived with him since he was ten years old, was "a thief, a liar, stubborn, and a glutton." Between 1493 and 1496, the artist took on another two apprentices. Later, at a time when Ludovico il Moro had commissioned work from him (and then revoked the order), Leonardo complained that he had "been feeding six mouths for thirty-six months" (Codex Atlanticus, fol. 867 recto [ex 315 v-b]).[3] He admits to making changes to drawings done by two pupils in his studio in Florence: "At times I do the work myself, that is in their portraits," or even in the copies they drew "to exercise the hand by copying drawings from the hand of a good master," as he puts it in his *Treatise on Painting* (§ 63).[4]

Hence the importance of the drawings by Leonardo's pupils. Some preserve traces of direct intervention by the master, as the above quotation confirms. They also reflect his teachings. Because his pupils constantly and faithfully adhered to his instructions on technique and style, their drawings were important vehicles for the dissemination of his ideas. There are so many of these drawings that it is often extremely difficult to identify the many and varied artists who formed the large yet homogenous group of the Leonardeschi, the adherents to Leonardo's style. In addition to his students, he had a great number of follow-

Negli ultimi anni della sua vita, trascorsi in Francia, Leonardo si dedica anche ad insegnare ai suoi allievi, come è documentato in modo esplicito da una lettera del 10 ottobre 1517, scritta dal segretario del Cardinale Luigi d'Aragona, dopo una visita allo studio di Leonardo nel castello di Clos Lucé ad Amboise: "et benché il predetto Messer Lunardo non possa colorir con quella dulceza che solea, pur serve ad far disegni et insegnar ad altri".[1] L'artista stesso, come si legge anche nella celebre lettera di Fra' Pietro da Novellara a Isabella d'Este del 1501, ammette di aver aiuti e nomina più volte i suoi garzoni e "maestri".[2]

Nel noto resoconto redatto verso il 1490 (Institut de France, *Ms. C*, foglio 15 v), Leonardo scrive di avere nel suo studio ben quattro "allievi", Boltraffio, Oggiono, Solario e Salai: quest'ultimo abitava con lui dall'età di 10 anni, "ladro, bugiardo, ostinato, ghiotto"; tra il 1493 e il 1496, poi, l'artista stipendiava altri "due maestri". E, ancora, in occasione di un'opera commissionatagli, poi interrotta, da Ludovico il Moro, Leonardo lamenta di aver "…tenuto sei bocche trentasei mesi…" (*Codice Atlantico*, foglio 867 *r* [ex 315 v-b]).[3] Quando a Firenze dice di avere due garzoni a bottega, ammette di intervenire lui stesso nei loro disegni: "a le volte in alcuno mette mano, cioè nei loro retrati"; ed anche in disegni copiati per esercizio, per "…suefare la mano col ritrarre disegni di mano di boni maestri…", secondo il primo dei suoi "Precetti di pittura" (*Libro di Pittura*, par. 63).[4]

Da qui l'importanza degli studi grafici degli allievi, a conferma di una pratica, quella "di far disegni", raccomandata da Leonardo nei "precetti": disegni che, a volte, possono conservare tracce dell'intervento diretto del maestro, oltre a rispecchiare i suoi insegnamenti e costituire pertanto, nel rispetto e nell'uniformità di adesione ai suoi dettami tecnici e stilistici, veicoli importanti di diffusione dei modelli leonardiani. Disegni tanto numerosi, da rendere complicata l'identificazione delle molte e diverse personalità artistiche, che formano il folto gruppo omogeneo dei Leonardeschi. Se al novero degli allievi veri e propri si aggiunge la folta schiera di seguaci, imitatori e copisti che, nella continuità della ripetizione di modelli e di modi, anche dopo l'affermarsi della scuola leonardesca, contribuiscono a perpetuare la diffusione dell'opera innovativa di Leonardo, si acquisiscono testimonianze importanti per

ers, imitators, and copyists, who continued to repeat his subjects and techniques even after the school of Leonardo was well established. They, too, furthered the dissemination of Leonardo's innovative work. All of these drawings provide us with significant material for the study of the complex movement known as Leonardism, which prevailed in Lombardy for almost a century.[5]

Leonardo did not have a workshop of his own, such as would have been fueled by substantial commissions requiring the help of numerous apprentices. The phenomenon of Leonardism emerged among artists in Milan who admired his work. It was in that city, rather than his native Florence, that his school developed. These followers, who spanned two generations, were very diverse artistically, but they were all linked to the works Leonardo produced in Milan. Certain of Leonardo's subjects were repeated by his followers, for example, *Salvator Mundi*, *Christ Carrying the Cross*, and the *Christ Child*. Their treatments of his subjects are important principally because they contain visual traces of paintings by Leonardo that have been lost and that can be reconstructed only through these copies or derivative works. Through them we have an invaluable record of certain works by the painter that would otherwise have been completely unknown.

The examples of drawing exercises executed by Leonardo's followers and students on exhibition at the Morgan Library & Museum demonstrate how deeply influential Leonardo's works were. We see this in his portraits, so esteemed at the time. The art historian Giorgio Vasari himself said that he owned, "a head drawn with the style in chiaroscuro, which is divine," a worthy expression of the drawing skills of Leonardo, who "drew on paper with such diligence and so well, that there is no one who has ever equalled him in perfection of finish."[6]

The highlight among the portraits from the Turin collection is the *Head of a Young Woman* (cat. 1), said to have been described by the art critic Bernard Berenson as "the most beautiful drawing in the world." (See pp. 27 and 32 where this is questioned.) The face of this exquisite young woman inspired many of his followers' portraits of young men and women, each an attempt to equal this peerless prototype.

The fascinating *Study of the Angel in Verrochio's "Baptism of Christ"* (cat. 10), attributed to Andrea del Verrocchio's workshop, is in a very poor state of preservation: there is a large part missing, filled in

lo studio di quel movimento complesso chiamato leonardismo, che per quasi un secolo è stato modulato dall'influenza di Leonardo in Lombardia.[5]

Il Vinciano, tuttavia, non aveva una vera e propria bottega, con commissioni impegnative che richiedessero l'impiego di molti garzoni: il fenomeno chiamato leonardismo si sviluppa piuttosto intorno alle sue opere, e soltanto a Milano. Qui, non nella patria fiorentina, nasce e cresce la scuola di Leonardo, sia con gli allievi di prima che di seconda generazione. Personalità artistiche diverse, ma ruotanti intorno all'attività milanese di Leonardo pittore. Le loro opere della scuola ripetono spesso tematiche comuni, alcune oggetto di numerose repliche, come *Salvator Mundi*, *Redentore*, *Cristo portacroce*, *Cristo fanciullo*, importanti soprattutto in quanto tracce pittoriche di dipinti del maestro ormai perduti, ricostruibili solo da copie e derivazioni, che restano, quindi, documenti preziosi di espressioni artistiche altrimenti ignote.

Gli esempi di prove grafiche di seguaci e allievi di Leonardo qui esposte sono, quindi, testimonianze importanti del diffondersi della sua opera, a partire dalla ritrattistica. Vasari stesso afferma di possedere "una testa di stile e chiaro scuro ch'è divina", degna espressione dell'abilità grafica del maestro di Vinci, che: "disegnò in carta con tanta diligenza e sì bene che in quelle finezze non è chi v'abbia aggiunto mai".[6]

La testa femminile (cat. 1), che Berenson avrebbe definito il "più bel disegno del mondo" (si veda alle pp. 27 e 32 dove questo problema è discusso), è il centro focale dei ritratti e dei volti della collezione grafica torinese qui esposti. Con la sua sfolgorante bellezza, la splendida giovane donna dà essenza ai ritratti di fanciulle e giovinetti che ruotano attorno a tale inarrivabile prototipo, imprescindibile fonte di ispirazione per allievi e seguaci.

Lo stato di conservazione dell'affascinante *Studio dell'angelo nel "Battesimo di Cristo"* (cat. 10), assegnato alla bottega di Andrea Verrocchio, è piuttosto precario: il disegno presenta una grande lacuna integrata dal restauro e alcune mancanze di colore, anche sulla parte alta della testa. Tuttavia la qualità del tratto emerge con forza dal segno preciso e delicato, con le ombreggiature ad acquerello ocra e i rialzi luminosi a biacca, stesa a punta di pennello. I tocchi di luce muovono soprattutto i lunghi ricci della folta capigliatura, che scendono sciolti sulle spalle. Il modo di arricciare in corte e soffici volute la ricca chioma, anticipa in parte quello che poi Leonardo complicherà in particolari acconciature a spirale, specie nei suoi studi per la *Leda*. I bordi della veste, avvolta sulle spalle con pieghe lumeggiate da lunghi tocchi di biacca, sono impreziositi da una raffinata decorazione con pietre preziose.

L'impostazione della figura vista girata di tre quarti di spalle, ma con il capo ruotato di profilo verso lo spettatore, esula dalle pose convenzionali, per manifestarsi in atteggiamen-

by restorers, and some loss of color, including the upper part of the head. Nevertheless, the quality of the drawing is clearly evident in the precise, delicate strokes, with ochre watercolor shading and white highlights applied with the tip of the brush; this is especially evident in the angel's thick curly hair, falling loosely over the shoulders. The hair's short, soft waves anticipate to some extent later hairstyles seen in Leonardo's drawings, those in which he added a complicated spiral detail, especially in his studies for *Leda*. The edges of the angel's garments, caught up in folds on the shoulder and heightened with long strokes of white, are decorated with a beautiful decorative band set with precious stones.

The attitude of the figure, a three-quarter view seen from behind, with the head turned in profile toward the viewer, breaks with convention, creating an innovative pose similar to one seen in the famous *Baptism of Christ* by Andrea del Verrocchio (Galleria degli Uffizi). According to Vasari's account, it was Leonardo, then an apprentice in Verrocchio's workshop, who painted that panel's delicately beautiful young angel, the inspiration for this ethereal representation. The soft shadowing that shapes the figure is constructed from strokes drawn in different directions. We are struck by the delicate, luminous face, gaze turned upward, enthralled by the divine scene.

In the final stages of planning for the *Last Supper* (ca. 1495), and also in his small codices of 1493–96 (Manuscript H and Codex Forster II and III), Leonardo adopts the distinctive technique of using red chalk on red-ochre prepared paper, which we find him using again in his second period in Milan (ca. 1508). The softness and flexibility of this medium allows the artist greater freedom of expression, and it was widely adopted by others, including Giovanni Agostino da Lodi, Giampietrino, Solario, Cesare da Sesto, and Francesco Melzi. One of the first artists to become aware of the extraordinary potential of red chalk to create effects very close to life, Melzi used this medium in the *Old Man Seated in Profile* (cat. 16). This drawing has been compared to others of the same subject, in particular to a Leonardo sheet now at Windsor (RL 12584; fig. 49), of which the Turin drawing may be a high-quality copy. Among the critics, Clark maintains that it is, in fact, a Leonardo original to which Melzi merely added some touches to the drapery. Berenson, too, recognizes its transcendent quality, while Möller[7] reiterates the attribution to Leonardo, identifying the drawing as a sketch for an apostle in the *Last*

FIG. 49
LEONARDO DA VINCI
*Old Man Seated in Profile /
Vecchio seduto visto di profilo*,
ca. 1495
Red chalk on paper /
Sanguigna su carta
180 x 127 mm
Windsor (RL 12584)

to del tutto innovativo, analogo a quello che si ammira nel celebre dipinto raffigurante il *Battesimo di Cristo* di Andrea Verrocchio degli Uffizi a Firenze, dove il giovane Leonardo, secondo la testimonianza vasariana, dipinge proprio la figura estremamente raffinata dell'angelo giovinetto: a quel prototipo l'artista della bottega di Verrocchio si ispira per il volto ritratto in questo disegno. Il modellato in morbidi toni di ombra, è costruito secondo diverse direzioni di movimento. L'eterea figura dell'angelo affascina per il volto delicato e luminoso, colto con lo sguardo rivolto all'insù, gli occhi rapiti dalla visione divina.

La particolare tecnica che utilizza la matita rossa su carta rossa, usata da Leonardo verso il 1495, nella fase finale della progettazione del *Cenacolo*, e nei piccoli codici del 1493-96 (*Ms. H o Cod. Foster II o III*), si afferma nel secondo soggiorno milanese, intorno al 1508: per la morbidezza e la flessibilità propria del mezzo permette una maggior libertà, e trova largo seguito in Giovanni Agostino da Lodi, Giampietrino, Solario, Cesare da Sesto e Francesco Melzi. Quest'ultimo, tra i primi ad avvertire le inusuali potenzialità della matita rossa nel raggiungere effetti naturali molto vicini alla realtà, la usa anche nel ritratto di *Vecchio seduto visto di profilo* (cat. 16), qui esposto. Il disegno è stato messo a confronto con altri

FIG. 50

LEONARDO DA VINCI

Head and Shoulders of Christ Being Held by the Hair /
Testa e spalle di Cristo afferrato per i capelli, ca. 1500
Silver and gold metalpoint on greyish-blue prepared
paper / Punta metallica d'argento e d'oro su carta
preparata di grigio-azzurro
116 x 91 mm
Venice, Gabinetto dei Disegni e Stampe delle Gallerie
dell'Accademia (231)

Supper. Pedretti supports the idea that the drawing
was done at the time the fresco was being executed,
particularly noting the link with a ca. 1495 drawing in
Bayonne (1325). He also remarks that the precision in
the drawing of the face recalls Leonardo's anatomical
drawings of 1510, now at Windsor Castle, namely RL
19003 verso and RL 19012 verso.[8]
In Melzi's drawing, the imposing figure is robed in
heavy drapery, highlighting the position of the legs,
which are crossed, and of the arms, with the right
hand raised and the left resting. Both positions are
accentuated with close hatching and shadowing with
strong chiaroscuro contrast. The garment, gathered

che ritraggono una figura di uomo anziano visto di profilo,
in particolare con l'immagine del foglio di Leonardo ora a
Windsor (RL 12584; fig. 49), di cui il disegno torinese potrebbe esserne una copia di alta qualità. Clark lo ritiene
addirittura un originale di Leonardo, ripassato poi da Melzi
nei panneggi. Anche Berenson ne riconosce la qualità ec-
celsa, mentre Möller[7] ripropone l'autografia e vi identifica
uno studio per un apostolo dell'*Ultima Cena*. Il riferimento
cronologico al tempo del grande affresco è condiviso da
Pedretti, in particolare per il collegamento con il disegno
di Bayonne (1325) del 1495 circa; lo studioso vi individua,
tuttavia, anche un'accuratezza nella definizione grafica del
volto di vecchio simile a quella dei disegni anatomici del
1510, quali i fogli RL 19003 v e 19012 v di Windsor Castle.[8]
Nello studio di Torino la monumentale figura è ricoperta
da un pesante panneggio, che sottolinea la posizione ao
cavallata delle gambe e delle braccia, con la mano destra
alzata e la sinistra appoggiata, posizioni entrambe ben
evidenziate da un fitto tratteggio e da un'ombreggiatura
contrastata da un forte risalto chiaroscurale. La veste, an-
nodata sul petto con un nodo sinistrorso, ricade in ampio
risvolto nella lunga manica e nelle pieghe sulla sedia. L'artista dedica grande attenzione alla descrizione anatomica
del cranio, calvo e arrotondato, con la fronte larga, il naso
adunco, il labbro inferiore accentuato, il mento sporgente,
la pelle rugosa sulle guance e sul collo. Simili fattezze si
ripetono sia nel disegno di Leonardo di Torino (15575 D.C.;
fig. 3) che nel foglio contemporaneo degli Uffizi 423 E.[9]
Prima che l'uso di matite colorate diventasse preminente,
la tecnica prediletta da Leonardo e i suoi allievi era la punta
metallica, di piombo, d'argento o d'oro: l'oro si può ammirare nell'esempio superbo della *Testa e spalle di Cristo
afferrato per i capelli* delle Gallerie dell'Accademia (231;
fig. 50). L'impiego della tradizionale tecnica a punta metallica su carta preparata, documentato nel noto brano del
Ms. C dell'Institut de France (foglio 15 v), dove Leonardo
nomina "uno grafio d'argiento", cioè uno stilo d'argento,
appartiene proprio agli allievi a lui più vicini fin dagli anni
Novanta del Quattrocento, Salai, Marco d'Oggiono, Francesco Napoletano, Ambrogio de' Predis e il Maestro della
Pala Sforzesca e Giovan Antonio Boltraffio.
Quest'ultimo, in particolare segue l'invito del maestro a
non fare mai "le teste dritte sopra le spalle, ma voltate in
traverso, a destra o a sinistra, ancora ch'elle guardino in
giù o in su, o a dritto […]", si rivolge con applicazione in-
tensa e sistematica ai modelli, studiati e resi secondo una
più diretta restituzione naturalistica ed espressiva insieme;
si qualifica come disegnatore sensibile al fascino della
bellezza sublimata e ai canoni di rarefatta perfezione, gli
stessi che ispirano anche il suo celebre disegno del Louvre

on the chest in a knot, falls in ample folds in the long sleeve and over the chair. The artist pays exacting anatomical attention to the bald skull, wide forehead, hooked nose, jutting lower lip, prominent chin, and the lined skin on the neck and cheek. Similar facial features can be seen in two drawings by Leonardo from the same period, one in Turin (15575 D.C.; fig. 3) and the other in the Galleria degli Uffizi (423 E).[9]

Before colored chalk became his principal medium, the technique preferred by Leonardo and his students was metalpoint, using a stylus made of lead, silver, or gold. A superb example of the use of a gold stylus can be seen in the *Head and Shoulders of Christ Being Held by the Hair* at the Gallerie dell'Accademia (231; fig. 50). This traditional drawing method, using a metalpoint on prepared paper, was recorded in Leonardo's writings as early as 1490, in the well-known passage of Manuscript C (fol. 15 verso), in which he mentions "uno grafio d'argiento," a silver pen or nib. The technique was characteristic of the students closest to him from the beginning of the 1490s: Salai, Marco d'Oggiono, Francesco Napoletano, Ambrogio de' Predis, the Maestro della Pala Sforzesca, and Boltraffio.

Boltraffio, in particular, adhered strictly to his master's injunction never to "place the head straight on the shoulders but a little turned, to the right or left, even if the figure should be looking up or down or straight ahead." Boltraffio applied himself intensely and systematically to learning from the models, which he studied and emulated, producing outstanding works that succeeded in being both naturalistic and expressive. The quality of his drawing demonstrated his sensitivity to the fascination of sublimated beauty and to the canons of rarefied perfection, the same canons that inspired his famous portrait in the Museé de Louvre (2251) of a young man with a classical profile, wearing a wreath of oak leaves. These oak leaves are probably the origin of the famous print adopted as the emblem of the "Achademia Leonardi Vinci," an institution for which there is little documentation, but whose existence is demonstrated by the work produced by Leonardo's followers.

The *Head of a Young Man with a Crown of Thorns and Vine Leaves* (cat. 12) is also the work of Boltraffio. It had been attributed to Leonardo until Müntz declared that it belonged to his circle. This opinion was supported by Bertini, who pointed to the drawings that Suida had defined as pseudo-Boltraffio as confirmation that the head should be attributed to the circle. The attribution to Boltraffio was put forward

FIG. 51

G.A. BOLTRAFFIO, attributed to / attribuito a
Head of a Young Man / *Testa di giovane*, ca. 1500
Black chalk and metalpoint on greyish blue prepared paper /
Matita nera e punta metallica su carta preparata
di grigio-azzurro
172 x 136 mm
Venice, Gabinetto dei Disegni e Stampe delle Gallerie
dell'Accademia (263)

(2251), che ritrae un profilo classicheggiante incoronato con fronde di quercia, probabile fonte della famosa incisione assunta ad emblema dell'"Achademia Leonardi Vinci", quell'Accademia poco documentata come istituzione ma la cui esistenza è testimoniata nei fatti dalla "scola" dei Leonardeschi.

È Boltraffio l'autore del *Busto di giovane coronato di spine e foglie di vite* (cat.12), attribuito allo stesso Leonardo fino a Müntz, che lo riporta alla scuola, seguito da Bertini, il quale, richiamandosi ai disegni che Suida assegna al cosiddetto Pseudo-Boltraffio, lo inserisce genericamente in quella cerchia. Il nome di Boltraffio è, invece, sostenuto da Andreina Griseri nel 1978, seguita da Susanna Zanuso nel 1985,[10] che propone l'identificazione del soggetto con un

FIG. 52
LEONARDO DA VINCI
Bust of a Woman /
Busto di donna, ca. 1501
Red chalk over
metalpoint on pale red
prepared paper /
Matita rossa su traccia
metallica su carta
preparata di rosso
221 x 159 mm
Windsor (RL 12514)

by Andreina Griseri in 1978 and supported in 1985 by Susanna Zanuso,[10] who suggested that the subject should be considered the young Christ, based on the presence of vine leaves entwined with thorns. The large leaves in the garland encircling the young man's forehead do, in fact, reveal glimpses of the crown of thorns, with one thorn piercing the center of his brow. These elements carry allusions to Christian and Dionysian symbols (wine of the Eucharist, blood of Christ, Bacchus).

As Pedretti points out, the image of the young Christ is present in Leonardo's iconography. Isabella d'Este first suggested the subject to Leonardo in a letter from May 14, 1504, in which she stipulated that Christ should be "about twelve years of age, which would be the age when he debated with the elders in the Temple." She referred to a "boy Christ" and a "young Christ, of about twelve years old" in two other letters, written between May and October 1504. It is therefore probable that Boltraffio was interpreting an idea of Leonardo's and that the student's drawing assumed the function of a model, perhaps even for paintings of the same subject by later artists. In the Turin sheet, the young man, who wears a low-necked garment gathered into many fine folds at the center, is seen in a three-quarter view slightly from the right. With his large, probing eyes gazing intensely at the viewer, he conveys confidence and an unusual degree of introspection.

Pedretti claims that the drawing has a dynamism that was unusual for a painter from Lombardy in general and for Boltraffio in particular. In fact, the artist is an excellent draftsman. In this sheet, he reveals an assurance and a capacity for expressiveness, conveyed through drawing so accomplished that it has a vibrant, almost sculptural effect. However, the brilliant qualities of this work are dimmed in a sheet in Venice (263; fig. 51). There, the vigor and artistry of the Turin drawing are reduced to a flat and colorless style. The difference between these sheets is so great that the Venice sheet has recently been reclassified as a pseudo-Boltraffio.

Boltraffio's *Head of a Young Man* is most compellingly compared to the drawing of the head of a woman at the Sterling and Francine Clark Art Institute (1955.1470), which was exhibited under the name of Boltraffio in the 2003 Leonardo exhibition in Paris. Pedretti notes the similar treatment of the shadow under the upper lip.[11] The Turin head has also been compared with the Windsor head of a woman (RL

Cristo giovinetto, vista la presenza nella corona delle foglie di vite insieme con le spine. Le grandi foglie di vite del serto che cinge la fronte, infatti, lasciano intravedere la corona di spine, una delle quali conficcata proprio in piena fronte. Tale compresenza favorisce un'interpretazione basata su una duplice valenza simbolica, cristiana, in quanto prefigurazione del vino dell'Eucarestia e del sangue della Passione di Cristo, e dionisiaca, per l'allusione a Bacco.

Il tema del "Cristo giovanetto", secondo la puntualizzazione di Pedretti, è presente nell'iconografia leonardiana: fu proposto da Isabella d'Este a Leonardo una prima volta il 14 maggio 1504, precisando: "da anni circa duodeci, che seria de quella età che l'haveva quando disputò nel tempio". La richiesta della marchesa di un "cristo piccolino" e un "Christo giovine de anni circa duodeci" è ripetuta in altre due lettere, del maggio e ottobre 1504, confermando l'interesse per tale soggetto. È probabile, quindi, che Boltraffio traduca un'idea di Leonardo, e che il disegno dell'allievo assuma, quasi, la funzione di modello, forse anche per derivazioni pittoriche. Il busto di giovane disegnato nel foglio torinese, con la veste molto scollata e riunita al centro in fitte pieghe, è ripreso di tre quarti leggermente girato verso destra, ma lo sguardo, molto intenso dei grandi occhi, penetrante e

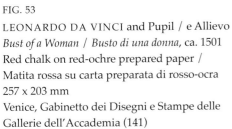

FIG. 53
LEONARDO DA VINCI and Pupil / e Allievo
Bust of a Woman / *Busto di una donna*, ca. 1501
Red chalk on red-ochre prepared paper /
Matita rossa su carta preparata di rosso-ocra
257 x 203 mm
Venice, Gabinetto dei Disegni e Stampe delle
Gallerie dell'Accademia (141)

FIG. 54
LEONARDO DA VINCI
The Head of Saint Anne / *Testa di donna,
studio per la Sant'Anna*, ca. 1501
Black chalk on paper / Matita nera su carta
188 x 130 mm
Windsor (RL 12533)

12510), attributed generically to the school of Leonardo. Similarities noted by Taglialagamba are the almost-sculptural drawing technique and the accentuation of facial features, achieved through shadowing on the full, prominent mouth, the broad nose, and the eyes with their frowning eyebrows.[12] The kind of portrait most congenial to Boltraffio is one that expresses Leonardo's "motions of the mind," that is, not a formal, heraldic manifestation of family prestige but a likeness closer to being a "portrait from nature."
Turin's *Bust of a Young Woman* (15716 D.C.; fig. 55)[13] is attributed to a follower of Leonardo. The woman in this small, delicate drawing in red chalk is turned slightly to the left, with her head turned three-quarters to the right, a pose assumed by many of Leonar-

scrutatore, è rivolto verso lo spettatore: l'espressione decisa denota un'inconsueta introspezione psicologica.
Pedretti ne riconosce un vigore insolito per un pittore lombardo, e per Boltraffio in particolare. L'artista, in realtà, è un eccellente disegnatore: in questa prova sprigiona infatti un piglio ed una carica espressiva, resa con sapiente tratto grafico, che sconfina in un'inflessione di vibrante plasticismo, quasi scultoreo, che diventa, invece, ad esempio, molto più sfumato nel foglio di Venezia 263 (fig. 51), dove il vigore e la qualità pittorica del disegno di Torino scolorano in una definizione stilistica molto più piatta ed incolore, tanto che l'attribuzione più recente del foglio veneziano, già ritenuto dello stesso Boltraffio, si indirizza piuttosto verso lo pseudo-Boltraffio per la più modesta resa grafica. Il confronto più calzante va instaurato con un disegno di Boltraf-

189

FIG. 55
Follower of / Seguace di
LEONARDO DA VINCI
Bust of a Young Woman /
Busto di giovane donna,
16th cent. / XVI sec.
Red chalk on paper /
Sanguigna su carta
90 x 68 mm
Turin, Biblioteca Reale
(15716 D.C.)

do's young women. This drawing includes two other elements from the master's female portraits. Her low-cut dress recalls the famous preparatory study at Windsor (RL 12514; fig. 52) for the lost painting *Madonna of the Yarnwinder* (ca. 1500). The cloth wrapped around her head like a turban is taken from another drawing by Leonardo at Windsor (RL 12533; fig. 54, ca. 1501), a study for the head of Saint Anne. The turban-like headdress repeats the one that Leonardo may have used in a third version of *Virgin and Child with Saint Anne*, a painting that we can reconstruct only through copies by the Leonardeschi. We see that the artist of the delicate Turin composition has blended motifs from two different drawings by Leonardo, both for works that have been lost. In all probability, this artist would have known the pictures, if they were actually ever painted, and would certainly have known the drawings and cartoons, to which only a close follower of Leonardo would have had access. Therefore, this delicate drawing must be regarded as having been produced in the sixteenth century by a member of Leonardo's large circle of students and followers, who used his preferred technique for preparatory sketches: fine lines and balanced chiaroscuro effects that highlight the volume of the body. Salvi and Pedretti both attribute it to a follower.[14] For Pedretti, the drawing proves "how much Leonardo contributed to the development of art in the high Renaissance, in terms of dynamism of forms perceived in

fio di una testa femminile dello Sterling and Francine Clark Art Institute (1955.1470), esposto con il nome di Boltraffio alla mostra di Parigi del 2003 (118), in particolare, come sottolinea Pedretti, per l'analoga ombreggiatura riflessa sotto il labbro superiore.[11] Altri punti di contatto con la testa femminile di Windsor (RL 12510), attribuita genericamente alla scuola di Leonardo, sono messi in risalto da Sara Taglialagamba, per lo stesso accento grafico che si caratterizza per il tratto quasi scultoreo; e, aggiunge la studiosa, in ambedue anche le ombre portate sulla bocca, carnosa e sporgente, sul naso, dalla larga base, sugli occhi, dalle sopracciglia corrucciate, valorizzano i lineamenti.[12] Il genere della ritrattistica, intesa come espressione dei "moti dell'animo", lontana, quindi, da qualsiasi intento araldico, ma vicina piuttosto a quel "retrato di naturale" di tipo leonardiano, è il più congeniale a Boltraffio.
Il *Busto di giovane donna* di Torino (15716 D.C; fig. 55),[13] è attribuito ad un seguace di Leonardo. Il piccolo e delicato disegno a sanguigna raffigura un busto di donna leggermente girato a sinistra, mentre il volto è ruotato di tre quarti a destra, riprendendo una posizione tipica delle giovani figure femminili leonardiane. Da esse sono ripresi, infatti, due motivi tipici espressi dal maestro in famosi disegni. L'ampia scollatura della veste della giovane è ripresa dal celebre studio per il busto della Madonna (Windsor RL 12514; fig. 52), preparatorio per il perduto dipinto con la *Madonna dei fusi*, del 1500 circa. Il capo ricoperto con un panno avvolto a turbante è copiato, invece, dal disegno di Leonardo a Windsor (RL 12533; fig. 54), del 1501 circa, per la testa della Sant'Anna, secondo una foggia del copricapo che l'artista utilizza, forse, in una terza versione della composizione con la *Madonna con il Bambino e la Sant'Anna*, oggi ricostruibile solo da copie di Leonardeschi. L'autore di questo delicato insieme, quindi, fonde motivi tipici di due disegni diversi, entrambi per opere perdute, e, pertanto, doveva forse conoscere l'opera del maestro, se mai realizzata, ma sicuramente i disegni o i cartoni, a cui solo gli allievi potevano accedere. L'attribuzione di questa delicata sanguigna dovrebbe rimanere, pertanto, in ambito cinquecentesco collocata nella folta cerchia di allievi e seguaci, opera di un artista che usa la tecnica preferita da Leonardo per gli studi preparatori, con un segno grafico sottile ed equilibrato nei giochi chiaroscurali, che fanno risaltare il volume del corpo. Ad un seguace lo assegnano, infatti, Paola Salvi e Carlo Pedretti;[14] quest'ultimo spiega come l'opera dimostri "quanto Leonardo ebbe a contribuire allo sviluppo dell'arte del pieno Rinascimento vitalità di forme volumetricamente percepite nello spazio e ineffabile dolcezza nell'espressione dei volti accesi di luce interiore".[15] Un altro importante documento artistico della bellezza dei

space as volumes and in the ineffable sweetness in the expressions of faces lit by an internal glow."[15] There are many works recording the beauty of women's faces by artists in Leonardo's sphere of influence. A splendid example of delicate expressivity achieved through superb technical skill is the *Head of a Young Woman* (cat. 11). The drawing was attributed to Melzi, but has recently been reclassified by Pedretti as a drawing by Leonardo that was reworked by one of his pupils.[16] Of Leonardo's students, one in particular often used red chalk on red-ochre prepared paper with exceptional skill, achieving artistic effects of notable quality and revealing himself to be an excellent draftsman: this was Cesare da Sesto. While the fine quality of this superb face suggests that it was made by Leonardo, it just as easily brings to mind Cesare, an artist who reached such heights as to compete with the master in the art of drawing. The young woman's head is turned three-quarters to the right, with the face slightly tilted and the eyes half closed; a narrow ribbon around her forehead holds back her long hair, which falls in light, ordered curls. The torso slightly leaning to the left, the curve of the shoulders, and the low-necked dress all establish a close relationship between this figure and Leonardo's studies for the *Madonna of the Yarnwinder*. That painting has been lost but is documented by copies painted by members of his workshop and by a single ca. 1500 drawing by Leonardo, now at Windsor (RL 12514; fig. 52). The comparison originated with Pedretti, who points out the similarities with another study of a young woman at the Gallerie dell'Accademia (141; fig. 53). In this drawing, the figure is in a pose comparable to that in the Windsor sheet: the torso, set at an angle to the face, is turned to the right, with the same pentimenti at the curve of the shoulder, where the outline has been redrawn several times and altered, probably by Cesare da Sesto himself. The artist was described as a "disciple and true imitator of the immortal Leonardo Vinci; he was among the most highly regarded painters of his time."[17]

The *Head of an Old Man* (cat. 15) is another sheet from the collection of drawings in the Biblioteca Reale, Turin that has been attributed to Cesare da Sesto.[18] It is a front view of an aging man who has slack, wrinkled skin, a balding head with sparse tufts of hair, and lifeless, staring eyes with no eyebrows. Pedretti's comparison of this sheet to two Leonar-

volti femminili e della loro grande diffusione nell'ambito leonardesco è la *Testa di fanciulla* (cat. 11), sempre di Torino, qui esposta, superbo esempio di raffinata espressività raggiunta con estrema sapienza grafica. Il disegno, attribuito anche a Francesco Melzi, è di recente considerato da Pedretti[16] un disegno di Leonardo "ripassato" da un allievo. Tra di loro, colui che più spesso usa con singolare sapienza la matita rossa su carta preparata di rosso-ocra, raggiungendo espressioni artistiche di particolare effetto, rivelandosi un eccellente disegnatore, è, in realtà, Cesare da Sesto. Se l'alta qualità di questo stupendo volto di fanciulla evoca il nome di Leonardo stesso, non di meno può richiamare quello di Cesare da Sesto, artista che arriva a competere con il maestro nell'arte del disegno. La testa della giovane donna è rivolta di tre quarti a destra, con il volto leggermente inclinato e abbassato e gli occhi socchiusi; un sottile nastro sulla fronte sostiene i lunghi capelli sciolti in leggeri riccioli ordinati. L'appena accennata inclinazione del busto verso sinistra, la curvatura delle spalle e l'ampia scollatura della veste, pongono la figura in stretto rapporto con gli studi di Leonardo per la *Madonna dei Fusi*, composizione perduta, ma documentata da copie pittoriche di bottega e da un unico disegno di Leonardo del 1500 circa, ora a Windsor (RL 12514; fig. 52). Il confronto è instaurato già da Pedretti, il quale sottolinea anche la vicinanza con un altro studio di busto di fanciulla del Gabinetto dei Disegni e Stampe delle Gallerie dell'Accademia di Venezia (141; fig. 53), dove la figura mostra una posizione analoga al foglio inglese: il busto, in scarto con il volto, è ruotato verso destra, con gli stessi evidenti pentimenti corretti o modificati del contorno delle spalle: lì la linea è ripassata più volte e modificata, probabilmente proprio da Cesare da Sesto, "discepolo e vero imitatore dell'immortale Leonardo Vinci, fu ne li più pregiati pittori dell'età sua".[17]

A lui è attribuito un altro foglio della collezione grafica della Biblioteca Reale di Torino, qui esposto: una *Testa di vecchio*[18] (cat. 15) in cui il volto senile è raffigurato frontalmente, con la pelle rugosa e cadente, stempiato e con radi ciuffi di capelli, gli occhi spenti e impressionanti, senza le arcate sopraciliari. Inevitabile il confronto, proposto da Pedretti, con due fogli autografi di Windsor (RL 12502 e 12503), databili al 1508-10, che ritraggono la stessa tipologia di vecchio, in analoga veduta frontale, con la pelle corrugata che sottolinea i tratti dello scheletro sottostante, il mento prominente, la bocca rientrata, il naso lungo, la fronte alta e la testa calva. In questo foglio torinese il personaggio, di indubbia matrice leonardesca, dagli occhi spenti e vacui, appare ancora più vecchio, con rari ciuffi di capelli sulle tempie e gli incavi ossei accentuati da una

FIG. 56
CESARE DA SESTO
Virgin and Child
(*Madonna of the
Tree*) / *Madonna
con il Bambino* detta
Madonna dell'albero,
ca. 1517
Oil on panel /
Olio su tavola
46 x 36 cm
Milan, Pinacoteca
di Brera

FIG. 57
CESARE DA SESTO
Virgin and Child / *Madonna con il Bambino*, ca. 1517
Pen and brown ink on paper /
Penna e inchiostro bruno su carta
Irregular shape / Forma irregolare, 190 x 150 mm
New York, Morgan Library & Museum (II, 62)

do sheets at Windsor, both ca. 1508–10 (RL 12502 and RL 12503) is inevitable. These sheets portray a bald old man in a similar front view, with lined skin accentuating the shape of the bones, underlying prominent chin, shrivelled mouth, long nose, and high forehead. In the Turin drawing, the figure, undoubtedly inspired by Leonardo, appears even older. He has very few tufts of hair at the temples and the hollows of his skull are emphasized by his slack, sagging skin. Recently, Pedretti[19] has stated his conviction that the artist is Leonardo, not Cesare da Sesto. He had supported the attribution to Cesare da Sesto in 1975 but called it into question in 1990.[20] Evidence that this superlative work is indeed by Cesare can be found in its technique, character, and style, all typical of that artist.

There are two other drawings in the Turin collection by Cesare da Sesto, both of the Christ Child (cat. 13 and cat. 14).[21] Morelli was the first to attribute these drawings to Cesare da Sesto, a classification supported by Loeser. Bertini recognized these drawings as studies for Cesare's *Virgin and Child*,

pelle floscia e cadente. Di recente, Pedretti[19] ne ha proposto la paternità di Leonardo, non più quella di Cesare da Sesto, da lui condivisa nel 1975 e poi messa in dubbio nel 1990.[20] Ad avvalorare l'intervento di Cesare per questo foglio, di indubbia qualità, concorrono la tecnica, il carattere e lo stile, espressioni tipiche del modus grafico dell'artista di Sesto.

Suoi sono anche altri due disegni qui esposti (catt. 13 e 14), raffiguranti la figura del Bambin Gesù,[21] entrambi attribuiti tradizionalmente a Cesare da Sesto da Morelli, seguito da Loeser. Bertini per primo vi riconosce degli studi per il Bambino raffigurato nel dipinto con la *Madonna con il Bambino* di Cesare ora a Brera, detta *Madonna dell'albero* (fig. 56). Nel secondo disegno il Bambino è ritratto a figura intera, inclinato verso destra e seduto su un parapetto, su cui poggia con il braccio sinistro, mentre rivolge lo sguardo verso lo spettatore. Nel primo, invece, il Bambino, rivolto di tre quarti verso destra, è seduto in braccio alla madre e appoggiato sul suo seno, in un atteggiamento che in realtà corrisponde con maggior esattezza a quello assunto nella variante pittorica della *Madonna con il Bambino*, nota ora da una copia a Strasburgo (fig. 59). Inoltre, come osserva

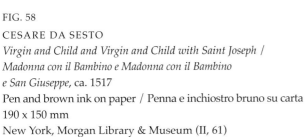

FIG. 58

CESARE DA SESTO

Virgin and Child and Virgin and Child with Saint Joseph /
Madonna con il Bambino e Madonna con il Bambino
e San Giuseppe, ca. 1517

Pen and brown ink on paper / Penna e inchiostro bruno su carta

190 x 150 mm

New York, Morgan Library & Museum (II, 61)

FIG. 59

CESARE DA SESTO

Virgin and Child / Madonna con il Bambino, ca. 1517

Oil on panel / Olio su tavola

61 x 45 cm

Strasbourg, Musée des Beaux-Arts

also known as the *Madonna of the Tree*, at the Pinacoteca di Brera in Milan (fig. 56). In the latter drawing, the Christ Child is depicted at full length, leaning to the right and seated on a parapet, on which he rests his left arm, while gazing at the viewer. In the former, he is seen in a three-quarter view, resting in his mother's arms and against her chest, a pose that closely corresponds to a version of the *Virgin and Child* at Strasbourg (fig. 59). Furthermore, as Pedretti notes,[22] this picture has an even closer connection to another sketch by Cesare da Sesto, originally from a sketchbook, now at the Morgan Library & Museum (II, 61; fig. 58), in which the Christ Child is sleeping and Saint Joseph

Pedretti[22] lo studio parrebbe in relazione più diretta con la composizione studiata da Cesare in un foglio del *Taccuino*, della Morgan Library, ora smembrato (II, 61; fig. 58), dove il Bambino dorme e San Giuseppe lo copre con un panno; nello stesso foglio è ripetuta la sola Madonna con il Bambino, sveglio, che la abbraccia o si appoggia con il piede destro al parapetto, in posa, quindi, diversa da entrambi gli studi come anche dal quadro. Altri schizzi preparatori per quel dipinto milanese si riconoscono in due fogli di Windsor, il RL 12565, dove è tagliata la testa del Bambino, e il RL 12566, dove il pentimento della gambetta destra appare più accentuato e il Bambino è raffigurato dormiente appoggiato al seno della madre, come appare già sia nel disegno di Torino 15588 D.C. (cat. 13), qui esposto, che

is covering him with a cloth. Another drawing on the same sheet shows only the figures of the Virgin and Child. Here, the Child is awake, with his arms around his mother and his left foot resting on the parapet, a pose that differs both from the other studies and from the painting. Other sketches preparatory for the painting at the Brera are at Windsor: one (RL 12565) does not include the Child's head. In the other (RL 12566), the pentimento on the right leg seems to be more accentuated; also, the Christ Child is asleep on his mother's breast, in the same pose that we find in the Turin *Study for the Christ Child* (cat. 13) and in the previously mentioned sketch at the Morgan (II, 61). In the Morgan sketch, however, the Christ Child is drawn twice, asleep and awake, proving that the artist continued to work on both solutions at the same time, considering them as possible alternatives. On yet another sheet at the Morgan (II, 62; fig. 57), we find a further sketch for the Brera *Madonna of the Tree*, which is substantially faithful to the final painting both in the pose of the Virgin and in the face of the Christ Child gazing directly at the viewer.

Cesare da Sesto made another study of the full-length figure of the Christ Child, with his hand on his mother's breast and his head turned toward the viewer, now at the Musée du Louvre (6814). Various aspects of the Virgin (her hands, face, and the left arm covered by full, softly falling drapery) can be found in a sheet at the Gallerie dell'Accademia (346; fig. 60). In addition, on a sheet at Windsor, he drew a tree with many branches and open, leafy fronds, much like the one he later painted in the background of the *Madonna of the Tree*. The composition seems to have been inspired by Leonardo's *Ginevra de' Benci*, in which the subject is set before a tree and has the same hairline as the Virgin in Cesare da Sesto's painting, with a slight smile that lends the face an expression of sweet serenity. The drawings record Cesare da Sesto's interest in the subject of the Virgin and Child at the time when he made his sketchbook, ca. 1513.

Traces of Madonnas in the style of Raphael, sketched earlier in the sketchbook, also recall the aloof beauty of Ginevra de' Benci. The motif of the Virgin holding the Christ Child's foot in her hand is an influence from the early works of Raphael, such as the *Holy Family* in Saint Petersburg and the so-called *Solly Madonna* in Berlin. In his small mas-

nel citato schizzo a penna del foglio della Morgan Library (II, 61; fig. 58): in esso, tuttavia, il Bambino è ritratto per due volte, una sveglio ed una addormentato, a documentazione di come le due soluzioni procedano insieme, alternative ma contemporanee. Anche in un altro foglio di New York (II, 62; fig. 57), compare un altro schizzo per il quadretto di Brera, piuttosto fedele, sia nella posa della Vergine, che nel volto del Bambino che guarda lo spettatore.

Cesare studia ancora l'intera figura del Bambino, con la mano sul seno della madre e il capo rivolto allo spettatore in un foglio del Louvre, Cabinet des Dessins 6814, e, invece, varie parti della figura della Vergine, le mani, il volto, il braccio sinistro coperto da un ricco e morbido panneggio, in un foglio delle Gallerie dell'Accademia (346; fig. 60). In uno studio di Windsor, inoltre, il da Sesto disegna un albero con molte ramificazioni e fronde aperte, sul tipo di quello che dipingerà alle spalle del gruppo sacro nella *Madonna dell'albero*. L'idea compositiva pare ispirata alla *Ginevra Benci*, la cui figura si staglia contro un albero e mostra la stessa attaccatura dei capelli della *Madonna* di Cesare, con un leggero sorriso che conferisce al volto un'espressione di pacata dolcezza. I disegni, quindi, documentano l'interesse per il tema della Madonna con il Bambino negli anni in cui lavora al taccuino, cioè intorno al 1513 circa.

Ricordi delle Madonne raffaellesche, schizzate già nel quadernetto, riaffiorano, infatti, all'interno dell'impostazione piramidale, che richiama ancora, invece, la distaccata bellezza della *Ginevra de' Benci*; il motivo della mano che tiene il piede di Gesù è ripreso, infatti, da opere giovanili di Raffaello, quali la *Sacra Famiglia* di San Pietroburgo e la *Madonna Solly* di Berlino. Nel piccolo capolavoro della *Madonna dell'albero* Cesare riesce più che mai a fondere mirabilmente lo sfumato di Leonardo con le tinte ormai sfrangiate del colorismo di Correggio e l'aulica nobiltà ed eleganza dei ritratti di Raffaello.

I due disegni di Bambino della Biblioteca Reale di Torino, entrambi eseguiti con la tipica tecnica di precisa ispirazione leonardesca a matita rossa su carta anch'essa preparata di rosso-ocra, sono un esempio del procedimento creativo di Cesare da Sesto, eccellente disegnatore, che, come in questo caso, abbina spesso lo studio del singolo particolare a matita allo schizzo a penna per l'intera composizione, prove con cui riempie le strabocchevoli pagine del celebre quadernetto della Morgan Library & Museum. Il *Taccuino* non trova uguali tra i contemporanei, per molteplicità di spunti, idee, motivi, nonché per raffinatezza ed eleganza di esecuzione. Costituisce un *unicum* grafico e artistico. Inoltre è particolarmente interessante poiché riflette l'attenzione dell'artista per le imprese che Michelangelo e Raffaello andavano realizzando nella Roma di Giulio II, in un mo-

terpiece, the *Madonna of the Tree*, Cesare succeeds more than ever in blending Leonardo's *sfumato* with Correggio's brilliant color effects and with the nobility and elegance of Raphael's portraits.

The two Turin drawings of the Christ Child, both executed in the artist's typical Leonardo-inspired red chalk on red-ochre prepared paper, exemplify Cesare da Sesto's creative process. A superb draftsman, he would often make a chalk study of a single detail and a pen and ink sketch of the entire composition (as he does in this case), and they fill sheet after sheet of the Morgan sketchbook. This sketchbook is unmatched by any contemporary artist, not only for the multitude of concepts, ideas and motifs, but also for the supremely skilled and elegant drawing. It stands as a comprehensive record of his drawing and his entire artistic oeuvre. The sketchbook is also extremely interesting because it reflects Cesare da Sesto's keen awareness of the masterpieces that Michelangelo and Raphael were accomplishing in Rome during the pontificate of Pope Julius II, a time when art was reaching unparalleled heights of splendor, and shows how his artistic development evolved in the face of that awareness. While he was undoubtedly fascinated by Michelangelo's expressivity, Cesare da Sesto was also greatly impressed by the harmony and proportions in Raphael's paintings and was certainly not impervious to the burgeoning interest in the art of classical antiquity. The visual sensations aroused by the masterpieces of the Renaissance in Rome found immediate expression in his drawings.

The pages of his sketchbook are also bursting with original ideas, perhaps never realized, or perhaps revised and modified at a later stage: from saints to satyrs, nymphs to angels, from Adam to Hercules, from Venus to Saint Lucy, from Mars to Saint George. On the same page, he combines derivative work from the great masters, adaptations of themes from antiquity, echoes of Leonardo, and original compositions. In all of the drawings, the style is so consistent and the energy in the execution so immediate that they form a coherent whole, produced in a limited time frame, from his years in Rome and his first journey to southern Italy to his return to Milan around 1517.[23]

At the time of the Morgan exhibition, Cesare da Sesto's *Madonna of the Tree* and the Venice study for the arms and face of the Virgin were on display at

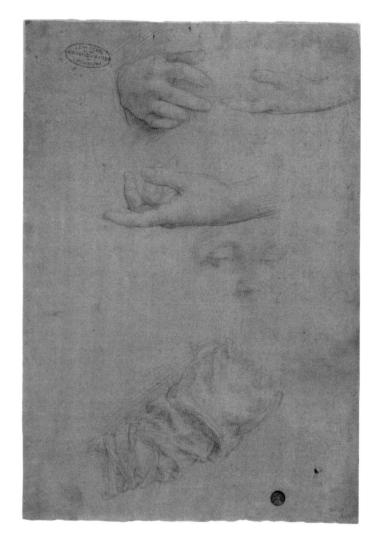

mento di eccezionale splendore artistico, e dimostra l'evoluzione in senso rinascimentale che esse determinano nel suo percorso artistico. Se l'espressività michelangiolesca lo affascina senza dubbio, il lombardo è particolarmente conquistato anche dall'armonia e dalla proporzione delle opere di Raffaello, pur non restando certo insensibile all'atmosfera di *revival* dell'antico: le sensazioni visive provate dinanzi ai capolavori del Rinascimento romano trovano nel disegno immediata possibilità di espressione.

Ma le pagine del suo inseparabile quadernetto sono ricolme anche di idee originali, forse mai realizzate, o riprese e modificate anche in tempi successivi, passando da santi a satiri, da ninfe ad angeli, dagli Adami agli Ercoli, dalle Veneri alle Sante Lucie, da Marte a San Giorgio. L'artista, quindi, intercala nello stesso foglio derivazioni dai grandi artisti, riprese dall'antico, ricordi leonardeschi e composizioni originali. Il tutto con un'omogeneità di stile e un'immediatezza d'esecuzione che fa di questi studi un gruppo compatto, frutto di una medesima ricerca formale, circoscritta in un limitato lasso di tempo, che dagli anni romani comprende il

FIG. 60

CESARE DA SESTO
Studies of Hands and of a Woman's Face / Studi di mani e di volto femminile,
ca. 1517
Red chalk on red-ochre prepared paper /
Sanguigna su carta preparata di rosso-ocra
380 x 265 mm
Venice, Gabinetto dei Disegni e Stampe delle Gallerie dell'Accademia
(346)

the Gallerie dell'Accademia in the exhibition *Leonardo da Vinci. L'uomo universale* (*Leonardo da Vinci: Universal Man*). May these two exhibitions create further reflections on the paintings and drawings of Cesare da Sesto, one of Leonardo's most interesting students.[24]

[1] Beltrami 1919, doc. 238.
[2] The letter, dated Florence, April 3, 1501, is held at the State Archives in Mantua, Archivio Gonzaga, b. 1103, c. 272 r-v, published in Beltrami 1919, p. 65, doc. 107.
[3] Marinoni 1973–80, vol. X, p. 80.
[4] Pedretti 1995, p. 175.
[5] Bernard Berenson and Roberto Longhi described the Leonardeschi as sad copyists of a *réchauffé* version of the beauty that appeared in the works of Leonardo. Recent studies of the Leonardeschi (in particular the essays by Marani in New York 2003, pp. 155–90 and Bora in Paris 2003, pp. 311–84) have reevaluated the importance of the school of Leonardo in Lombardy, emphasizing individual artistic personalities, dedicating to them many monographic case studies and documenting the influence of Leonardo on followers and imitators through the end of the sixteenth century.
[6] Vasari (1568) 1963, vol. III, p. 388.
[7] Berenson 1903, p. 1262, fig. 566; Möller 1916; Clark and Pedretti 1968–69, p. 115.
[8] Pedretti 1990, pp. 102–3, no. 16.
[9] As suggested by Dalli Regoli, in Pedretti and Dalli Regoli 1985, cat. 16.
[10] Müntz 1899, p. 518, no. XVII; Suida 1929; Bertini 1958, p. 33; Griseri 1978, no. 12; Zanuso in Bologna 1985.
[11] Pedretti 1990, p. 104.
[12] Taglialagamba in Venaria Reale (Turin) 2011–12, pp. 124–25, cat. 1.30.
[13] Biblioteca Reale, Turin (15716 D.C.), red chalk on paper, 90 x 68 mm. See Salvi in Turin 2006, pp. 92–93, cat. II.5.
[14] Pedretti 1990, p. 105; Salvi in Turin 2006, p. 92, cat. II.5.
[15] Pedretti 1990, p. 105.
[16] Taglialagamba in Venaria Reale (Turin) 2011–12, p. 124, cat. 1.29.
[17] Morigia 1595, p. 277.
[18] Taglialagamba in Venaria Reale (Turin) 2011–12, pp. 123–24, cat. 1.28.
[19] Pedretti in Venaria Reale (Turin) 2011–12, pp. 42–44.
[20] Pedretti 1990, p. 183.
[21] Carminati 1994, pp. 294–95.
[22] Pedretti 1990, p. 94.
[23] Among the drawings in the sketchbook are preparatory studies for works from his first journey to southern Italy and from the period immediately afterward, spent in Milan.
[24] The exhibition at the Gallerie dell'Accademia, in Venice, curated by the author, was on display from September 1 to December 1, 2013.

primo viaggio al sud e il rientro a Milano, intorno al 1517.[23] In contemporanea all'esposizione dei due studi torinesi preparatori per il Bambino per la *Madonna dell'albero*, il dipinto e lo studio veneziano per le braccia e il volto della Vergine, sono stati esposti insieme a Venezia alla mostra *Leonardo da Vinci. L'uomo universale*,[24] quasi a creare un momento unitario di riflessione su un'opera pittorica (e la sua genesi grafica) di Cesare da Sesto, tra i più interessanti allievi di Leonardo.

[1] Beltrami 1919, doc. 238.
[2] La lettera, datata Firenze 3 aprile 1501, è conservata nell'Archivio di Stato di Mantova, *Archivio Gonzaga*, b.1103, c. 272 r-v, pubblicata in Beltrami 1919, p. 65, doc. 107.
[3] Marinoni 1973-80, vol. X, p. 80.
[4] Pedretti 1995, p. 175.
[5] Da quando Bernard Berenson e Roberto Longhi demolirono i Leonardeschi quali "tristi descrittori di bellà rifredde" che tanto avevano vibrato nelle opere del maestro di Vinci, gli studi sui Leonardeschi (in particolare i saggi di Marani in New York 2003, pp. 155-90 e Bora in Parigi 2003, pp. 311-84), hanno rivalutato l'importanza della scuola di Leonardo in Lombardia, delineando singole personalità artistiche (dedicandovi in molti casi studi monografici) e documentando l'influenza sino a seguaci e imitatori di fine secolo.
[6] Vasari (1568) 1963, vol. III, p. 388.
[7] Berenson 1903, p. 1262, fig. 566; Möller 1916; Clark-Pedretti 1968-69, p. 115.
[8] Pedretti 1990, pp. 102-3, no. 16.
[9] Come ha suggerito Gigetta Dalli Regoli, in Pedretti and Dalli Regoli 1985, no. 16.
[10] Müntz 1899, p. 518, no. XVII; Suida 1929; Bertini 1958, p. 33; Griseri 1978, no.12; Zanuso in Bologna 1985.
[11] Pedretti 1990, p. 104.
[12] Taglialagamba in Venaria Reale (Turin) 2011-12, pp. 124-25, cat. 1.30.
[13] Biblioteca Reale di Torino, 15716 D.C. Sanguigna, carta bianca, mm 90 x 68; Salvi in Turin 2006, pp. 92-93, cat. II.5.
[14] Pedretti 1990, p. 105; Salvi in Turin 2006, p. 92, cat. II.5.
[15] Pedretti 1990, p. 105.
[16] Taglialagamba, in Venaria Reale (Turin) 2011-12, p. 124, cat. 1.29.
[17] Morigia 1595, p. 277.
[18] Taglialagamba in Venaria Reale (Turin) 2011-12, pp. 123-24, cat. 1.28.
[19] Pedretti in Venaria Reale (Turin) 2011-12, pp. 42-44.
[20] Pedretti 1990, p. 183.
[21] Carminati 1994, pp. 294-95.
[22] Pedretti 1990, p. 94.
[23] Tra gli schizzi dello sketchbook, infatti, affiorano studi preparatori per le opere del primo soggiorno meridionale e per quelle milanesi immediatamente successive.
[24] La mostra, a cura di Annalisa Perissa Torrini, è stata aperta alle Gallerie dell'Accademia di Venezia dal 1 settembre al 1 dicembre 2013.

10

Workshop of/Bottega di ANDREA DEL VERROCCHIO

Study of the Angel in Verrocchio's "Baptism of Christ"
Studio dell'angelo nel "Battesimo di Cristo" del Verrocchio
1470s

Metalpoint and wash heightened with white on buff prepared paper
Punta metallica, acquarello e biacca su carta preparata di ocra chiara
231 x 171 mm (9 $\frac{1}{16}$ x 6 $\frac{3}{4}$ inches)
Turin, Biblioteca Reale
(15635 D.C.)

Literature/Bibliografia: Bertini 1958, p. 37, no. 232; Pedretti 1973, pp. 31–32; Pedretti in Turin 1975, p. 32, cat. 15; Pedretti and Dalli Regoli 1985, pp. 101–2, no. 15; Pedretti 1987, p. 6; Pedretti 1990, pp. 32–33, 101–2, no. 15; Turin 1998–99, pp. 104–5, cat. II.15; Marani 1999, pp. 62–65; Marani in Milan 2001, pp. 116–17, cat. 23; Pedretti in Turin 2006, pp. 84–85, cat. II.1; Vezzosi in Fukuoka and Tokyo 2012, pp. 38–39, cat. 003; Taglialagamba in Venaria Reale (Turin) 2011–12, pp. 118–19, cat. 1.23.

11

Attributed to / Attribuito a LEONARDO DA VINCI and Follower / e Seguace

Head of a Young Woman
Testa di fanciulla
ca. 1510

Red chalk heightened with white on red-ochre prepared paper
Sanguigna e biacca su carta preparata di rosso-ocra
222 x 175 mm (8 ¾ x 6 ⅞ inches)

Turin, Biblioteca Reale
(15586 D.C.)

Literature / Bibliografia: Pedretti in Turin 1975, p. 34, cat. 17; Pedretti in Vinci 1982, p. 22, cat. 16; Sciolla 1985, pp. 40–42; Bora 1987, p. 145; Pedretti 1990, p. 103, no. 17; Turin 1998–89, pp. 108–9, cat. II.17; Pedretti in Turin 2006, pp. 88–89, cat. II.3; Taglialagamba in Venaria Reale (Turin) 2011–12, p. 124, cat. 1.29; Pedretti in Fukuoka and Tokyo 2012, p. 42, cat. 005.

12

GIOVANNI ANTONIO BOLTRAFFIO (ca. 1467–1516)

Head of a Young Man with a Crown of Thorns and Vine Leaves
Testa di giovane incoronato di spine e foglie di vite
ca. 1495

Metalpoint on blue prepared paper
Punta metallica su carta preparata di azzurro
305 x 220 mm (12 x 8 ¹¹⁄₁₆ inches)

Turin, Biblioteca Reale
(15587 D.C.)

Literature/Bibliografia: Bertini in Turin 1950, p. 17, cat. 33; Bertini 1958, p. 19, no. 60; Pedretti in Turin 1975, p. 35, cat. 18; Griseri 1978, no. 12; Zanuso in Bologna 1985, pp. 157, 199, cat. 5; Pedretti 1990, p. 104, no. 18; Pedretti in Turin 1990, pp. 54–55, cat. 17; Caroli 1991, pp. 237–38; Pedretti 1991, pp. 43–44; Fiorio in Lugano 1998, pp. 143–44, cat. 11; Pedretti 1998, pp. 40–41; Turin 1998–99, pp. 110–11, cat. II.18; Fiorio 2000, pp. 146–50; Bora in Paris 2003, pp. 348–49, cat. 119; Pedretti in Turin 2006, pp. 90–91, cat. II.4; Taglialagamba in Venaria Reale (Turin) 2011–12, pp. 124–25, cat. 1.30.

13

CESARE DA SESTO (1477–1523)

Study for the Christ Child
Studio per Gesù Bambino
ca. 1510

Red chalk on red-ochre prepared paper
Matita rossa su carta preparata di rosso-ocra
380 x 275 mm (14 $^{15}/_{16}$ x 10 $^{13}/_{16}$ inches)

Turin, Biblioteca Reale
(15988 D.C.)

Literature/Bibliografia: Bertini in Turin 1950, p. 16, cat. 31; Bertini 1958, p. 25, no. 115; Clark 1968–69, p. 108; Pedretti in Turin 1975, p. 38, cat. 21; Griseri 1978, no. 13; Pedretti 1990, p. 106, no. 21; Turin 1998–99, pp. 112–13, cat. II.19; Pedretti in Turin 2006, pp. 94–95, cat. II.6.

14

CESARE DA SESTO (1477–1523)

Study for the Blessing Christ Child
Studio per Gesù Bambino benedicente
ca. 1510

Red chalk on red-ochre prepared paper
Matita rossa su carta preparata di rosso-ocra
360 x 240 mm (14 ³⁄₁₆ x 9 ⁷⁄₁₆ inches)

Turin, Biblioteca Reale
(15987 D.C.)

Literature/Bibliografia: Bertini in Turin 1950, p. 16, cat. 32; Bertini 1958, p. 25, no. 116; Clark 1968–69, p. 108; Pedretti in Turin 1975, p. 39, cat. 22; Pedretti 1990, p. 106, no. 22.

15

CESARE DA SESTO (1477–1523)

Head of an Old Man
Testa di vecchio
ca. 1515

Red chalk on red-ochre prepared paper
Sanguigna su carta preparata di rosso-ocra
190 x 130 mm (7 ½ x 5 ⅛ inches)

Turin, Biblioteca Reale
(15585 D.C.)

Literature / Bibliografia: Pedretti 1953, p. 59; Pedretti in Turin 1975, p. 37, cat. 20; Pedretti and Dalli Regoli 1985, p. 74; Bora 1987, p. 145; Pedretti 1990, p. 105, no. 20; Perissa 2006, p. 81; Taglialagamba in Venaria Reale (Turin) 2011–12, pp. 123–24, cat. 1.28.

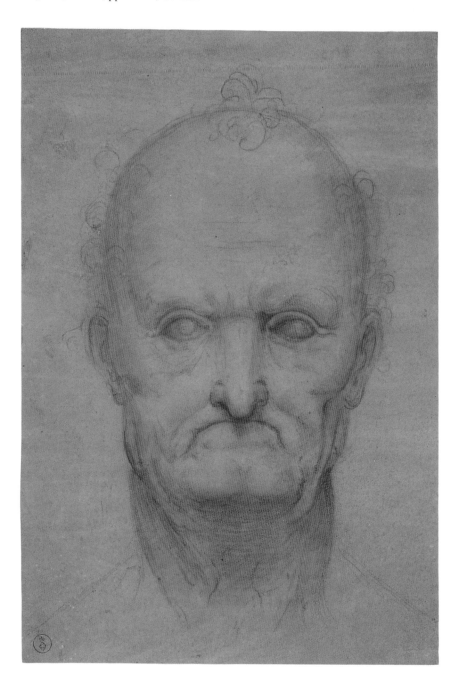

16

Pupil of/Allievo di LEONARDO DA VINCI

Old Man Seated in Profile
Vecchio seduto visto di profilo
ca. 1495

Red chalk on paper
Sanguigna su carta
180 x 130 mm (7 ¹/₁₆ x 5 ⅛ inches)

Turin, Biblioteca Reale
(15584 D.C.)

Literature/Bibliografia: Berenson 1903, vol. 2, p. 68, no. 1262; Bertini 1958, p. 37, no. 230; Clark 1968–69, p. 115; Pedretti in Turin 1975, p. 33, cat. 16; Pedretti in Milan 1983, p. 128; Pedretti 1990, pp. 102–3, no. 16; Turin 1998–99, pp. 106–7, cat. II.16; Marani in Milan 2001, pp. 128–29, cat. 29; Pedretti in Turin 2006, pp. 86–87, cat. II.2; Taglialagamba in Venaria Reale (Turin) 2011–12, pp. 119–20, cat. 1.24.

SELECT BIBLIOGRAPHY
BIBLIOGRAFIA DI RIFERIMENTO

Ancona 2005–6
Leonardo. Genio e visione in terra marchigiana, ed. Carlo Pedretti, exh. cat., Mole Vanvitelliana, Ancona, Foligno (Perugia) 2005

Badia Polesine (da) 1946
Jotti da Badia Polesine, ed., *Il Codice sul volo degli uccelli*, facsimile, Milan 1946

Bambach 2001
Carmen C. Bambach, "A Leonardo Drawing for the Metropolitan Museum of Art: Studies for a Statue of Hercules," *Apollo* 153 (2001), pp. 16–23

Bambach 2009
Carmen C. Bambach, *Un'eredità difficile: i disegni ed i manoscritti di Leonardo tra mito e documento*, XLVII Lettura Vinciana (2007), Biblioteca Leonardiana, Vinci, Florence 2009

Barone and Kemp 2008
Juliana Barone and Martin Kemp, "What is Leonardo's Codex on the Flight of Birds Really About?," in Birmingham and San Francisco 2008–9, pp. 97–109

Baselica 2005
Giulia Baselica, "Fëdor Sabašnikov e il *Codice sul volo degli uccelli* di Leonardo da Vinci alla Biblioteca Reale di Torino," *Centro Studi Piemontesi* 34, 1 (2005), pp. 97–103

Beltrami 1912
Luca Beltrami, *Leonardo da Vinci e l'aviazione*, Milan 1912

Beltrami 1919
Luca Beltrami, ed., *Documenti e memorie riguardanti la vita e le opere di Leonardo da Vinci*, Milan 1919

Berenson 1903
Bernard Berenson, *The Drawings of the Florentine Painters*, 2 vols., London 1903

Berenson 1938
Bernard Berenson, *The Drawings of the Florentine Painters*, 3 vols., Chicago 1938

Bertini 1958
Aldo Bertini, ed., *I disegni italiani della Biblioteca Reale di Torino*, Rome 1958

Birmingham and San Francisco 2008–9
Leonardo da Vinci: Drawings from the Biblioteca Reale in Turin, ed. Jeannine A. O'Grody, exh. cat., The Birmingham Museum of Art, Birmingham, Alabama, and The Legion of Honor, San Francisco, Birmingham 2008

Bodenheimer 1956
Friedrich S. Bodenheimer, "Léonard de Vinci et les insects," *Revue de Synthèse* 77 (1956), pp. 147–53

Bologna 1985
Leonardo: il codice Hammer e la Mappa di Imola. Arte e scienza a Bologna in Emilia e Romagna nel primo Cinquecento, eds. Carlo Pedretti, Alessandro Vezzosi, Susanna Zanuso, exh. cat., Palazzo del Podestà, Bologna, Florence 1985

Bora 1987
Giulio Bora, "Per un catalogo dei disegni dei leonardeschi lombardi: indicazioni e problemi di metodo," *Raccolta Vinciana* 22 (1987), pp. 139–82

Bora 2003
Giulio Bora, "Les léonardesques. Léonard de Vinci et les léonardesques lombards: les difficultés d'une conquête du naturel," in Paris 2003, pp. 310–83

Bottari 1754–73
Giovanni Gaetano Bottari, *Raccolta di lettere sulla pittura, scultura ed architettura, scritte da più celebri professori che in dette arti fiorirono dal sec. XV al XVII*, 7 vols., Rome 1754–73

Caroli 1991
Flavio Caroli, *Leonardo. Studi di fisiognomica*, Milan 1991

Carminati 1994
Marco Carminati, *Cesare da Sesto. 1477-1523*, Milan 1994

Carusi 1926
Enrico Carusi, ed., *Leonardo da Vinci. I fogli mancanti al codice di Leonardo su 'l volo degli uccelli nella Biblioteca Reale di Torino*, Rome 1926

Chastel 1982
André Chastel, "Les limites du savoir scientifique chez Léonard," in *Leonardo e l'età della ragione*, ed. Enrico Bellone, Milan 1982, pp. 7–14

Clark 1935
Kenneth Clark, *A Catalogue of the Drawings of Leonardo da Vinci in the Collection of His Majesty the King at Windsor Castle*, Cambridge 1935

Clark 1939
Kenneth Clark, *Leonardo da Vinci: An Account of His Development as an Artist*, Cambridge 1939

Clark 1968–69
Kenneth Clark and Carlo Pedretti, *The Drawings of Leonardo da Vinci in the Collection of Her Majesty the Queen at Windsor Castle*, 3 vols., London 1968–69

Clark 1969
Kenneth Clark, "Leonardo and the Antique," in *Leonardo's Legacy*, ed. Charles Donald O'Malley, Berkeley 1969, pp. 1–34

Dondi 1975a
Giuseppe Dondi, "In margine al codice vinciano della Biblioteca Reale di Torino: note storico-codicologiche," *Accademie e Biblioteche d'Italia* 43, 4 (1975), pp. 252–71

Dondi 1975b
Giuseppe Dondi, "Leonardo, il Piemonte e i Piemontesi," *Cronache economiche* 7/8 (1975), pp. 3–23

Dondi 1991
Giuseppe Dondi, "Il Codice vinciano della Biblioteca Reale di Torino," in *Il Codice sul volo degli uccelli*, facsimile, Turin 1991, pp. XI–XVII

Fiorio 2000
Maria Teresa Fiorio, *Giovanni Antonio Boltraffio: un pittore milanese nel lume di Leonardo*, Milan 2000

Firpo 1975
Luigi Firpo, "Leonardo a Torino," in Turin 1975, pp. XI–XXIV

Firpo 1978
Luigi Firpo, "Il Codice sul volo," *Attualità Leonardiane* 1978, pp. 4–19

Firpo 1991
Luigi Firpo, "Il Codice vinciano della Biblioteca Reale di Torino," in *Il Codice sul volo degli uccelli*, facsimile, Turin 1991, pp. XIX–XXXII

Florence 1952
Mostra di disegni, manoscritti e documenti. Quinto centenario della nascita di Leonardo da Vinci, ed. Giulia Brunetti, exh. cat., Biblioteca Medicea Laurenziana, Florence 1952

Florence 1992
Il disegno fiorentino del tempo di Lorenzo il Magnifico, ed. Annamaria Petrioli Tofani, exh. cat., Gabinetto Disegni e Stampe della Galleria degli Uffizi, Florence, Cinisello Balsamo (Milan) 1992

Florence 2001
Nel segno di Masaccio. L'invenzione della prospettiva, ed. Filippo Camerota, exh. cat., Galleria degli Uffizi, Florence 2001

Florence 2005
Leonardo da Vinci. La vera immagine, eds. Vanna Arrighi, Anna Bellinazzi, Edoardo Villata, exh. cat., Archivio di Stato, Florence 2005

Florence 2006–7a
La mente di Leonardo. Nel laboratorio del Genio Universale, ed. Paolo Galluzzi, exh. cat., Galleria degli Uffizi, Florence 2006

Florence 2006–7b
La mente di Leonardo. Al tempo della Battaglia di Anghiari, ed. Carlo Pedretti, exh. cat., Gabinetto Disegni e Stampe degli Uffizi, Florence 2006

Fontani 1792
Francesco Fontani, ed., *Trattato della pittura di Lionardo Da Vinci, ridotto alla sua vera lezione sopra una copia a penna di mano di Stefano Della Bella con le figure disegnate dal medesimo, corredato delle memorie per la vita dell'autore e del copiatore di Francesco Fontani*, Florence 1792

Fukuoka and Tokyo 2012
Leonardo da Vinci e l'idea della bellezza, eds. Alessandro Vezzosi and Shunsuke Kijima, exh. cat., Shizuoka City Museum of Art; Fukuoka Art Museum; The Bunkamura Museum of Art, Tokyo 2011

Fumagalli 1939
Giuseppina Fumagalli, ed., *Leonardo omo sanza lettere*, Florence 1939

Galluzzi 1979
Paolo Galluzzi, *Momento. Studi galileiani*, Rome 1979

Galluzzi 1989
Paolo Galluzzi, *Leonardo e i proporzionanti*, XXVIII Lettura Vinciana (1988), Biblioteca Leonardiana, Vinci, Florence 1989

Galluzzi 2006
"Leonardo e la 'ventilazione' delle bilance," in Turin 2006, pp. 20–22

Genoa 2001
Viaggio in Italia. Un corteo magico dal Cinquecento al Novecento, eds. Giuseppe Marcenaro and Piero Boragina, exh. cat., Palazzo Ducale, Genoa, Milan 2001

Giacobello Bernard 1990
Giovanna Giacobello Bernard, ed., *Biblioteca Reale di Torino*, Florence 1990

Giacomelli 1936
Raffaele Giacomelli, *Gli scritti di Leonardo da Vinci sul volo*, Rome 1936

Giglioli 1944
Odoardo H. Giglioli, *Leonardo. Iniziazione alla conoscenza di lui e delle questioni vinciane*, Florence 1944

Griseri 1978
Andreina Griseri, ed., *I grandi disegni italiani della Biblioteca Reale*, Milan 1978

Kant (1783) 1982
Immanuel Kant, *Prolegomeni ad ogni futura metafisica*, Rome and Bari 1982

Keele and Pedretti 1979–80
Kenneth D. Keele and Carlo Pedretti, eds., *Leonardo da Vinci: Corpus of the Anatomical Studies in the Collection of Her Majesty the Queen at Windsor Castle*, 3 vols., facsimile, London 1979–80

Keele and Pedretti 1980–84
Kenneth D. Keele and Carlo Pedretti, eds., *Leonardo da Vinci. Corpus degli studi anatomici nella collezione di sua Maestà la Regina Elisabetta II nel castello di Windsor*, 3 vols., facsimile, Florence 1980–84

Lacaita 1879
James Philippe Lacaita, *Catalogue of the Library* [of William, VII Duke of Devonshire] *at Chatsworth*, London 1879

Laurenza 2004
Domenico Laurenza, *Leonardo. Il volo*, Florence 2004

London 2011–12
Leonardo da Vinci: Painter at the Court of Milan, ed. Luke Syson, exh. cat., The National Gallery, London 2011

London 2012
Leonardo da Vinci: Anatomist, eds. Martin Clayton and Ron Philo, exh. cat., The Queen's Gallery, Buckingham Palace, London 2012

Lugano 1998
Rabisch. Il grottesco nell'arte del Cinquecento; L'Accademia della Val di Blenio; Lomazzo e l'ambiente milanese, eds. Giulio Bora, Manuela Kahn-Rossi and Francesco Porzio, exh. cat., Museo Cantonale d'Arte, Lugano, Milan 1998

Luporini 1953
Cesare Luporini, *La mente di Leonardo*, Florence 1953

MacCurdy 1955
Edward MacCurdy, ed., *The Notebooks of Leonardo da Vinci*, New York 1955

Maffei 1999
Sonia Maffei, ed., *Paolo Giovio. Scritti d'arte: lessico ed ecfrasi*, Pisa 1999

Marani 1997
Pietro C. Marani, "Dalla natura al simbolo: osservazione della natura, imitazione dell'antico e visualizzazione del moto nell'opera di Leonardo," *Raccolta Vinciana* 27 (1997), pp. 155–85

Marani 1999
Pietro C. Marani, *Leonardo. Una carriera di pittore*, Milan 1999

Marani 2003
Pietro C. Marani, "Leonardo's Drawings in Milan and their Influence on the Graphic Work of Milanese Artists," in New York 2003, pp. 155–90

Marani 2010
Pietro C. Marani, *Leonardiana. Studi e saggi su Leonardo*, Milan 2010

Marani 2011a
Pietro C. Marani, "Una traccia per l'evoluzione del disegno in Leonardo: dalla copia dei disegni dei 'boni maestri' alla 'scuola del mondo'," in *La scuola del mondo. Leonardo e Michelangelo: disegni a confronto*, eds. Pietro C. Marani and Pina Ragionieri, exh. cat., Casa Buonarroti, Florence, Cinisello Balsamo (Milan) 2011, pp. 13–33

Marani 2011b
Pietro C. Marani, "Una traccia per l'evoluzione del disegno in Leonardo: dalla copia dei disegni dei 'boni maestri' alla 'scuola del mondo'," in *Leonardo e Michelangelo: capolavori della grafica e studi romani*, eds. Pietro C. Marani and Pina Ragionieri, exh. cat., Musei Capitolini, Rome 2011–12, Cinisello Balsamo (Milan) 2011, pp. 18–31

Mariette 1730
Pierre Jean Mariette, ed., *Recueil de Testes de caractere et de charges dessinées par Leonard de Vinci florentin & gravées par M. de le C. de C[aylus]*, Paris 1730

Mariette 1767
Pierre Jean Mariette, ed., *Recueil de charges et de têtes de différens caracteres, gravees à l'eau forte d'après les desseins de Leonard de Vinci*, Nouvelle édition, revue & augmentée par l'Auteur, Paris 1767

Marinoni 1973–80
Augusto Marinoni, ed., *Il Codice Atlantico della Biblioteca Ambrosiana di Milano*, 12 vols., facsimile, Florence 1973–80

Marinoni 1976
Augusto Marinoni, ed., *Il Codice sul volo degli uccelli nella Biblioteca Reale di Torino*, facsimile, Florence 1976

Marinoni 1982
Augusto Marinoni, ed., *Leonardo da Vinci: The Codex on the Flight of Birds*, facsimile, New York 1982

Marinoni 1986–90
Augusto Marinoni, ed., *Leonardo da Vinci. I manoscritti dell'Institut de France*, facsimile, Florence 1986–90

Milan 1939
Mostra di Leonardo da Vinci e delle invenzioni italiane, exh. cat., Palazzo dell'Arte, Milan 1939

Milan 1983
Leonardo. Studi per il Cenacolo dalla Biblioteca Reale nel Castello di Windsor, ed. Carlo Pedretti, exh. cat., Santa Maria delle Grazie, Milan 1983

Milan 2001
Il Genio e le Passioni. Leonardo e il Cenacolo, ed. Pietro C. Marani, exh. cat., Civico Museo d'Arte Contemporanea, Milan 2001

Milan 2012
Il volo degli uccelli e il volo meccanico. Disegni di Leonardo dal Codice Atlantico, ed. Edoardo Villata, exh. cat., Biblioteca-Pinacoteca-Accademia Ambrosiana and Sacrestia del Bramante, Milan, Novara 2012

Milan 2013
Leonardo: favole e facezie, ed. Carlo Vecce, exh. cat., Biblioteca-Pinacoteca-Accademia Ambrosiana and Sacrestia del Bramante, Milan, Novara 2013

Milan and Washington, D.C. 1983–84
Leonardo: Studies for the Last Supper from the Royal Library at Windsor Castle, ed. Carlo Pedretti, exh. cat., Santa Maria delle Grazie, Milan, and The National Gallery of Art, Washington, D.C., Milan 1983

Möller 1916
Emil Möller, "Leonardos Bildnis der Cecilia Gallerani in der Galerie des Fürsten Czartoryski in Krakau," *Monatshefte für Kunstwissenschaft* 9, 9 (1916), pp. 313 26

Morigia 1595
Paolo Morigia, *La nobiltà di Milano*, Milan 1595

Moscow 2012–13
Kodeks o polëte ptic Leonardo da Vinci, exh. cat., and facsimile, Pushing Arts Museum, Moscow 2012–13

Müller-Walde 1897
Paul Müller-Walde, "Beiträge zur Kenntnis des Leonardo da Vinci," *Jahrbuch der Königlich Preussischen Kunstsammlungen* 18, 2/3 (1897), pp. 92–169

Müntz 1899
Eugène Müntz, *Léonard de Vinci. L'artiste, le penseur, le savant*, Paris 1899

New York 2003
Leonardo da Vinci: Master Draftsman, ed. Carmen C. Bambach, exh. cat., The Metropolitan Museum of Art, New York 2003

Ochenkowski (D') 1919
Henri D'Ochenkowski, "La 'donna coll'ermellino' è una composizione di Leonardo da Vinci," *Raccolta Vinciana* X (1919), pp. 65–111

Panofsky 1940
Erwin Panofsky, *The Codex Huygens and Leonardo da Vinci's Art Theory*, London 1940

Panofsky (1955) 1962
Erwin Panofsky, *Il significato nelle arti visive*, Turin 1962

Paris 2003
Léonard de Vinci. Dessins et manuscrits, eds. Françoise Viatte and Varena Forcione, exh. cat., Musée National du Louvre, Paris 2003

Paris 2012
La "Sainte Anne" l'ultime chef-d'œuvre de Léonard de Vinci, ed. Vincent Delieuvin, exh. cat., Musée National du Louvre, Paris 2012

Pedretti 1953
Carlo Pedretti, *Documenti e memorie riguardanti Leonardo da Vinci a Bologna e in Emilia*, Bologna 1953

Pedretti 1958
Carlo Pedretti, "L'Ercole di Leonardo," *L'Arte* 57, 23 (1958), pp. 163–72

Pedretti 1965
Carlo Pedretti, "Excerpts from the Codex Huygens, published in London in 1720," *Journal of the Warburg and Courtauld Institutes* 28 (1965), pp. 336–38

Pedretti 1973
Carlo Pedretti, *Leonardo: A Study in Chronology and Style*, London 1973

Pedretti 1977
Carlo Pedretti, ed., *The Literary Works of Leonardo da Vinci Compiled and Edited from the Original Manuscripts by Jean Paul Richter, Commentary* by Carlo Pedretti, 2 vols., Los Angeles 1977

Pedretti 1978
Carlo Pedretti, *Leonardo architetto*, Milan 1978

Pedretti and Dalli Regoli 1985
Carlo Pedretti and Gigetta Dalli Regoli, eds., *I disegni di Leonardo da Vinci e della sua cerchia nel Gabinetto Disegni e Stampe della Galleria degli Uffizi a Firenze*, Florence 1985

Pedretti 1987a
Carlo Pedretti, "Il nuovo Apelle," *Art e Dossier* 12 (1987), pp. 5–21

Pedretti 1987b
Carlo Pedretti, "'Impacientissimo al pennello'," *Art e Dossier* 12 (1987), pp. 22–39

Pedretti 1990
Carlo Pedretti, *I disegni di Leonardo da Vinci e della sua cerchia nella Biblioteca Reale di Torino*, Florence 1990

Pedretti 1991
Carlo Pedretti, "Il tema del profilo, o quasi," in *I leonardeschi a Milano. Fortuna e collezionismo*; Atti del Convegno Internazionale, ed. Maria Teresa Fiorio and Pietro C. Marani, Milan 1991, pp. 14–24

Pedretti 1993
Carlo Pedretti, *The Drawings of Leonardo da Vinci and His Circle in America*, Florence 1993

Pedretti 1995
Carlo Pedretti, ed., *Leonardo da Vinci. Libro di Pittura: Codice Urbinate lat. 1270 nella Biblioteca Apostolica Vaticana*, Florence 1995

Pedretti 1998a
Carlo Pedretti, "Leonardo: il ritratto," *Art e Dossier* 138 (1998)

Pedretti 1998b
Carlo Pedretti, ed., *Leonardo da Vinci. Il Codice Arundel nella British Library*, 2 vols., facsimile, Florence 1998

Pedretti 2005
Carlo Pedretti, ed., *L'anatomia di Leonardo da Vinci fra Mondino e Berengario*, Florence 2005

Pedretti 2007
Carlo Pedretti, *Il tempio dell'anima*, Foligno (Perugia) 2007

Pedretti 2011
Carlo Pedretti, "I disegni di Leonardo 'ripassati' da allievi o seguaci," in Venaria Reale (Turin) 2011–12, pp. 41–51

Pedretti 2012
Carlo Pedretti, *Leonardo da Vinci. I cento disegni più belli delle raccolte di tutto il mondo*, Florence 2012

Perissa 2006
Annalisa Perissa Torrini, *Leonardo: la sua scuola e il disegno*, in Turin 2006, pp. 80–83

Prum 2008
Richard O. Prum, "Leonardo and the Science of Bird Flight," in Birmingham and San Francisco 2008–9, pp. 111–17

Reti 1974a
Ladislao Reti, ed., *Leonardo da Vinci: The Madrid Codices*, 5 vols., New York 1974

Reti 1974b
Ladislao Reti, ed., *I Codici di Madrid nella Biblioteca Nazionale di Madrid*, 5 vols., Florence 1974

Richter (1883) 1939
Jean Paul Richter, ed., *The Literary Works of Leonardo da Vinci*, 2 vols., Oxford 1939

Richter (1883) 1970
Jean Paul Richter, ed., *The Notebooks of Leonardo da Vinci*, 2 vols., New York 1970

Richter I.A. 1941
Irma A. Richter, "Erwin Panofsky: The Codex Huygens and Leonardo da Vinci's Art Theory: The Pierpont Morgan Library Codex M.A. 1139, London 1940," *The Art Bulletin* 23 (1941), pp. 335–38

Sabachnikoff and Piumati 1893
Teodoro Sabachnikoff and Giovanni Piumati, eds., *Codice sul volo degli uccelli e varie altre materie*, facsimile, Paris 1893

Salvi 2005a
Paola Salvi, "Leonardo e la scienza anatomica del pittore," in Pedretti 2005, pp. xiii–xliii

Salvi 2005b
Paola Salvi, "Alle origini dell'anatomia artistica," *Art e Dossier* 207 (2005), pp. 32–48

Salvi 2006
Paola Salvi, "Atleti e guerrieri: Leonardo e la potenza del corpo," in Turin 2006, pp. 23–25

Salvi 2011
Paola Salvi, "Leonardo attraverso la collezione della Biblioteca Reale," in Venaria Reale (Turin) 2011–12, pp. 27–40

Salvi 2012a
Paola Salvi, "L'*Uomo vitruviano* e il *De statua* di Leon Battista Alberti: la misura dell'armonia," in Paola Salvi, ed., *Approfondimenti sull'*Uomo vitruviano *di Leonardo da Vinci*, Poggio a Caiano (Florence) 2012, pp. 21–60

Salvi 2012b
Paola Salvi, "Leonardo da Vinci e il *Paragone delle arti*: le vie dell'anima attraverso il 'miglior senso'," in Rocco Sinisgalli, ed., *Ut pictura poësis. Per una storia delle arti visive*, Poggio a Caiano (Florence) 2012, pp. 59–82

Salvi 2013a
Paola Salvi, *L'anatomia di Leonardo: "figurare e descrivere,"* Poggio a Caiano (Florence) 2013

Salvi 2013b
Paola Salvi, "L'*Uomo Vitruviano* di Leonardo, il *De statua* di Alberti e altre proporzioni del corpo umano," in Venice 2013, pp. 40–57

Sciolla 1985
Gianni Carlo Sciolla, ed., *Le collezioni d'arte della Biblioteca Reale di Torino. Disegni, incisioni, manoscritti figurati*, Turin 1985

Sciolla 1990
Gianni Carlo Sciolla, "I disegni della Biblioteca Reale: linee per una storia delle collezioni," in Turin 1990, pp. 3–13

Suida 1929
Wilhelm Suida, *Leonardo und sein Kreis*, München 1929

Turin 1950
Prima mostra dei disegni italiani della Biblioteca Reale di Torino, ed. Aldo Bertini, exh. cat., Biblioteca Reale, Turin 1950

Turin 1975
Disegni di Leonardo da Vinci e della sua scuola alla Biblioteca Reale di Torino, ed. Carlo Pedretti, exh. cat., Biblioteca Reale, Turin, Florence 1975

Turin 1990
Da Leonardo a Rembrandt. Disegni della Biblioteca Reale di Torino, ed. Gianni Carlo Sciolla, Palazzo Reale, Turin 1990

Turin 1998–99
Leonardo e le meraviglie della Biblioteca Reale di Torino, ed. Giovanna Giacobello Bernard, exh. cat., Biblioteca Reale, Turin, Milan 1998

Turin 2003–4
Van Eyck, Antonello, Leonardo. Tre capolavori del Rinascimento, eds. Giovanna Giacobello Bernard and Enrica Pagella, exh. cat., Biblioteca Reale, Turin 2003

Turin 2006
Leonardo da Vinci. Capolavori in mostra, ed. Giovanna Giacobello Bernard, exh. cat., Biblioteca Reale, Turin, Milan 2006

Uccelli and Zammattio 1952
Arturo Uccelli and Carlo Zammattio, *I libri del volo di Leonardo da Vinci*, Milan 1952

Uzielli 1872
Gustavo Uzielli, *Ricerche intorno a Leonardo da Vinci*, Florence 1872

Uzielli 1884
Gustavo Uzielli, *Ricerche intorno a Leonardo da Vinci*, Rome 1884

Valentiner 1930
Wilhelm R. Valentiner, "Leonardo as Verrocchio's Coworker," *The Art Bulletin* 12, 1 (1930), pp. 43–89

Valentiner 1950
Wilhelm R. Valentiner, *Studies of Italian Renaissance Sculpture*, London 1950

Valéry (1894) 1996
Paul Valéry, *Introduzione al metodo di Leonardo da Vinci*, Milan 1996

Vasari (1568) 1878–85
Giorgio Vasari, *Le vite de' più eccellenti pittori, scultori ed architettori*, ed. Gaetano Milanesi, 9 vols., Florence 1878–85

Vasari (1568) 1963
Giorgio Vasari, *The Lives of the Painters, Sculptors and Architects*, ed. William Gaunt, 4 vols., London 1963

Vasari (1568) 1996
Giorgio Vasari, *Lives of the Painters, Sculptors and Architects*, trans. Gaston du C. de Vere, ed. David Ekserdjian, 2 vols., London 1996

Venaria Reale (Turin) 2011–12
Leonardo. Il Genio e il Mito, eds. Carlo Pedretti, Paola Salvi, Clara Vitulo, Pietro C. Marani, Renato Barilli, Arnaldo Colasanti, exh. cat., Reggia di Venaria Reale, Venaria Reale (Turin), Cinisello Balsamo (Milan) 2011

Venice 1992
Leonardo & Venezia, eds. Giovanna Nepi Scirè and Pietro C. Marani, exh. cat., Istituto di Cultura di Palazzo Grassi, Venice, Milan 1992

Venice 2013
Leonardo da Vinci. L'uomo universale, ed. Annalisa Perissa Torrini, exh. cat., Gallerie dell'Accademia di Venezia, Venice, Florence 2013

Venturi 1797
Giambattista Venturi, *Essai sur les ouvrages physico-mathématiques de Léonard de Vinci, avec des fragmens tirés de ses manuscrits, apportés de l'Italie*, Paris 1797

Verga 1931
Ettore Verga, *Bibliografia Vinciana. 1493–1930*, 2 vols., Bologna 1931

Vinci 1982
Leonardo dopo Milano. La Madonna dei fusi, ed. Alessandro Vezzosi, exh. cat., Biblioteca Comunale, Vinci, Florence 1982

Wallace 1966
Robert Wallace, *The World of Leonardo: 1452–1519*, New York 1966

Washington, D.C. 1991–92
Circa 1492: Art in the Age of Exploration, ed. Jay A. Levenson, exh. cat., The National Gallery of Art, Washington, D.C., New Haven and London 1991

Zanon 2009
Edoardo Zanon, *Il libro del Codice del volo di Leonardo da Vinci*, Milan 2009

Zöllner 1985
Frank Zöllner, "Agrippa, Leonardo and the Codex Huygens," *Journal of the Warburg and Courtauld Institutes* 48 (1985), pp. 229–34

Zöllner 1989
Frank Zöllner, "Die Bedeutung von Codex Huygens und Codex Urbinas für die Proportions- und Bewegungsstudien Leonardo da Vincis," *Zeitschrift für Kunstgeschichte* 52, 3 (1989), pp. 334–52

Zuccaro 1607
Federico Zuccaro *L'Idea de' pittori, scultori et architetti*, Turin 1607